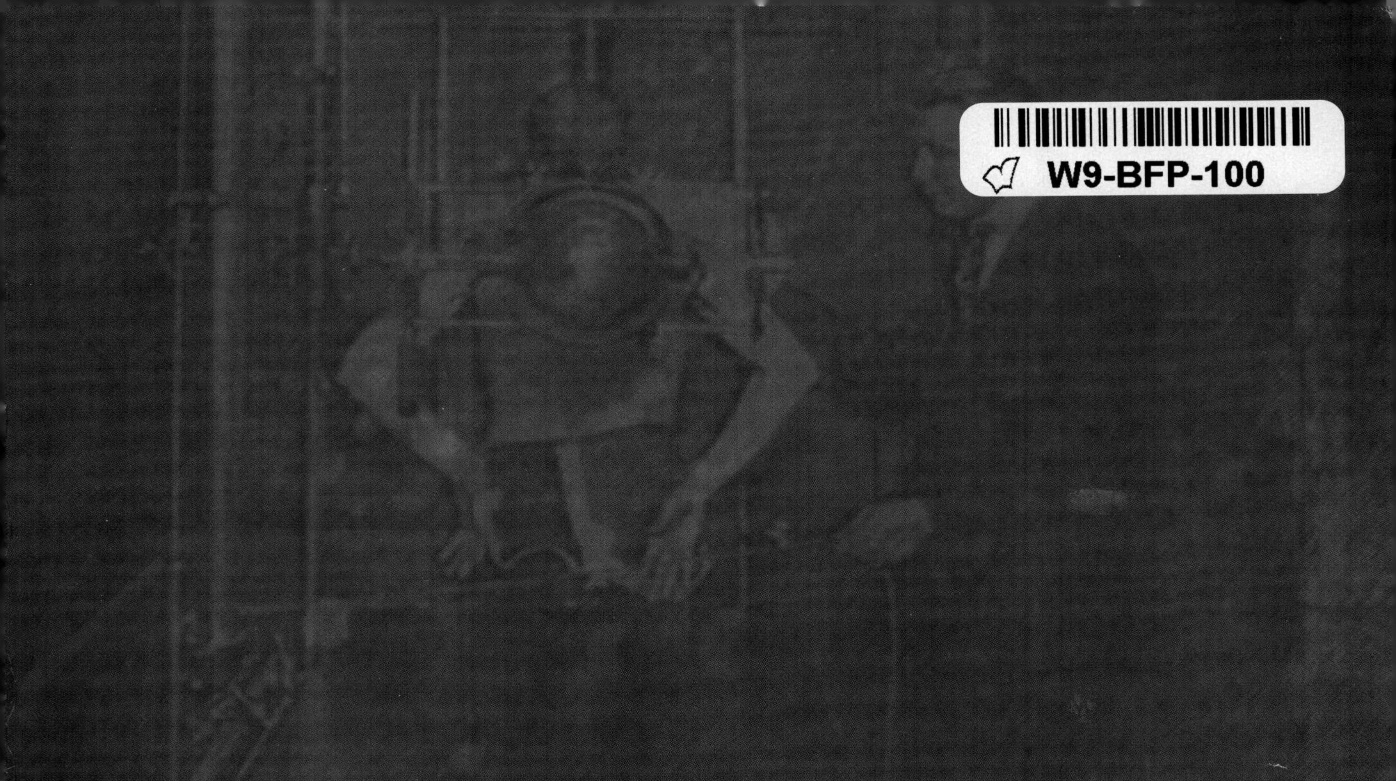

Christophe Bec - Stefano Raffaele

PANDEMONIUM

HUMANOIDS

Christophe Bec
Writer

Stefano Raffaele
Artist

Marie-Paule Alluard (Volume #1)
Bruno Pradelle (Volume #2 and 3)
Colorists

Cover Art *by* Olivier Peru *and* Christophe Bec

Quinn *and* Katia Donoghue
Translators

Alex Donoghue
U.S. Edition Editor

Jerry Frissen
Book Designer

HUMANOIDS:
Fabrice Giger, Publisher
Alex Donoghue, Director & Editor
Jerry Frissen, Senior Art Director
Edmond Lee, Rights & Licensing - licensing@humano.com

PANDEMONIUM. This title is a publication of Humanoids, Inc. 8033 Sunset Blvd. #628, Los Angeles, CA 90046.

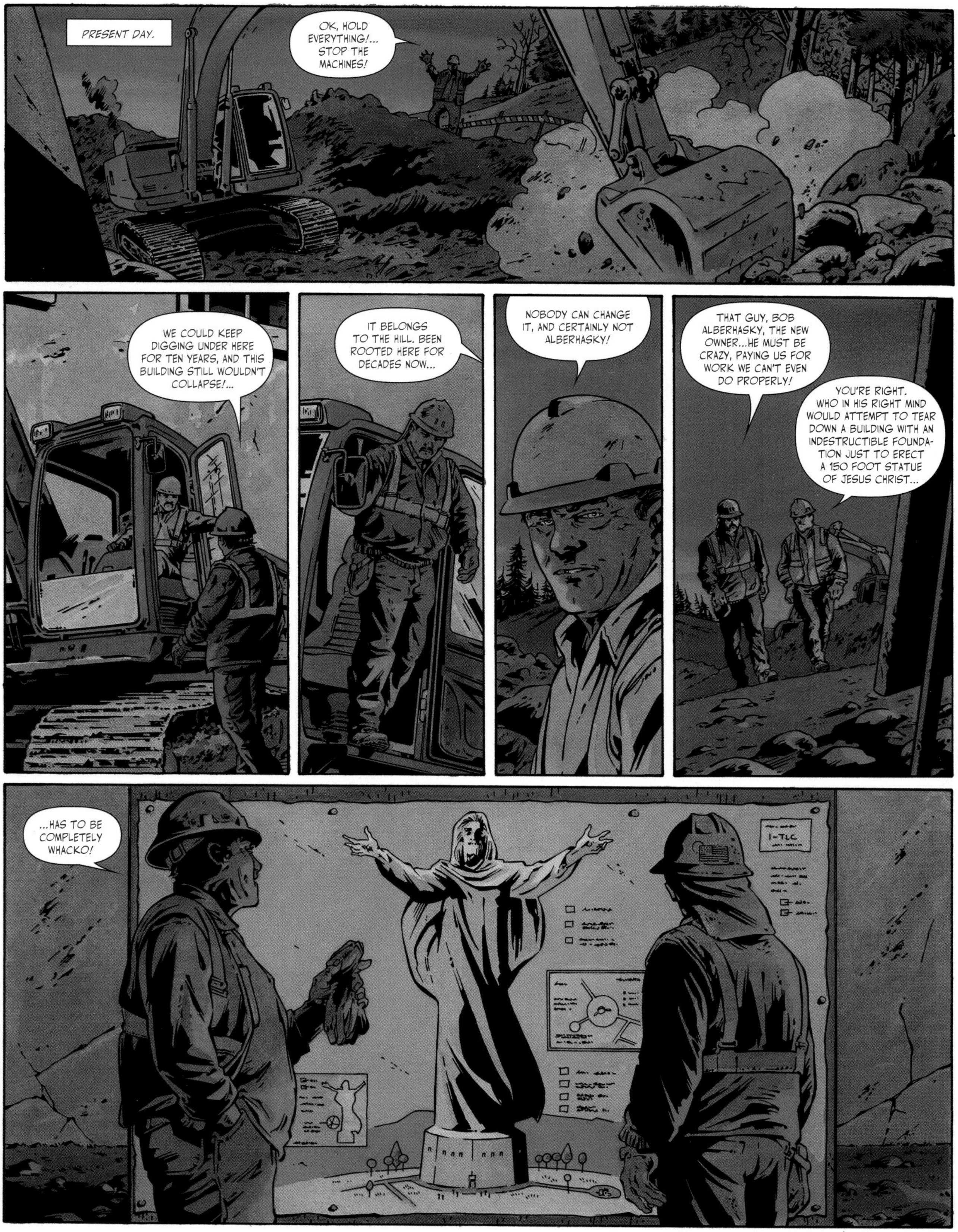
PRESENT DAY.
OK, HOLD EVERYTHING!... STOP THE MACHINES!
WE COULD KEEP DIGGING UNDER HERE FOR TEN YEARS, AND THIS BUILDING STILL WOULDN'T COLLAPSE!...
IT BELONGS TO THE HILL. BEEN ROOTED HERE FOR DECADES NOW...
NOBODY CAN CHANGE IT, AND CERTAINLY NOT ALBERHASKY!
THAT GUY, BOB ALBERHASKY, THE NEW OWNER...HE MUST BE CRAZY, PAYING US FOR WORK WE CAN'T EVEN DO PROPERLY!
YOU'RE RIGHT. WHO IN HIS RIGHT MIND WOULD ATTEMPT TO TEAR DOWN A BUILDING WITH AN INDESTRUCTIBLE FOUNDATION JUST TO ERECT A 150 FOOT STATUE OF JESUS CHRIST...
...HAS TO BE COMPLETELY WHACKO!
I-TLC

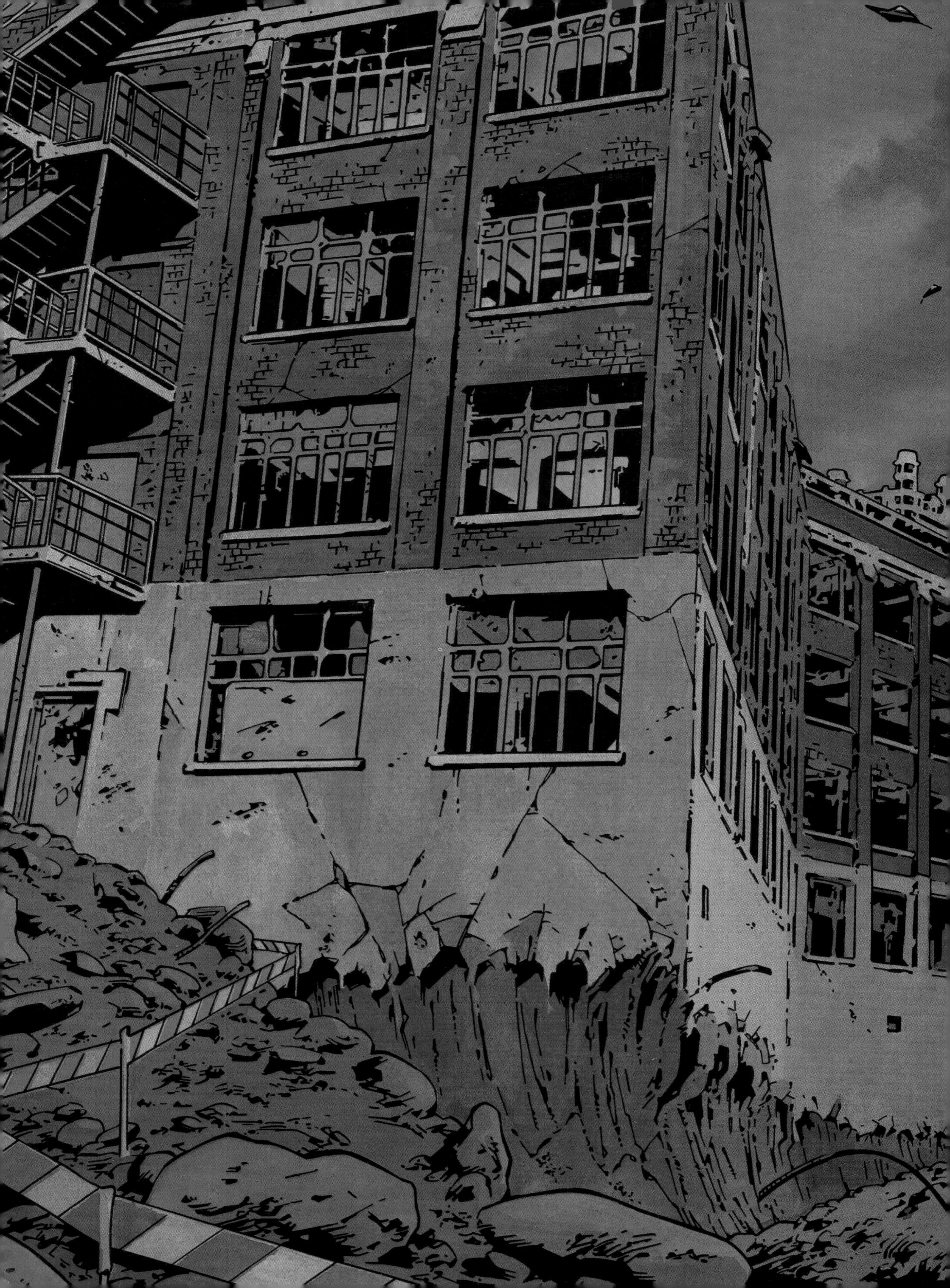

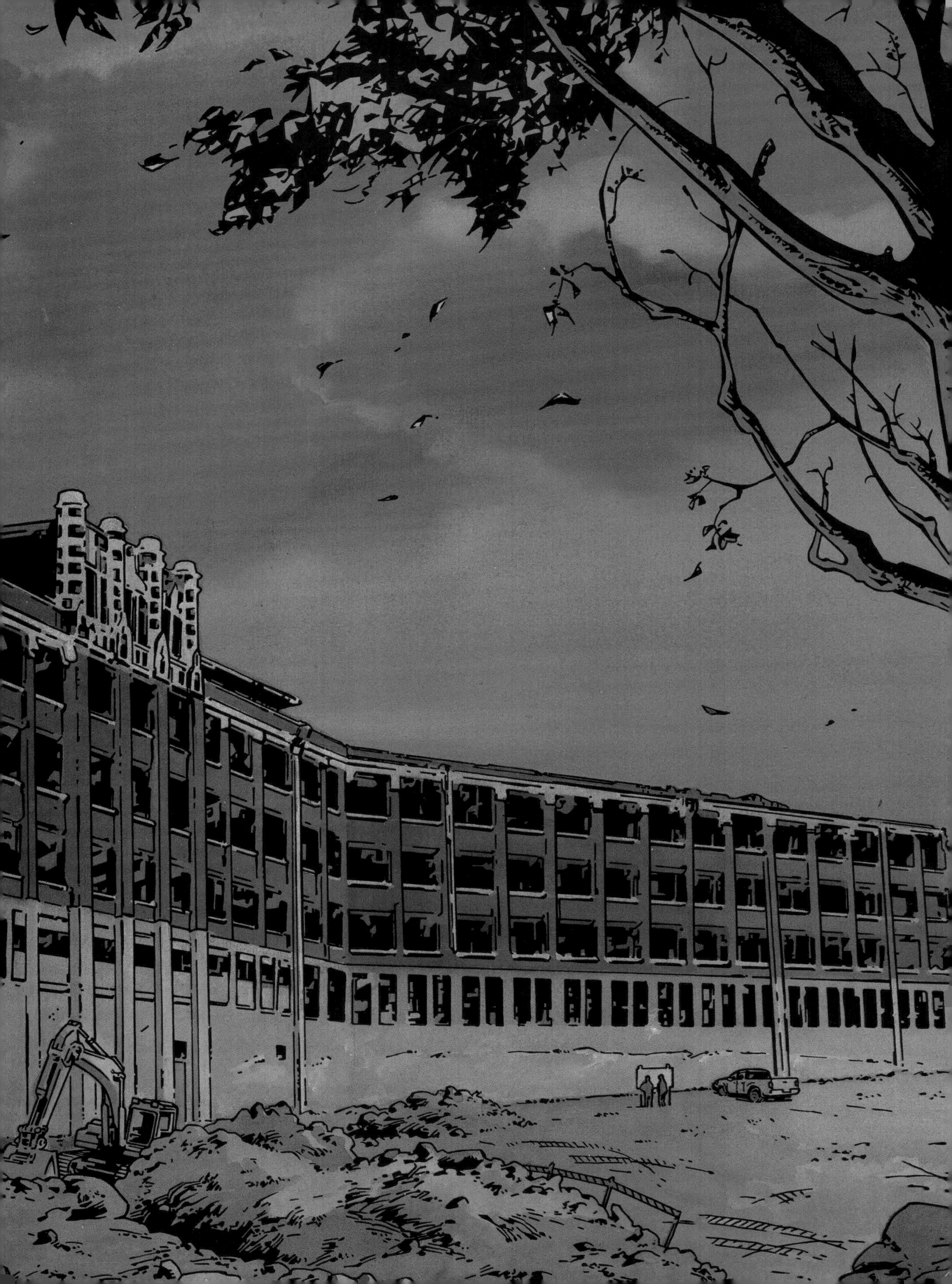

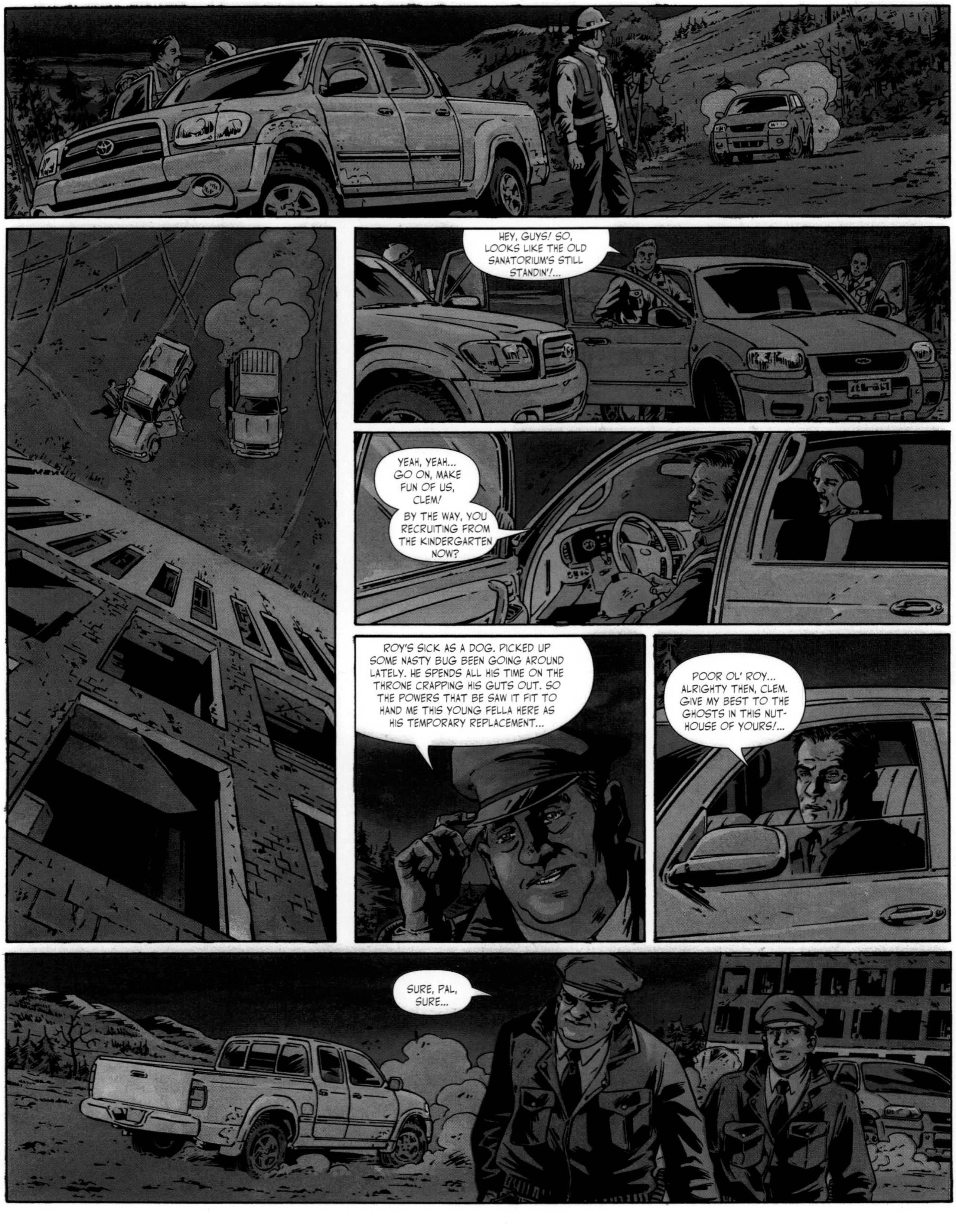
HEY, GUYS! SO, LOOKS LIKE THE OLD SANATORIUM'S STILL STANDIN'!...
YEAH, YEAH... GO ON, MAKE FUN OF US, CLEM!
BY THE WAY, YOU RECRUITING FROM THE KINDERGARTEN NOW?
ROY'S SICK AS A DOG. PICKED UP SOME NASTY BUG BEEN GOING AROUND LATELY. HE SPENDS ALL HIS TIME ON THE THRONE CRAPPING HIS GUTS OUT. SO THE POWERS THAT BE SAW IT FIT TO HAND ME THIS YOUNG FELLA HERE AS HIS TEMPORARY REPLACEMENT...
POOR OL' ROY... ALRIGHTY THEN, CLEM. GIVE MY BEST TO THE GHOSTS IN THIS NUT-HOUSE OF YOURS!...
SURE, PAL, SURE...

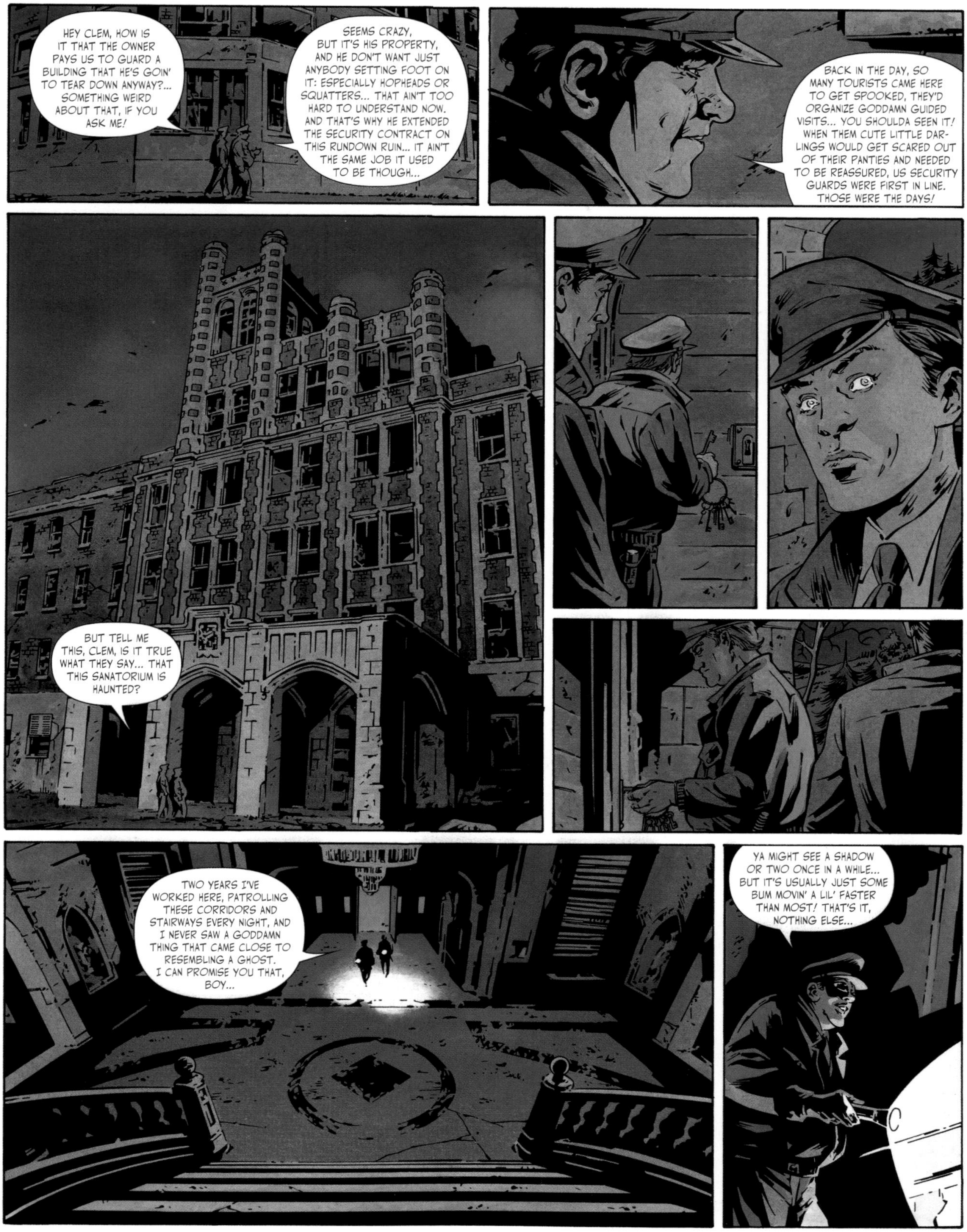
HEY CLEM, HOW IS IT THAT THE OWNER PAYS US TO GUARD A BUILDING THAT HE'S GOIN' TO TEAR DOWN ANYWAY?... SOMETHING WEIRD ABOUT THAT, IF YOU ASK ME!
SEEMS CRAZY, BUT IT'S HIS PROPERTY, AND HE DON'T WANT JUST ANYBODY SETTING FOOT ON IT: ESPECIALLY HOPHEADS OR SQUATTERS... THAT AIN'T TOO HARD TO UNDERSTAND NOW. AND THAT'S WHY HE EXTENDED THE SECURITY CONTRACT ON THIS RUNDOWN RUIN... IT AIN'T THE SAME JOB IT USED TO BE THOUGH...
BACK IN THE DAY, SO MANY TOURISTS CAME HERE TO GET SPOOKED, THEY'D ORGANIZE GODDAMN GUIDED VISITS... YOU SHOULDA SEEN IT! WHEN THEM CUTE LITTLE DARLINGS WOULD GET SCARED OUT OF THEIR PANTIES AND NEEDED TO BE REASSURED, US SECURITY GUARDS WERE FIRST IN LINE. THOSE WERE THE DAYS!
BUT TELL ME THIS, CLEM, IS IT TRUE WHAT THEY SAY... THAT THIS SANATORIUM IS HAUNTED?
TWO YEARS I'VE WORKED HERE, PATROLLING THESE CORRIDORS AND STAIRWAYS EVERY NIGHT, AND I NEVER SAW A GODDAMN THING THAT CAME CLOSE TO RESEMBLING A GHOST. I CAN PROMISE YOU THAT, BOY...
YA MIGHT SEE A SHADOW OR TWO ONCE IN A WHILE... BUT IT'S USUALLY JUST SOME BUM MOVIN' A LIL' FASTER THAN MOST! THAT'S IT, NOTHING ELSE...

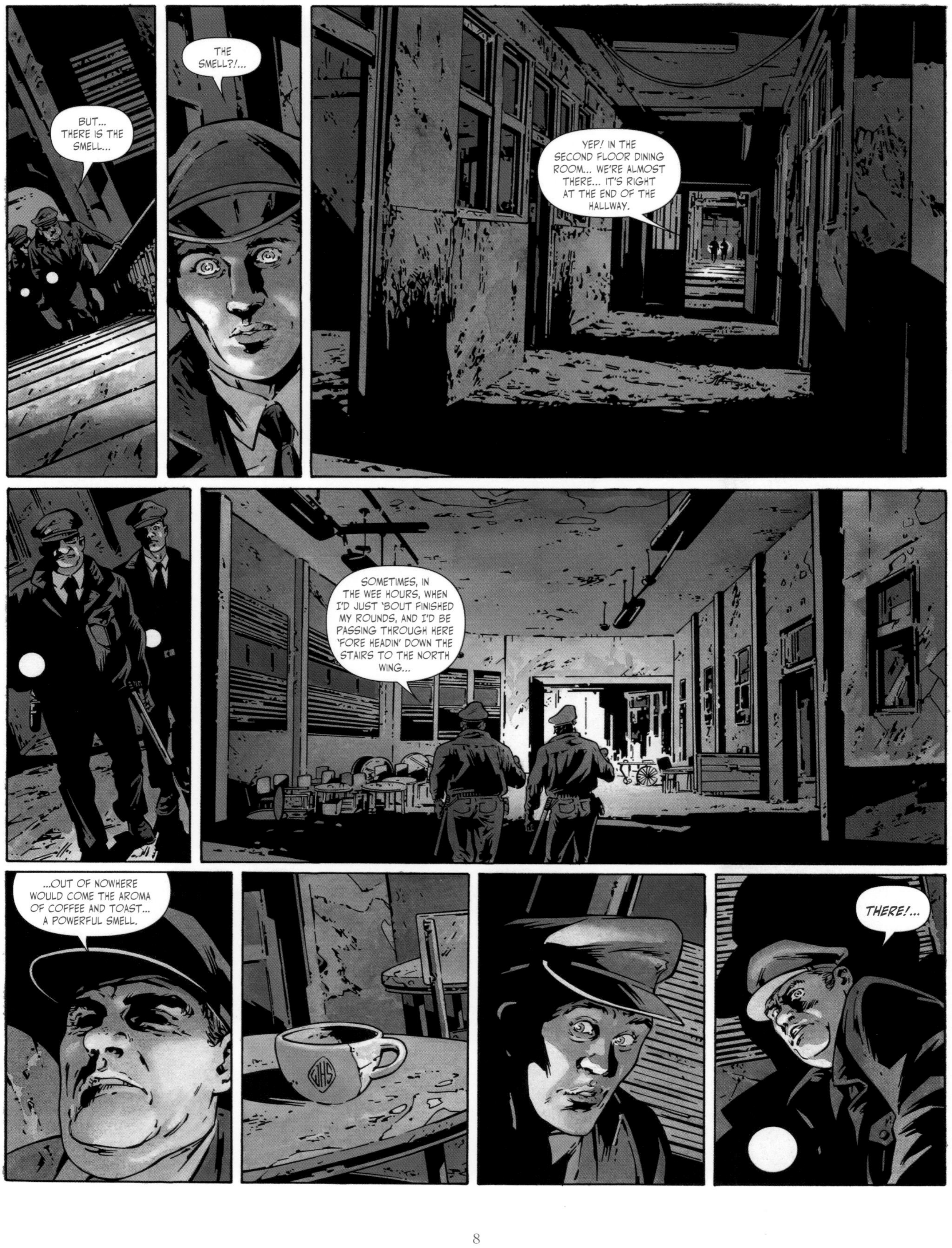
BUT... THERE IS THE SMELL...
THE SMELL?!...
YEP! IN THE SECOND FLOOR DINING ROOM... WE'RE ALMOST THERE... IT'S RIGHT AT THE END OF THE HALLWAY.
SOMETIMES, IN THE WEE HOURS, WHEN I'D JUST 'BOUT FINISHED MY ROUNDS, AND I'D BE PASSING THROUGH HERE 'FORE HEADIN' DOWN THE STAIRS TO THE NORTH WING...
...OUT OF NOWHERE WOULD COME THE AROMA OF COFFEE AND TOAST... A POWERFUL SMELL.
THERE!...

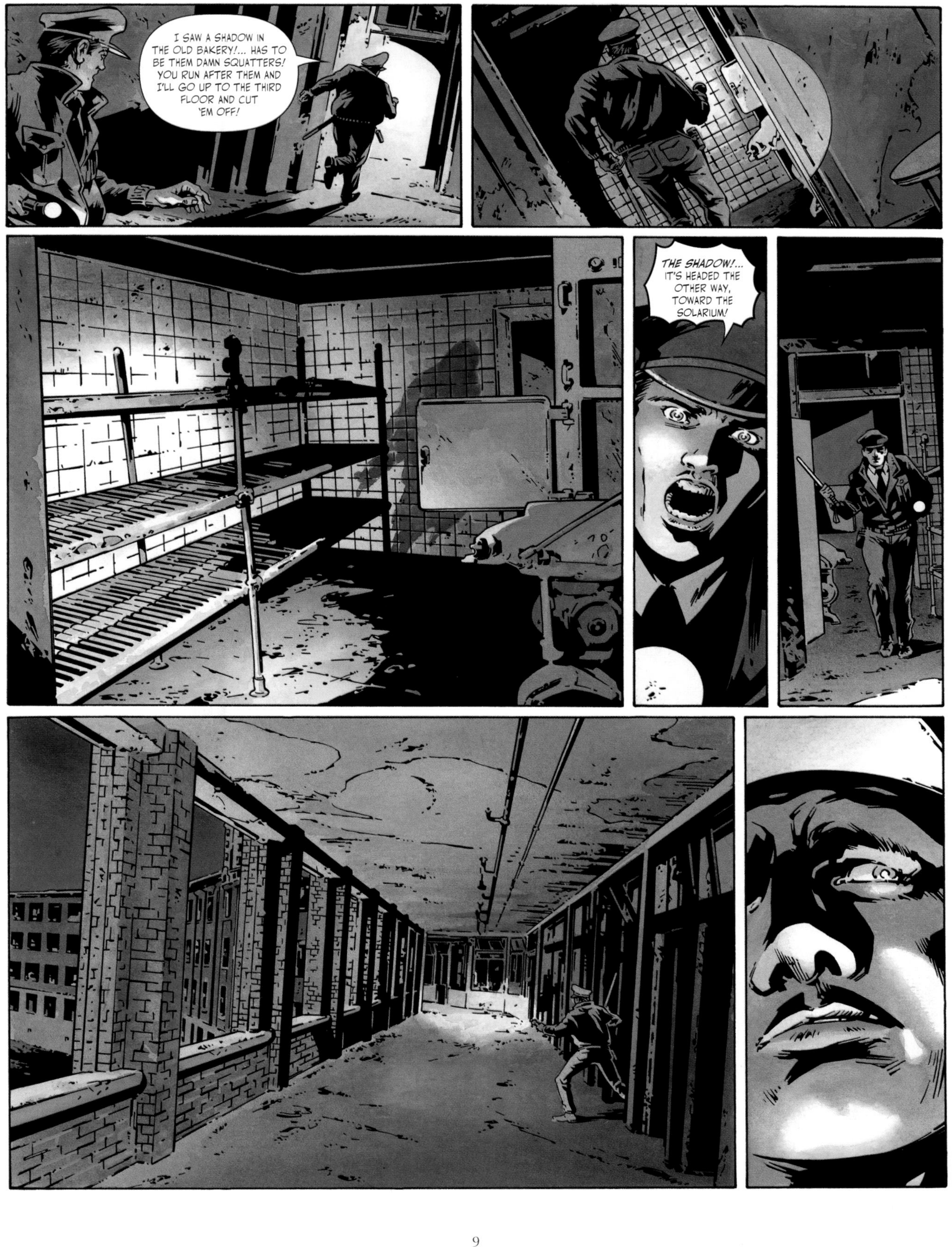
I SAW A SHADOW IN THE OLD BAKERY!... HAS TO BE THEM DAMN SQUATTERS! YOU RUN AFTER THEM AND I'LL GO UP TO THE THIRD FLOOR AND CUT 'EM OFF!
THE SHADOW!... IT'S HEADED THE OTHER WAY, TOWARD THE SOLARIUM!

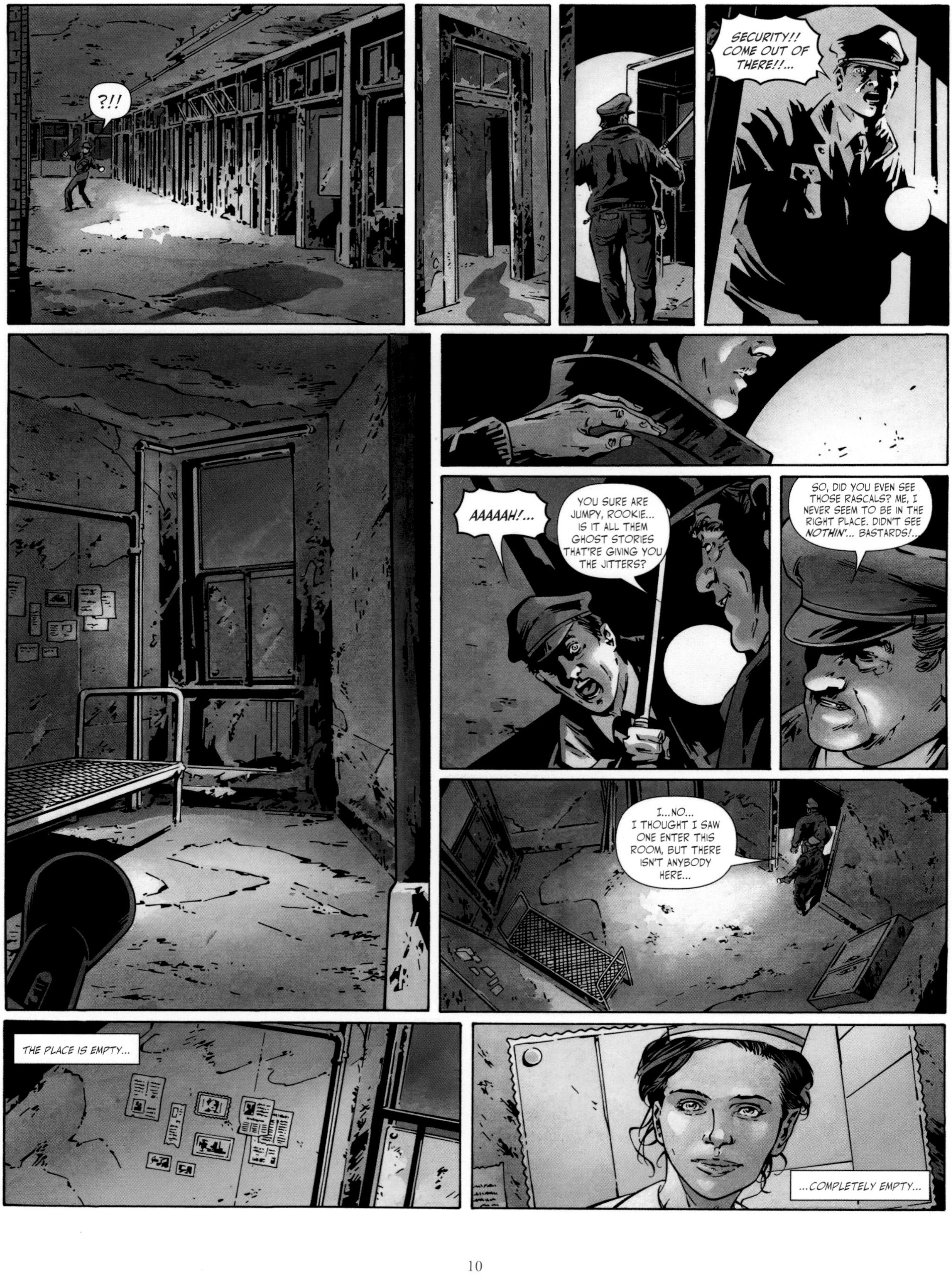
?!!
SECURITY!! COME OUT OF THERE!!...
AAAAAH!...
YOU SURE ARE JUMPY, ROOKIE... IS IT ALL THEM GHOST STORIES THAT'RE GIVING YOU THE JITTERS?
SO, DID YOU EVEN SEE THOSE RASCALS? ME, I NEVER SEEM TO BE IN THE RIGHT PLACE. DIDN'T SEE NOTHIN'... BASTARDS!...
I...NO... I THOUGHT I SAW ONE ENTER THIS ROOM, BUT THERE ISN'T ANYBODY HERE...
THE PLACE IS EMPTY...
...COMPLETELY EMPTY...

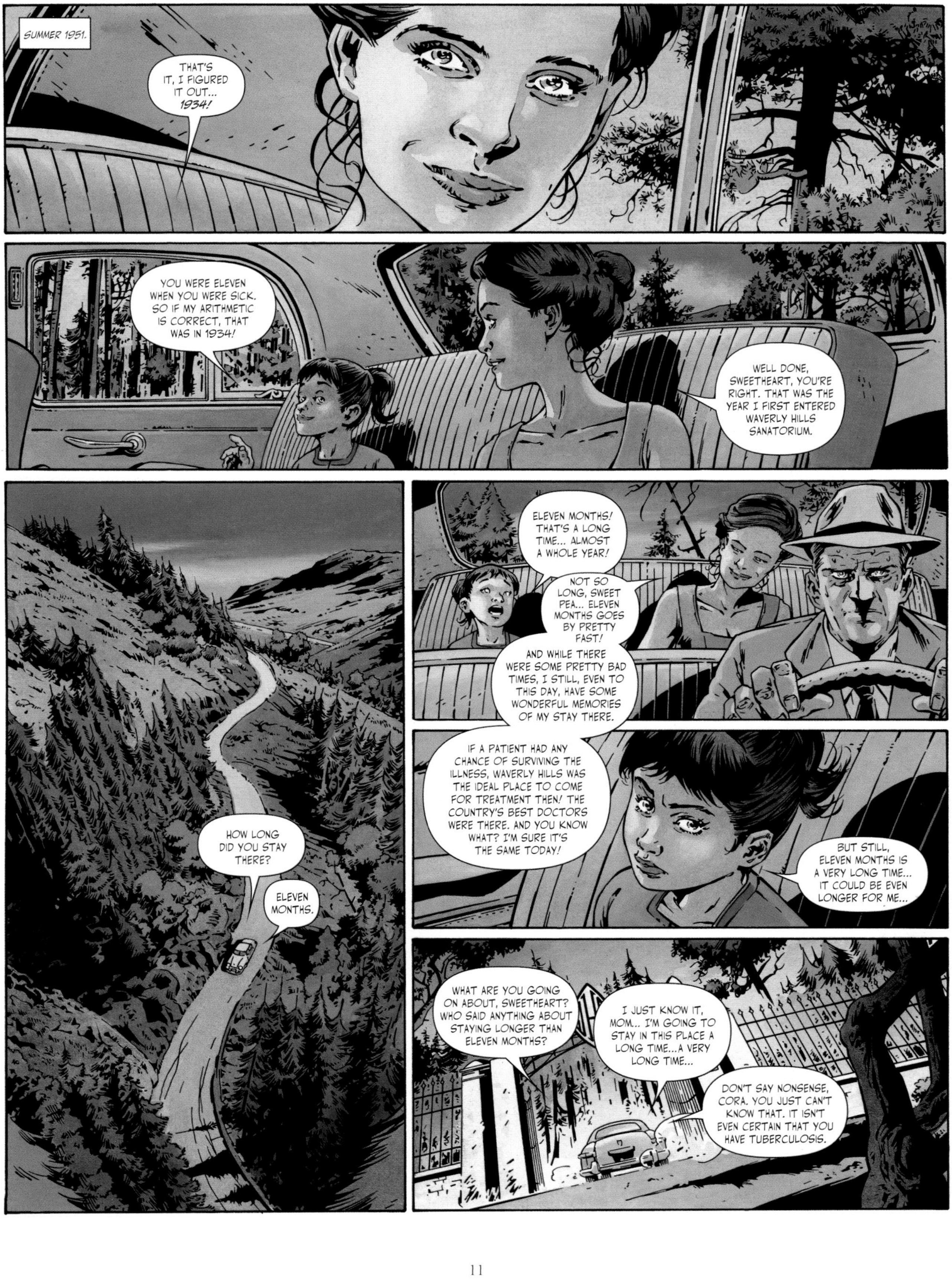
SUMMER 1951.
THAT'S IT, I FIGURED IT OUT... 1934!
YOU WERE ELEVEN WHEN YOU WERE SICK. SO IF MY ARITHMETIC IS CORRECT, THAT WAS IN 1934!
WELL DONE, SWEETHEART, YOU'RE RIGHT. THAT WAS THE YEAR I FIRST ENTERED WAVERLY HILLS SANATORIUM.
HOW LONG DID YOU STAY THERE?
ELEVEN MONTHS.
ELEVEN MONTHS! THAT'S A LONG TIME... ALMOST A WHOLE YEAR!
NOT SO LONG, SWEET PEA... ELEVEN MONTHS GOES BY PRETTY FAST!
AND WHILE THERE WERE SOME PRETTY BAD TIMES, I STILL, EVEN TO THIS DAY, HAVE SOME WONDERFUL MEMORIES OF MY STAY THERE.
IF A PATIENT HAD ANY CHANCE OF SURVIVING THE ILLNESS, WAVERLY HILLS WAS THE IDEAL PLACE TO COME FOR TREATMENT THEN! THE COUNTRY'S BEST DOCTORS WERE THERE. AND YOU KNOW WHAT? I'M SURE IT'S THE SAME TODAY!
BUT STILL, ELEVEN MONTHS IS A VERY LONG TIME... IT COULD BE EVEN LONGER FOR ME...
WHAT ARE YOU GOING ON ABOUT, SWEETHEART? WHO SAID ANYTHING ABOUT STAYING LONGER THAN ELEVEN MONTHS?
I JUST KNOW IT, MOM... I'M GOING TO STAY IN THIS PLACE A LONG TIME...A VERY LONG TIME...
DON'T SAY NONSENSE, CORA. YOU JUST CAN'T KNOW THAT. IT ISN'T EVEN CERTAIN THAT YOU HAVE TUBERCULOSIS.

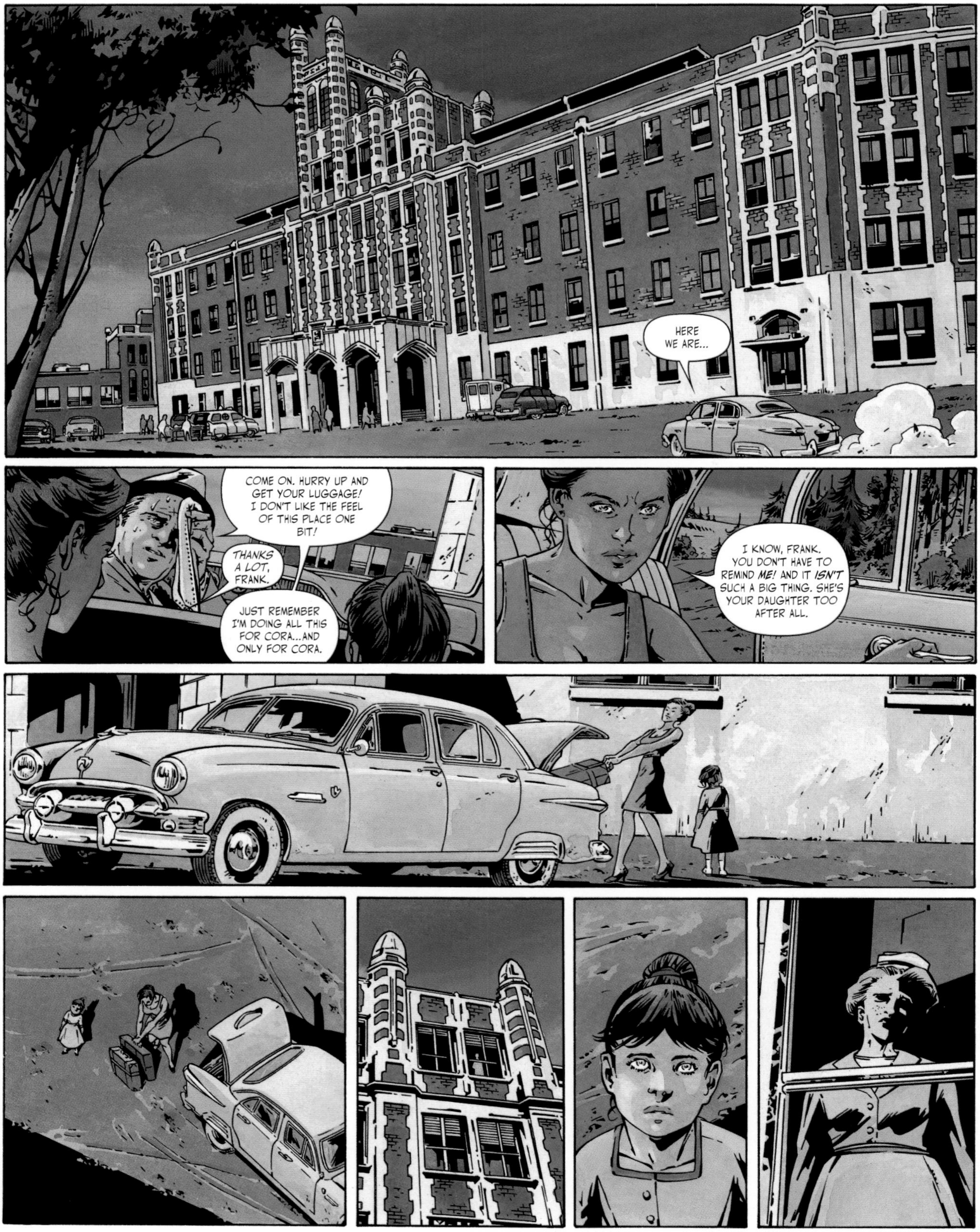
HERE WE ARE...
COME ON. HURRY UP AND GET YOUR LUGGAGE! I DON'T LIKE THE FEEL OF THIS PLACE ONE BIT!
THANKS A LOT, FRANK.
JUST REMEMBER I'M DOING ALL THIS FOR CORA...AND ONLY FOR CORA.
I KNOW, FRANK. YOU DON'T HAVE TO REMIND ME! AND IT ISN'T SUCH A BIG THING. SHE'S YOUR DAUGHTER TOO AFTER ALL.

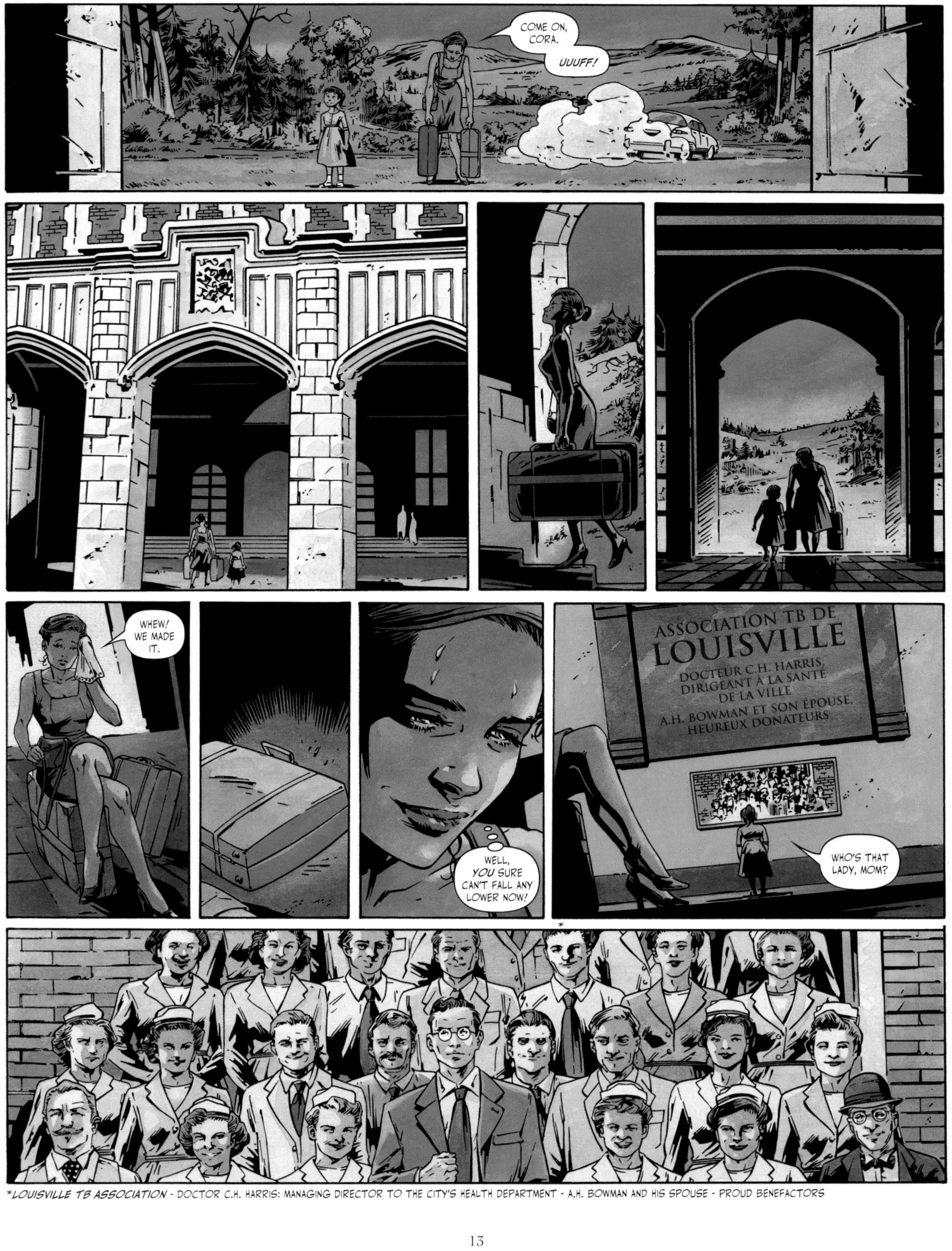
COME ON, CORA.
UUUFF!
WHEW! WE MADE IT.
WELL, YOU SURE CAN'T FALL ANY LOWER NOW!
ASSOCIATION TB DE LOUISVILLE
DOCTEUR C.H. HARRIS, DIRIGEANT À LA SANTÉ DE LA VILLE
A.H. BOWMAN ET SON ÉPOUSE, HEUREUX DONATEURS
WHO'S THAT LADY, MOM?
*

**LOUISVILLE TB ASSOCIATION* - DOCTOR C.H. HARRIS: MANAGING DIRECTOR TO THE CITY'S HEALTH DEPARTMENT - A.H. BOWMAN AND HIS SPOUSE - PROUD BENEFACTORS

WHOM DO YOU MEAN, SWEETHEART?

HER!

I HAVE NO IDEA, HON.... SURELY ONE OF THE NURSES THAT WORKED HERE WHEN THE SANATORIUM JUST OPENED.

I JUST SAW HER, MOM.

YOU SAW HER?... WHERE DID YOU SEE HER?

JUST NOW, WHEN YOU WERE UNLOADING THE SUITCASES... SHE WAS AT A WINDOW, WAY UP THERE, NEAR THE BELL-TOWER... SHE SEEMED REALLY SAD.

BUT CORA, THIS PHOTOGRAPH WAS TAKEN 25 YEARS AGO. HOW CAN YOU BE SURE IT'S THE SAME WOMAN? SHE HAD TO HAVE CHANGED A LOT SINCE...

I'M SURE, MOM. IT WAS HER! SHE HAS THE SAME FACE, EXACTLY THE SAME FACE. SHE HASN'T CHANGED AT ALL!

LOUISVILLE
DOCTEUR C.H. HARRIS
DIRIGEANT A LA SANTÉ
DE LA VILLE
A.H. BOWMAN ET SONS ET
HEUREUX ...

LET'S GO, CORA, JUST BEHA--

CAN I HELP YOU?

14

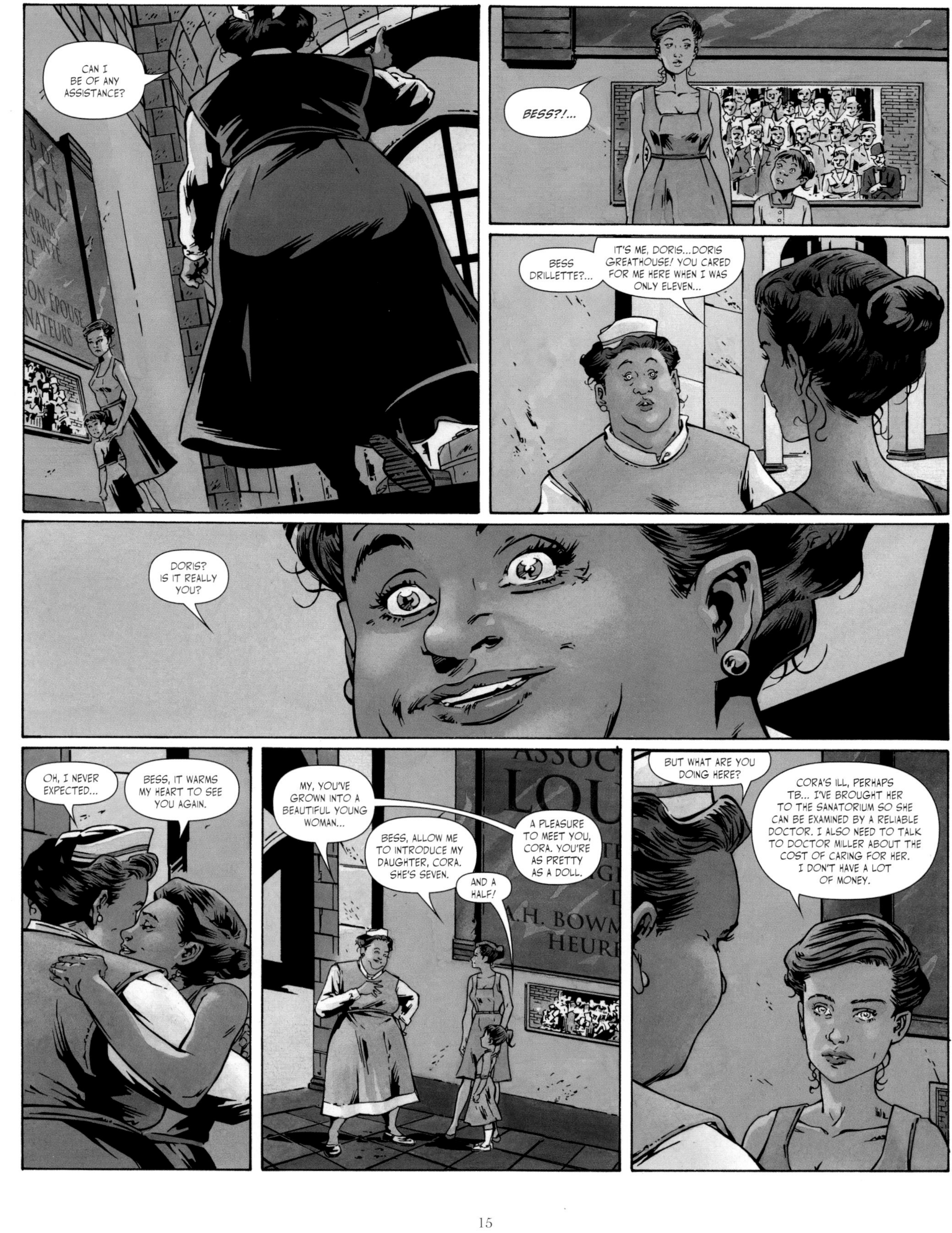
CAN I BE OF ANY ASSISTANCE?
BESS?!...
BESS DRILLETTE?...
IT'S ME, DORIS...DORIS GREATHOUSE! YOU CARED FOR ME HERE WHEN I WAS ONLY ELEVEN...
DORIS? IS IT REALLY YOU?
OH, I NEVER EXPECTED...
BESS, IT WARMS MY HEART TO SEE YOU AGAIN.
MY, YOU'VE GROWN INTO A BEAUTIFUL YOUNG WOMAN...
BESS, ALLOW ME TO INTRODUCE MY DAUGHTER, CORA. SHE'S SEVEN.
A PLEASURE TO MEET YOU, CORA. YOU'RE AS PRETTY AS A DOLL.
AND A HALF!
BUT WHAT ARE YOU DOING HERE?
CORA'S ILL, PERHAPS TB... I'VE BROUGHT HER TO THE SANATORIUM SO SHE CAN BE EXAMINED BY A RELIABLE DOCTOR. I ALSO NEED TO TALK TO DOCTOR MILLER ABOUT THE COST OF CARING FOR HER. I DON'T HAVE A LOT OF MONEY.

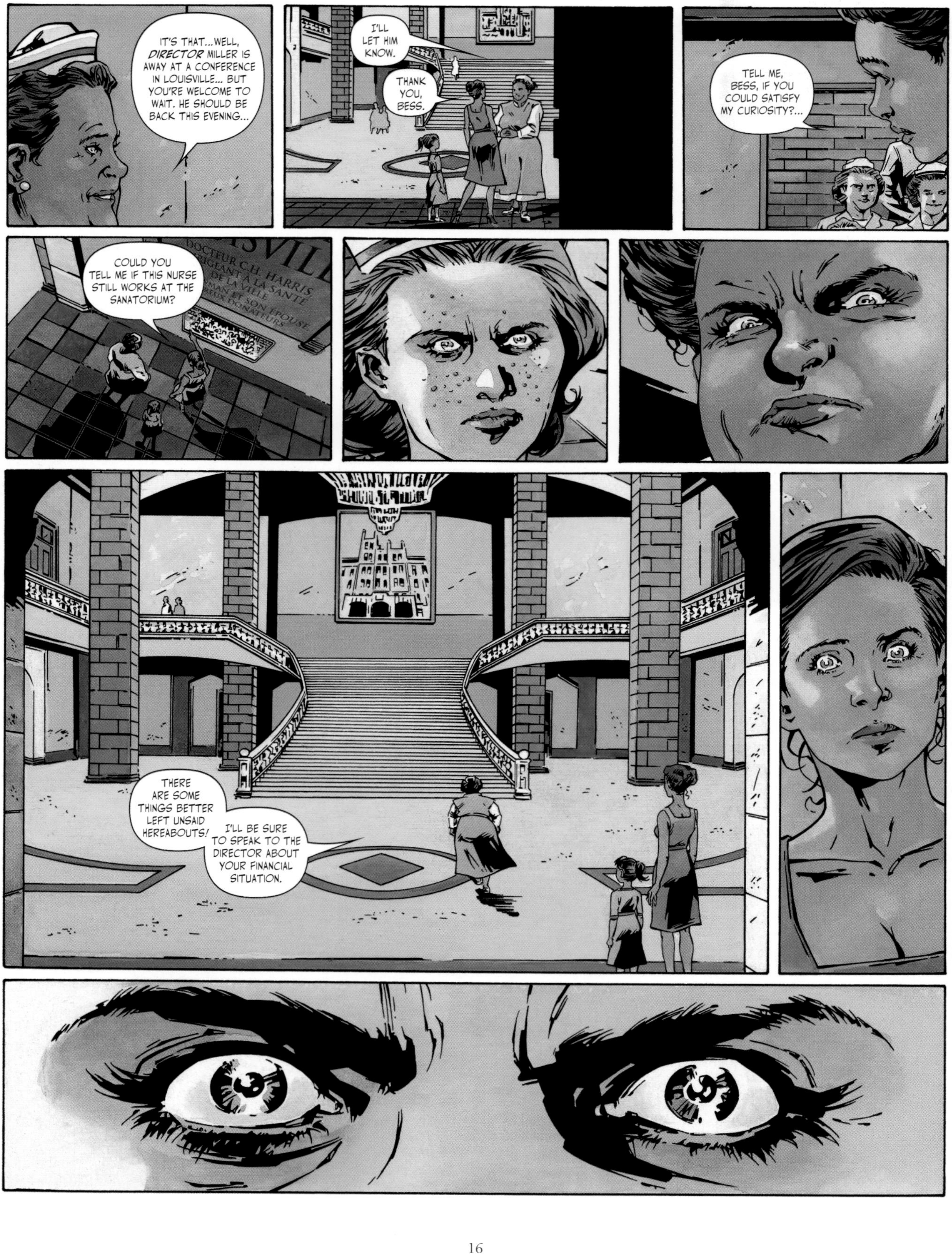
IT'S THAT...WELL, DIRECTOR MILLER IS AWAY AT A CONFERENCE IN LOUISVILLE... BUT YOU'RE WELCOME TO WAIT. HE SHOULD BE BACK THIS EVENING...
I'LL LET HIM KNOW.
THANK YOU, BESS.
TELL ME, BESS, IF YOU COULD SATISFY MY CURIOSITY?...
COULD YOU TELL ME IF THIS NURSE STILL WORKS AT THE SANATORIUM?
DOCTEUR C.H. HARRIS
DE LA VILLE
THERE ARE SOME THINGS BETTER LEFT UNSAID HEREABOUTS!
I'LL BE SURE TO SPEAK TO THE DIRECTOR ABOUT YOUR FINANCIAL SITUATION.

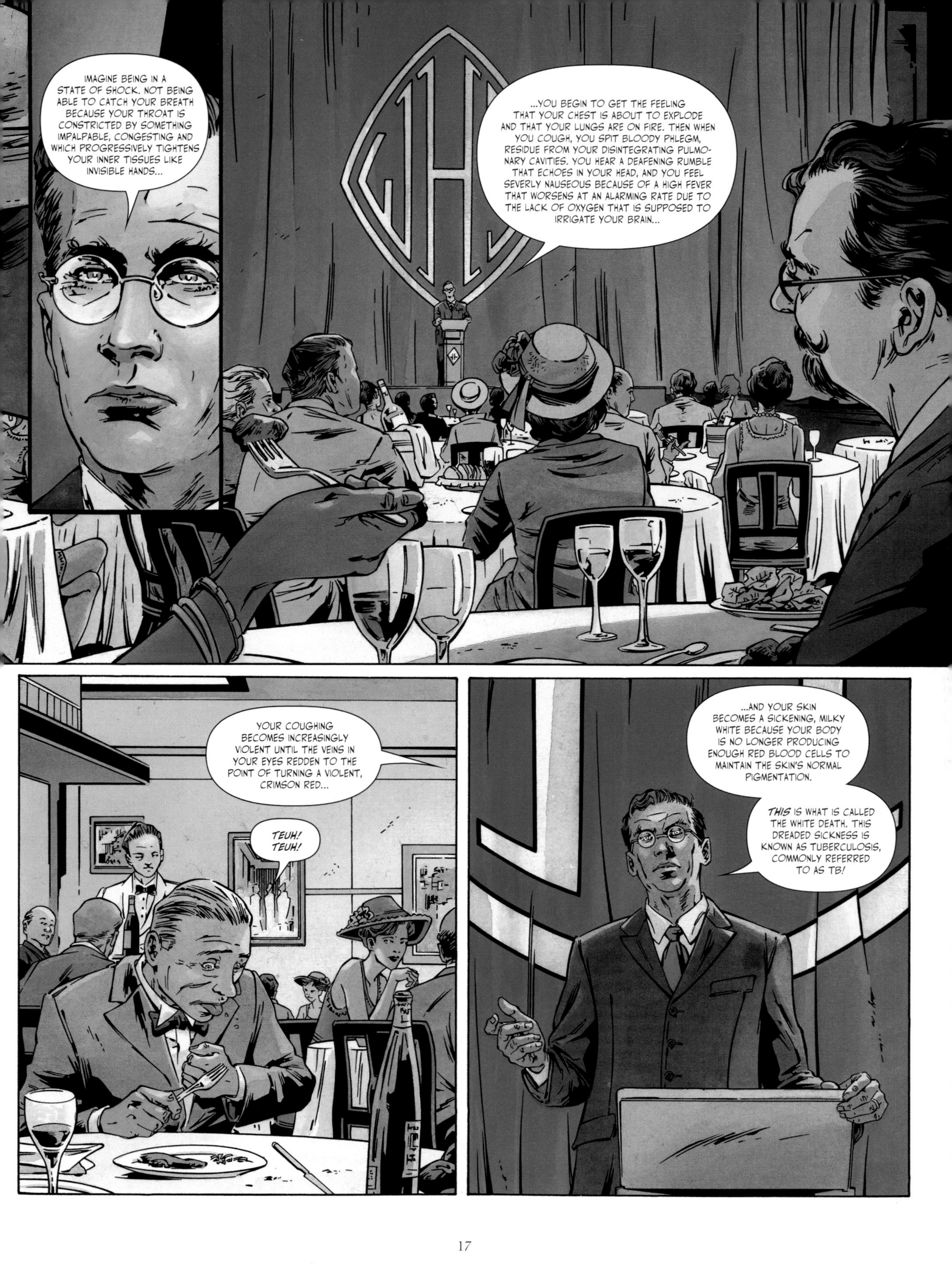
IMAGINE BEING IN A STATE OF SHOCK. NOT BEING ABLE TO CATCH YOUR BREATH BECAUSE YOUR THROAT IS CONSTRICTED BY SOMETHING IMPALPABLE, CONGESTING AND WHICH PROGRESSIVELY TIGHTENS YOUR INNER TISSUES LIKE INVISIBLE HANDS...
...YOU BEGIN TO GET THE FEELING THAT YOUR CHEST IS ABOUT TO EXPLODE AND THAT YOUR LUNGS ARE ON FIRE. THEN WHEN YOU COUGH, YOU SPIT BLOODY PHLEGM, RESIDUE FROM YOUR DISINTEGRATING PULMONARY CAVITIES. YOU HEAR A DEAFENING RUMBLE THAT ECHOES IN YOUR HEAD, AND YOU FEEL SEVERLY NAUSEOUS BECAUSE OF A HIGH FEVER THAT WORSENS AT AN ALARMING RATE DUE TO THE LACK OF OXYGEN THAT IS SUPPOSED TO IRRIGATE YOUR BRAIN...
YOUR COUGHING BECOMES INCREASINGLY VIOLENT UNTIL THE VEINS IN YOUR EYES REDDEN TO THE POINT OF TURNING A VIOLENT, CRIMSON RED...
TEUH! TEUH!
...AND YOUR SKIN BECOMES A SICKENING, MILKY WHITE BECAUSE YOUR BODY IS NO LONGER PRODUCING ENOUGH RED BLOOD CELLS TO MAINTAIN THE SKIN'S NORMAL PIGMENTATION.
THIS IS WHAT IS CALLED THE WHITE DEATH. THIS DREADED SICKNESS IS KNOWN AS TUBERCULOSIS, COMMONLY REFERRED TO AS TB!

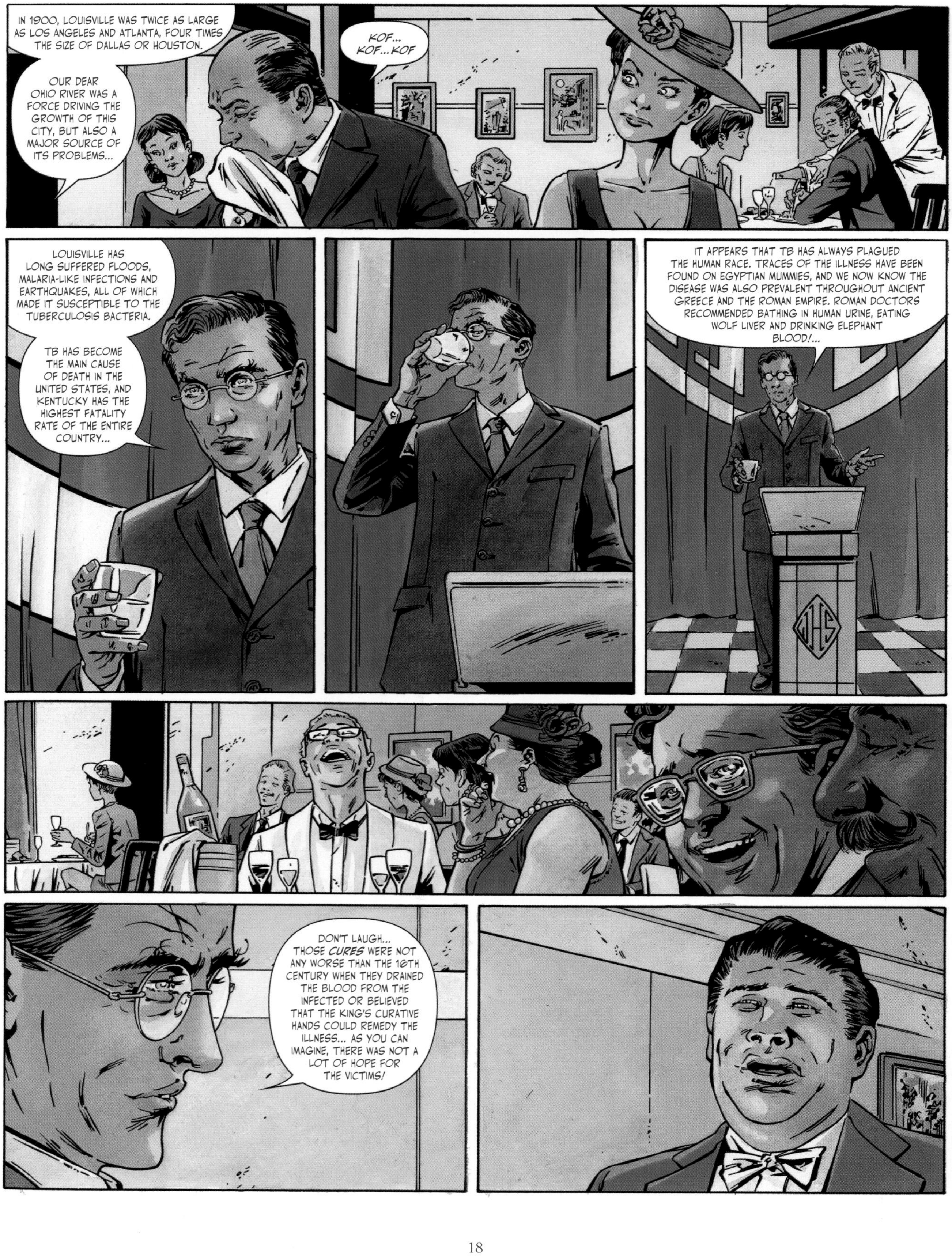
IN 1900, LOUISVILLE WAS TWICE AS LARGE AS LOS ANGELES AND ATLANTA, FOUR TIMES THE SIZE OF DALLAS OR HOUSTON.
OUR DEAR OHIO RIVER WAS A FORCE DRIVING THE GROWTH OF THIS CITY, BUT ALSO A MAJOR SOURCE OF ITS PROBLEMS...
KOF... KOF...KOF
LOUISVILLE HAS LONG SUFFERED FLOODS, MALARIA-LIKE INFECTIONS AND EARTHQUAKES, ALL OF WHICH MADE IT SUSCEPTIBLE TO THE TUBERCULOSIS BACTERIA.
TB HAS BECOME THE MAIN CAUSE OF DEATH IN THE UNITED STATES, AND KENTUCKY HAS THE HIGHEST FATALITY RATE OF THE ENTIRE COUNTRY...
IT APPEARS THAT TB HAS ALWAYS PLAGUED THE HUMAN RACE. TRACES OF THE ILLNESS HAVE BEEN FOUND ON EGYPTIAN MUMMIES, AND WE NOW KNOW THE DISEASE WAS ALSO PREVALENT THROUGHOUT ANCIENT GREECE AND THE ROMAN EMPIRE. ROMAN DOCTORS RECOMMENDED BATHING IN HUMAN URINE, EATING WOLF LIVER AND DRINKING ELEPHANT BLOOD!...
DON'T LAUGH... THOSE CURES WERE NOT ANY WORSE THAN THE 16TH CENTURY WHEN THEY DRAINED THE BLOOD FROM THE INFECTED OR BELIEVED THAT THE KING'S CURATIVE HANDS COULD REMEDY THE ILLNESS... AS YOU CAN IMAGINE, THERE WAS NOT A LOT OF HOPE FOR THE VICTIMS!

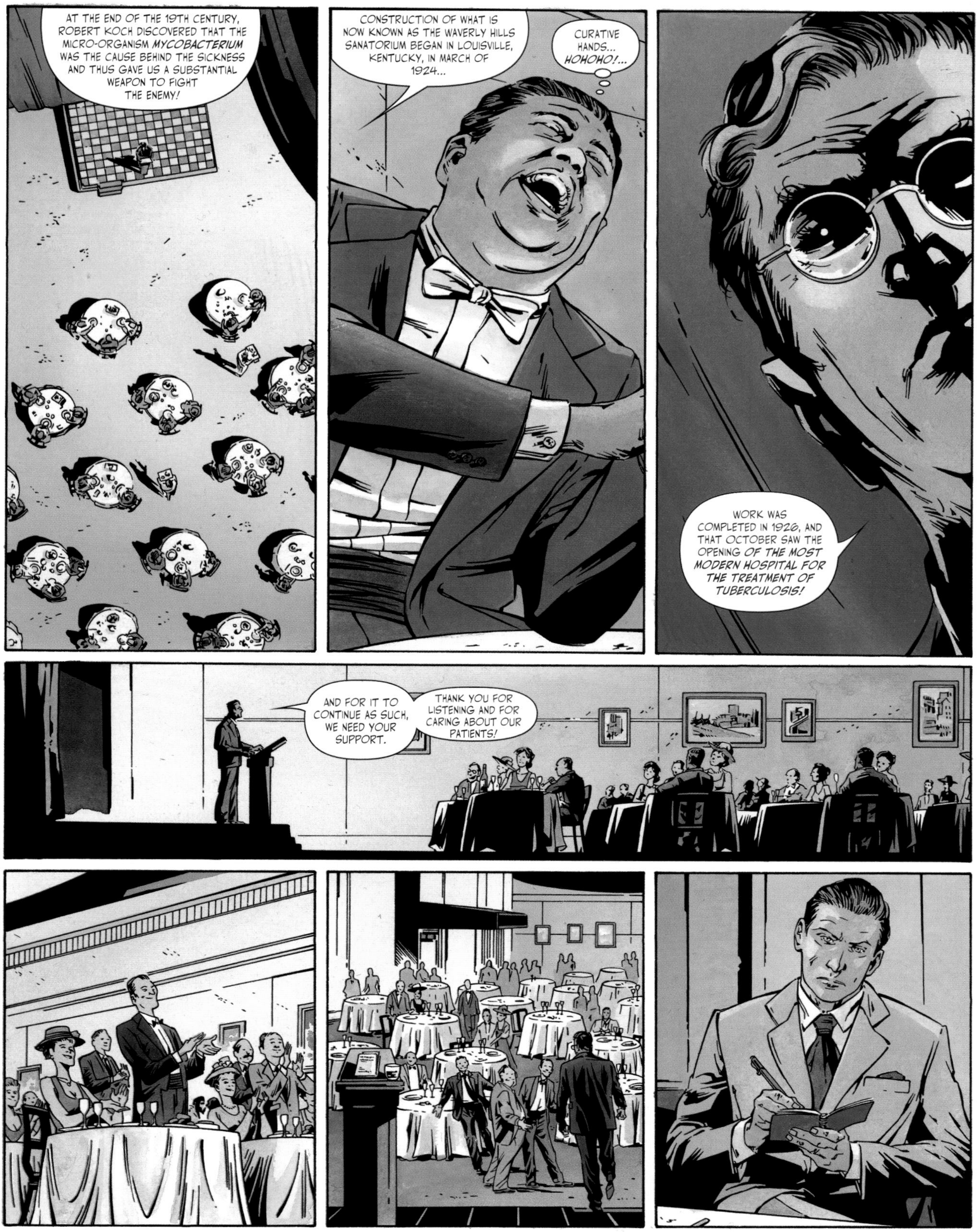
AT THE END OF THE 19TH CENTURY, ROBERT KOCH DISCOVERED THAT THE MICRO-ORGANISM MYCOBACTERIUM WAS THE CAUSE BEHIND THE SICKNESS AND THUS GAVE US A SUBSTANTIAL WEAPON TO FIGHT THE ENEMY!
CONSTRUCTION OF WHAT IS NOW KNOWN AS THE WAVERLY HILLS SANATORIUM BEGAN IN LOUISVILLE, KENTUCKY, IN MARCH OF 1924...
CURATIVE HANDS... HOHOHO!...
WORK WAS COMPLETED IN 1926, AND THAT OCTOBER SAW THE OPENING OF THE MOST MODERN HOSPITAL FOR THE TREATMENT OF TUBERCULOSIS!
AND FOR IT TO CONTINUE AS SUCH, WE NEED YOUR SUPPORT.
THANK YOU FOR LISTENING AND FOR CARING ABOUT OUR PATIENTS!

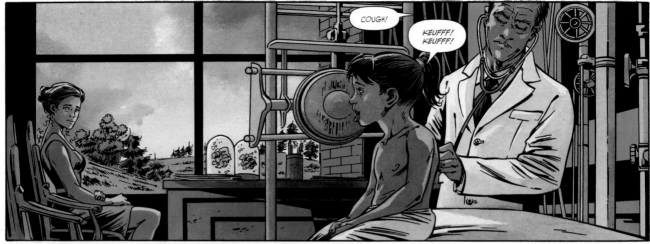

COUGH!

KEUFFF! KEUFFF!

IT IS INDEED TUBERCULOSIS, MRS. GREATHOUSE. AND IT IS IN A VERY ADVANCED STATE THAT DEMANDS IMMEDIATE TREATMENT!

THE LUNGS CONSTITUTE THE INITIAL ENTRYWAY, BUT IT IS PROBABLE THAT THE GERMS WILL RAPIDLY SPREAD TO OTHER PARTS OF THE BODY VIA THE CIRCULATION OF THE BLOOD.

YOUR DAUGHTER SHOULD BE PLACED IN IMMEDIATE ISOLATION. TB IS SPREAD THROUGH THE AIR, AND BY BEING EXPOSED TO GERMS PRESENT IN SALIVA AND PULMONARY EXPECTO-RATIONS. IF SHE COUGHS OR SNEEZES, THE MINISCULE, INFECTED DROPLETS CAN BE INHALED BY EVERYONE IN HER PROXIMITY. YOUR DAUGHTER IS A VERITABLE DANGER TO THE POPULATION AT LARGE!

THE BEST POSSIBLE TREATMENT IS HERE AT WAVERLY HILLS SANATORIUM, OF COURSE. AT THE COST OF FIVE DOLLARS PER DAY... WHAT DO YOU WISH TO DO, MISS GREATHOUSE?

I KNOW THAT THE BEST TREATMENT IS HERE. I MYSELF WAS CURED HERE AS A CHILD.

I DON'T HAVE THE MONEY, BUT I HAVE REACHED AN ARRANGEMENT WITH DIRECTOR MILLER. I AM GOING TO WORK HERE AS A NURSE'S AIDE TOWARDS WHAT THE HOSPITAL WILL CHARGE FOR MY DAUGHTER'S CARE.

THAT'S FINE... IF YOU HAVE REACHED AN AGREEMENT WITH DIRECTOR MILLER, THEN I WILL DRAW UP A LETTER OF ADMISSION FOR THE CHILDREN'S HOSPITAL. HOWEVER, YOU STILL ARE REQUIRED TO PAY FOR THIS CONSULTATION...

THANK YOU VERY MUCH, DOCTOR.

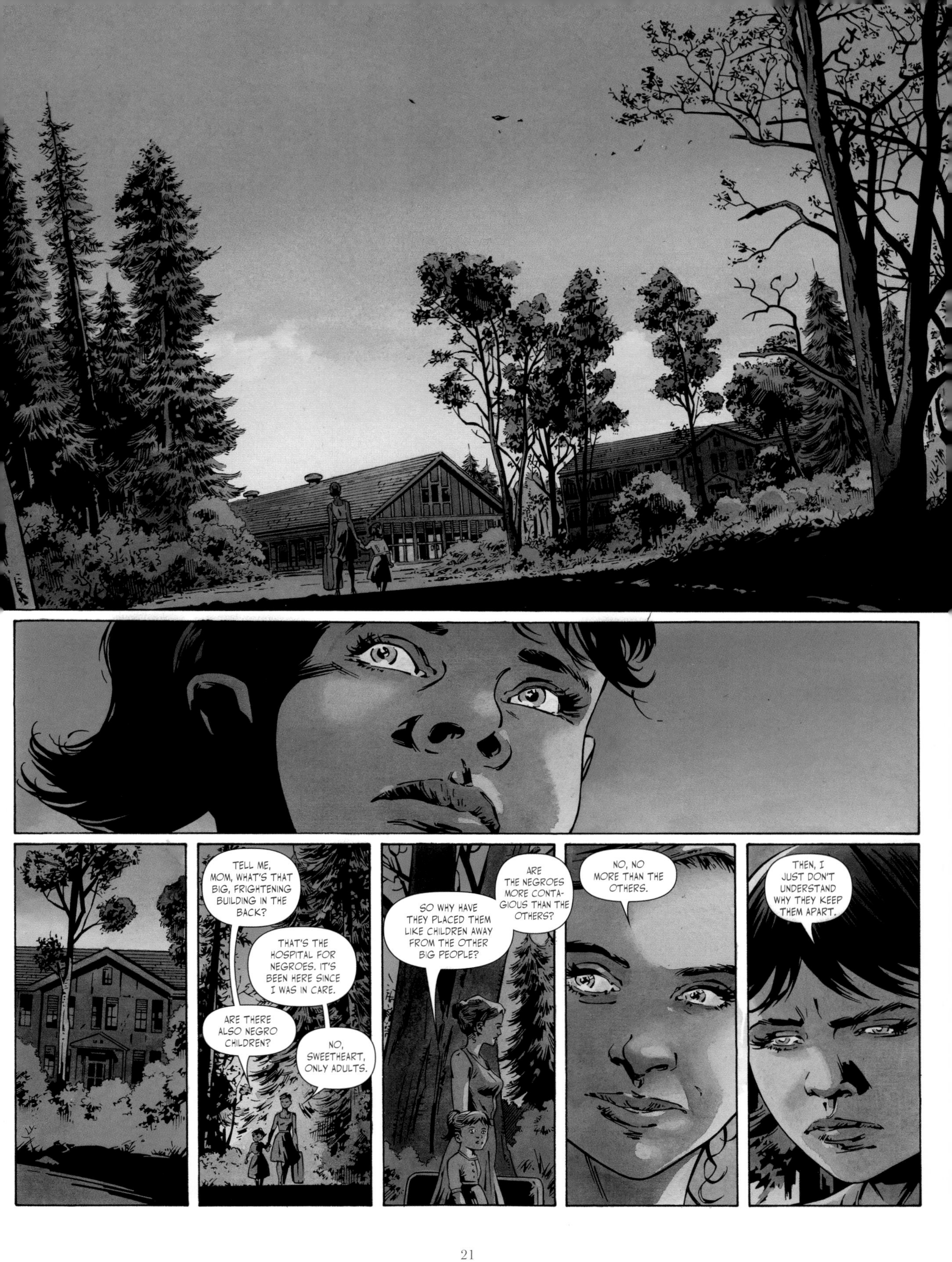
TELL ME, MOM, WHAT'S THAT BIG, FRIGHTENING BUILDING IN THE BACK?
THAT'S THE HOSPITAL FOR NEGROES. IT'S BEEN HERE SINCE I WAS IN CARE.
ARE THERE ALSO NEGRO CHILDREN?
NO, SWEETHEART, ONLY ADULTS.
SO WHY HAVE THEY PLACED THEM LIKE CHILDREN AWAY FROM THE OTHER BIG PEOPLE?
ARE THE NEGROES MORE CONTAGIOUS THAN THE OTHERS?
NO, NO MORE THAN THE OTHERS.
THEN, I JUST DON'T UNDERSTAND WHY THEY KEEP THEM APART.

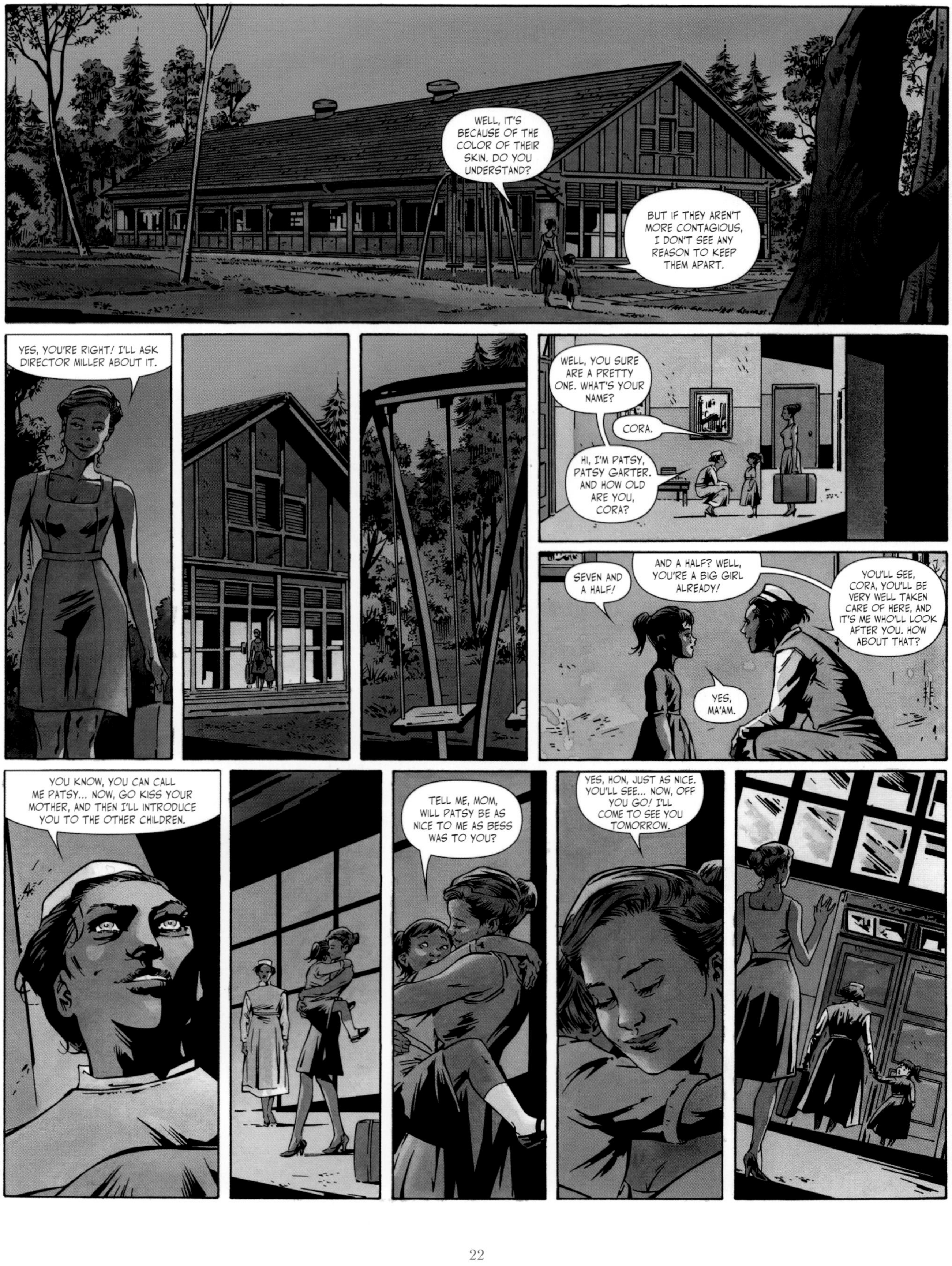

WELL, IT'S BECAUSE OF THE COLOR OF THEIR SKIN. DO YOU UNDERSTAND?
BUT IF THEY AREN'T MORE CONTAGIOUS, I DON'T SEE ANY REASON TO KEEP THEM APART.
YES, YOU'RE RIGHT! I'LL ASK DIRECTOR MILLER ABOUT IT.
WELL, YOU SURE ARE A PRETTY ONE. WHAT'S YOUR NAME?
CORA.
HI, I'M PATSY, PATSY GARTER. AND HOW OLD ARE YOU, CORA?
SEVEN AND A HALF!
AND A HALF? WELL, YOU'RE A BIG GIRL ALREADY!
YOU'LL SEE, CORA, YOU'LL BE VERY WELL TAKEN CARE OF HERE, AND IT'S ME WHO'LL LOOK AFTER YOU. HOW ABOUT THAT?
YES, MA'AM.
YOU KNOW, YOU CAN CALL ME PATSY... NOW, GO KISS YOUR MOTHER, AND THEN I'LL INTRODUCE YOU TO THE OTHER CHILDREN.
TELL ME, MOM, WILL PATSY BE AS NICE TO ME AS BESS WAS TO YOU?
YES, HON, JUST AS NICE. YOU'LL SEE... NOW, OFF YOU GO! I'LL COME TO SEE YOU TOMORROW.

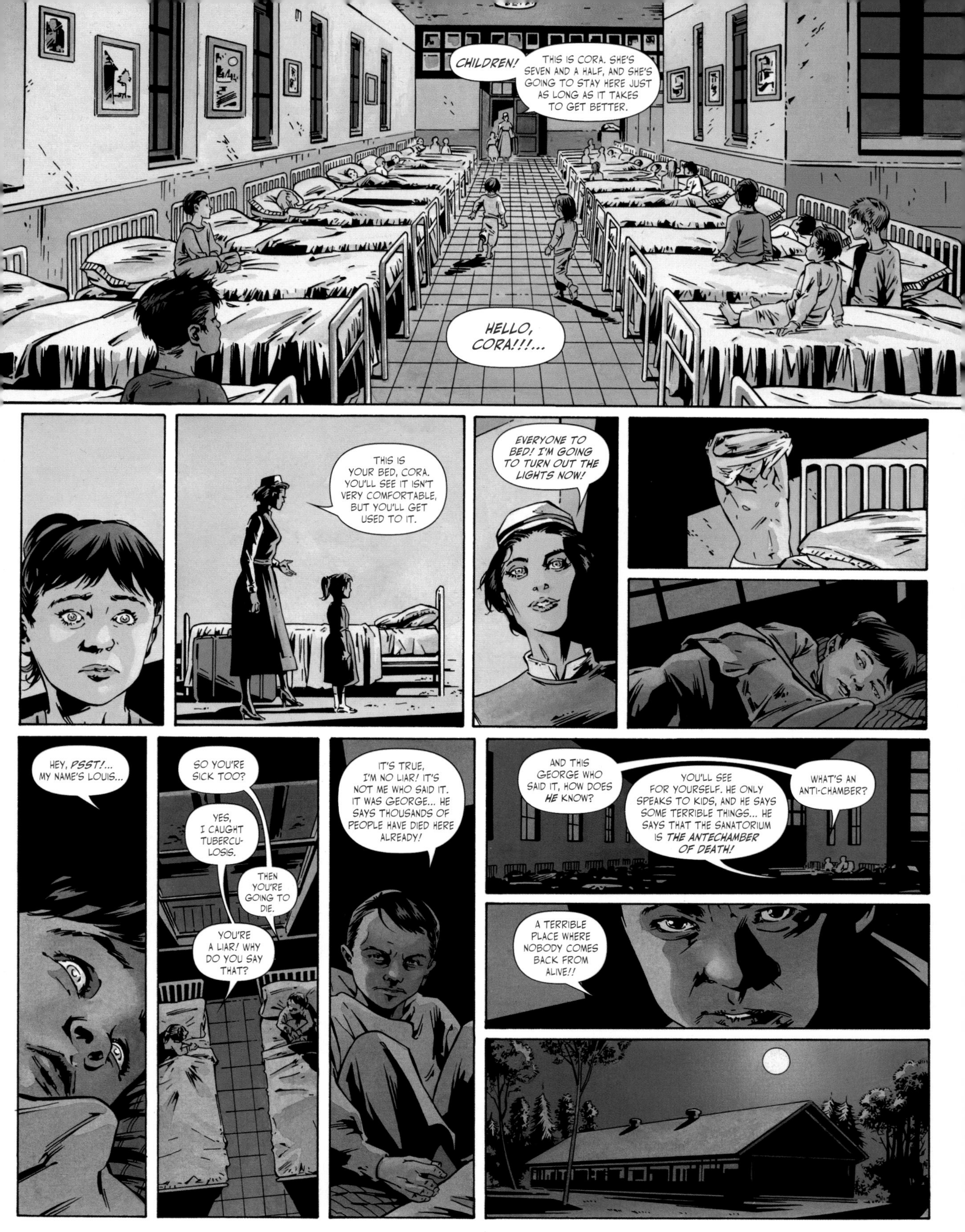
CHILDREN!
THIS IS CORA. SHE'S SEVEN AND A HALF, AND SHE'S GOING TO STAY HERE JUST AS LONG AS IT TAKES TO GET BETTER.
HELLO, CORA!!!...
THIS IS YOUR BED, CORA. YOU'LL SEE IT ISN'T VERY COMFORTABLE, BUT YOU'LL GET USED TO IT.
EVERYONE TO BED! I'M GOING TO TURN OUT THE LIGHTS NOW!
HEY, PSST!... MY NAME'S LOUIS...
SO YOU'RE SICK TOO?
YES, I CAUGHT TUBERCU-LOSIS.
THEN YOU'RE GOING TO DIE.
YOU'RE A LIAR! WHY DO YOU SAY THAT?
IT'S TRUE, I'M NO LIAR! IT'S NOT ME WHO SAID IT. IT WAS GEORGE... HE SAYS THOUSANDS OF PEOPLE HAVE DIED HERE ALREADY!
AND THIS GEORGE WHO SAID IT, HOW DOES HE KNOW?
YOU'LL SEE FOR YOURSELF. HE ONLY SPEAKS TO KIDS, AND HE SAYS SOME TERRIBLE THINGS... HE SAYS THAT THE SANATORIUM IS THE ANTECHAMBER OF DEATH!
WHAT'S AN ANTI-CHAMBER?
A TERRIBLE PLACE WHERE NOBODY COMES BACK FROM ALIVE!!

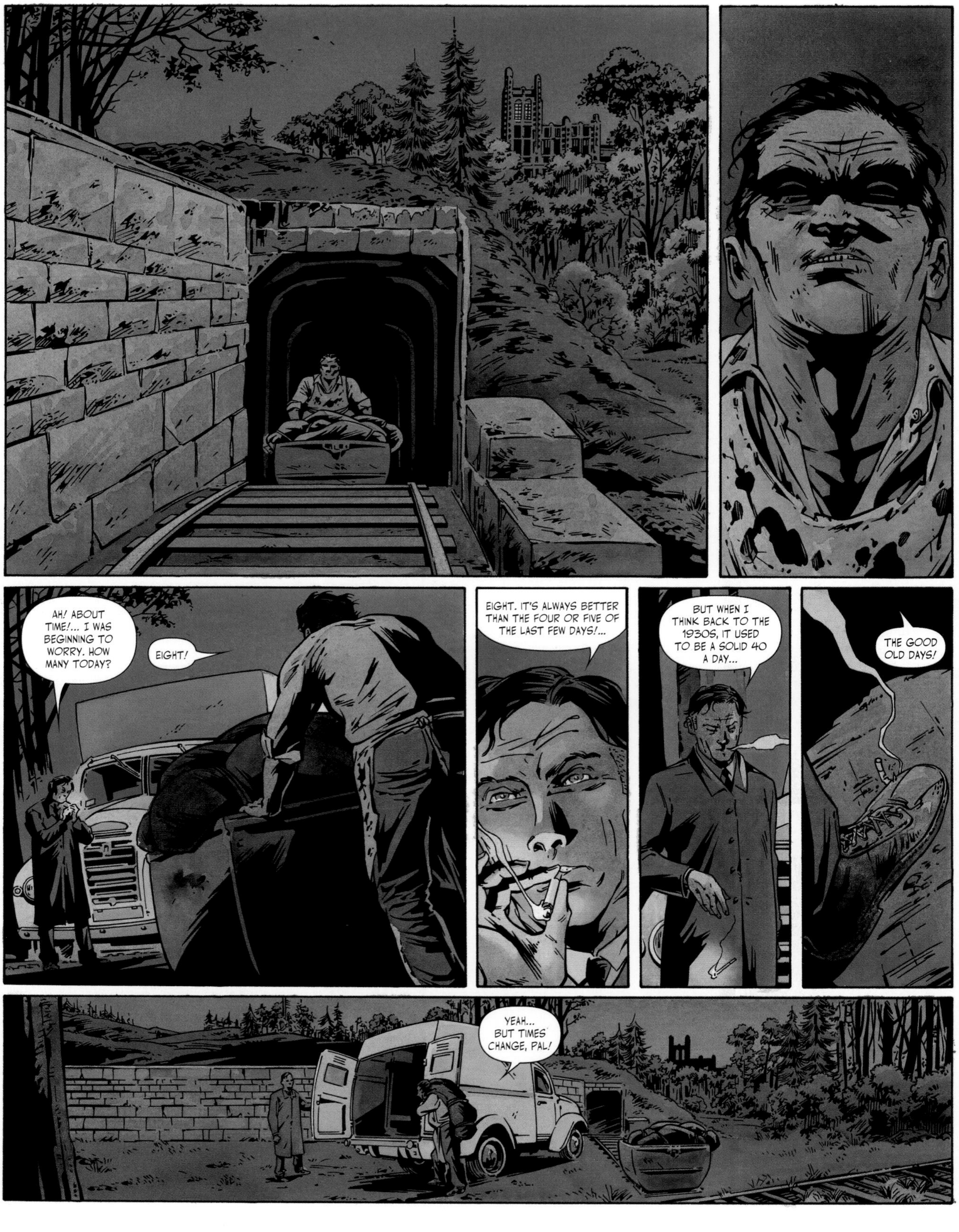
AH! ABOUT TIME!... I WAS BEGINNING TO WORRY. HOW MANY TODAY?
EIGHT!
EIGHT. IT'S ALWAYS BETTER THAN THE FOUR OR FIVE OF THE LAST FEW DAYS!...
BUT WHEN I THINK BACK TO THE 1930S, IT USED TO BE A SOLID 40 A DAY...
THE GOOD OLD DAYS!
YEAH... BUT TIMES CHANGE, PAL!

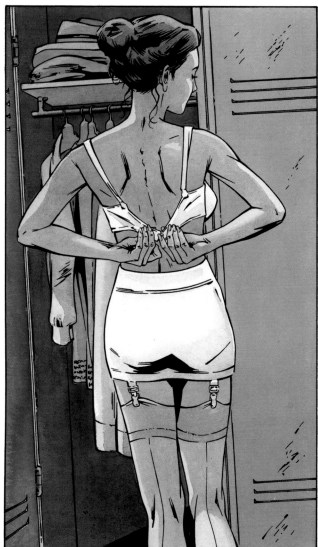

MISS GREATHOUSE, DOCTOR C.B. SEVERS WISHES TO--

I...I'M SORRY. I THOUGHT YOU'D BE READY BY NOW...

IT'S OK, DOCTOR WHITE. DON'T WORRY YOURSELF.

I WANTED TO NOTIFY YOU THAT THE EMINENT DOCTOR CHARLES B. SEVERS ASKED ME FOR A NURSE'S AIDE TO BE ON HAND FOR THIS MORNING'S ROUNDS OF THE PATIENTS IN THE SOLARIUM... AND I THOUGHT THAT YOU COULD DO IT.

WELL, THANK YOU, DOCTOR WHITE. IT WAS VERY NICE OF YOU TO THINK OF ME.

ONLY IF YOU AGREE TO CALL ME DORIS. ESPECIALLY NOW THAT YOU'VE SEEN ME PRACTICALLY NAKED.

SURE. PLEASE CALL ME FRED, MISS GREATHOUSE.

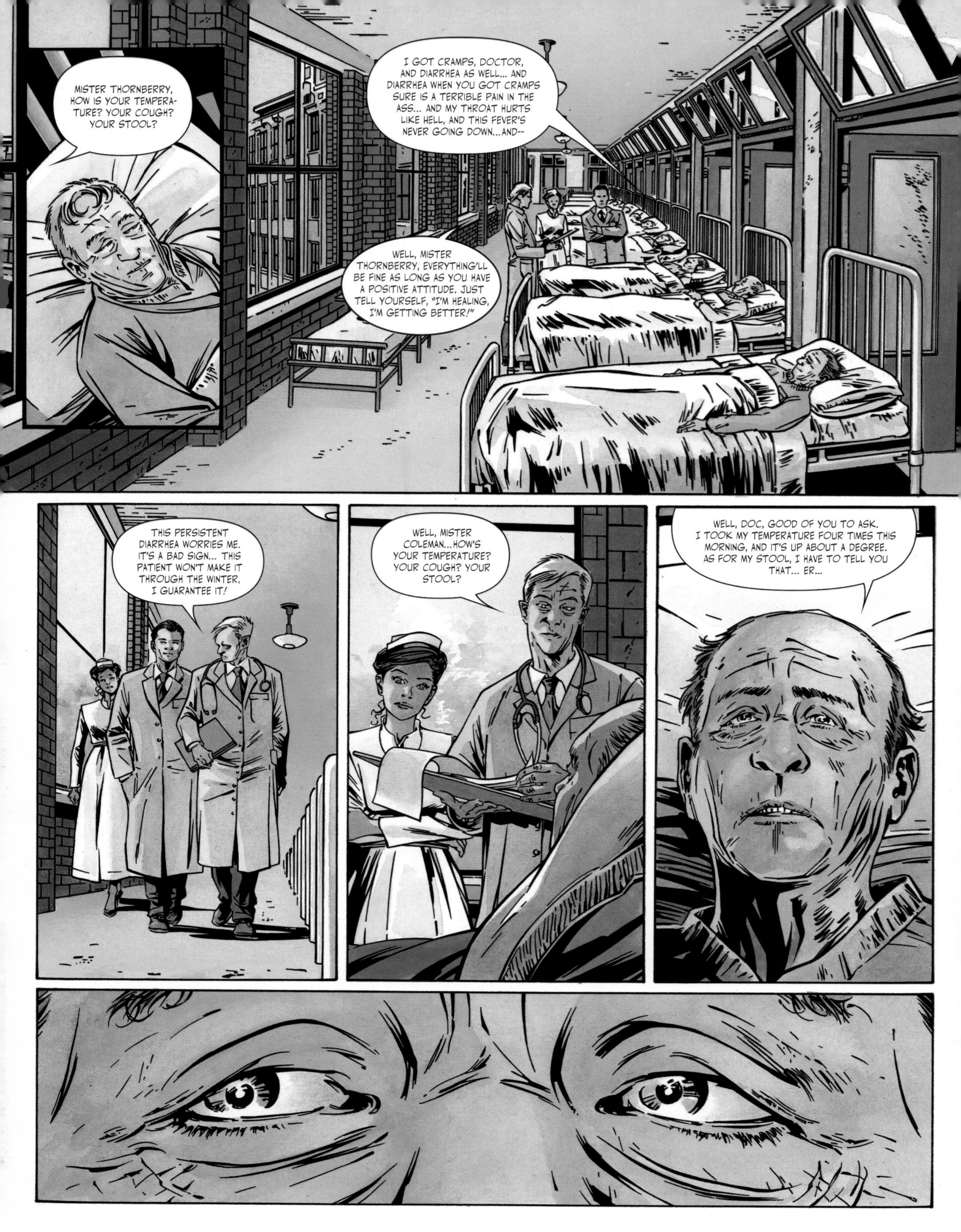
MISTER THORNBERRY, HOW IS YOUR TEMPERA-TURE? YOUR COUGH? YOUR STOOL?
I GOT CRAMPS, DOCTOR, AND DIARRHEA AS WELL... AND DIARRHEA WHEN YOU GOT CRAMPS SURE IS A TERRIBLE PAIN IN THE ASS... AND MY THROAT HURTS LIKE HELL, AND THIS FEVER'S NEVER GOING DOWN...AND--
WELL, MISTER THORNBERRY, EVERYTHING'LL BE FINE AS LONG AS YOU HAVE A POSITIVE ATTITUDE. JUST TELL YOURSELF, "I'M HEALING, I'M GETTING BETTER!"
THIS PERSISTENT DIARRHEA WORRIES ME. IT'S A BAD SIGN... THIS PATIENT WON'T MAKE IT THROUGH THE WINTER, I GUARANTEE IT!
WELL, MISTER COLEMAN...HOW'S YOUR TEMPERATURE? YOUR COUGH? YOUR STOOL?
WELL, DOC, GOOD OF YOU TO ASK. I TOOK MY TEMPERATURE FOUR TIMES THIS MORNING, AND IT'S UP ABOUT A DEGREE. AS FOR MY STOOL, I HAVE TO TELL YOU THAT... ER...

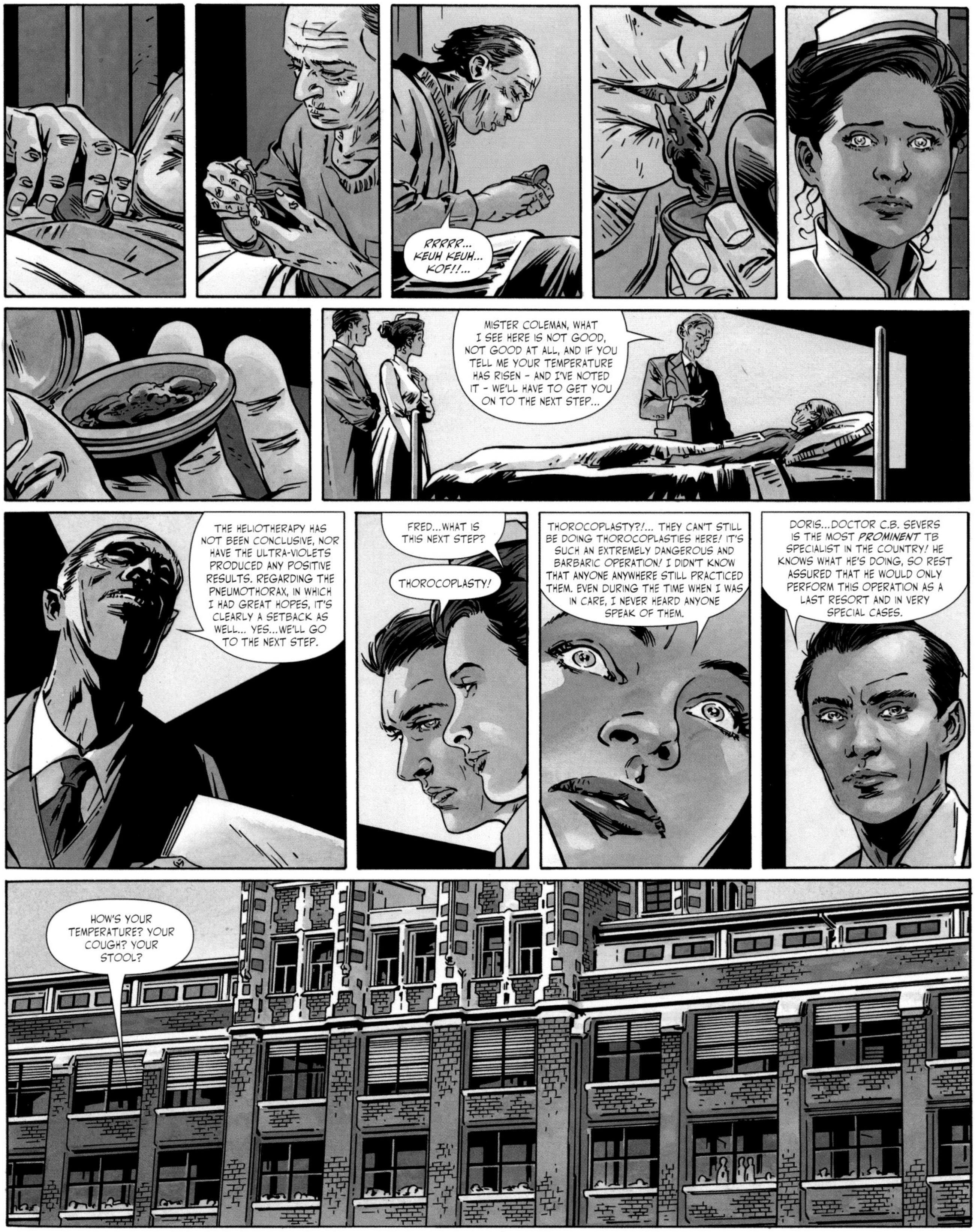
RRRRR... KEUH KEUH... KOF!!...
MISTER COLEMAN, WHAT I SEE HERE IS NOT GOOD, NOT GOOD AT ALL, AND IF YOU TELL ME YOUR TEMPERATURE HAS RISEN - AND I'VE NOTED IT - WE'LL HAVE TO GET YOU ON TO THE NEXT STEP...
THE HELIOTHERAPY HAS NOT BEEN CONCLUSIVE, NOR HAVE THE ULTRA-VIOLETS PRODUCED ANY POSITIVE RESULTS. REGARDING THE PNEUMOTHORAX, IN WHICH I HAD GREAT HOPES, IT'S CLEARLY A SETBACK AS WELL... YES...WE'LL GO TO THE NEXT STEP.
FRED...WHAT IS THIS NEXT STEP?
THOROCOPLASTY!
THOROCOPLASTY?!... THEY CAN'T STILL BE DOING THOROCOPLASTIES HERE! IT'S SUCH AN EXTREMELY DANGEROUS AND BARBARIC OPERATION! I DIDN'T KNOW THAT ANYONE ANYWHERE STILL PRACTICED THEM. EVEN DURING THE TIME WHEN I WAS IN CARE, I NEVER HEARD ANYONE SPEAK OF THEM.
DORIS...DOCTOR C.B. SEVERS IS THE MOST PROMINENT TB SPECIALIST IN THE COUNTRY! HE KNOWS WHAT HE'S DOING, SO REST ASSURED THAT HE WOULD ONLY PERFORM THIS OPERATION AS A LAST RESORT AND IN VERY SPECIAL CASES.
HOW'S YOUR TEMPERATURE? YOUR COUGH? YOUR STOOL?

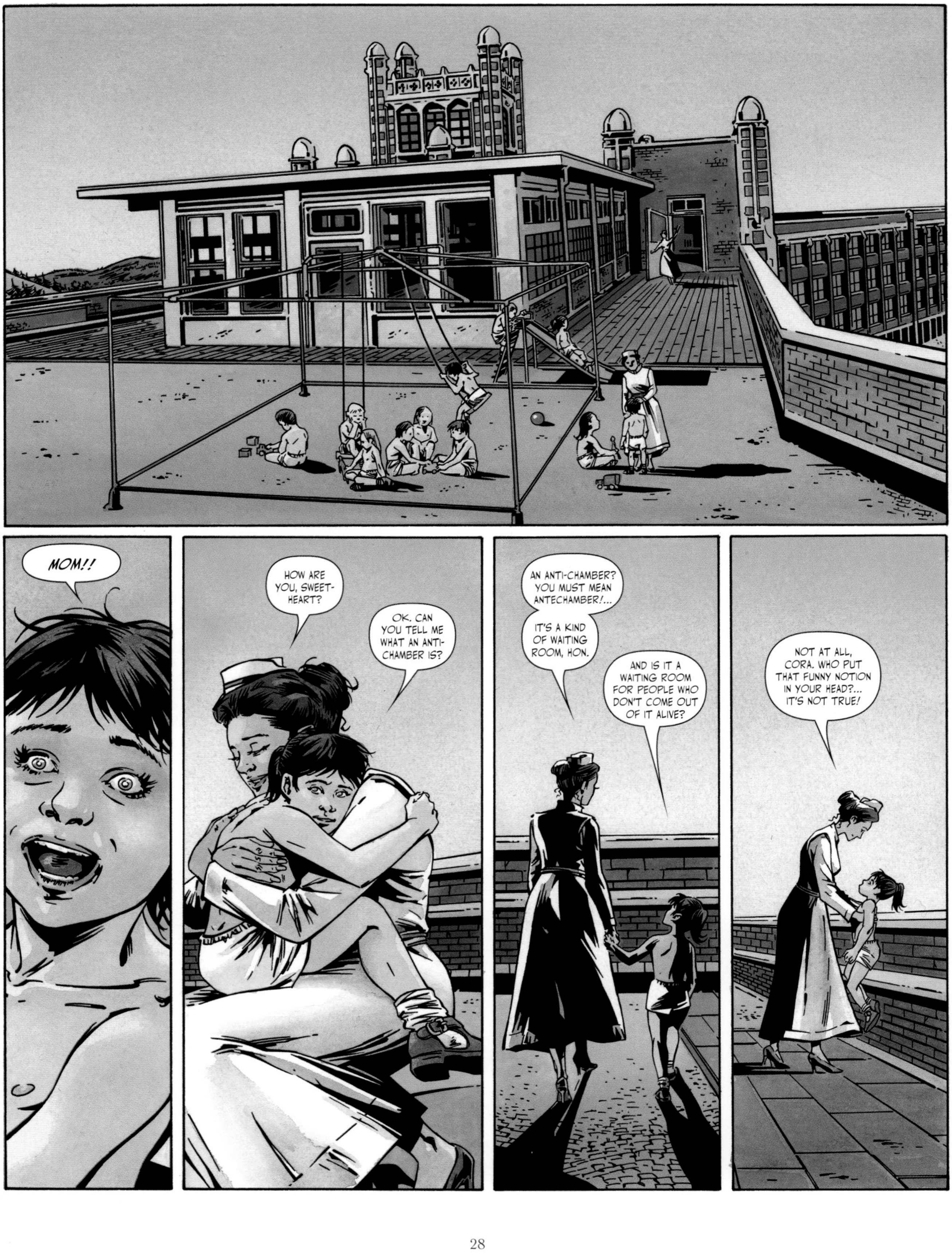
MOM!!
HOW ARE YOU, SWEET-HEART?
OK. CAN YOU TELL ME WHAT AN ANTI-CHAMBER IS?
AN ANTI-CHAMBER? YOU MUST MEAN ANTECHAMBER!...
IT'S A KIND OF WAITING ROOM, HON.
AND IS IT A WAITING ROOM FOR PEOPLE WHO DON'T COME OUT OF IT ALIVE?
NOT AT ALL, CORA. WHO PUT THAT FUNNY NOTION IN YOUR HEAD?... IT'S NOT TRUE!

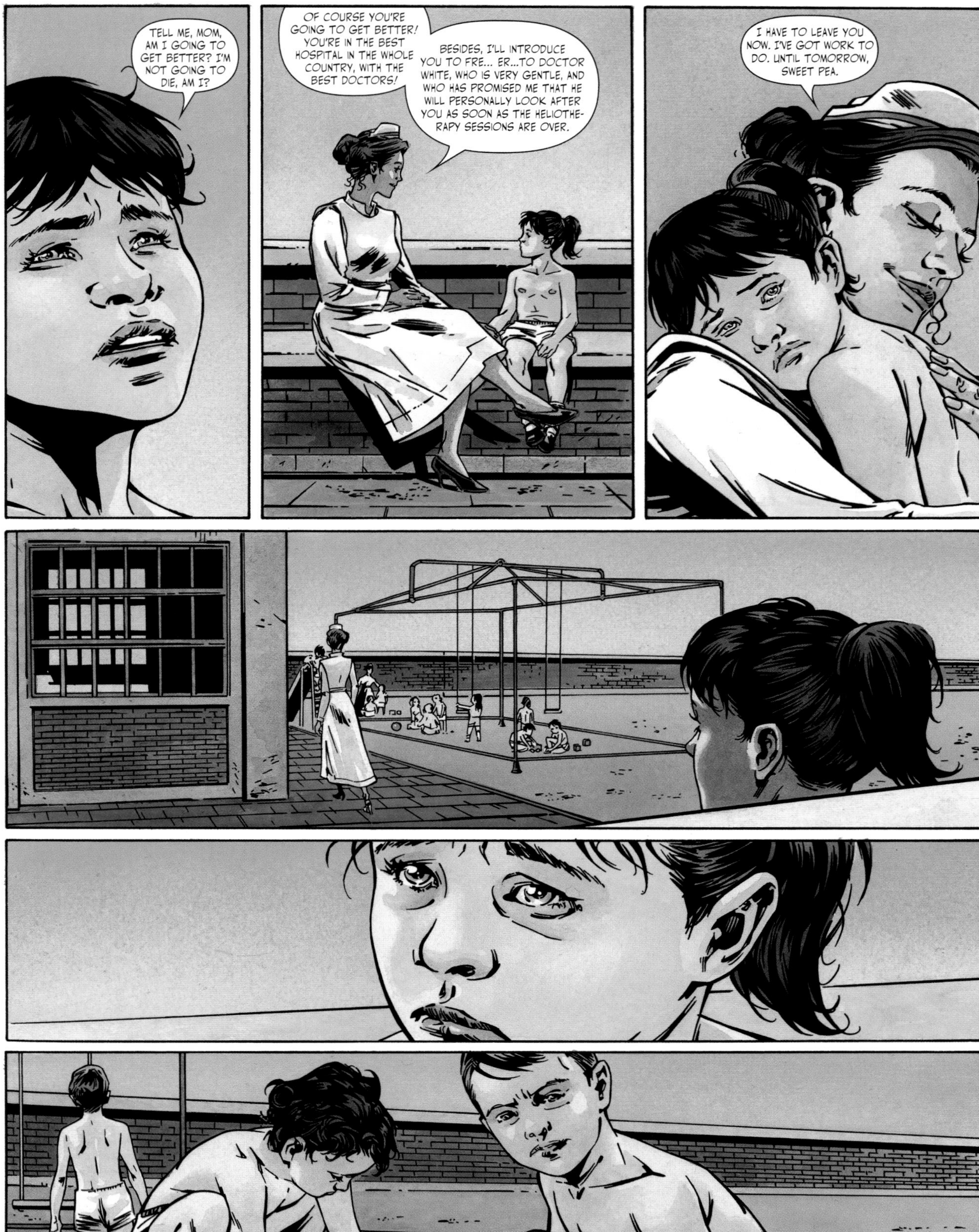
TELL ME, MOM, AM I GOING TO GET BETTER? I'M NOT GOING TO DIE, AM I?
OF COURSE YOU'RE GOING TO GET BETTER! YOU'RE IN THE BEST HOSPITAL IN THE WHOLE COUNTRY, WITH THE BEST DOCTORS!
BESIDES, I'LL INTRODUCE YOU TO FRE... ER...TO DOCTOR WHITE, WHO IS VERY GENTLE, AND WHO HAS PROMISED ME THAT HE WILL PERSONALLY LOOK AFTER YOU AS SOON AS THE HELIOTHE-RAPY SESSIONS ARE OVER.
I HAVE TO LEAVE YOU NOW. I'VE GOT WORK TO DO. UNTIL TOMORROW, SWEET PEA.

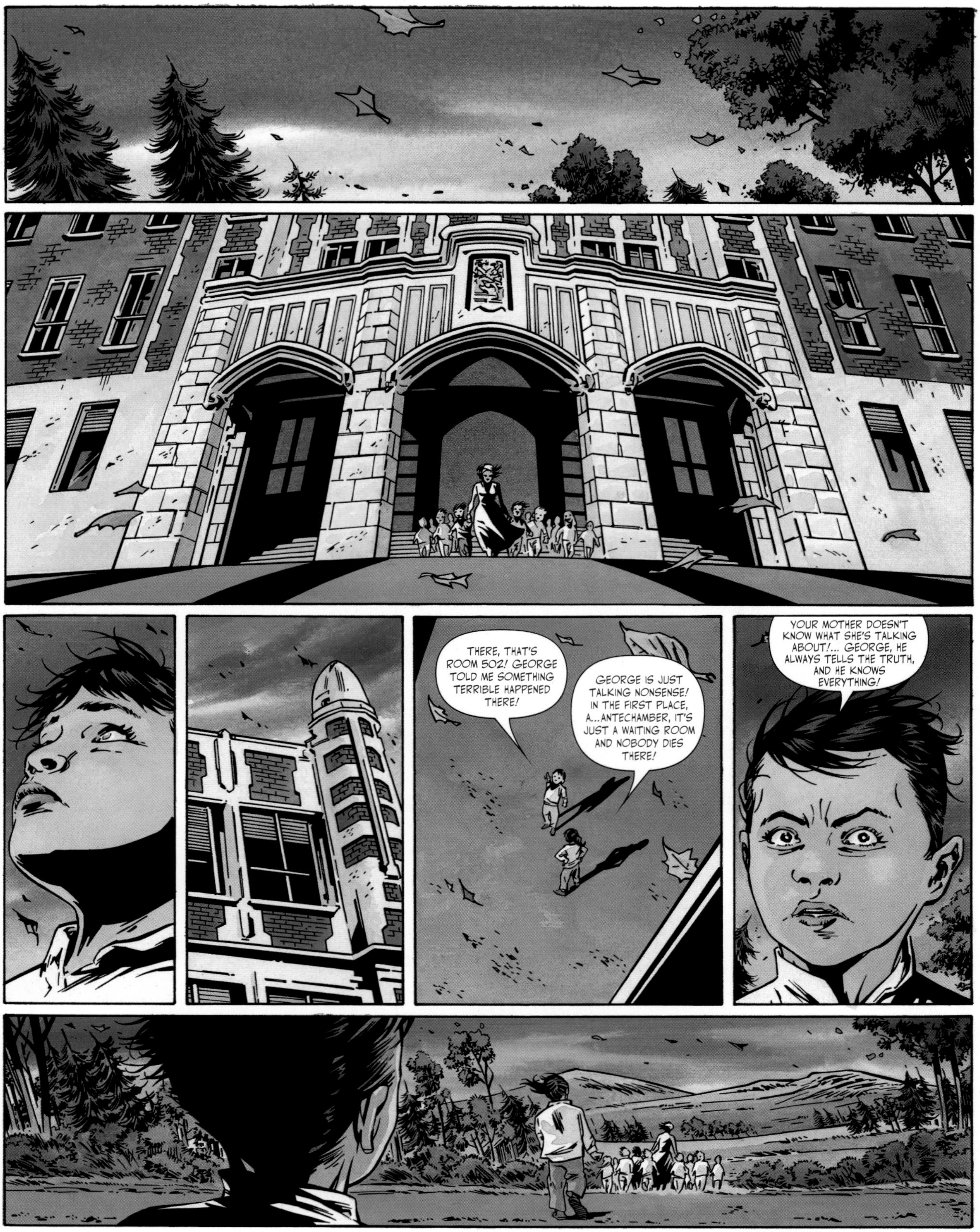
THERE, THAT'S ROOM 502! GEORGE TOLD ME SOMETHING TERRIBLE HAPPENED THERE!
GEORGE IS JUST TALKING NONSENSE! IN THE FIRST PLACE, A...ANTECHAMBER, IT'S JUST A WAITING ROOM AND NOBODY DIES THERE!
YOUR MOTHER DOESN'T KNOW WHAT SHE'S TALKING ABOUT!... GEORGE, HE ALWAYS TELLS THE TRUTH, AND HE KNOWS EVERYTHING!

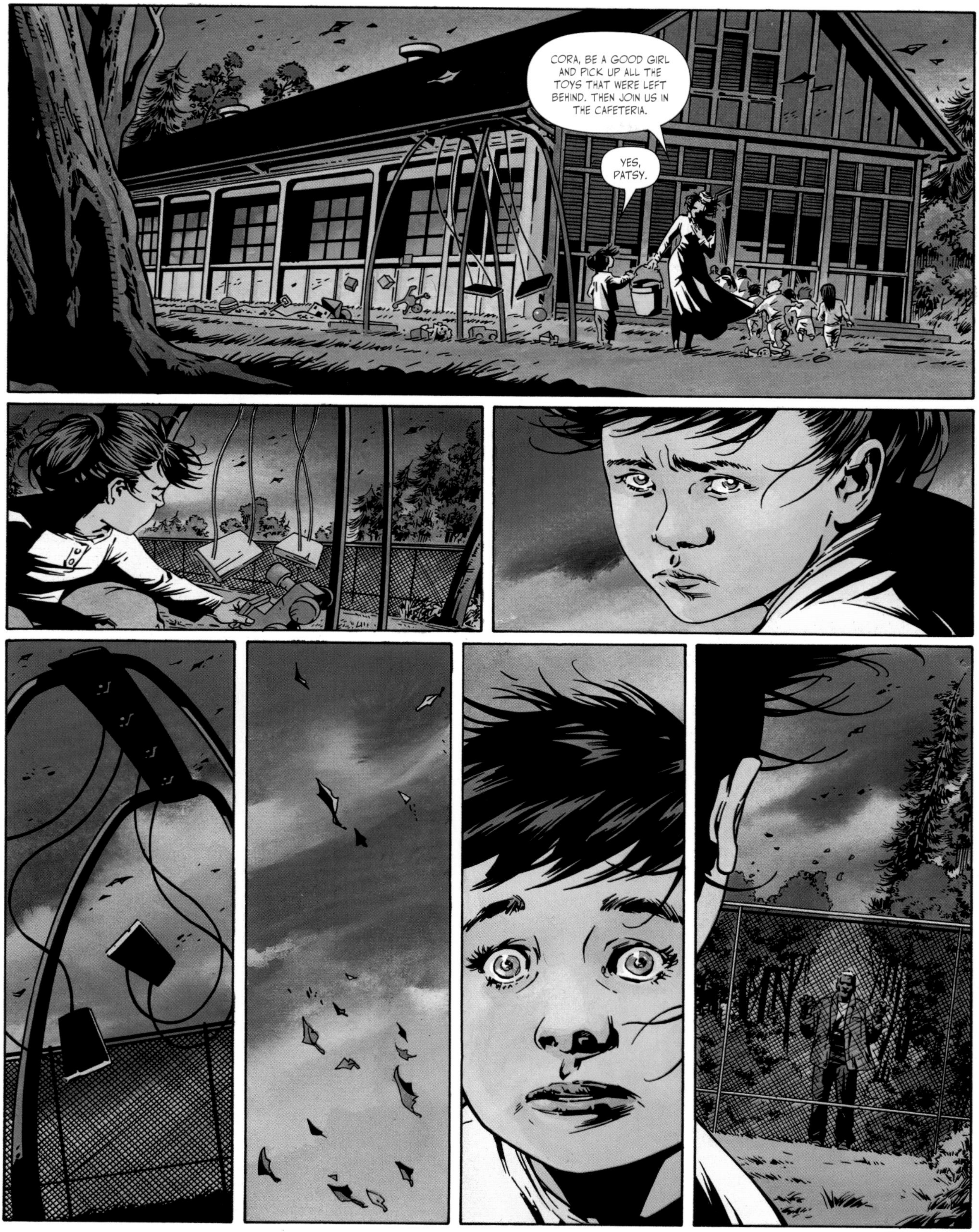
CORA, BE A GOOD GIRL AND PICK UP ALL THE TOYS THAT WERE LEFT BEHIND. THEN JOIN US IN THE CAFETERIA.
YES, PATSY.

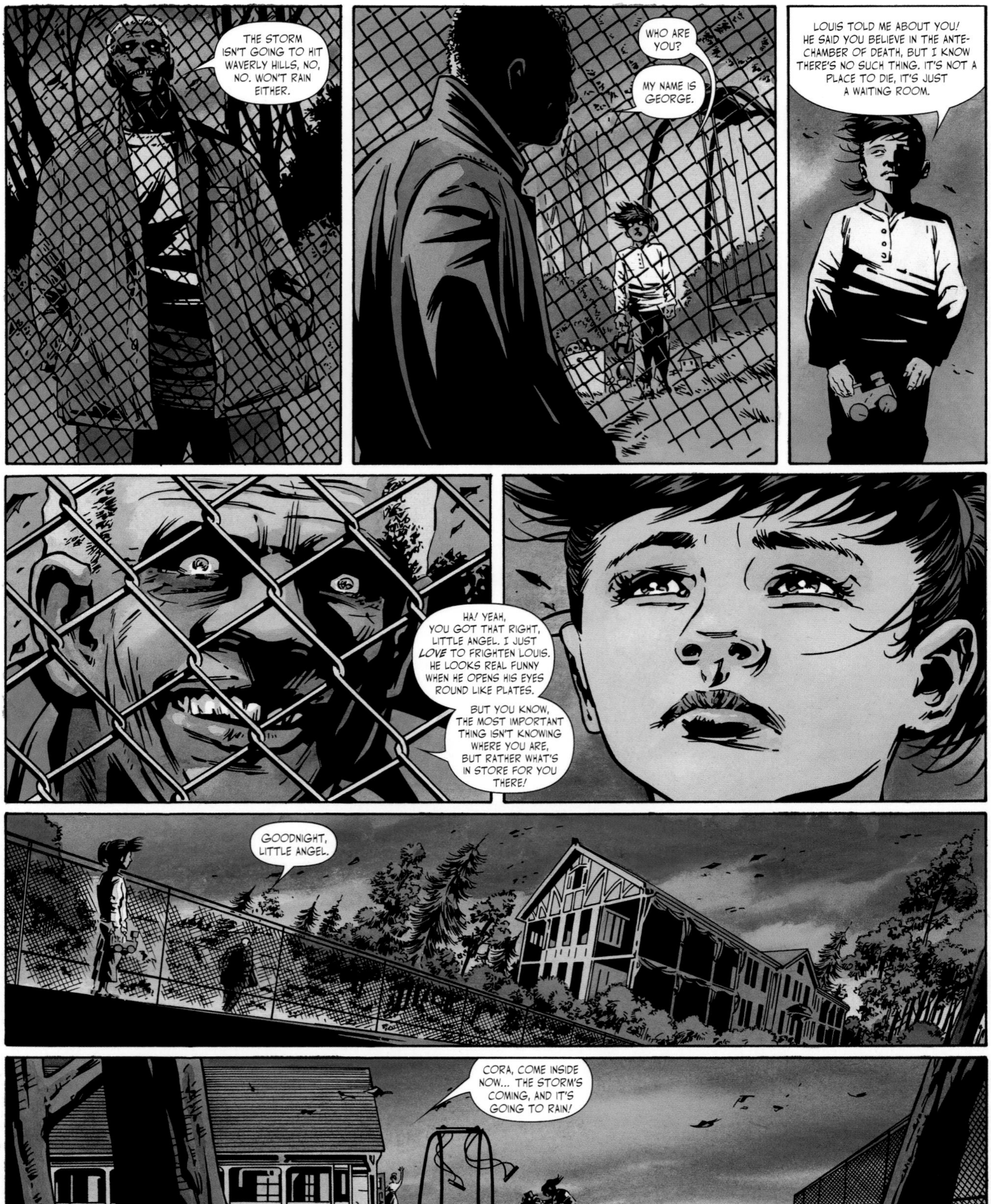
THE STORM ISN'T GOING TO HIT WAVERLY HILLS, NO, NO. WON'T RAIN EITHER.
WHO ARE YOU?
MY NAME IS GEORGE.
LOUIS TOLD ME ABOUT YOU! HE SAID YOU BELIEVE IN THE ANTE-CHAMBER OF DEATH, BUT I KNOW THERE'S NO SUCH THING. IT'S NOT A PLACE TO DIE, IT'S JUST A WAITING ROOM.
HA! YEAH, YOU GOT THAT RIGHT, LITTLE ANGEL. I JUST LOVE TO FRIGHTEN LOUIS. HE LOOKS REAL FUNNY WHEN HE OPENS HIS EYES ROUND LIKE PLATES.
BUT YOU KNOW, THE MOST IMPORTANT THING ISN'T KNOWING WHERE YOU ARE, BUT RATHER WHAT'S IN STORE FOR YOU THERE!
GOODNIGHT, LITTLE ANGEL.
CORA, COME INSIDE NOW... THE STORM'S COMING, AND IT'S GOING TO RAIN!

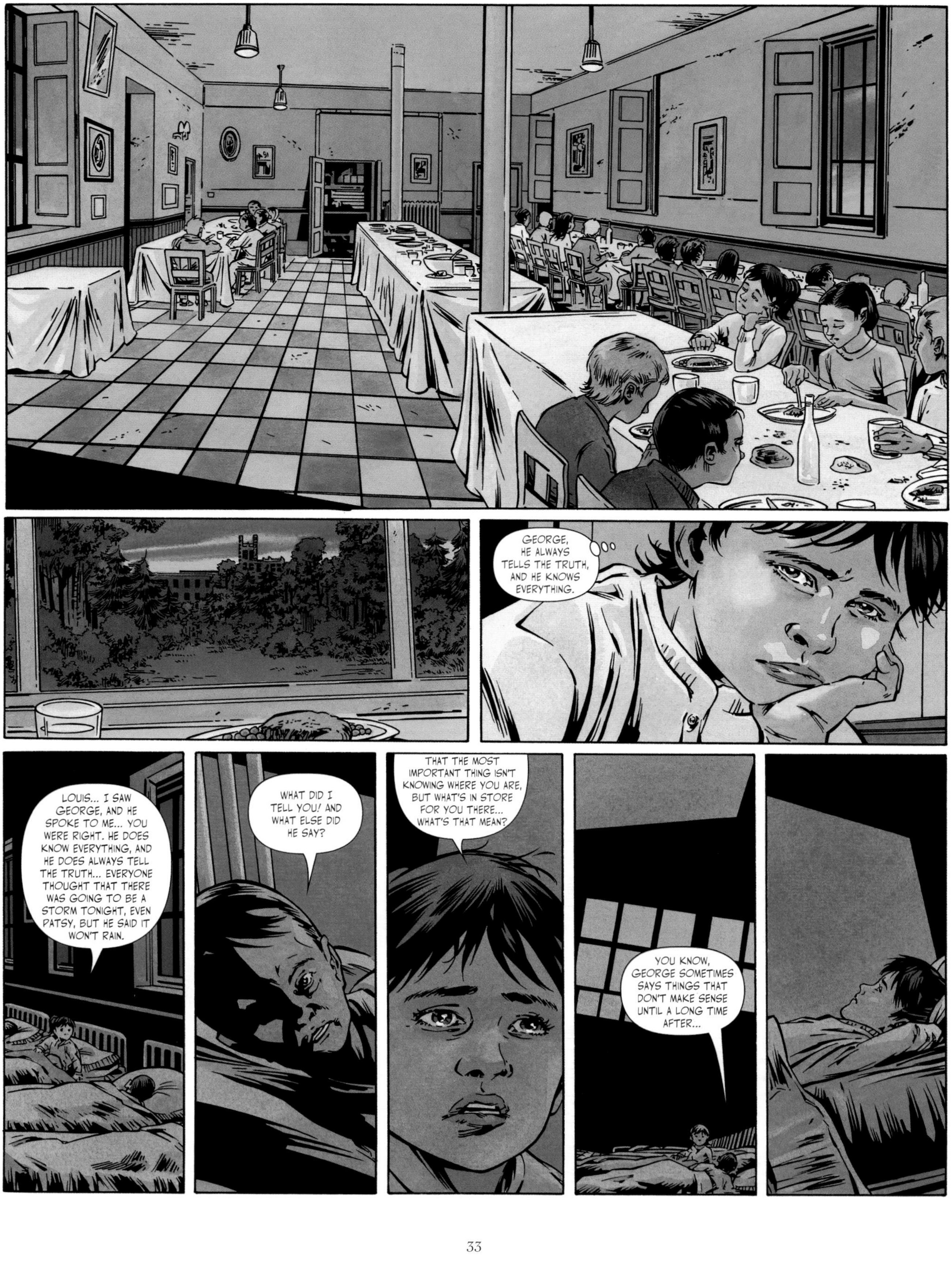
GEORGE, HE ALWAYS TELLS THE TRUTH, AND HE KNOWS EVERYTHING.
LOUIS... I SAW GEORGE, AND HE SPOKE TO ME... YOU WERE RIGHT. HE DOES KNOW EVERYTHING, AND HE DOES ALWAYS TELL THE TRUTH... EVERYONE THOUGHT THAT THERE WAS GOING TO BE A STORM TONIGHT, EVEN PATSY, BUT HE SAID IT WON'T RAIN.
WHAT DID I TELL YOU! AND WHAT ELSE DID HE SAY?
THAT THE MOST IMPORTANT THING ISN'T KNOWING WHERE YOU ARE, BUT WHAT'S IN STORE FOR YOU THERE... WHAT'S THAT MEAN?
YOU KNOW, GEORGE SOMETIMES SAYS THINGS THAT DON'T MAKE SENSE UNTIL A LONG TIME AFTER...

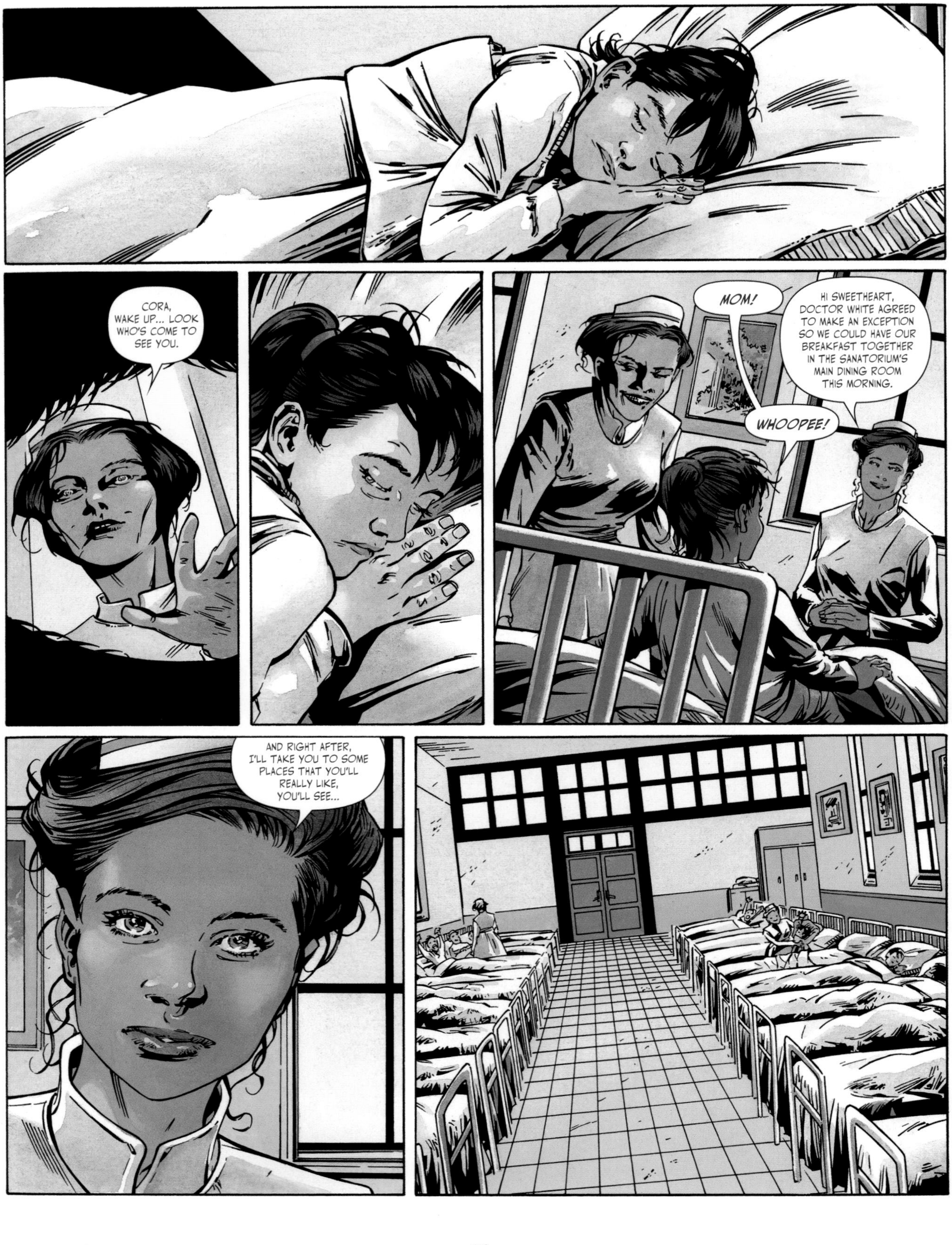

CORA, WAKE UP... LOOK WHO'S COME TO SEE YOU.
MOM!
HI SWEETHEART, DOCTOR WHITE AGREED TO MAKE AN EXCEPTION SO WE COULD HAVE OUR BREAKFAST TOGETHER IN THE SANATORIUM'S MAIN DINING ROOM THIS MORNING.
WHOOPEE!
AND RIGHT AFTER, I'LL TAKE YOU TO SOME PLACES THAT YOU'LL REALLY LIKE, YOU'LL SEE...

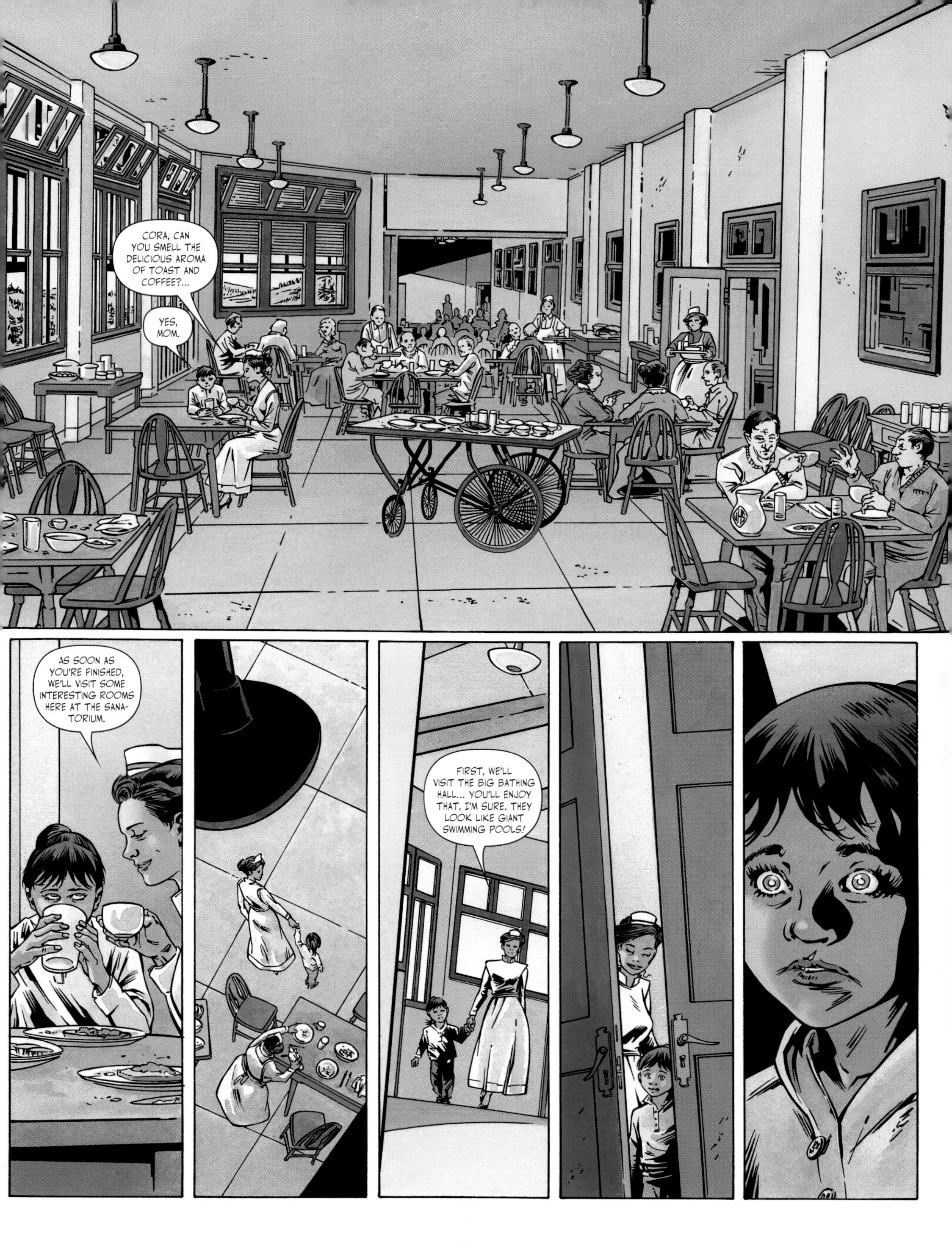
CORA, CAN YOU SMELL THE DELICIOUS AROMA OF TOAST AND COFFEE?...
YES, MOM.
AS SOON AS YOU'RE FINISHED, WE'LL VISIT SOME INTERESTING ROOMS HERE AT THE SANA-TORIUM.
FIRST, WE'LL VISIT THE BIG BATHING HALL... YOU'LL ENJOY THAT, I'M SURE. THEY LOOK LIKE GIANT SWIMMING POOLS!

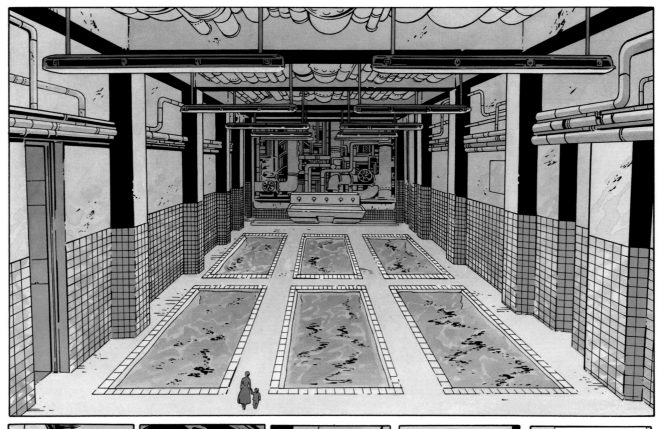

WHAT'S WRONG, SWEETHEART?

MOM... THE POOLS... THEY'RE FILLED WITH BLOOD!...

36

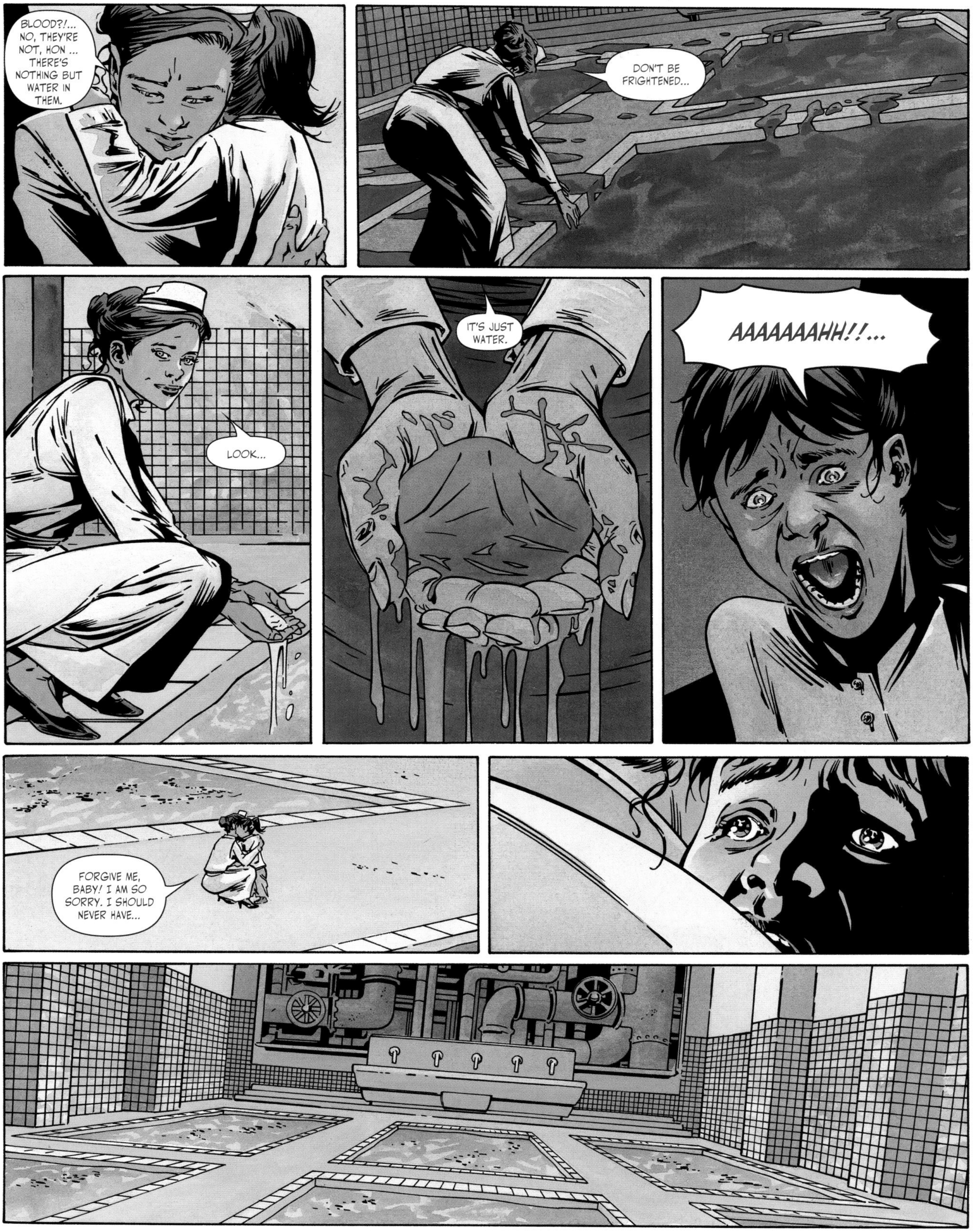
BLOOD?!... NO, THEY'RE NOT, HON ... THERE'S NOTHING BUT WATER IN THEM.
DON'T BE FRIGHTENED...
LOOK...
IT'S JUST WATER.
AAAAAAAHH!!...
FORGIVE ME, BABY! I AM SO SORRY. I SHOULD NEVER HAVE...

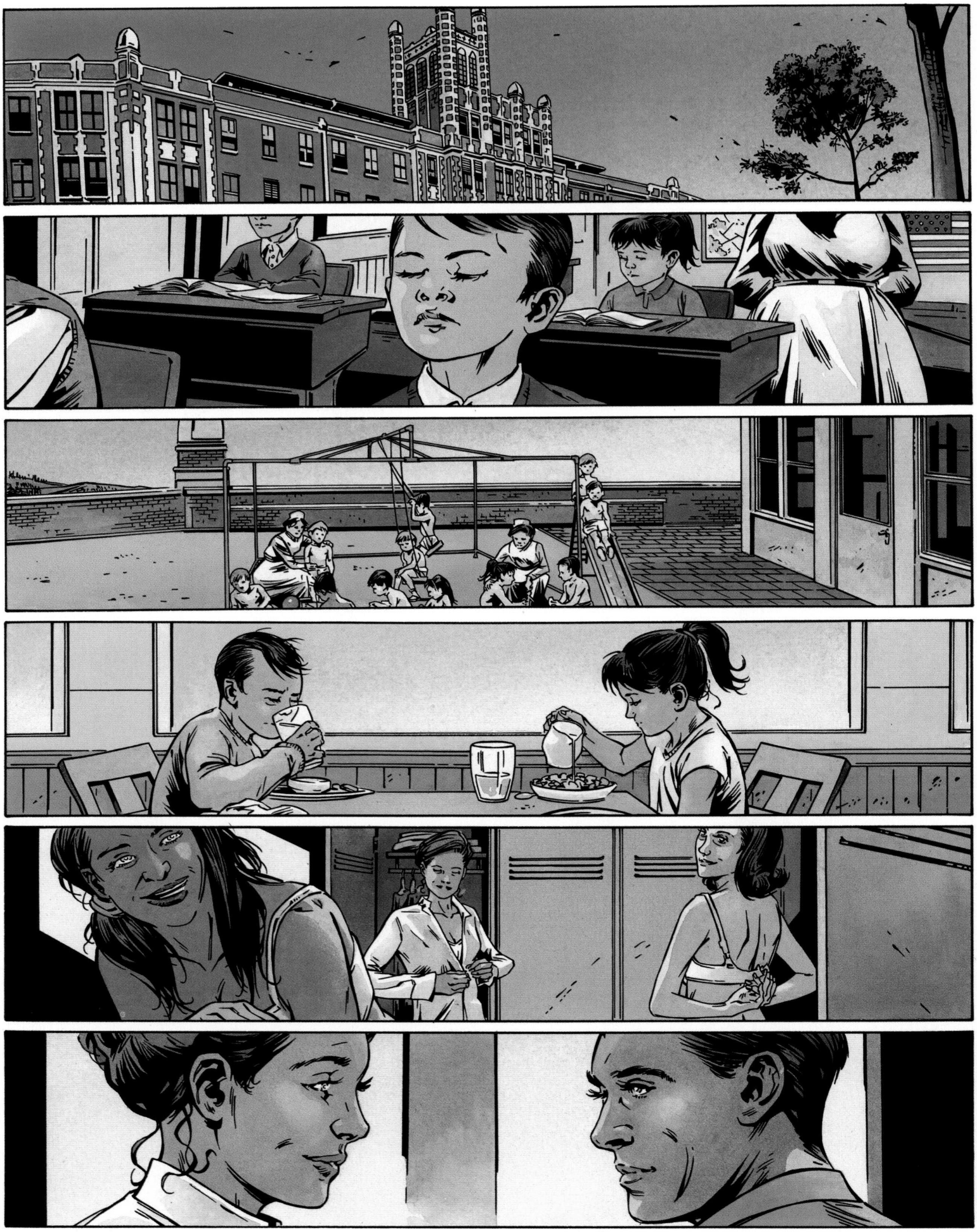

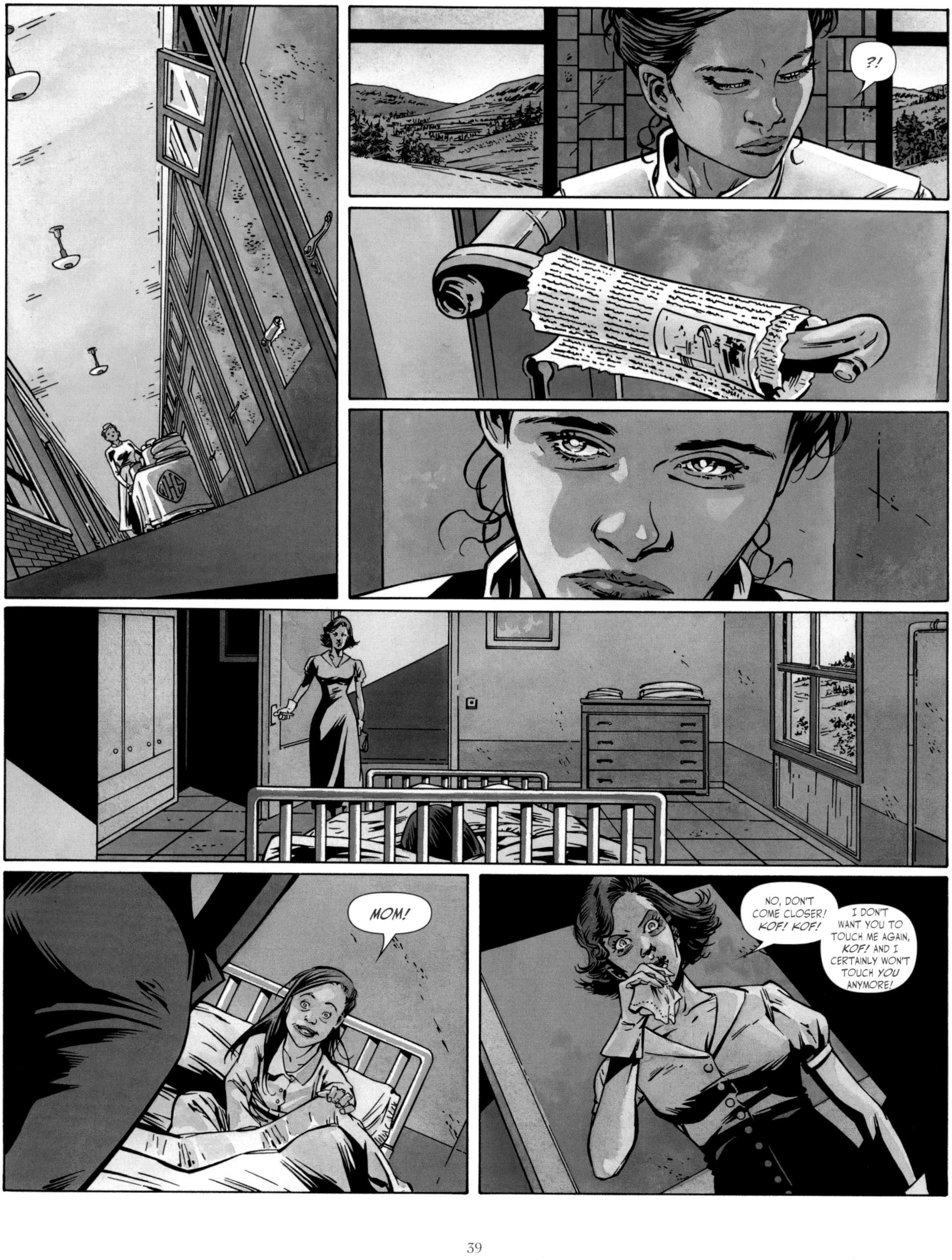
?!
MOM!
NO, DON'T COME CLOSER! KOF! KOF!
I DON'T WANT YOU TO TOUCH ME AGAIN, KOF! AND I CERTAINLY WON'T TOUCH YOU ANYMORE!

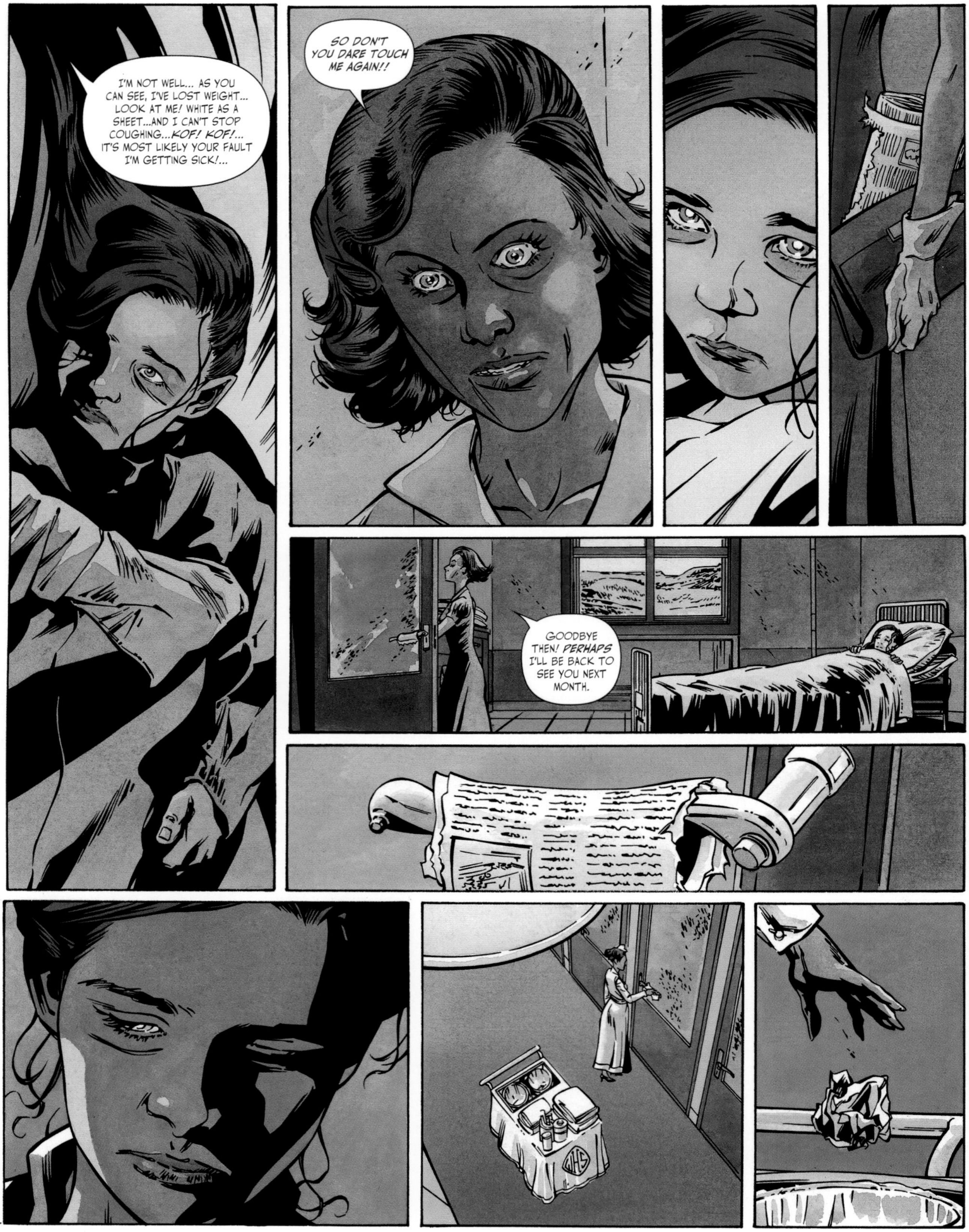
I'M NOT WELL... AS YOU CAN SEE, I'VE LOST WEIGHT... LOOK AT ME! WHITE AS A SHEET...AND I CAN'T STOP COUGHING...KOF! KOF!... IT'S MOST LIKELY YOUR FAULT I'M GETTING SICK!...
SO DON'T YOU DARE TOUCH ME AGAIN!!
GOODBYE THEN! PERHAPS I'LL BE BACK TO SEE YOU NEXT MONTH.

HI MISTER COLEMAN. HOW ARE YOU THIS MORNING?

BETTER, DORIS, BETTER! YOU KNOW I HAD A VISIT FROM MY DAUGHTER THIS MORNING. JUST SEEING THAT GIRL MAKES ME FEEL BETTER!

YOU KNOW SOMETHING, I REALLY LOVE THAT GIRL, AND SHE LOVES ME TOO.

I'M SURE OF THAT, MISTER COLEMAN...

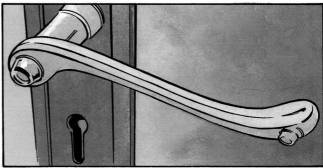

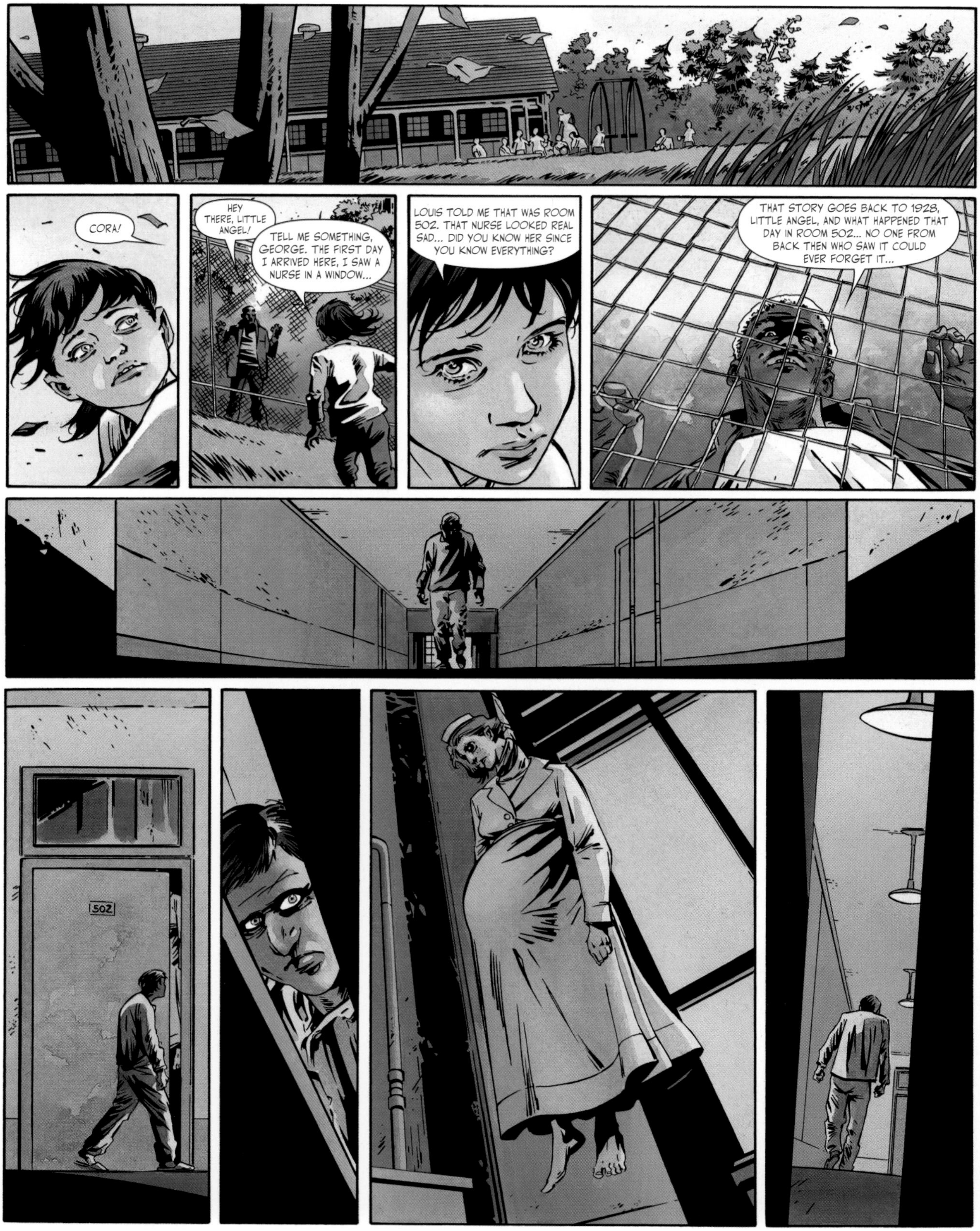
CORA!
HEY THERE, LITTLE ANGEL!
TELL ME SOMETHING, GEORGE. THE FIRST DAY I ARRIVED HERE, I SAW A NURSE IN A WINDOW...
LOUIS TOLD ME THAT WAS ROOM 502. THAT NURSE LOOKED REAL SAD... DID YOU KNOW HER SINCE YOU KNOW EVERYTHING?
THAT STORY GOES BACK TO 1928, LITTLE ANGEL, AND WHAT HAPPENED THAT DAY IN ROOM 502... NO ONE FROM BACK THEN WHO SAW IT COULD EVER FORGET IT...
502

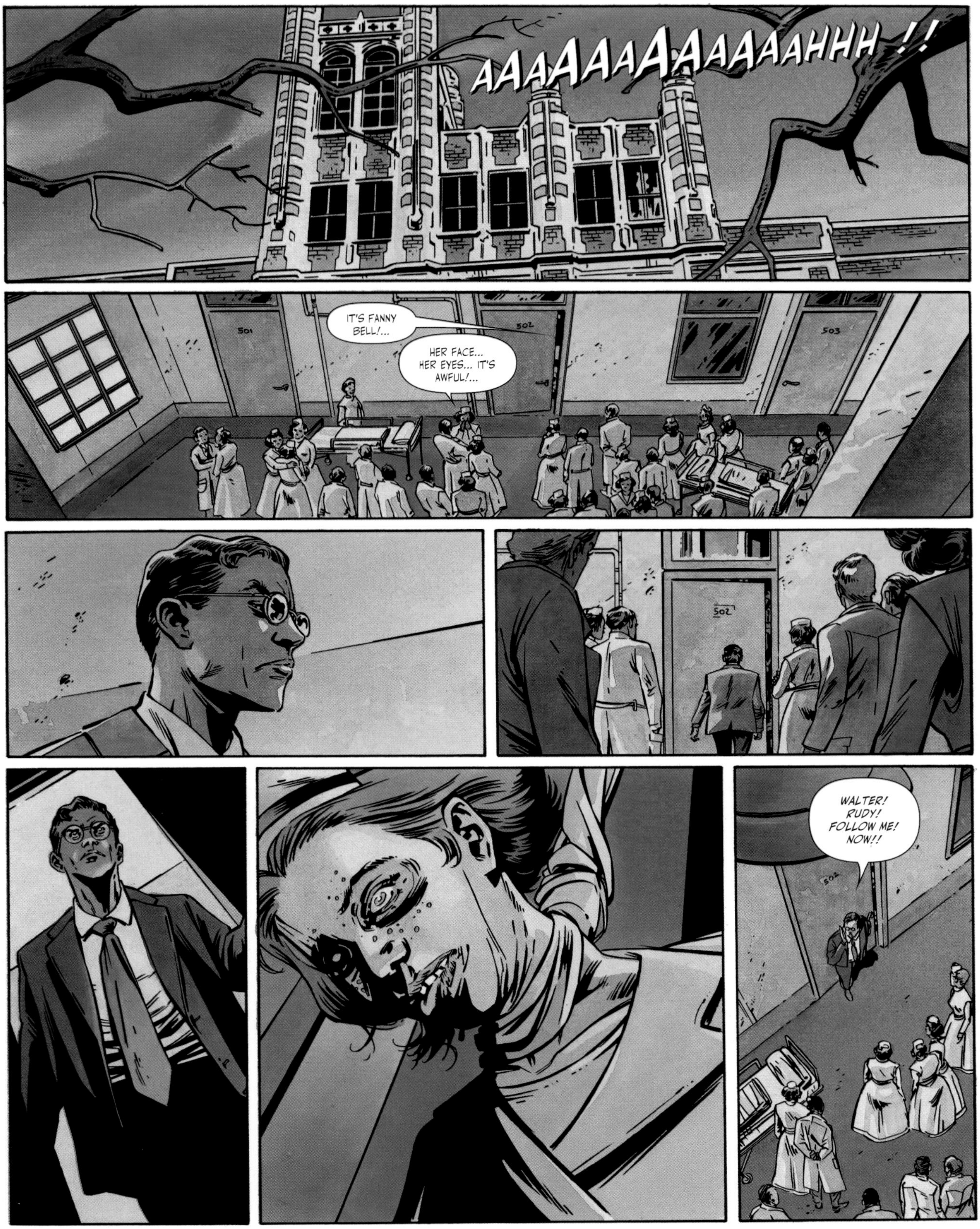
AAAAAAAAAAAAAHHH !!
IT'S FANNY BELL!...
HER FACE... HER EYES... IT'S AWFUL!...
WALTER! RUDY! FOLLOW ME! NOW!!

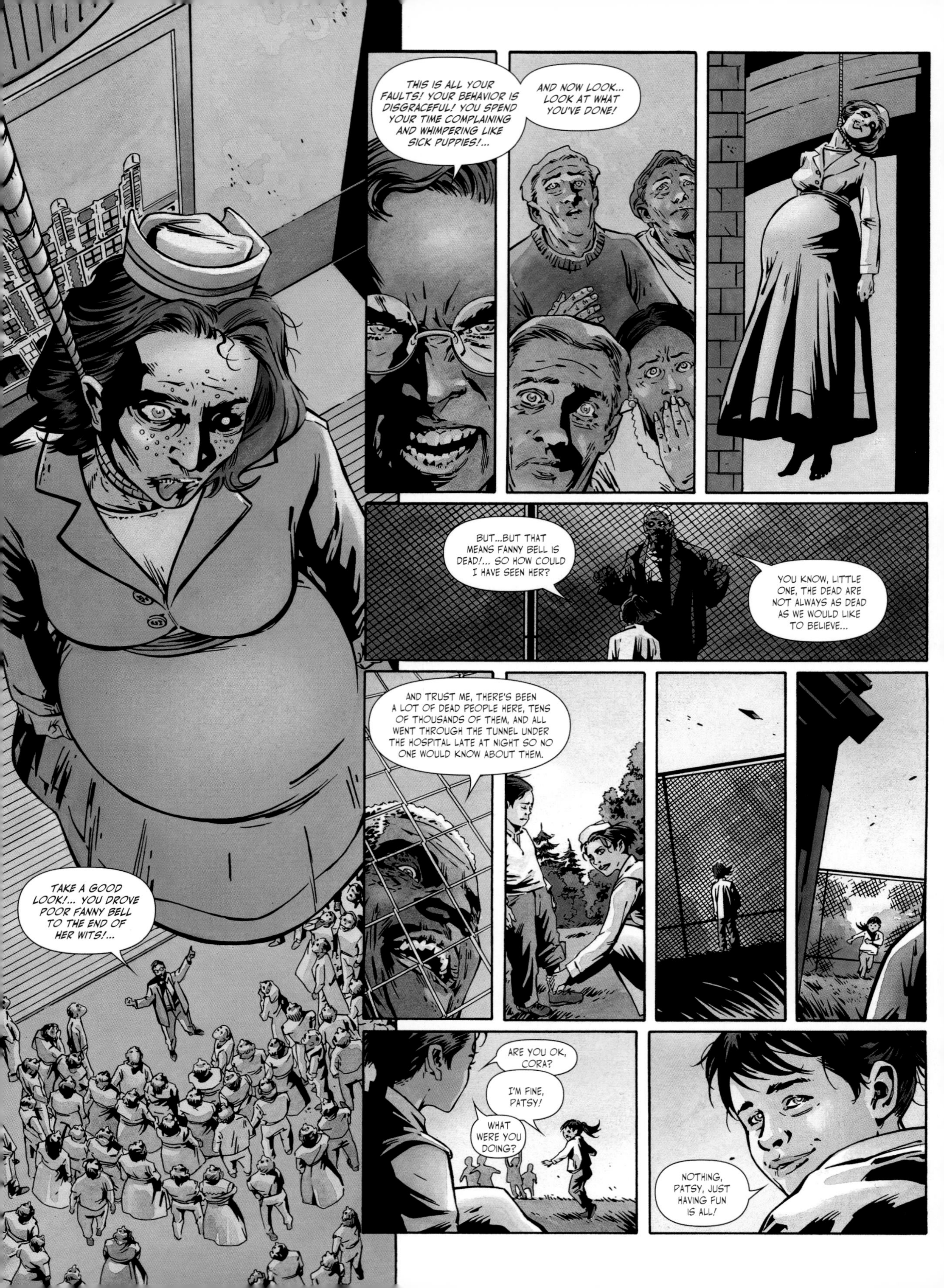
TAKE A GOOD LOOK!... YOU DROVE POOR FANNY BELL TO THE END OF HER WITS!...
THIS IS ALL YOUR FAULTS! YOUR BEHAVIOR IS DISGRACEFUL! YOU SPEND YOUR TIME COMPLAINING AND WHIMPERING LIKE SICK PUPPIES!...
AND NOW LOOK... LOOK AT WHAT YOU'VE DONE!
BUT...BUT THAT MEANS FANNY BELL IS DEAD!... SO HOW COULD I HAVE SEEN HER?
YOU KNOW, LITTLE ONE, THE DEAD ARE NOT ALWAYS AS DEAD AS WE WOULD LIKE TO BELIEVE...
AND TRUST ME, THERE'S BEEN A LOT OF DEAD PEOPLE HERE, TENS OF THOUSANDS OF THEM, AND ALL WENT THROUGH THE TUNNEL UNDER THE HOSPITAL LATE AT NIGHT SO NO ONE WOULD KNOW ABOUT THEM.
ARE YOU OK, CORA?
I'M FINE, PATSY!
WHAT WERE YOU DOING?
NOTHING, PATSY, JUST HAVING FUN IS ALL!

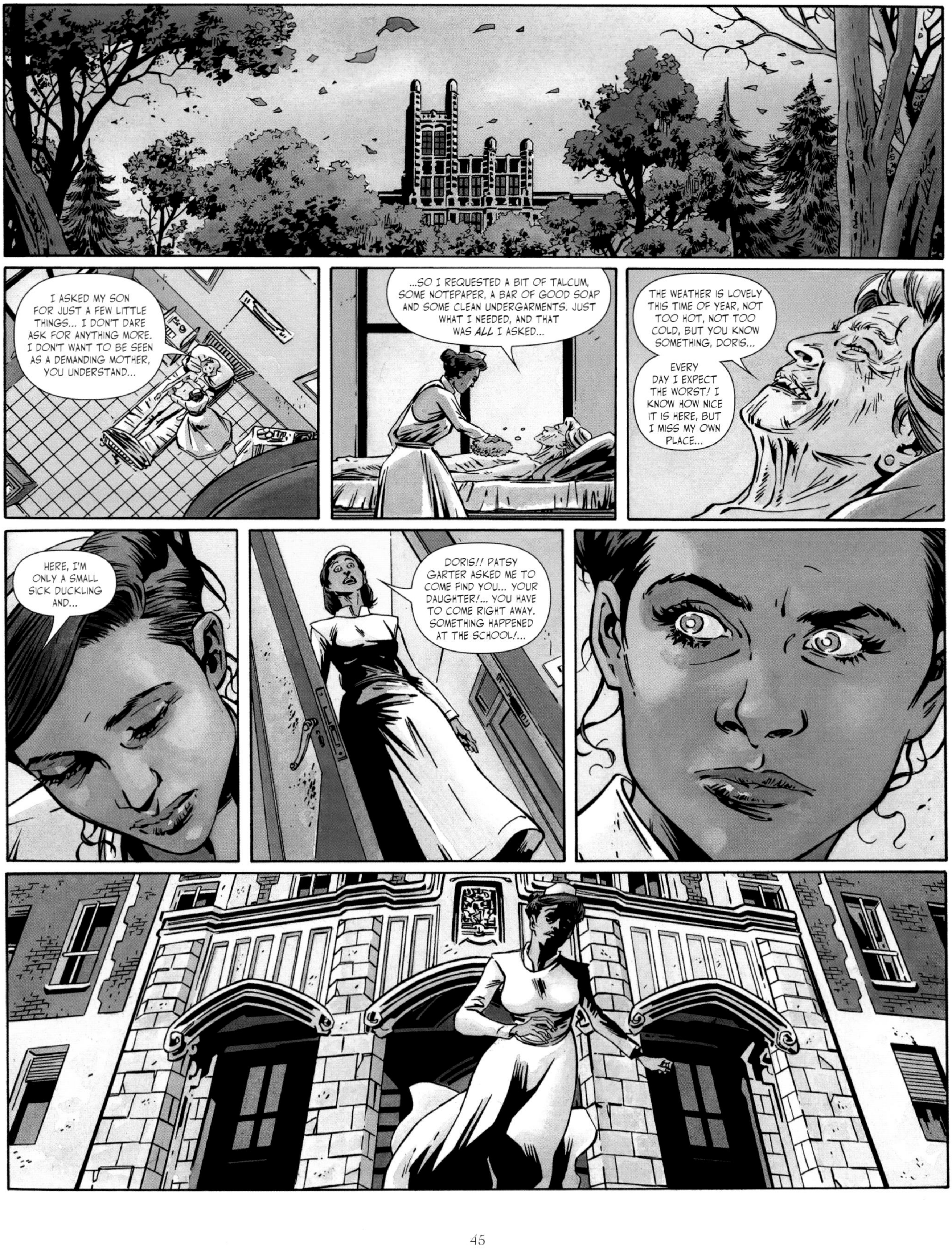
I ASKED MY SON FOR JUST A FEW LITTLE THINGS... I DON'T DARE ASK FOR ANYTHING MORE. I DON'T WANT TO BE SEEN AS A DEMANDING MOTHER, YOU UNDERSTAND...
...SO I REQUESTED A BIT OF TALCUM, SOME NOTEPAPER, A BAR OF GOOD SOAP AND SOME CLEAN UNDERGARMENTS. JUST WHAT I NEEDED, AND THAT WAS ALL I ASKED...
THE WEATHER IS LOVELY THIS TIME OF YEAR, NOT TOO HOT, NOT TOO COLD, BUT YOU KNOW SOMETHING, DORIS...
EVERY DAY I EXPECT THE WORST! I KNOW HOW NICE IT IS HERE, BUT I MISS MY OWN PLACE...
HERE, I'M ONLY A SMALL SICK DUCKLING AND...
DORIS!! PATSY GARTER ASKED ME TO COME FIND YOU... YOUR DAUGHTER!... YOU HAVE TO COME RIGHT AWAY. SOMETHING HAPPENED AT THE SCHOOL!...

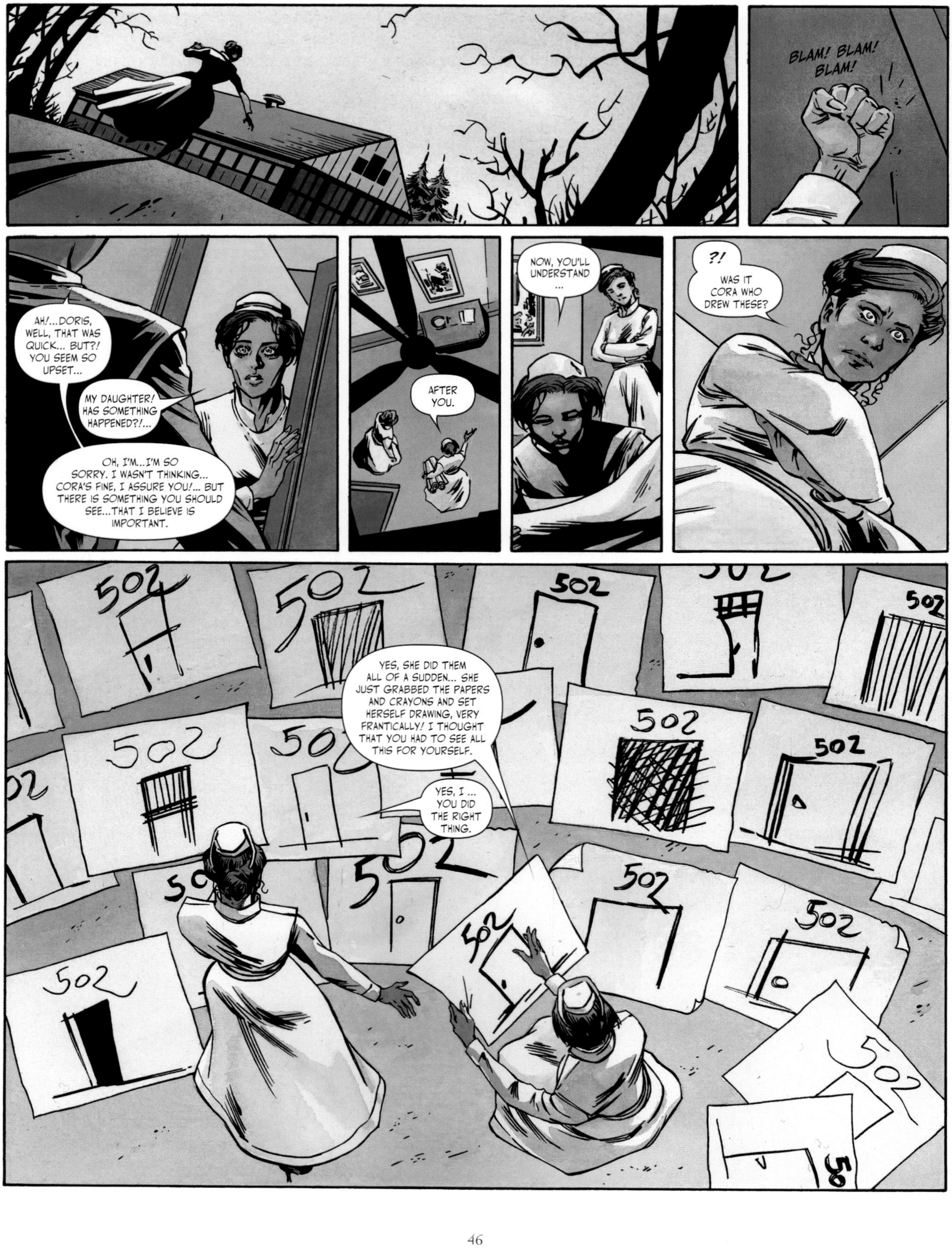
BLAM! BLAM! BLAM!
AH!...DORIS, WELL, THAT WAS QUICK... BUT?! YOU SEEM SO UPSET...
MY DAUGHTER! HAS SOMETHING HAPPENED?!...
OH, I'M...I'M SO SORRY. I WASN'T THINKING... CORA'S FINE, I ASSURE YOU!... BUT THERE IS SOMETHING YOU SHOULD SEE...THAT I BELIEVE IS IMPORTANT.
AFTER YOU.
NOW, YOU'LL UNDERSTAND ...
?!
WAS IT CORA WHO DREW THESE?
YES, SHE DID THEM ALL OF A SUDDEN... SHE JUST GRABBED THE PAPERS AND CRAYONS AND SET HERSELF DRAWING, VERY FRANTICALLY! I THOUGHT THAT YOU HAD TO SEE ALL THIS FOR YOURSELF.
YES, I ... YOU DID THE RIGHT THING.

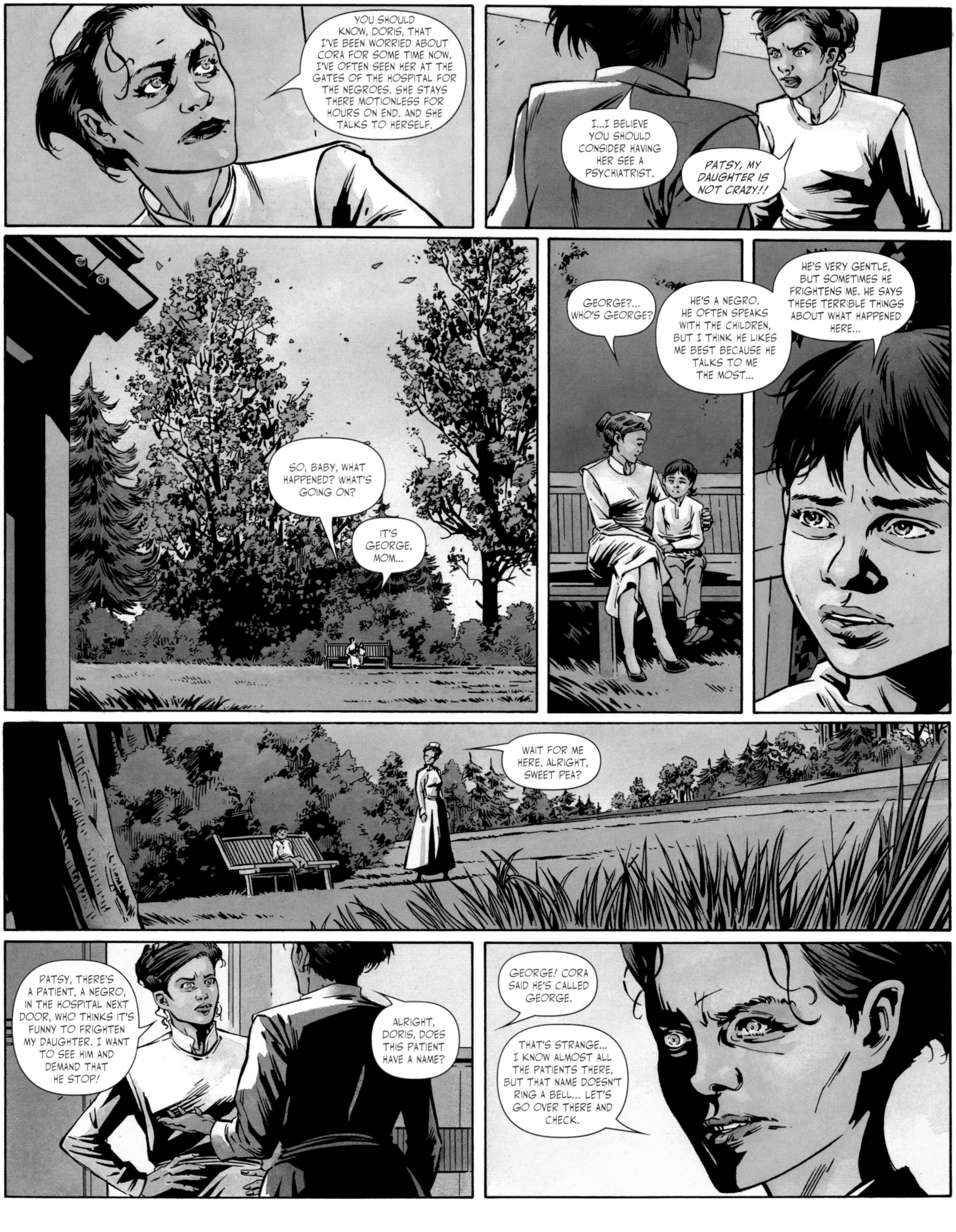
YOU SHOULD KNOW, DORIS, THAT I'VE BEEN WORRIED ABOUT CORA FOR SOME TIME NOW. I'VE OFTEN SEEN HER AT THE GATES OF THE HOSPITAL FOR THE NEGROES. SHE STAYS THERE MOTIONLESS FOR HOURS ON END. AND SHE TALKS TO HERSELF.
I...I BELIEVE YOU SHOULD CONSIDER HAVING HER SEE A PSYCHIATRIST.
PATSY, MY DAUGHTER IS NOT CRAZY!!
SO, BABY, WHAT HAPPENED? WHAT'S GOING ON?
IT'S GEORGE, MOM...
GEORGE?... WHO'S GEORGE?
HE'S A NEGRO. HE OFTEN SPEAKS WITH THE CHILDREN, BUT I THINK HE LIKES ME BEST BECAUSE HE TALKS TO ME THE MOST...
HE'S VERY GENTLE, BUT SOMETIMES HE FRIGHTENS ME. HE SAYS THESE TERRIBLE THINGS ABOUT WHAT HAPPENED HERE...
WAIT FOR ME HERE. ALRIGHT, SWEET PEA?
PATSY, THERE'S A PATIENT, A NEGRO, IN THE HOSPITAL NEXT DOOR, WHO THINKS IT'S FUNNY TO FRIGHTEN MY DAUGHTER. I WANT TO SEE HIM AND DEMAND THAT HE STOP!
ALRIGHT, DORIS, DOES THIS PATIENT HAVE A NAME?
GEORGE! CORA SAID HE'S CALLED GEORGE.
THAT'S STRANGE... I KNOW ALMOST ALL THE PATIENTS THERE, BUT THAT NAME DOESN'T RING A BELL... LET'S GO OVER THERE AND CHECK.

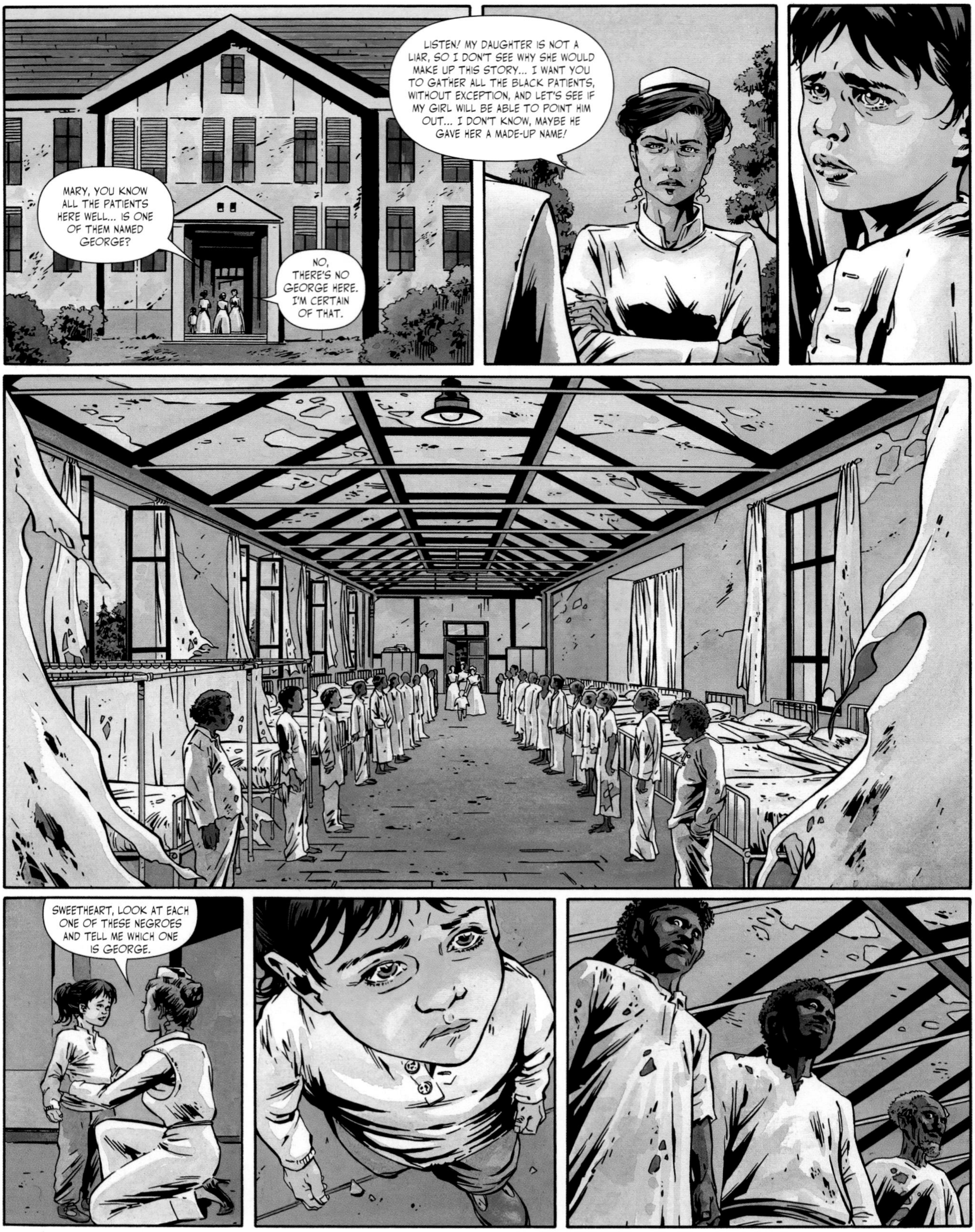
MARY, YOU KNOW ALL THE PATIENTS HERE WELL... IS ONE OF THEM NAMED GEORGE?
NO, THERE'S NO GEORGE HERE. I'M CERTAIN OF THAT.
LISTEN! MY DAUGHTER IS NOT A LIAR, SO I DON'T SEE WHY SHE WOULD MAKE UP THIS STORY... I WANT YOU TO GATHER ALL THE BLACK PATIENTS, WITHOUT EXCEPTION, AND LET'S SEE IF MY GIRL WILL BE ABLE TO POINT HIM OUT... I DON'T KNOW, MAYBE HE GAVE HER A MADE-UP NAME!
SWEETHEART, LOOK AT EACH ONE OF THESE NEGROES AND TELL ME WHICH ONE IS GEORGE.

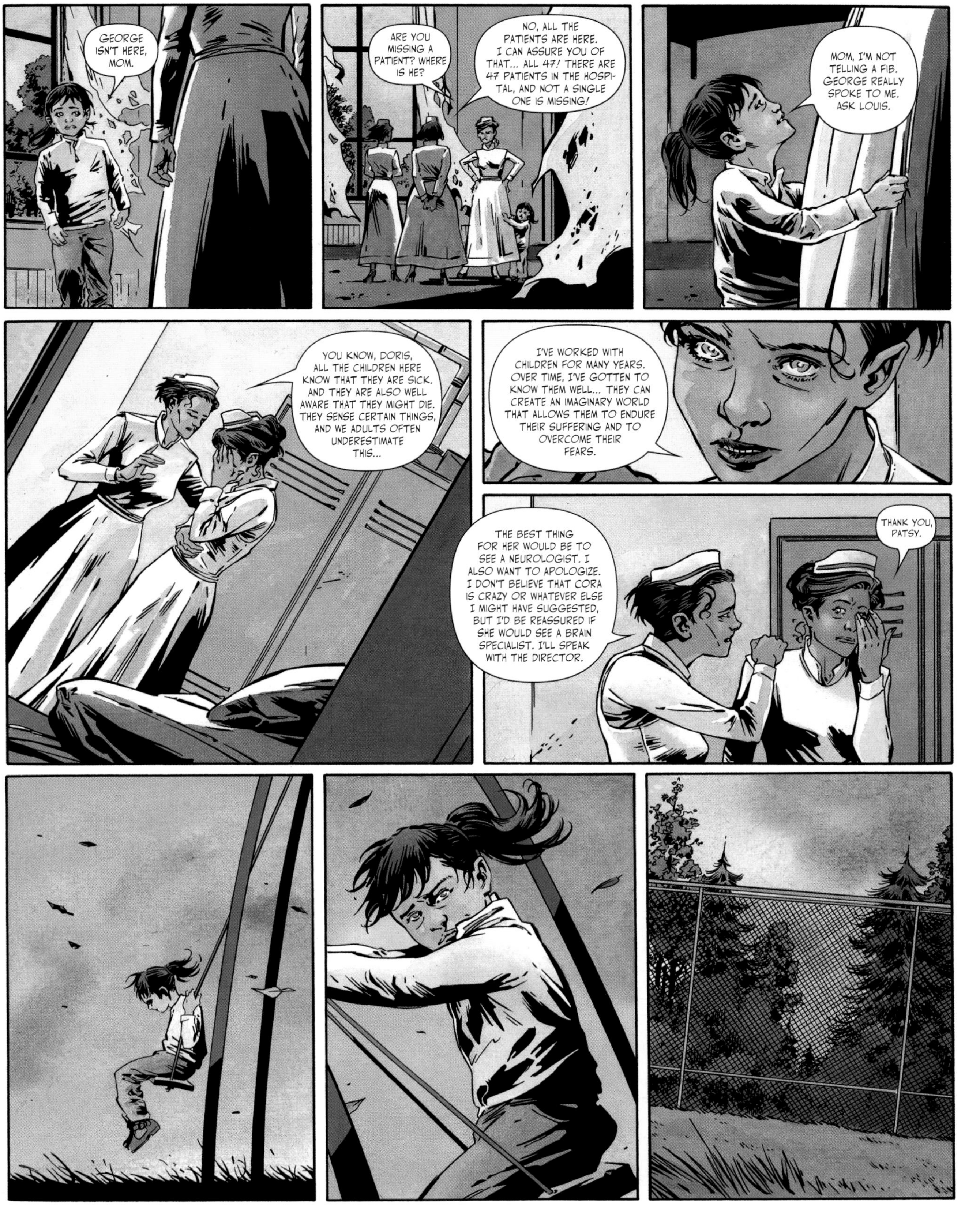
GEORGE ISN'T HERE, MOM.
ARE YOU MISSING A PATIENT? WHERE IS HE?
NO, ALL THE PATIENTS ARE HERE. I CAN ASSURE YOU OF THAT... ALL 47! THERE ARE 47 PATIENTS IN THE HOSPITAL, AND NOT A SINGLE ONE IS MISSING!
MOM, I'M NOT TELLING A FIB. GEORGE REALLY SPOKE TO ME. ASK LOUIS.
YOU KNOW, DORIS, ALL THE CHILDREN HERE KNOW THAT THEY ARE SICK. AND THEY ARE ALSO WELL AWARE THAT THEY MIGHT DIE. THEY SENSE CERTAIN THINGS, AND WE ADULTS OFTEN UNDERESTIMATE THIS...
I'VE WORKED WITH CHILDREN FOR MANY YEARS. OVER TIME, I'VE GOTTEN TO KNOW THEM WELL... THEY CAN CREATE AN IMAGINARY WORLD THAT ALLOWS THEM TO ENDURE THEIR SUFFERING AND TO OVERCOME THEIR FEARS.
THE BEST THING FOR HER WOULD BE TO SEE A NEUROLOGIST. I ALSO WANT TO APOLOGIZE. I DON'T BELIEVE THAT CORA IS CRAZY OR WHATEVER ELSE I MIGHT HAVE SUGGESTED, BUT I'D BE REASSURED IF SHE WOULD SEE A BRAIN SPECIALIST. I'LL SPEAK WITH THE DIRECTOR.
THANK YOU, PATSY.

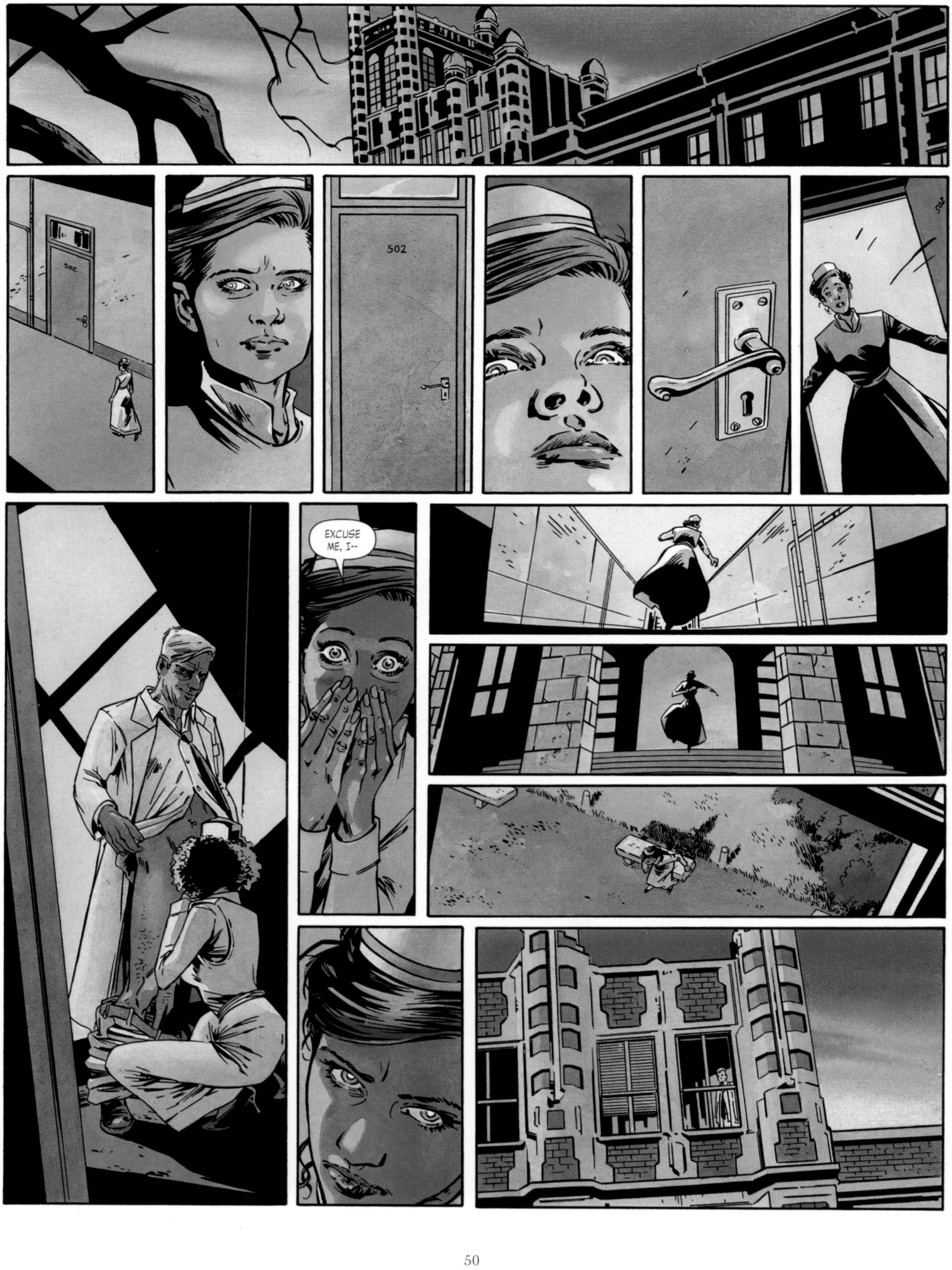
502
502
502
EXCUSE ME, I--

*DOCTOR EARNEST STADIA: NEUROLOGY, STUDY OF THE HUMAN BRAIN

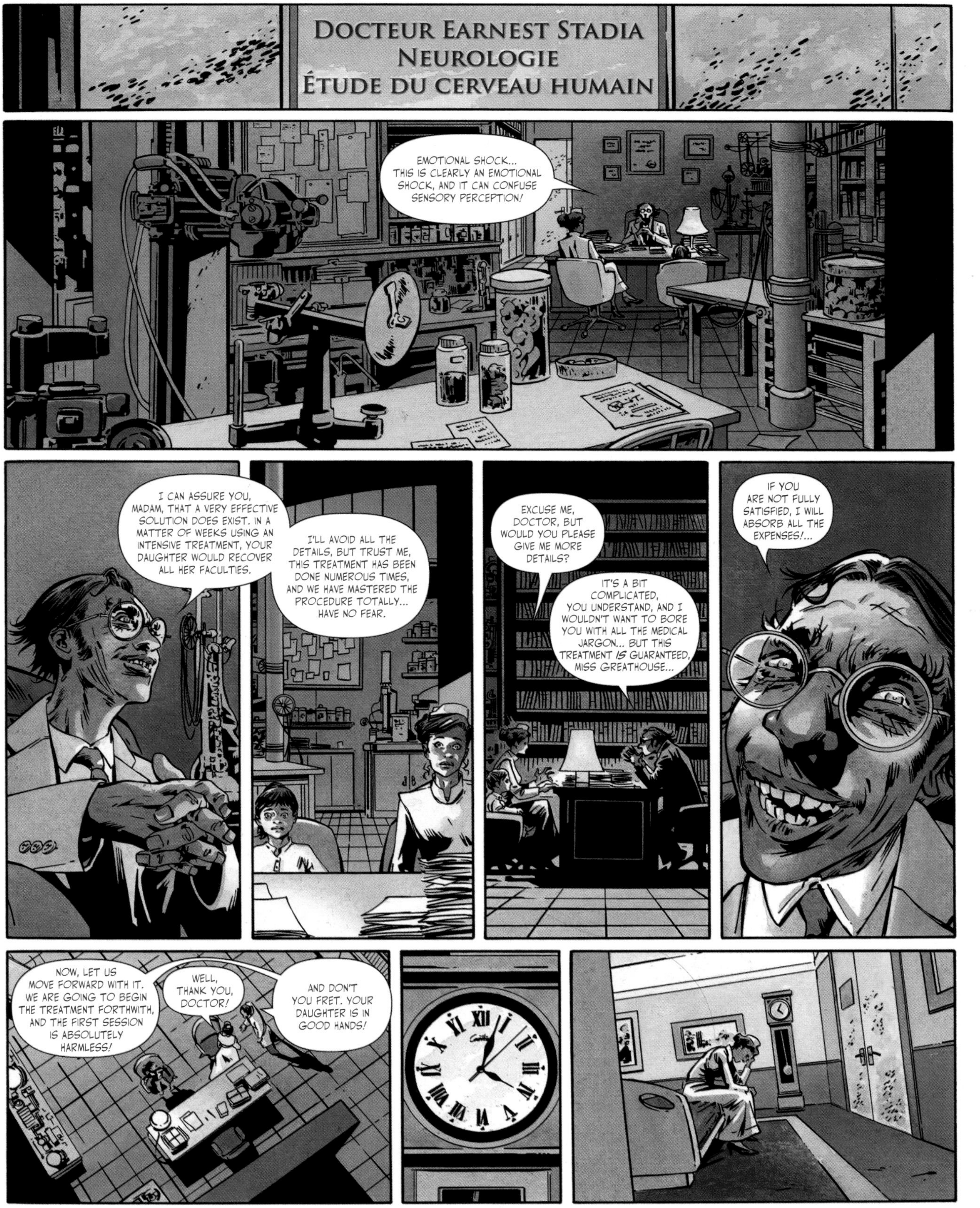

DOCTEUR EARNEST STADIA
NEUROLOGIE
ÉTUDE DU CERVEAU HUMAIN
EMOTIONAL SHOCK... THIS IS CLEARLY AN EMOTIONAL SHOCK, AND IT CAN CONFUSE SENSORY PERCEPTION!
I CAN ASSURE YOU, MADAM, THAT A VERY EFFECTIVE SOLUTION DOES EXIST. IN A MATTER OF WEEKS USING AN INTENSIVE TREATMENT, YOUR DAUGHTER WOULD RECOVER ALL HER FACULTIES.
I'LL AVOID ALL THE DETAILS, BUT TRUST ME, THIS TREATMENT HAS BEEN DONE NUMEROUS TIMES, AND WE HAVE MASTERED THE PROCEDURE TOTALLY... HAVE NO FEAR.
EXCUSE ME, DOCTOR, BUT WOULD YOU PLEASE GIVE ME MORE DETAILS?
IT'S A BIT COMPLICATED, YOU UNDERSTAND, AND I WOULDN'T WANT TO BORE YOU WITH ALL THE MEDICAL JARGON... BUT THIS TREATMENT IS GUARANTEED, MISS GREATHOUSE...
IF YOU ARE NOT FULLY SATISFIED, I WILL ABSORB ALL THE EXPENSES!...
NOW, LET US MOVE FORWARD WITH IT. WE ARE GOING TO BEGIN THE TREATMENT FORTHWITH, AND THE FIRST SESSION IS ABSOLUTELY HARMLESS!
WELL, THANK YOU, DOCTOR!
AND DON'T YOU FRET. YOUR DAUGHTER IS IN GOOD HANDS!

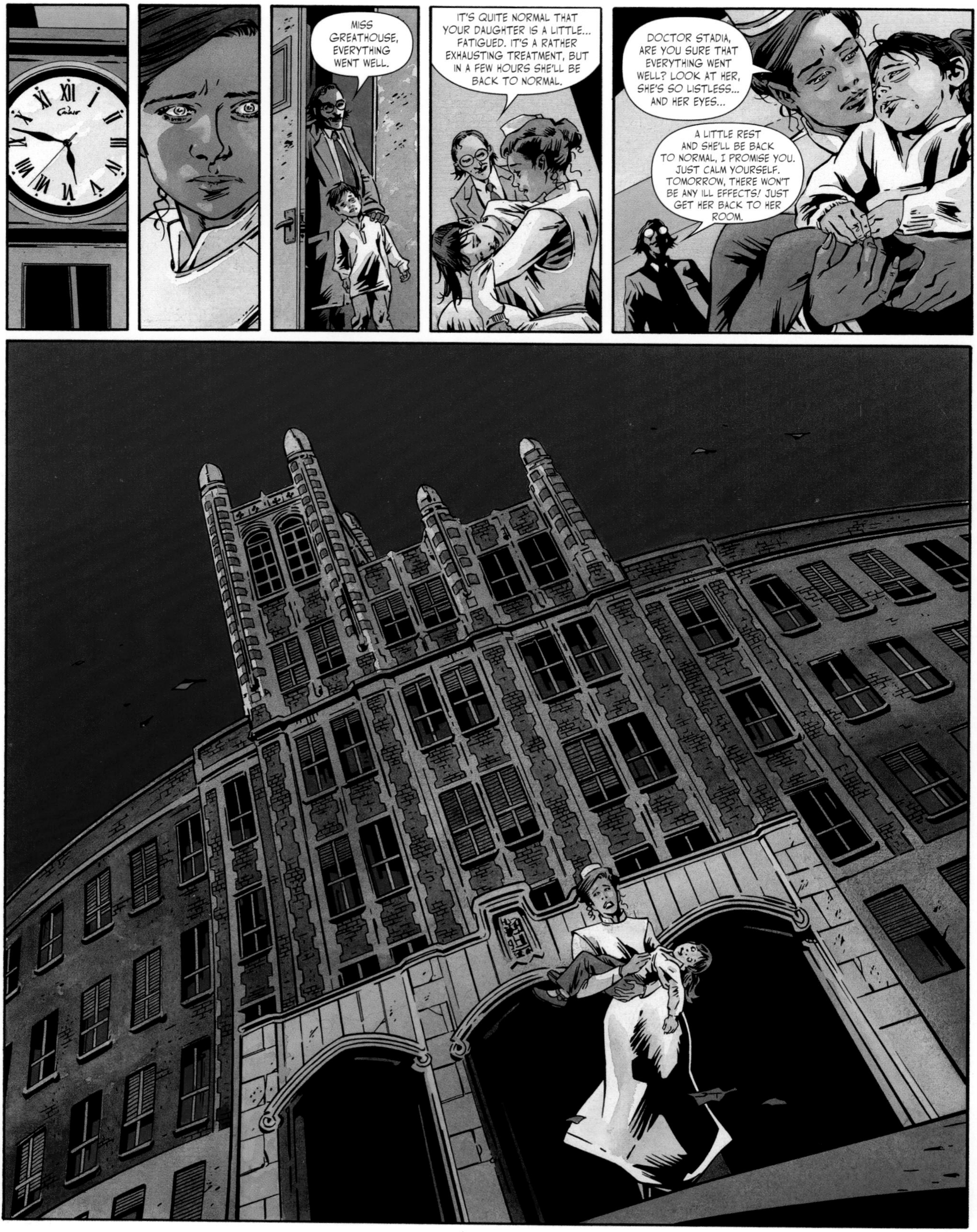
MISS GREATHOUSE, EVERYTHING WENT WELL.
IT'S QUITE NORMAL THAT YOUR DAUGHTER IS A LITTLE... FATIGUED. IT'S A RATHER EXHAUSTING TREATMENT, BUT IN A FEW HOURS SHE'LL BE BACK TO NORMAL.
DOCTOR STADIA, ARE YOU SURE THAT EVERYTHING WENT WELL? LOOK AT HER, SHE'S SO LISTLESS... AND HER EYES...
A LITTLE REST AND SHE'LL BE BACK TO NORMAL, I PROMISE YOU. JUST CALM YOURSELF. TOMORROW, THERE WON'T BE ANY ILL EFFECTS! JUST GET HER BACK TO HER ROOM.

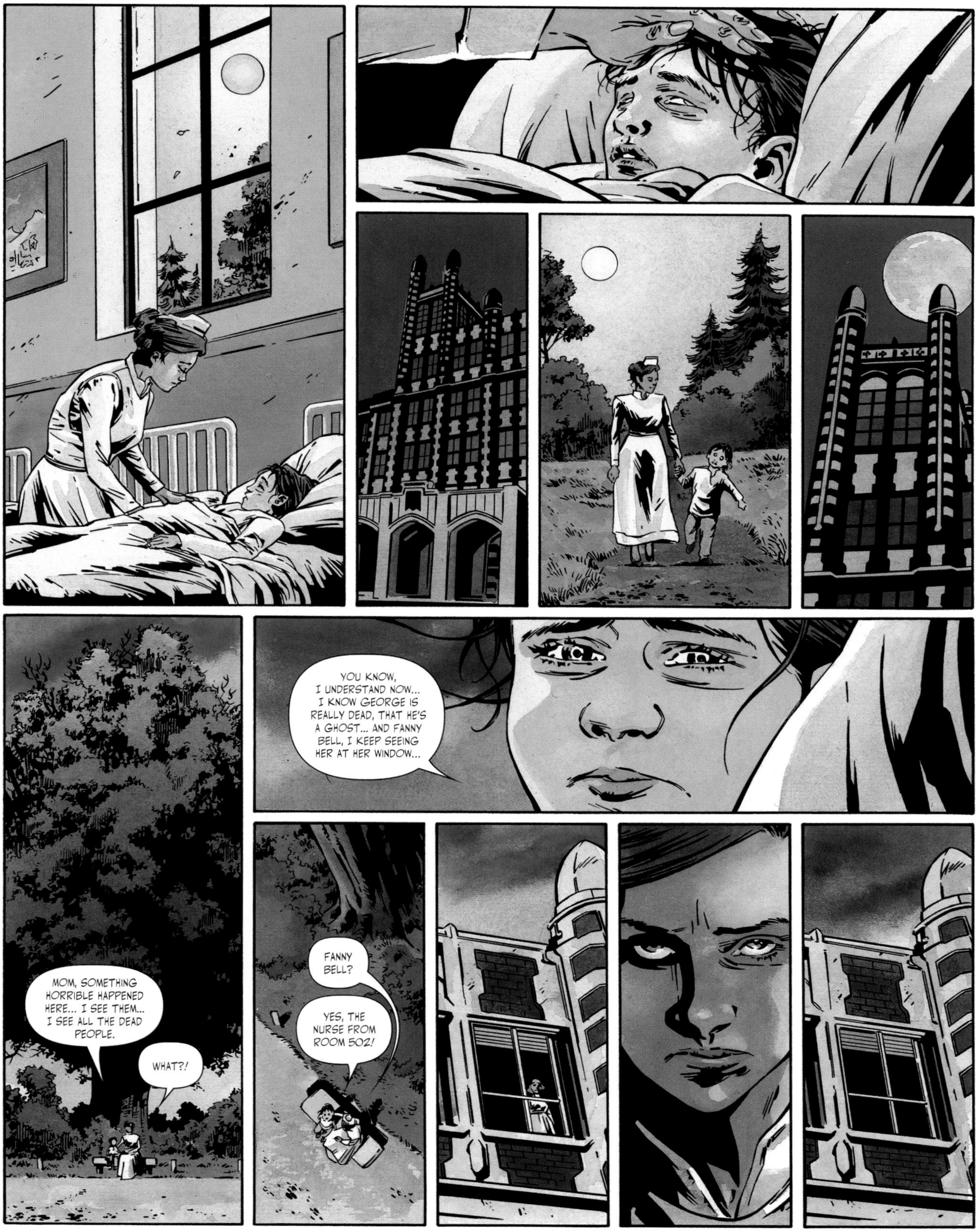
YOU KNOW, I UNDERSTAND NOW... I KNOW GEORGE IS REALLY DEAD, THAT HE'S A GHOST... AND FANNY BELL, I KEEP SEEING HER AT HER WINDOW...
MOM, SOMETHING HORRIBLE HAPPENED HERE... I SEE THEM... I SEE ALL THE DEAD PEOPLE.
WHAT?!
FANNY BELL?
YES, THE NURSE FROM ROOM 502!

WHAT HAVE YOU DONE TO MY DAUGHTER?!!

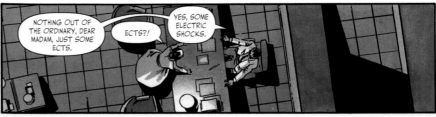

NOTHING OUT OF THE ORDINARY, DEAR MADAM, JUST SOME ECTS.

ECTS?!

YES, SOME ELECTRIC SHOCKS.

WHAT?!! ELECTRO-SHOCKS!... ON A SEVEN-YEAR-OLD!!...

GET A GRIP ON YOURSELF, MISS GREAT-HOUSE!...

AN ECT CREATES CONVULSIONS IN THE NERVOUS SYSTEM AND PRO-VOKES A RHYTHMIC ACTIVITY IN THE BRAIN'S DAMAGED CELLS. THE SECONDARY EFFECTS EXPERIENCED BY YOUR DAUGHTER ARE NORMAL: SHORT-TERM MEMORY LOSS, DISORIENTATION, ETC.

SURE, ECTS CAN AFFECT CERTAIN AREAS IN A HAZARDOUS FASHION. IF THAT IS THE CASE HERE, IT CAN BE QUICKLY ALLEVIATED SO YOUR DAUGHTER WOULD NOT EXPERIENCE THESE SECONDARY EFFECTS ANY FURTHER. IT IS A...LOCALIZED PROCEDURE, WHEREBY A PHYSIOLOGICAL SERUM IS INJECTED THAT ERASES THE NEUROLOGICAL ANOMALY.

AND WHAT DOES THIS OPERATION ENTAIL?

IT ENTAILS DRILLING A LITTLE HOLE...!

DOCTOR STADIA! YOU WILL NEVER AGAIN TOUCH MY DAUGHTER! DO I MAKE MYSELF CLEAR?! FROM NOW ON, I FORBID YOU TO GO NEAR HER!

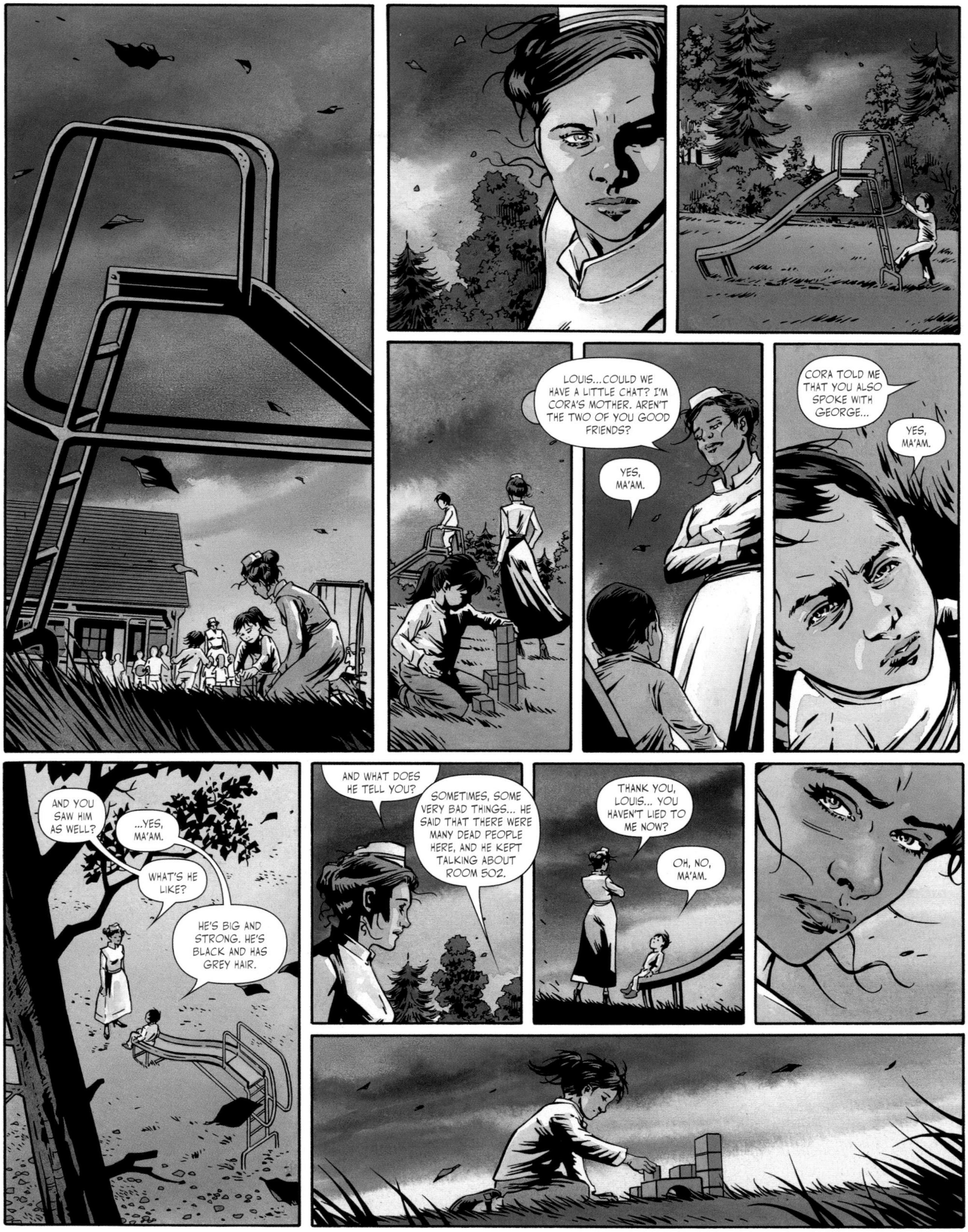
LOUIS...COULD WE HAVE A LITTLE CHAT? I'M CORA'S MOTHER. AREN'T THE TWO OF YOU GOOD FRIENDS?
YES, MA'AM.
CORA TOLD ME THAT YOU ALSO SPOKE WITH GEORGE...
YES, MA'AM.
AND YOU SAW HIM AS WELL?
...YES, MA'AM.
WHAT'S HE LIKE?
HE'S BIG AND STRONG. HE'S BLACK AND HAS GREY HAIR.
AND WHAT DOES HE TELL YOU?
SOMETIMES, SOME VERY BAD THINGS... HE SAID THAT THERE WERE MANY DEAD PEOPLE HERE, AND HE KEPT TALKING ABOUT ROOM 502.
THANK YOU, LOUIS... YOU HAVEN'T LIED TO ME NOW?
OH, NO, MA'AM.

BESS, I NEED HELP... I REALLY NEED YOU. IT'S NOT FOR ME, IT'S FOR CORA. MY DAUGHTER IS SEEING THINGS, AND HEARING THINGS. SHE TALKS ABOUT TERRIFYING EVENTS THAT SUPPOSEDLY HAPPENED HERE, MOSTLY IN ROOM 502!

YOU SAID THERE WERE THINGS BETTER LEFT UNSAID... WHAT WERE THOSE THINGS, BESS? WHAT HAPPENED IN ROOM 502?

I CAN'T SAY ANYTHING!

BESS, TELL ME THE TRUTH...FOR CORA'S SAKE... I BEG YOU.

YOU WANT TO KNOW WHAT HAPPENED IN ROOM 502?... YOU REALLY WANT TO KNOW?

YES, BESS.

THEN FOLLOW ME.

IN THE WINTER OF 1928, A YOUNG NURSE, ONLY 29 YEARS OLD, KILLED HERSELF IN ROOM 502. SHE HUNG HERSELF WITH DRAPES TIED INTO A KNOT. NO ONE KNOWS HOW LONG SHE WAS HANGING IN THAT ROOM BEFORE HER BODY WAS FINALLY DISCOVERED...

FOLLOWING AN AUTOPSY, HER DEATH WAS DECLARED A SUICIDE...

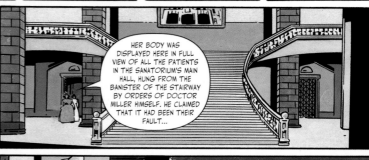

HER BODY WAS DISPLAYED HERE IN FULL VIEW OF ALL THE PATIENTS IN THE SANATORIUM'S MAIN HALL, HUNG FROM THE BANISTER OF THE STAIRWAY BY ORDERS OF DOCTOR MILLER HIMSELF. HE CLAIMED THAT IT HAD BEEN THEIR FAULT...

TRUTH WAS SHE WAS PREGNANT AND UNMARRIED, REJECTED BY HER FAMILY, AND DEEPLY DEPRESSED...

HER NAME WAS FANNY BELL.

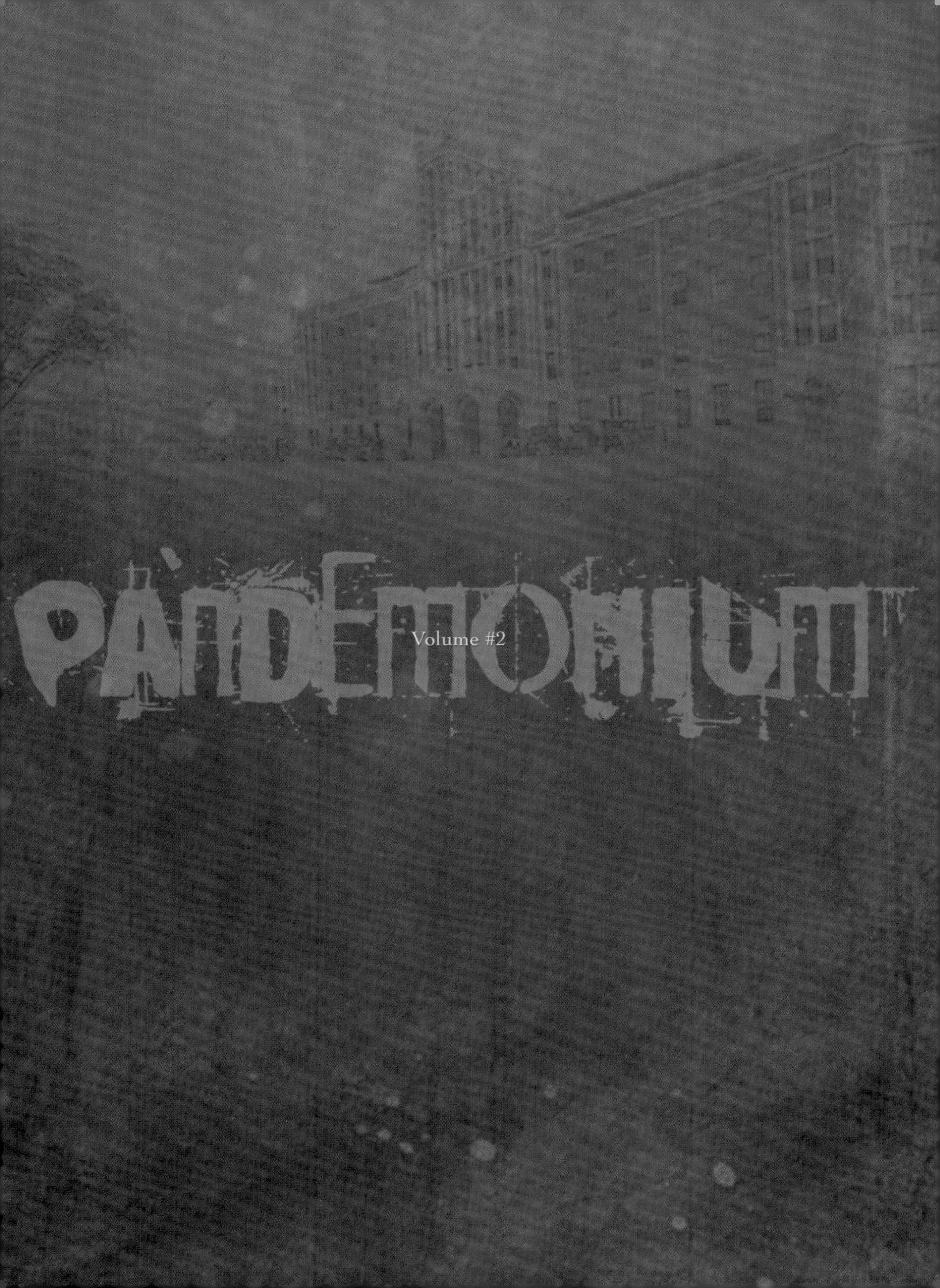
PANDEMONIUM
Volume #2

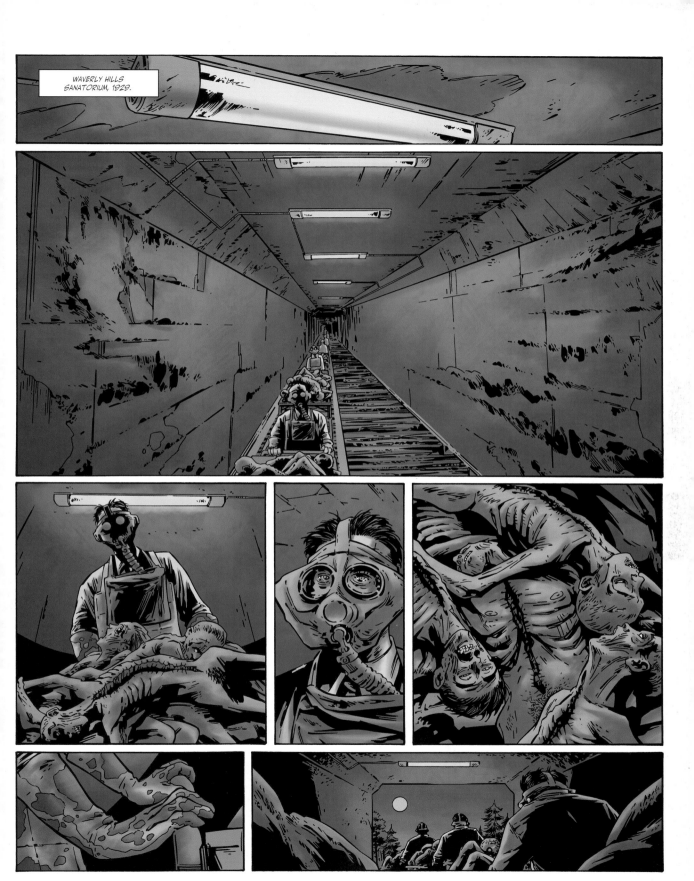

WAVERLY HILLS
SANATORIUM, 1929.

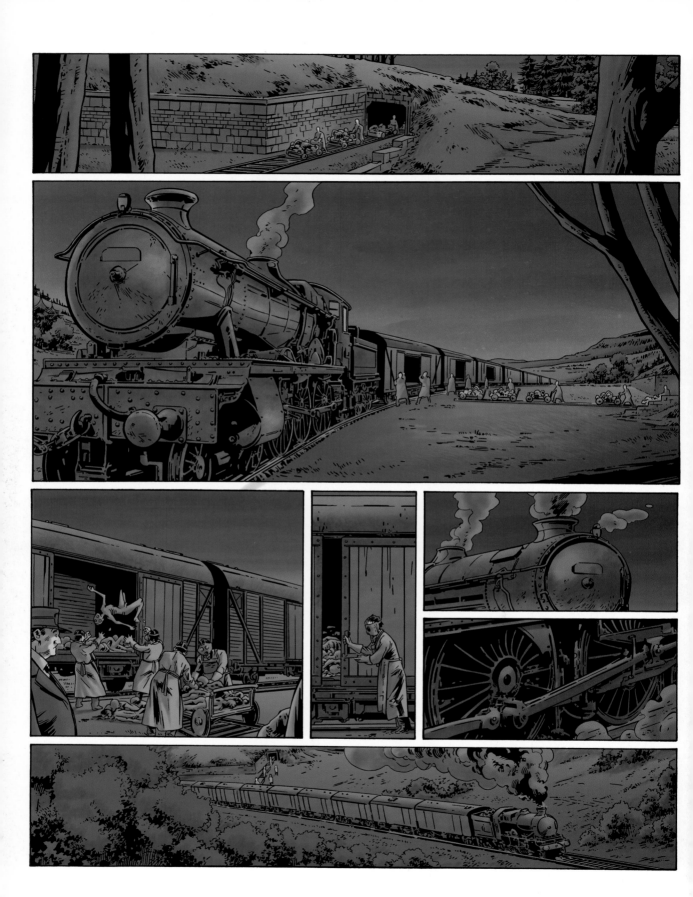

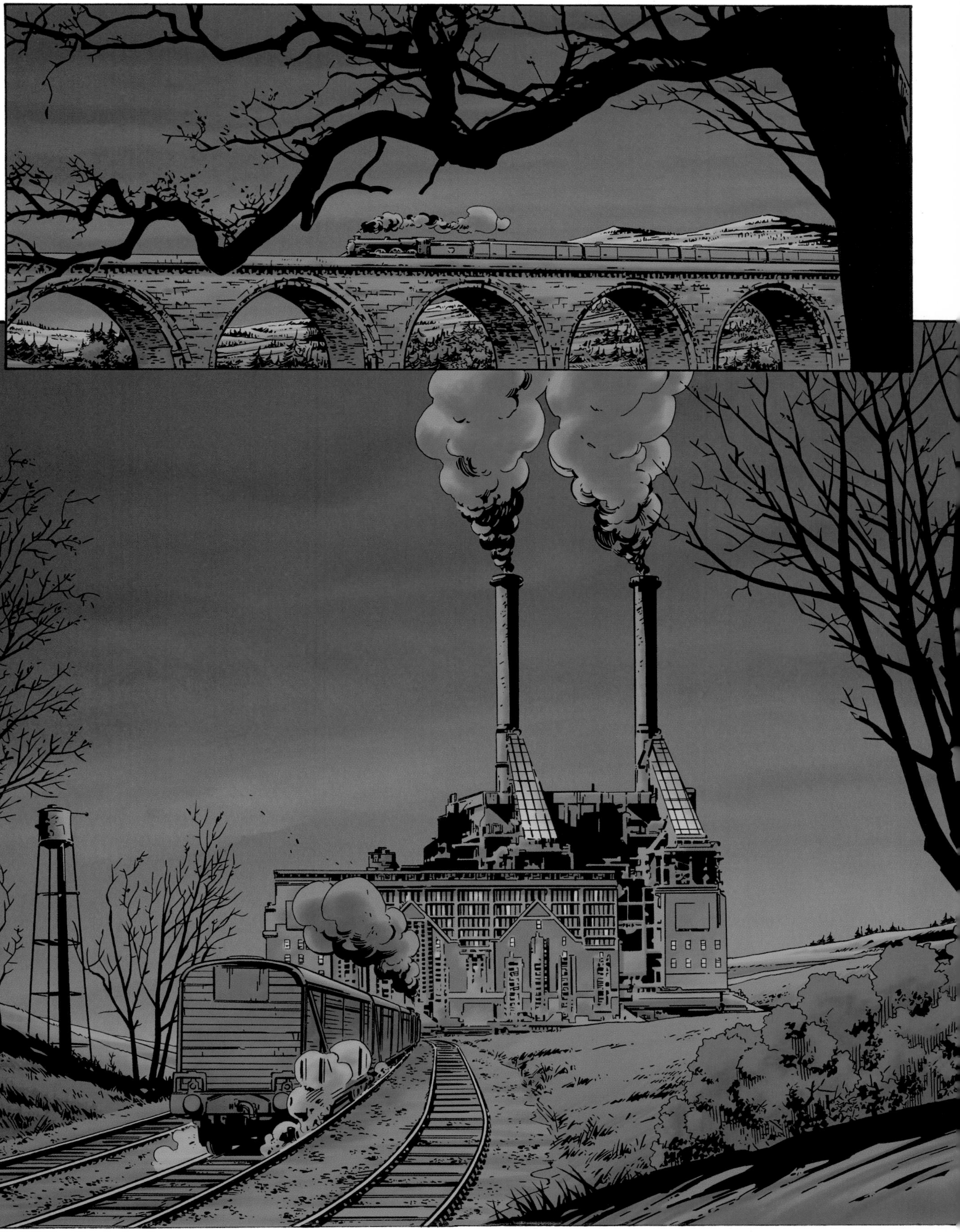

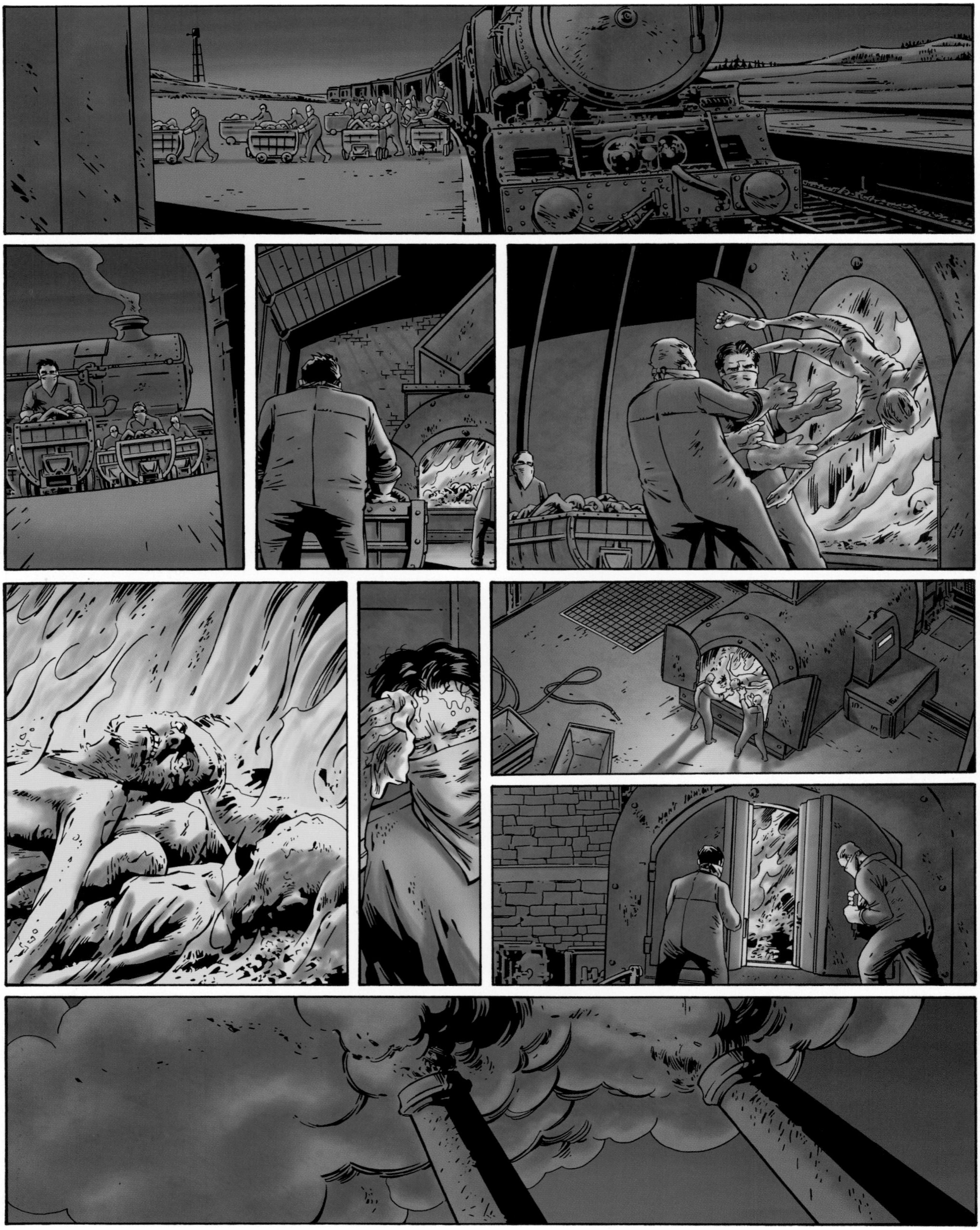

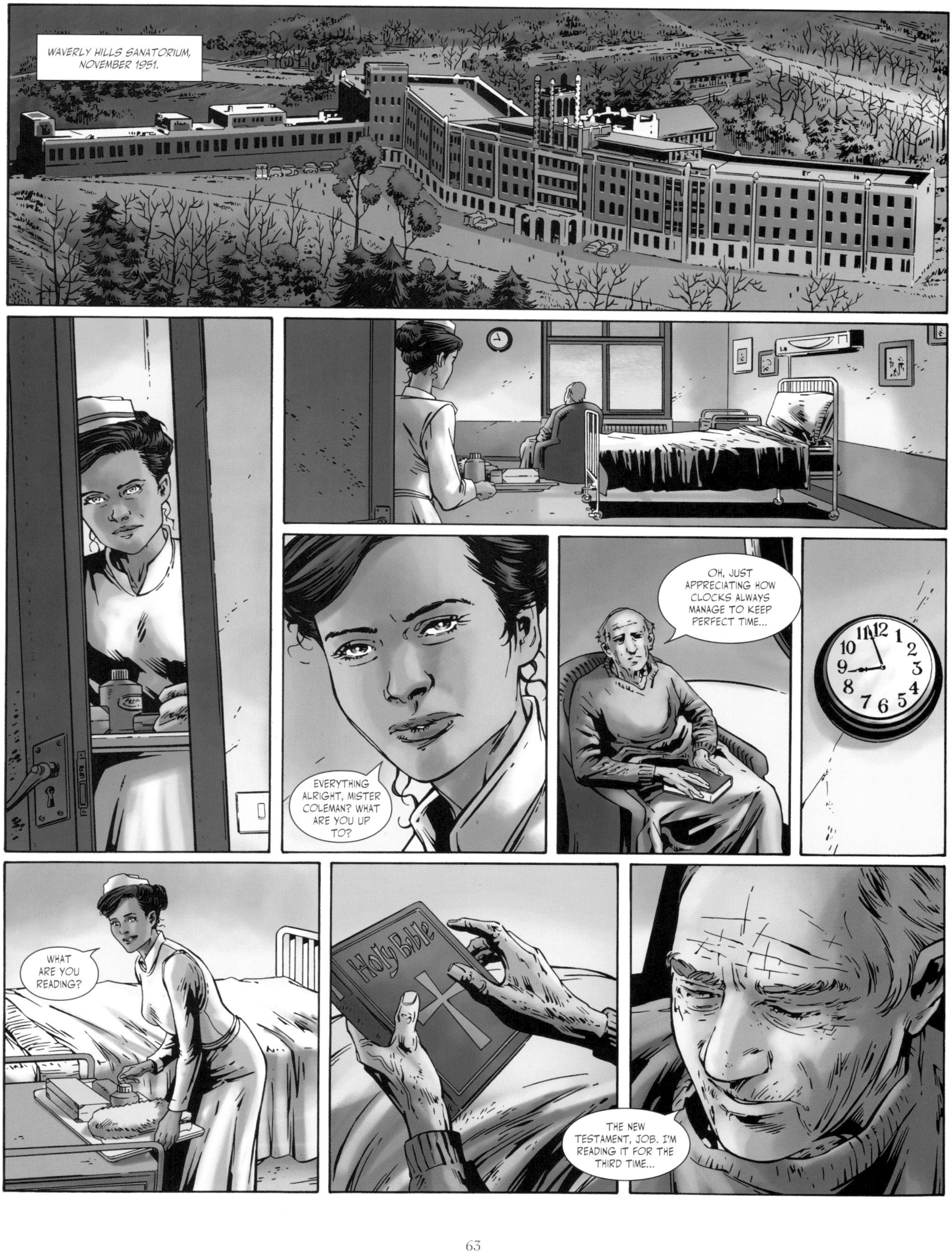
WAVERLY HILLS SANATORIUM, NOVEMBER 1951.
EVERYTHING ALRIGHT, MISTER COLEMAN? WHAT ARE YOU UP TO?
OH, JUST APPRECIATING HOW CLOCKS ALWAYS MANAGE TO KEEP PERFECT TIME...
WHAT ARE YOU READING?
Holy Bible
THE NEW TESTAMENT, JOB. I'M READING IT FOR THE THIRD TIME...

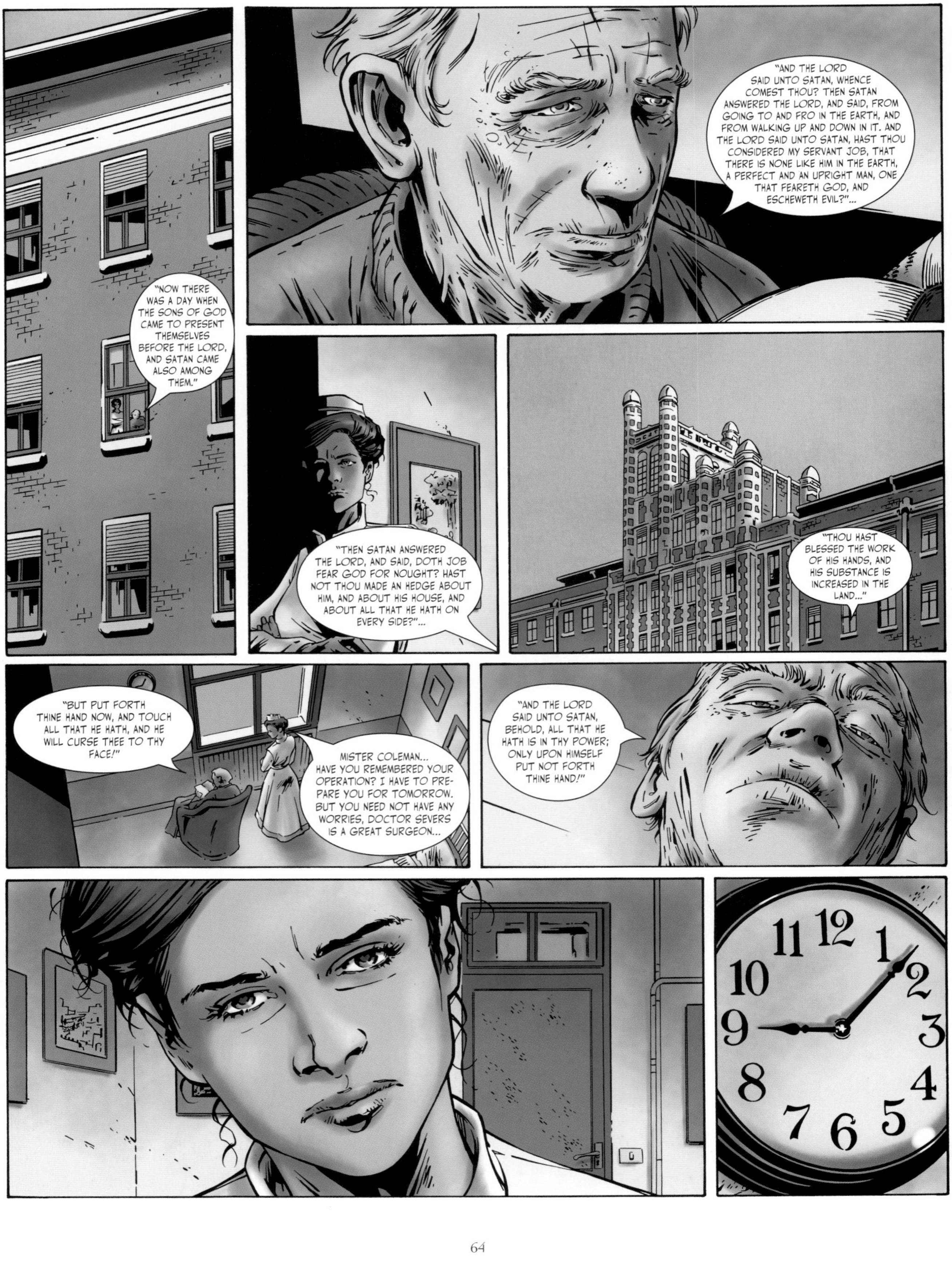
"NOW THERE WAS A DAY WHEN THE SONS OF GOD CAME TO PRESENT THEMSELVES BEFORE THE LORD, AND SATAN CAME ALSO AMONG THEM."
"AND THE LORD SAID UNTO SATAN, WHENCE COMEST THOU? THEN SATAN ANSWERED THE LORD, AND SAID, FROM GOING TO AND FRO IN THE EARTH, AND FROM WALKING UP AND DOWN IN IT. AND THE LORD SAID UNTO SATAN, HAST THOU CONSIDERED MY SERVANT JOB, THAT THERE IS NONE LIKE HIM IN THE EARTH, A PERFECT AND AN UPRIGHT MAN, ONE THAT FEARETH GOD, AND ESCHEWETH EVIL?"...
"THEN SATAN ANSWERED THE LORD, AND SAID, DOTH JOB FEAR GOD FOR NOUGHT? HAST NOT THOU MADE AN HEDGE ABOUT HIM, AND ABOUT HIS HOUSE, AND ABOUT ALL THAT HE HATH ON EVERY SIDE?"...
"THOU HAST BLESSED THE WORK OF HIS HANDS, AND HIS SUBSTANCE IS INCREASED IN THE LAND..."
"BUT PUT FORTH THINE HAND NOW, AND TOUCH ALL THAT HE HATH, AND HE WILL CURSE THEE TO THY FACE!"
MISTER COLEMAN... HAVE YOU REMEMBERED YOUR OPERATION? I HAVE TO PRE-PARE YOU FOR TOMORROW. BUT YOU NEED NOT HAVE ANY WORRIES, DOCTOR SEVERS IS A GREAT SURGEON...
"AND THE LORD SAID UNTO SATAN, BEHOLD, ALL THAT HE HATH IS IN THY POWER; ONLY UPON HIMSELF PUT NOT FORTH THINE HAND!"
11 12 1 2 3 4 5 6 7 8 9 10

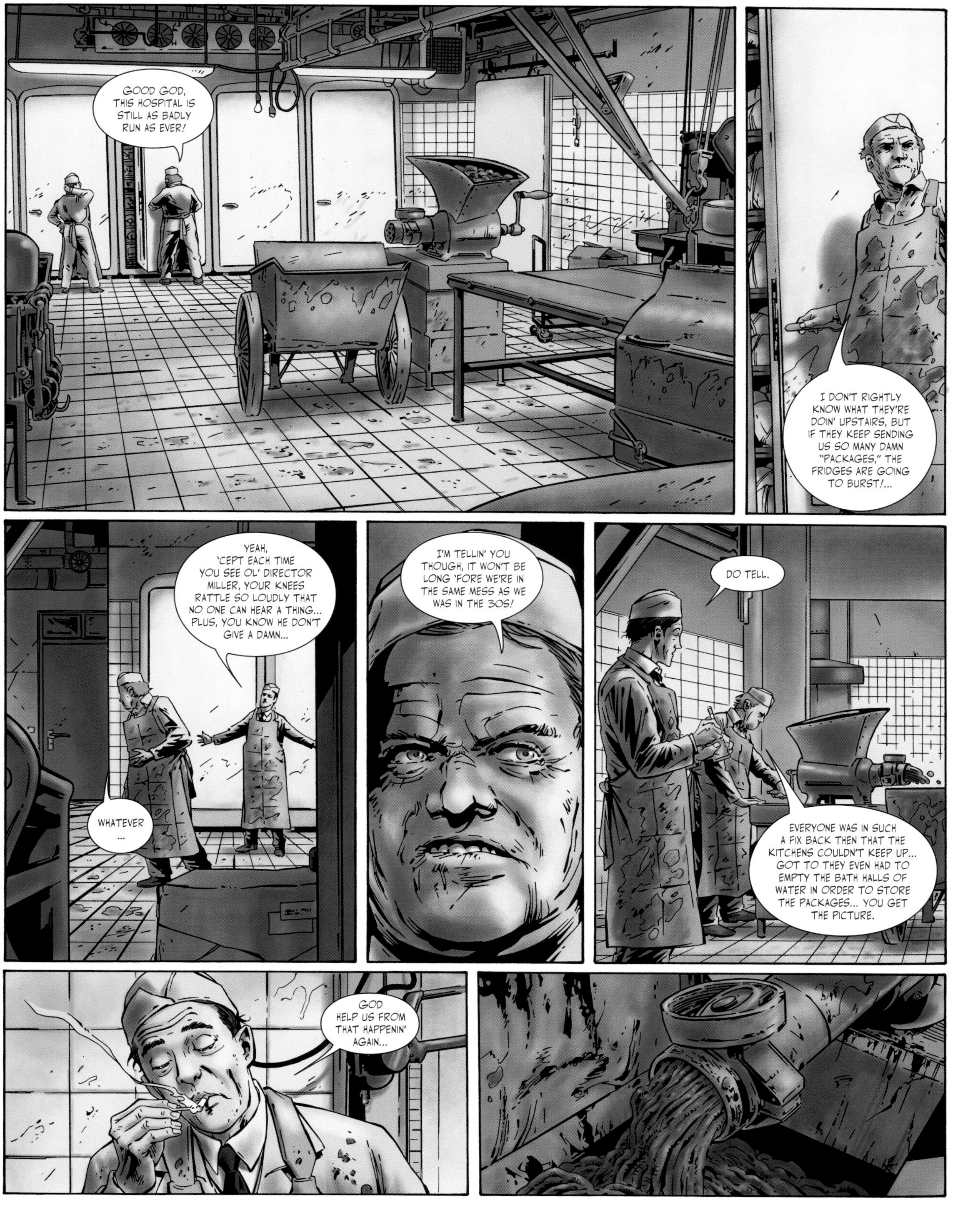
GOOD GOD, THIS HOSPITAL IS STILL AS BADLY RUN AS EVER!
I DON'T RIGHTLY KNOW WHAT THEY'RE DOIN' UPSTAIRS, BUT IF THEY KEEP SENDING US SO MANY DAMN "PACKAGES," THE FRIDGES ARE GOING TO BURST!...
YEAH, 'CEPT EACH TIME YOU SEE OL' DIRECTOR MILLER, YOUR KNEES RATTLE SO LOUDLY THAT NO ONE CAN HEAR A THING... PLUS, YOU KNOW HE DON'T GIVE A DAMN...
WHATEVER ...
I'M TELLIN' YOU THOUGH, IT WON'T BE LONG 'FORE WE'RE IN THE SAME MESS AS WE WAS IN THE 30S!
DO TELL.
EVERYONE WAS IN SUCH A FIX BACK THEN THAT THE KITCHENS COULDN'T KEEP UP... GOT TO THEY EVEN HAD TO EMPTY THE BATH HALLS OF WATER IN ORDER TO STORE THE PACKAGES... YOU GET THE PICTURE.
GOD HELP US FROM THAT HAPPENIN' AGAIN...

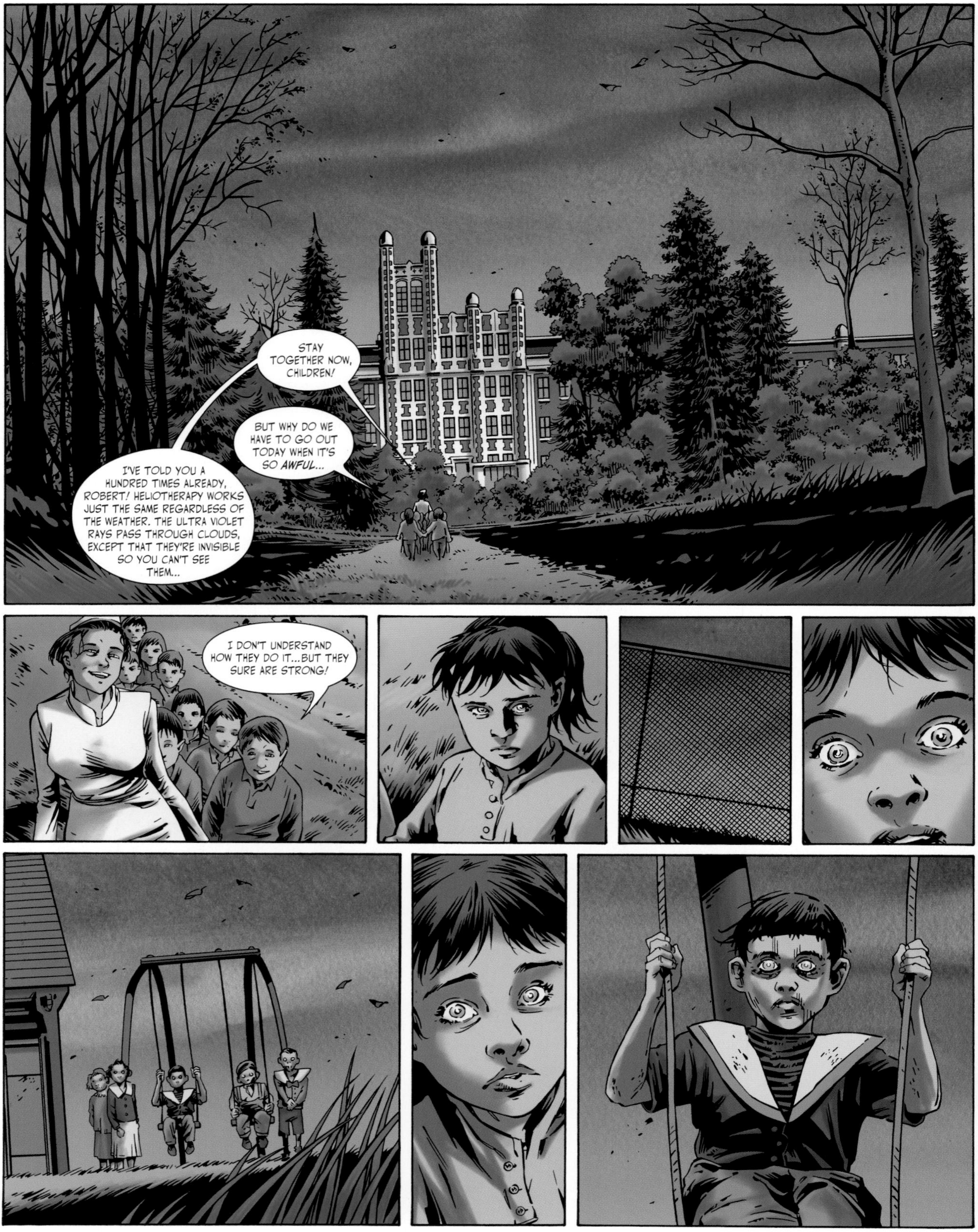
STAY TOGETHER NOW, CHILDREN!
BUT WHY DO WE HAVE TO GO OUT TODAY WHEN IT'S SO *AWFUL*...
I'VE TOLD YOU A HUNDRED TIMES ALREADY, ROBERT! HELIOTHERAPY WORKS JUST THE SAME REGARDLESS OF THE WEATHER. THE ULTRA VIOLET RAYS PASS THROUGH CLOUDS, EXCEPT THAT THEY'RE INVISIBLE SO YOU CAN'T SEE THEM...
I DON'T UNDERSTAND HOW THEY DO IT...BUT THEY SURE ARE STRONG!

LOUIS! DID YOU SEE THOSE STRANGE KIDS BY THE SWINGS?

THAT'S NOT FUNNY! NOBODY'S THERE!

BUT THERE IS, I SWEAR. THERE'S FIVE OF THEM, AND ONE OF THEM WON'T STOP STARING AT ME WITH HIS FUNNY EYES.

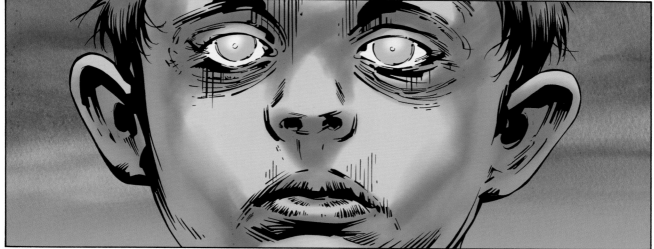

I TOLD YOU, I DON'T SEE ANYONE!

AND THE TRAIN, YOU DID HEAR THE TRAIN LAST NIGHT, RIGHT?

NO, I DIDN'T HEAR ANY TRAIN. YOU'RE GETTING ANNOYING.

BUT GEORGE, YOU SAID YOU SAW HIM TOO...

SO WHAT?! I DIDN'T HEAR ANY TRAIN!!...

YOU'RE A LIAR!

AND YOU, YOU'RE AS CRAZY AS YOUR MOTHER!

THAT'S NOT TRUE!... MY MOTHER ISN'T CRAZY!

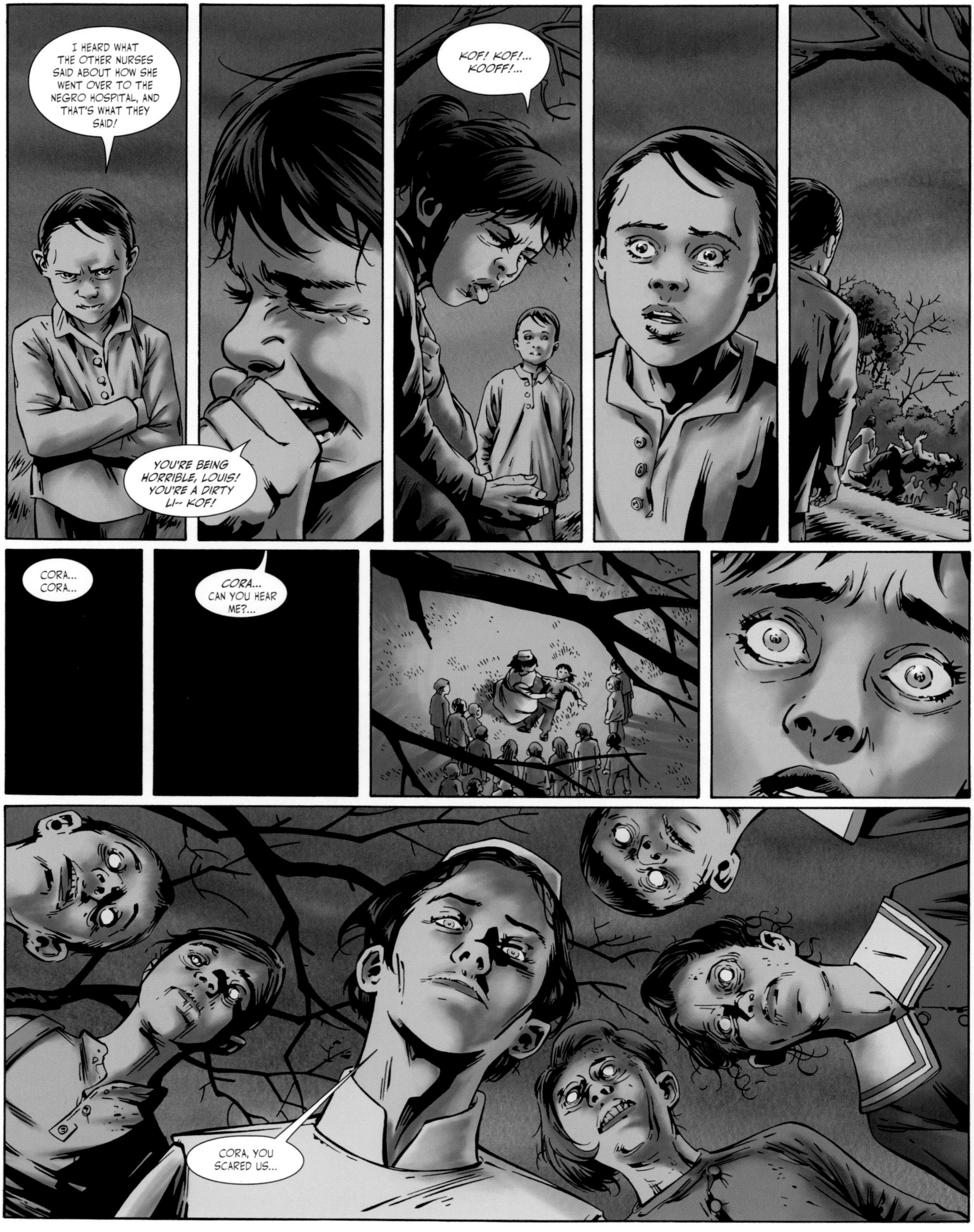
I HEARD WHAT THE OTHER NURSES SAID ABOUT HOW SHE WENT OVER TO THE NEGRO HOSPITAL, AND THAT'S WHAT THEY SAID!
YOU'RE BEING HORRIBLE, LOUIS! YOU'RE A DIRTY LI-- KOF!
KOF! KOF!... KOOFF!...
CORA... CORA...
CORA... CAN YOU HEAR ME?...
CORA, YOU SCARED US...

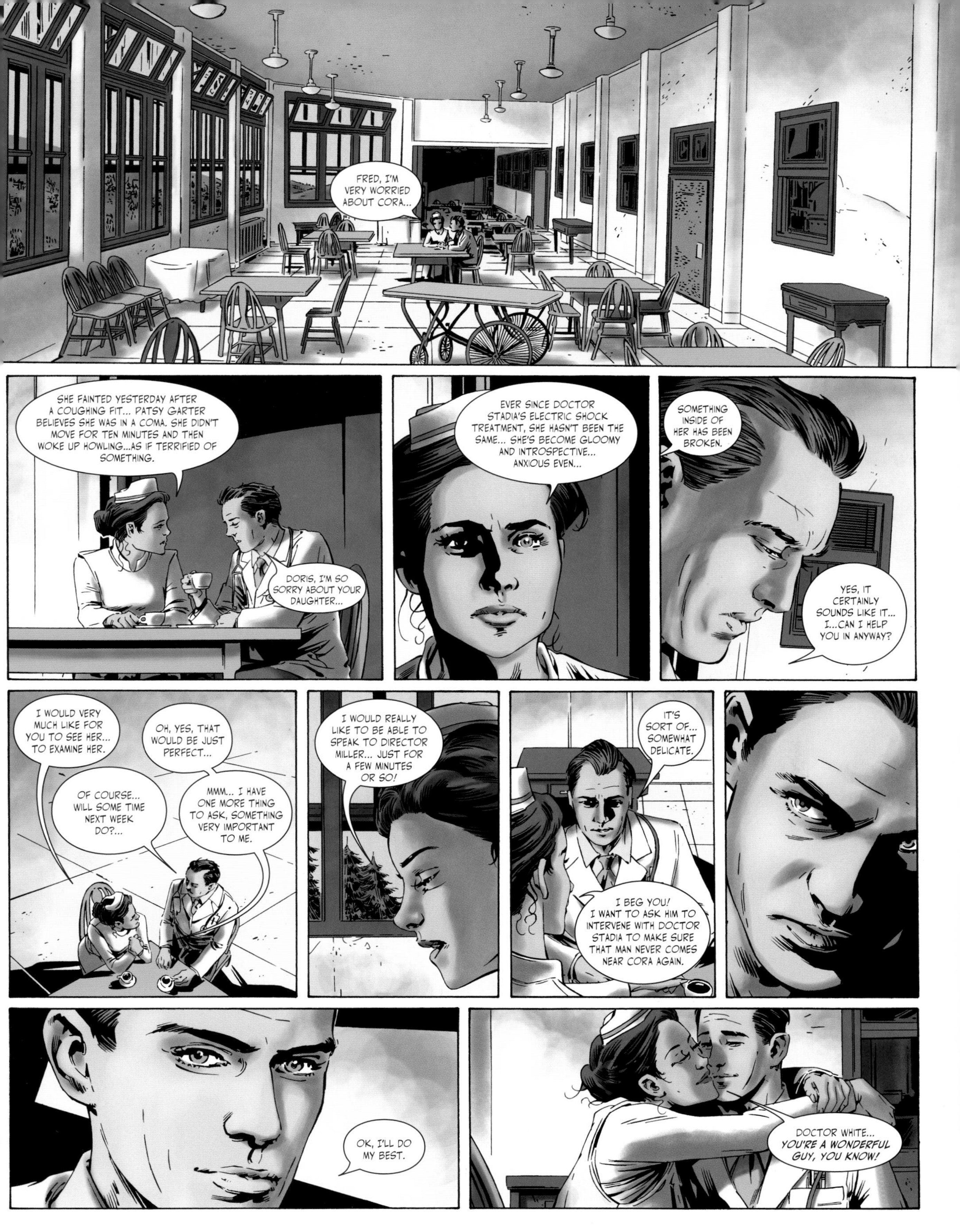
FRED, I'M VERY WORRIED ABOUT CORA...
SHE FAINTED YESTERDAY AFTER A COUGHING FIT... PATSY GARTER BELIEVES SHE WAS IN A COMA. SHE DIDN'T MOVE FOR TEN MINUTES AND THEN WOKE UP HOWLING...AS IF TERRIFIED OF SOMETHING.
DORIS, I'M SO SORRY ABOUT YOUR DAUGHTER...
EVER SINCE DOCTOR STADIA'S ELECTRIC SHOCK TREATMENT, SHE HASN'T BEEN THE SAME... SHE'S BECOME GLOOMY AND INTROSPECTIVE... ANXIOUS EVEN...
SOMETHING INSIDE OF HER HAS BEEN BROKEN.
YES, IT CERTAINLY SOUNDS LIKE IT... I...CAN I HELP YOU IN ANYWAY?
I WOULD VERY MUCH LIKE FOR YOU TO SEE HER... TO EXAMINE HER.
OF COURSE... WILL SOME TIME NEXT WEEK DO?...
OH, YES, THAT WOULD BE JUST PERFECT...
MMM... I HAVE ONE MORE THING TO ASK, SOMETHING VERY IMPORTANT TO ME.
I WOULD REALLY LIKE TO BE ABLE TO SPEAK TO DIRECTOR MILLER... JUST FOR A FEW MINUTES OR SO!
IT'S SORT OF... SOMEWHAT DELICATE.
I BEG YOU! I WANT TO ASK HIM TO INTERVENE WITH DOCTOR STADIA TO MAKE SURE THAT MAN NEVER COMES NEAR CORA AGAIN.
OK, I'LL DO MY BEST.
DOCTOR WHITE... *YOU'RE A WONDERFUL GUY, YOU KNOW!*

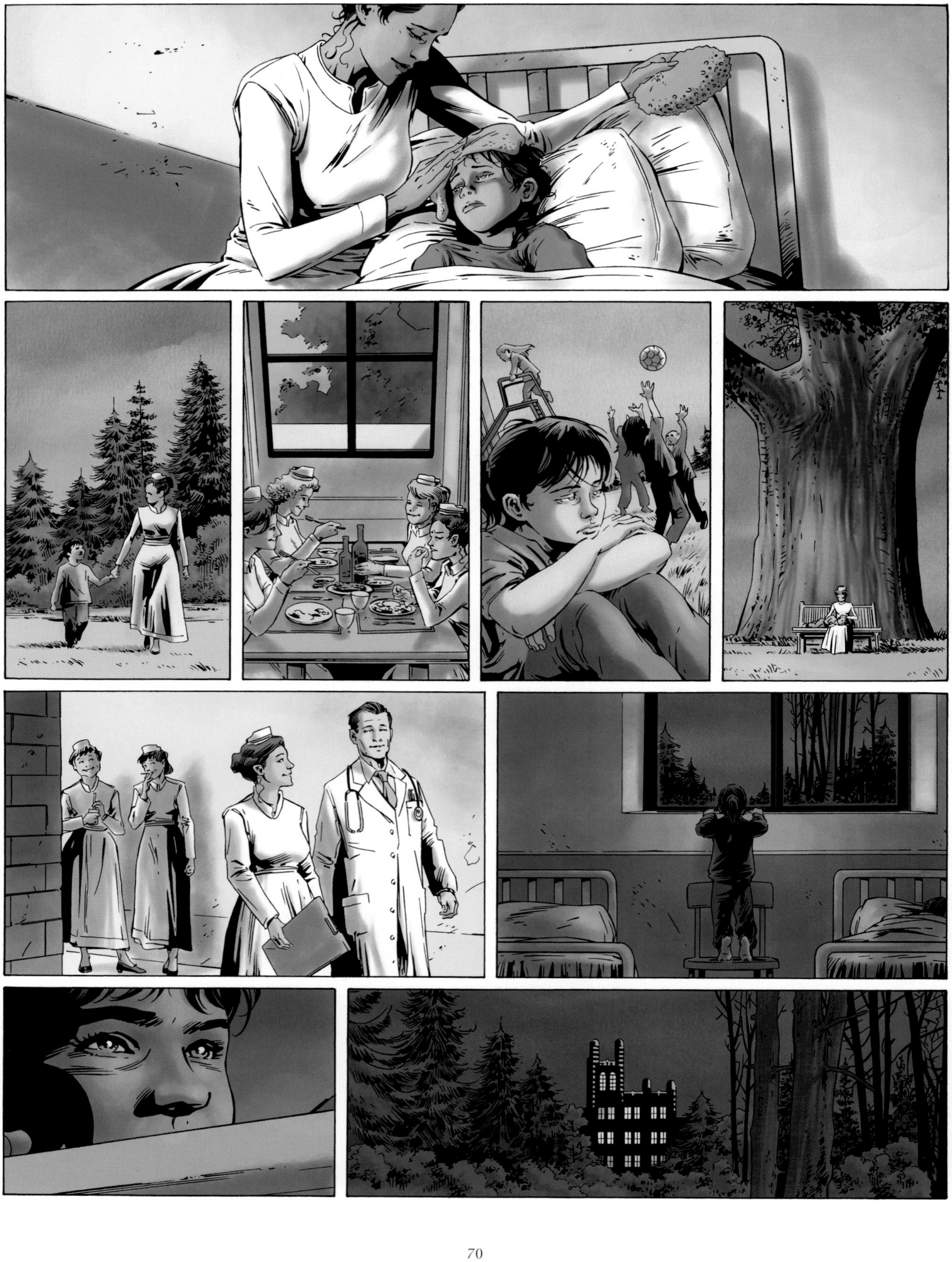

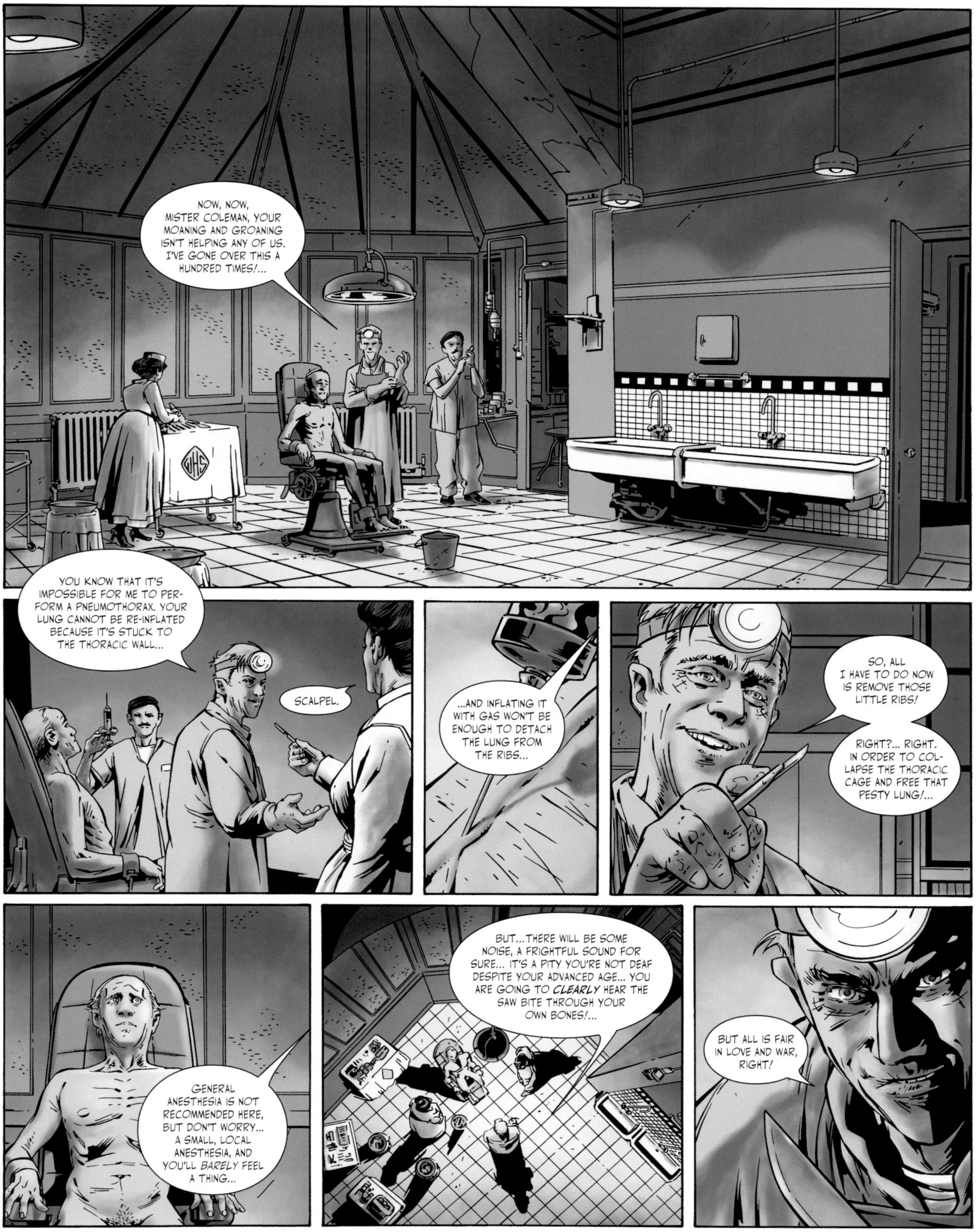
NOW, NOW, MISTER COLEMAN, YOUR MOANING AND GROANING ISN'T HELPING ANY OF US. I'VE GONE OVER THIS A HUNDRED TIMES!...
YOU KNOW THAT IT'S IMPOSSIBLE FOR ME TO PERFORM A PNEUMOTHORAX. YOUR LUNG CANNOT BE RE-INFLATED BECAUSE IT'S STUCK TO THE THORACIC WALL...
SCALPEL.
...AND INFLATING IT WITH GAS WON'T BE ENOUGH TO DETACH THE LUNG FROM THE RIBS...
SO, ALL I HAVE TO DO NOW IS REMOVE THOSE LITTLE RIBS!
RIGHT?... RIGHT. IN ORDER TO COLLAPSE THE THORACIC CAGE AND FREE THAT PESTY LUNG!...
GENERAL ANESTHESIA IS NOT RECOMMENDED HERE, BUT DON'T WORRY... A SMALL, LOCAL ANESTHESIA, AND YOU'LL *BARELY* FEEL A THING...
BUT...THERE WILL BE SOME NOISE, A FRIGHTFUL SOUND FOR SURE... IT'S A PITY YOU'RE NOT DEAF DESPITE YOUR ADVANCED AGE... YOU ARE GOING TO *CLEARLY* HEAR THE SAW BITE THROUGH YOUR OWN BONES!...
BUT ALL IS FAIR IN LOVE AND WAR, RIGHT!

HERE WE GO. I'LL BEGIN BY OPENING YOU UP FROM TOP TO BOTTOM, FROM NECK TO BELLY BUTTON.

RETRACTOR!

HERE YOU ARE, DOCTOR!

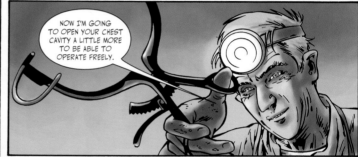

NOW I'M GOING TO OPEN YOUR CHEST CAVITY A LITTLE MORE TO BE ABLE TO OPERATE FREELY.

SAW!

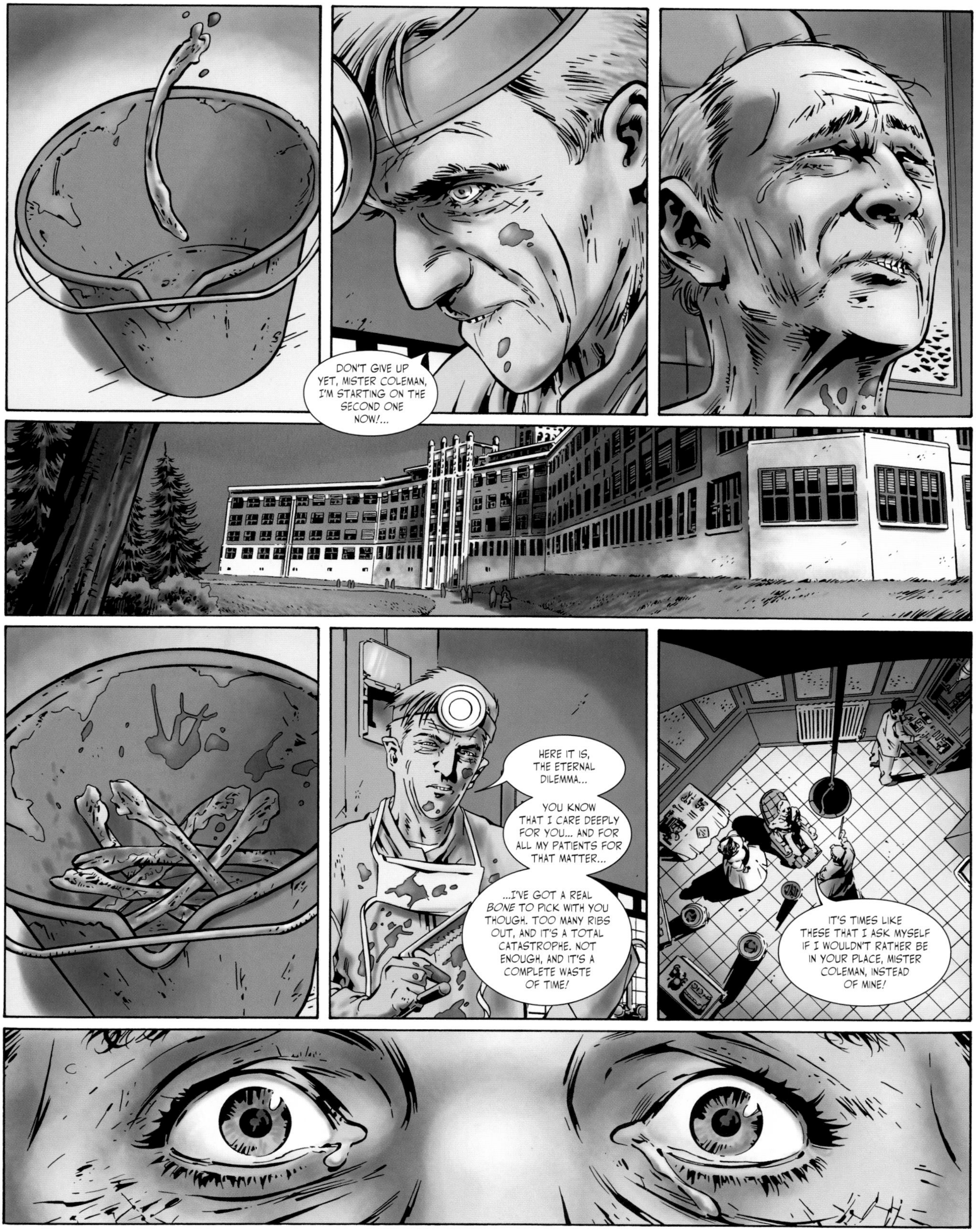
DON'T GIVE UP YET, MISTER COLEMAN, I'M STARTING ON THE SECOND ONE NOW!...
HERE IT IS, THE ETERNAL DILEMMA...
YOU KNOW THAT I CARE DEEPLY FOR YOU... AND FOR ALL MY PATIENTS FOR THAT MATTER...
...I'VE GOT A REAL *BONE* TO PICK WITH YOU THOUGH. TOO MANY RIBS OUT, AND IT'S A TOTAL CATASTROPHE. NOT ENOUGH, AND IT'S A COMPLETE WASTE OF TIME!
IT'S TIMES LIKE THESE THAT I ASK MYSELF IF I WOULDN'T RATHER BE IN YOUR PLACE, MISTER COLEMAN, INSTEAD OF MINE!

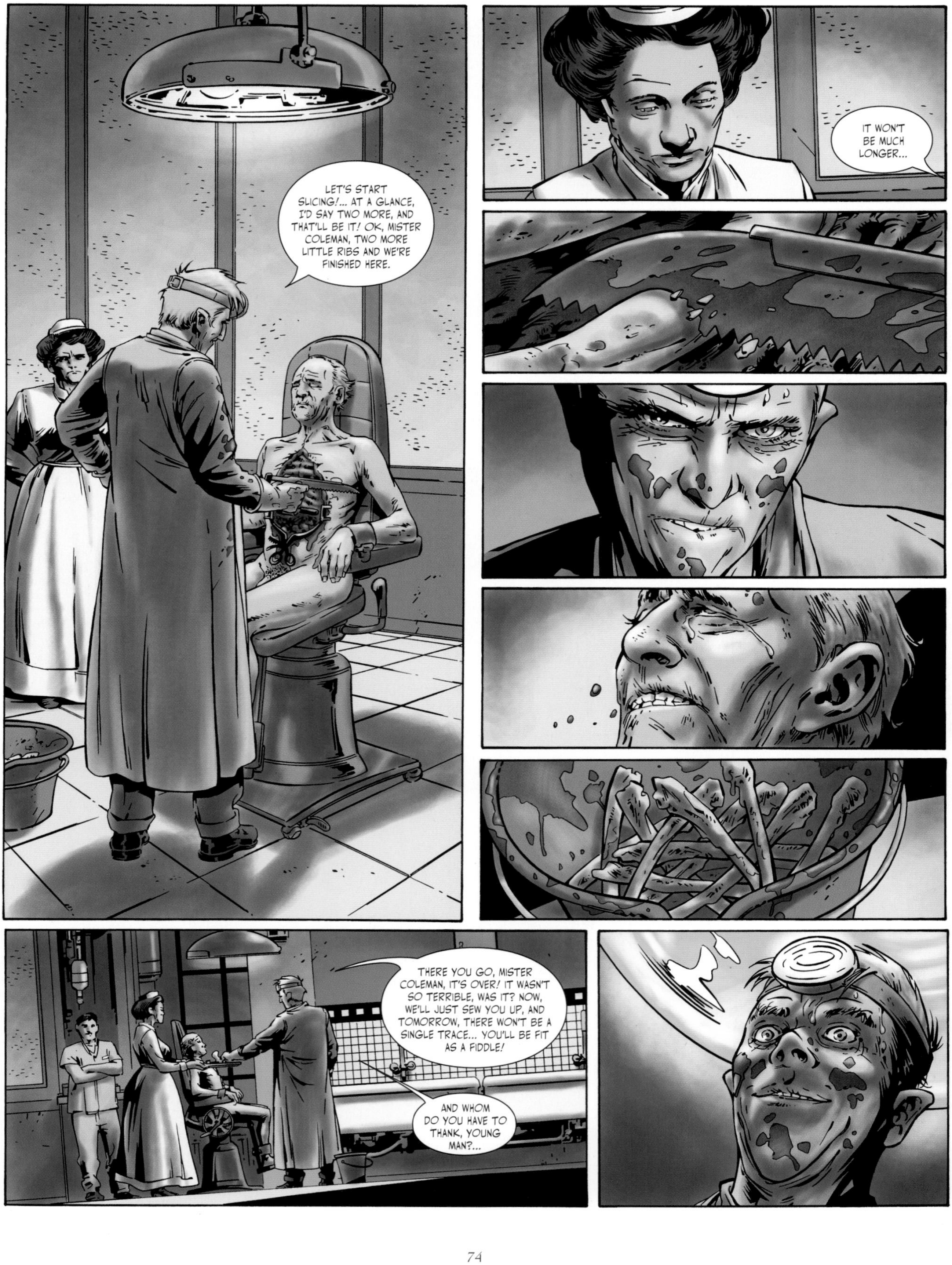
LET'S START SLICING!... AT A GLANCE, I'D SAY TWO MORE, AND THAT'LL BE IT! OK, MISTER COLEMAN, TWO MORE LITTLE RIBS AND WE'RE FINISHED HERE.
IT WON'T BE MUCH LONGER...
THERE YOU GO, MISTER COLEMAN, IT'S OVER! IT WASN'T SO TERRIBLE, WAS IT? NOW, WE'LL JUST SEW YOU UP, AND TOMORROW, THERE WON'T BE A SINGLE TRACE... YOU'LL BE FIT AS A FIDDLE!
AND WHOM DO YOU HAVE TO THANK, YOUNG MAN?...

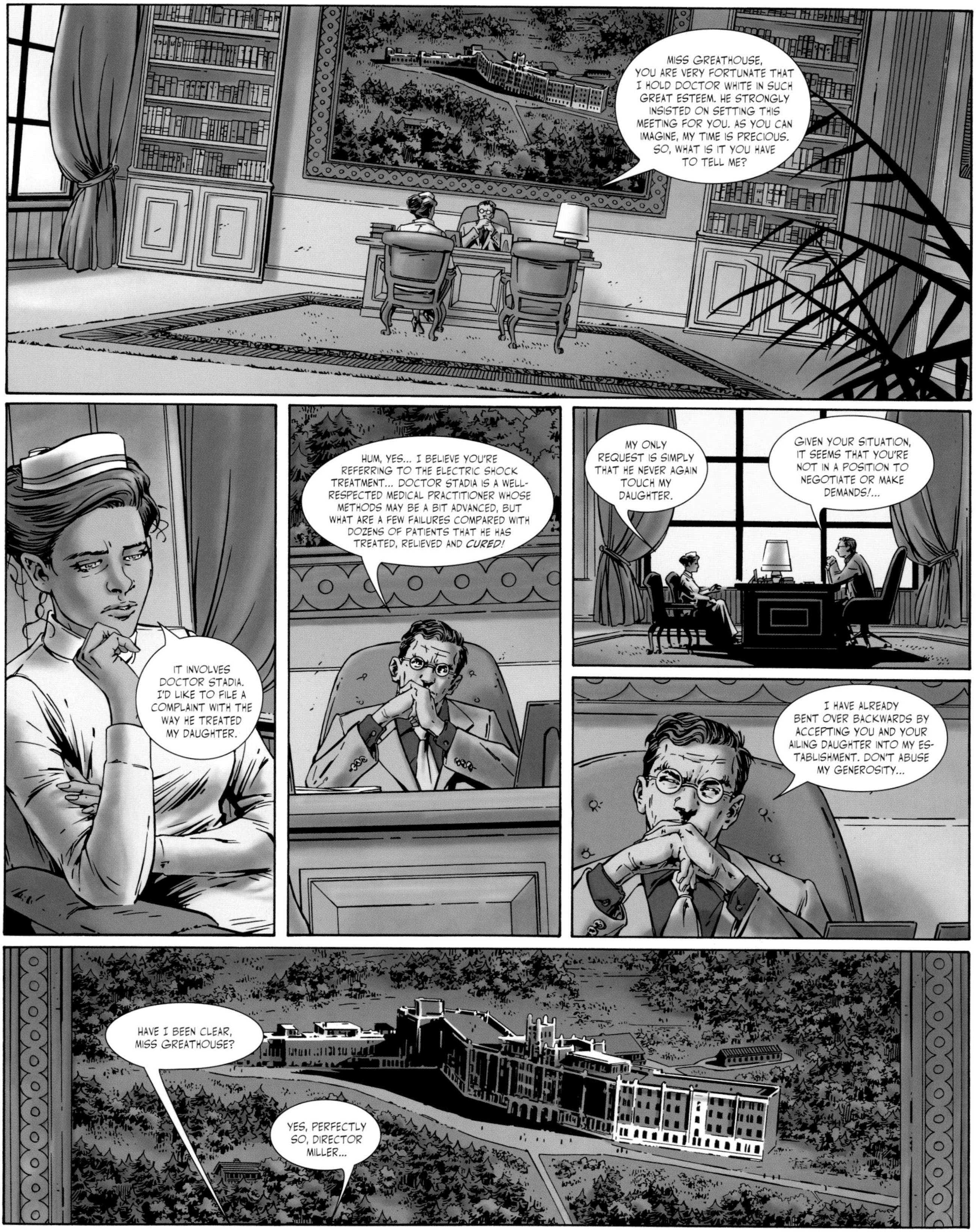
MISS GREATHOUSE, YOU ARE VERY FORTUNATE THAT I HOLD DOCTOR WHITE IN SUCH GREAT ESTEEM. HE STRONGLY INSISTED ON SETTING THIS MEETING FOR YOU. AS YOU CAN IMAGINE, MY TIME IS PRECIOUS. SO, WHAT IS IT YOU HAVE TO TELL ME?
IT INVOLVES DOCTOR STADIA. I'D LIKE TO FILE A COMPLAINT WITH THE WAY HE TREATED MY DAUGHTER.
HUM, YES... I BELIEVE YOU'RE REFERRING TO THE ELECTRIC SHOCK TREATMENT... DOCTOR STADIA IS A WELL-RESPECTED MEDICAL PRACTITIONER WHOSE METHODS MAY BE A BIT ADVANCED, BUT WHAT ARE A FEW FAILURES COMPARED WITH DOZENS OF PATIENTS THAT HE HAS TREATED, RELIEVED AND *CURED!*
MY ONLY REQUEST IS SIMPLY THAT HE NEVER AGAIN TOUCH MY DAUGHTER.
GIVEN YOUR SITUATION, IT SEEMS THAT YOU'RE NOT IN A POSITION TO NEGOTIATE OR MAKE DEMANDS!...
I HAVE ALREADY BENT OVER BACKWARDS BY ACCEPTING YOU AND YOUR AILING DAUGHTER INTO MY ESTABLISHMENT. DON'T ABUSE MY GENEROSITY...
HAVE I BEEN CLEAR, MISS GREATHOUSE?
YES, PERFECTLY SO, DIRECTOR MILLER...

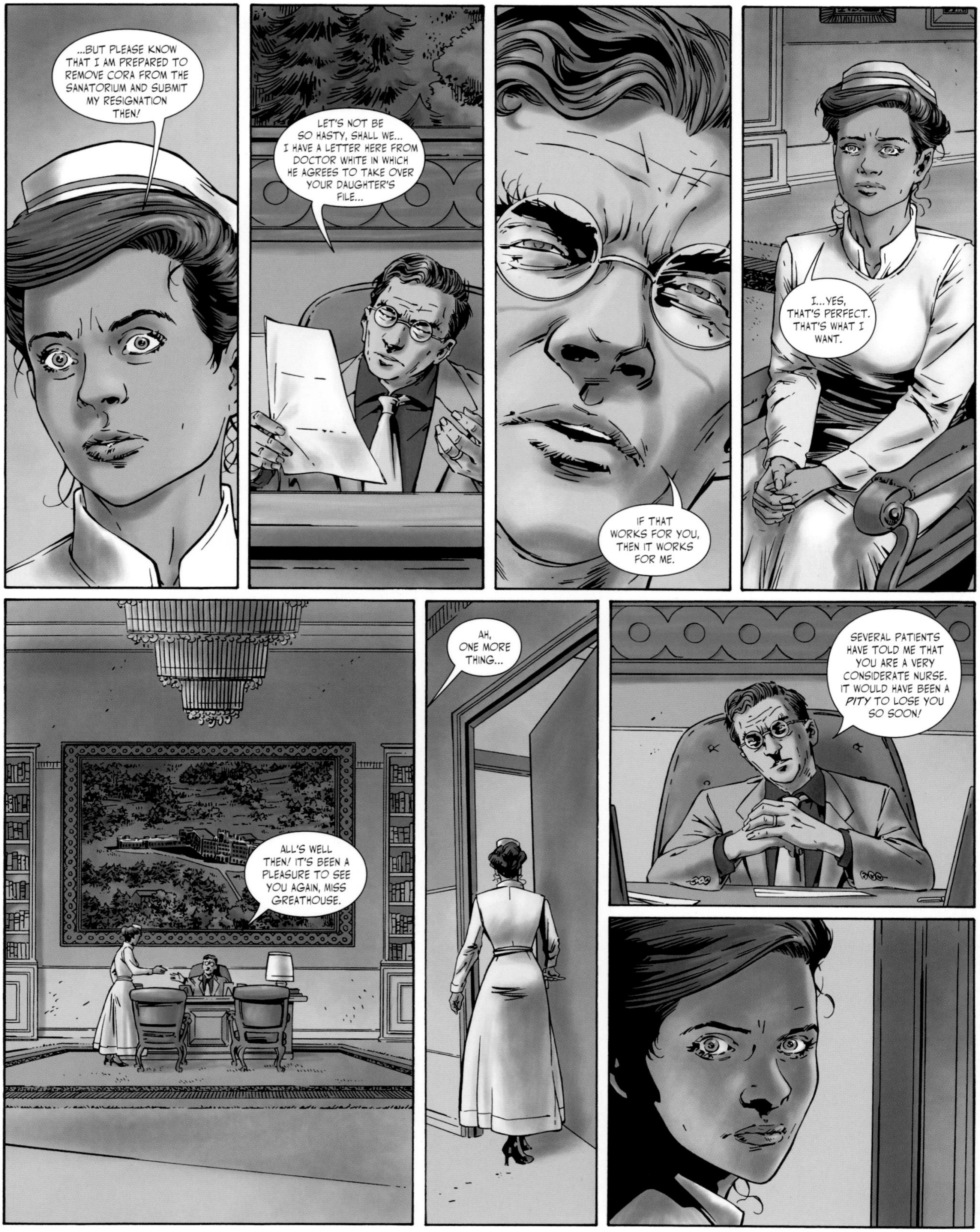
...BUT PLEASE KNOW THAT I AM PREPARED TO REMOVE CORA FROM THE SANATORIUM AND SUBMIT MY RESIGNATION THEN!
LET'S NOT BE SO HASTY, SHALL WE... I HAVE A LETTER HERE FROM DOCTOR WHITE IN WHICH HE AGREES TO TAKE OVER YOUR DAUGHTER'S FILE...
IF THAT WORKS FOR YOU, THEN IT WORKS FOR ME.
I...YES, THAT'S PERFECT. THAT'S WHAT I WANT.
ALL'S WELL THEN! IT'S BEEN A PLEASURE TO SEE YOU AGAIN, MISS GREATHOUSE.
AH, ONE MORE THING...
SEVERAL PATIENTS HAVE TOLD ME THAT YOU ARE A VERY CONSIDERATE NURSE. IT WOULD HAVE BEEN A *PITY* TO LOSE YOU SO SOON!

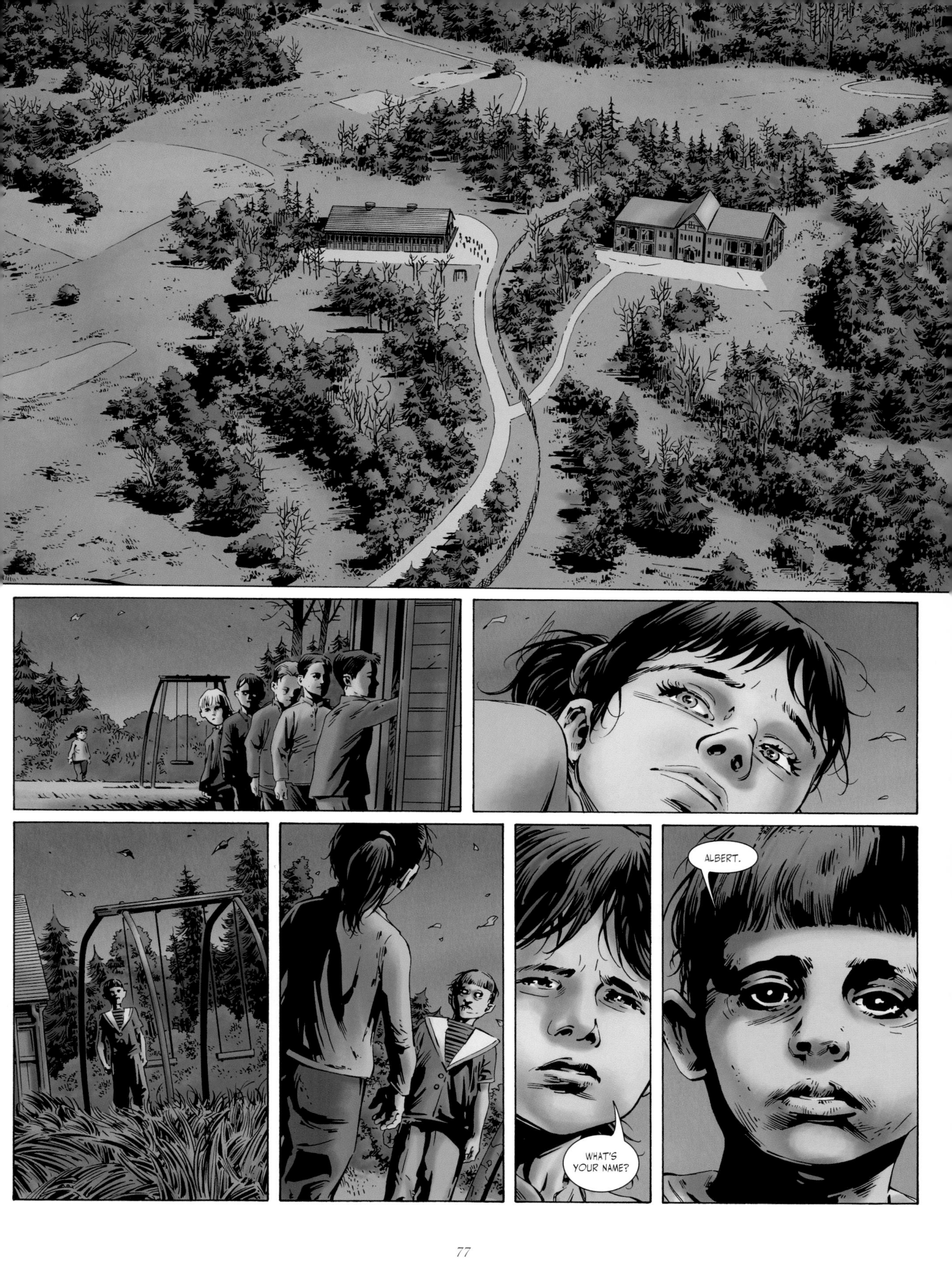
WHAT'S YOUR NAME?
ALBERT.

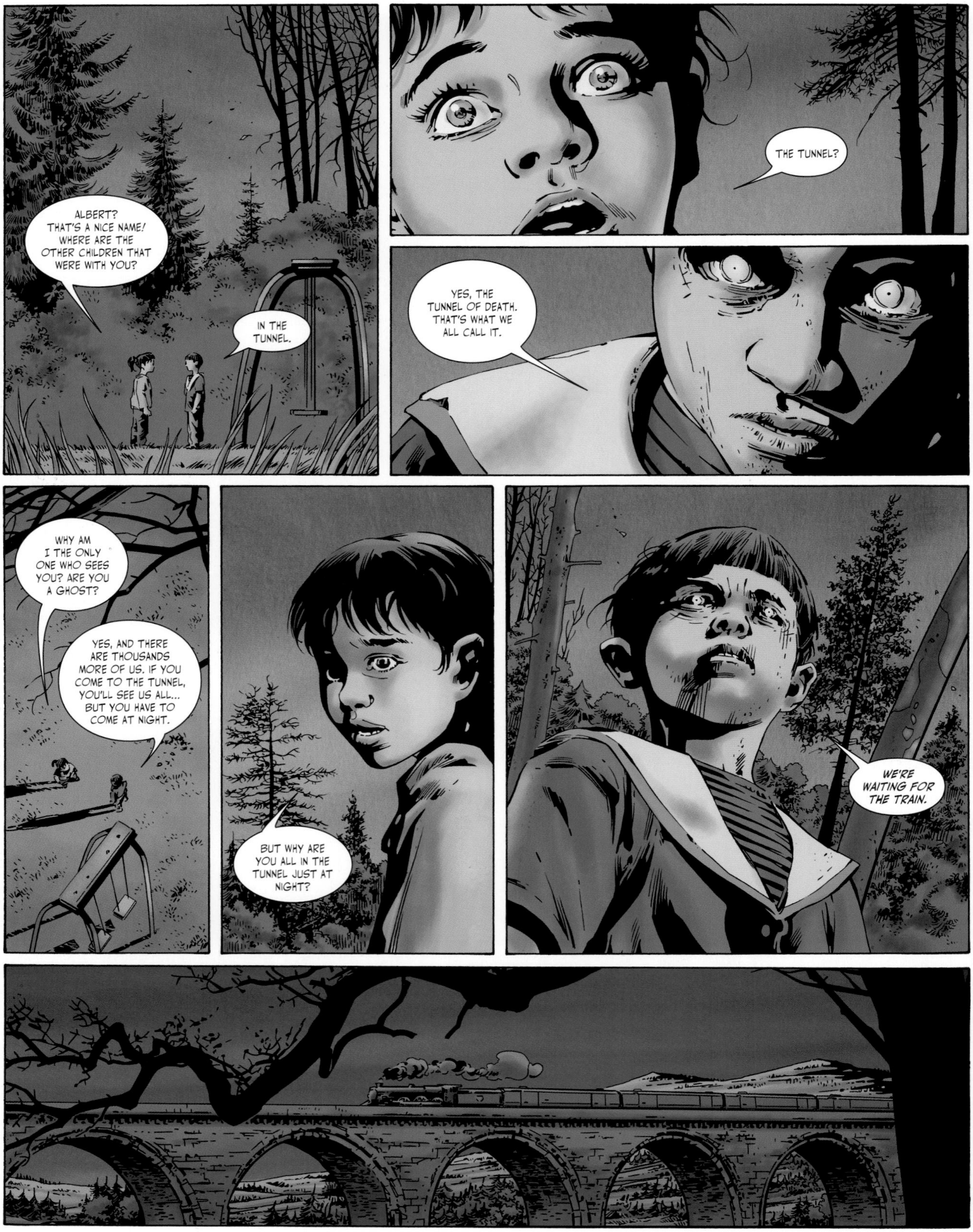
ALBERT? THAT'S A NICE NAME! WHERE ARE THE OTHER CHILDREN THAT WERE WITH YOU?
IN THE TUNNEL.
THE TUNNEL?
YES, THE TUNNEL OF DEATH. THAT'S WHAT WE ALL CALL IT.
WHY AM I THE ONLY ONE WHO SEES YOU? ARE YOU A GHOST?
YES, AND THERE ARE THOUSANDS MORE OF US. IF YOU COME TO THE TUNNEL, YOU'LL SEE US ALL... BUT YOU HAVE TO COME AT NIGHT.
BUT WHY ARE YOU ALL IN THE TUNNEL JUST AT NIGHT?
WE'RE WAITING FOR THE TRAIN.

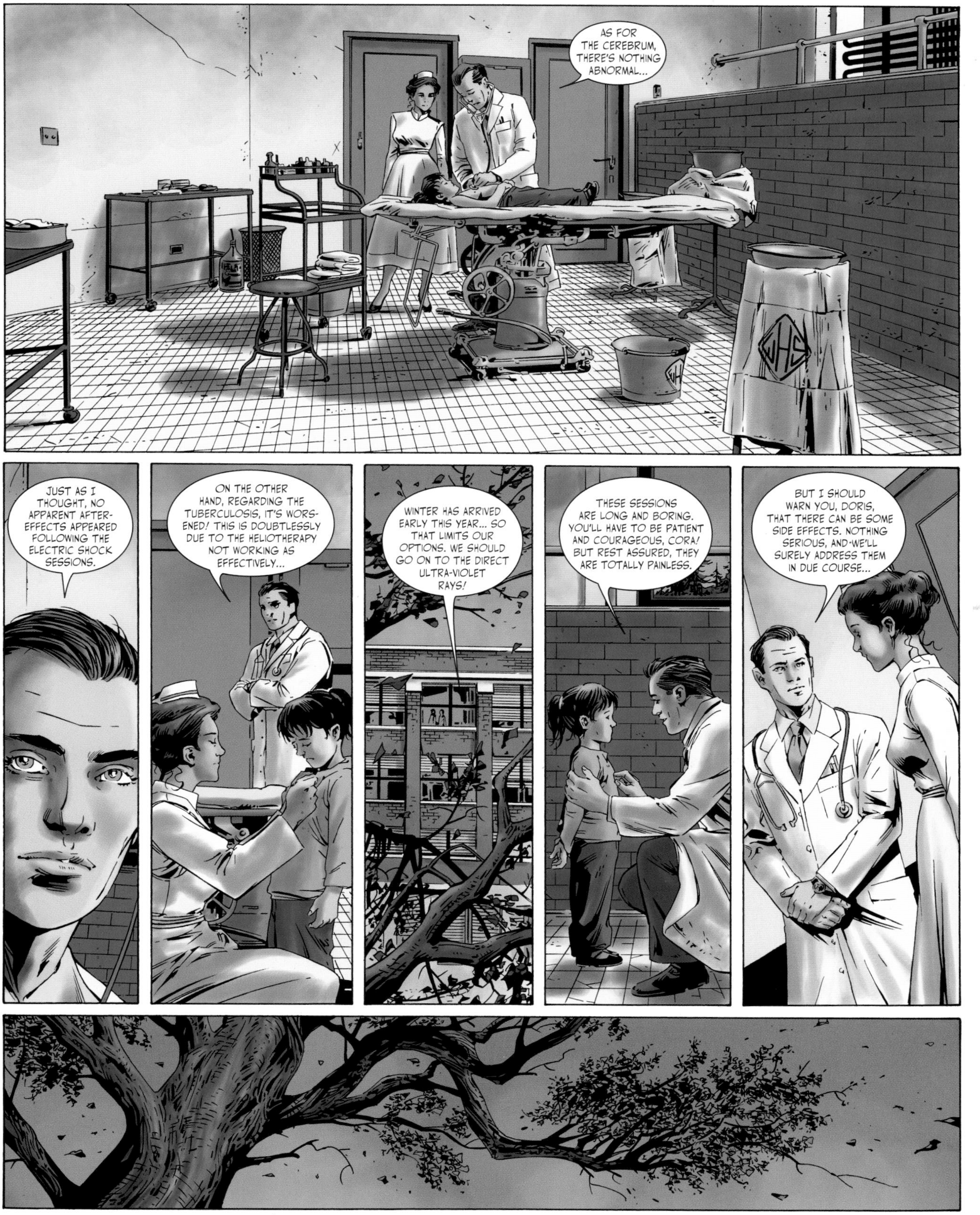
AS FOR THE CEREBRUM, THERE'S NOTHING ABNORMAL...
JUST AS I THOUGHT, NO APPARENT AFTER-EFFECTS APPEARED FOLLOWING THE ELECTRIC SHOCK SESSIONS.
ON THE OTHER HAND, REGARDING THE TUBERCULOSIS, IT'S WORSENED! THIS IS DOUBTLESSLY DUE TO THE HELIOTHERAPY NOT WORKING AS EFFECTIVELY...
WINTER HAS ARRIVED EARLY THIS YEAR... SO THAT LIMITS OUR OPTIONS. WE SHOULD GO ON TO THE DIRECT ULTRA-VIOLET RAYS!
THESE SESSIONS ARE LONG AND BORING. YOU'LL HAVE TO BE PATIENT AND COURAGEOUS, CORA! BUT REST ASSURED, THEY ARE TOTALLY PAINLESS.
BUT I SHOULD WARN YOU, DORIS, THAT THERE CAN BE SOME SIDE EFFECTS. NOTHING SERIOUS, AND WE'LL SURELY ADDRESS THEM IN DUE COURSE...

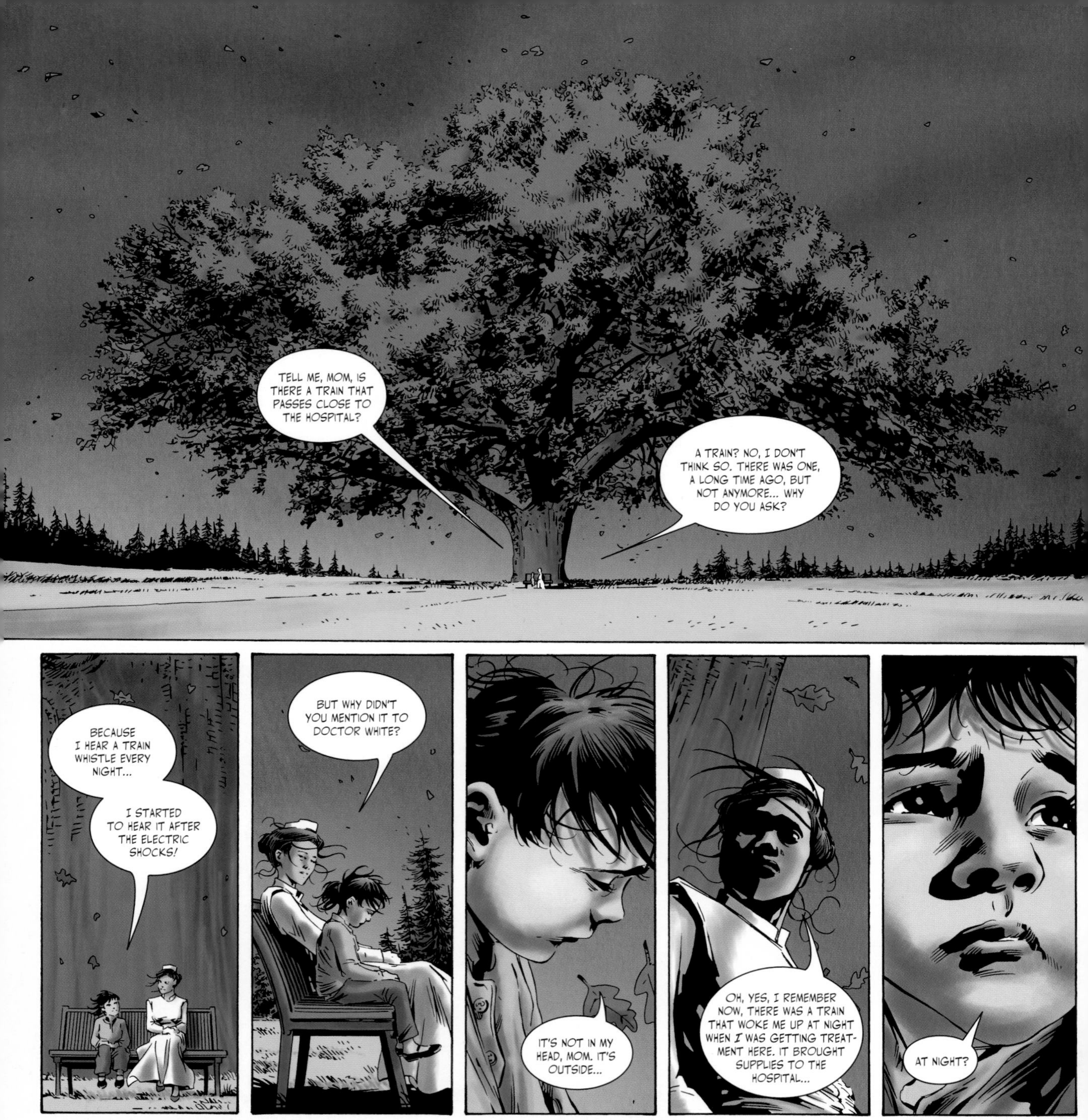
TELL ME, MOM, IS THERE A TRAIN THAT PASSES CLOSE TO THE HOSPITAL?
A TRAIN? NO, I DON'T THINK SO. THERE WAS ONE, A LONG TIME AGO, BUT NOT ANYMORE... WHY DO YOU ASK?
BECAUSE I HEAR A TRAIN WHISTLE EVERY NIGHT...
I STARTED TO HEAR IT AFTER THE ELECTRIC SHOCKS!
BUT WHY DIDN'T YOU MENTION IT TO DOCTOR WHITE?
IT'S NOT IN MY HEAD, MOM. IT'S OUTSIDE...
OH, YES, I REMEMBER NOW, THERE WAS A TRAIN THAT WOKE ME UP AT NIGHT WHEN I WAS GETTING TREAT-MENT HERE. IT BROUGHT SUPPLIES TO THE HOSPITAL...
AT NIGHT?
YES, THOUGH THAT IS STRANGE... WHY BRING SUPPLIES AT NIGHT? I'LL ASK BESS. THERE MUST BE A GOOD REASON.

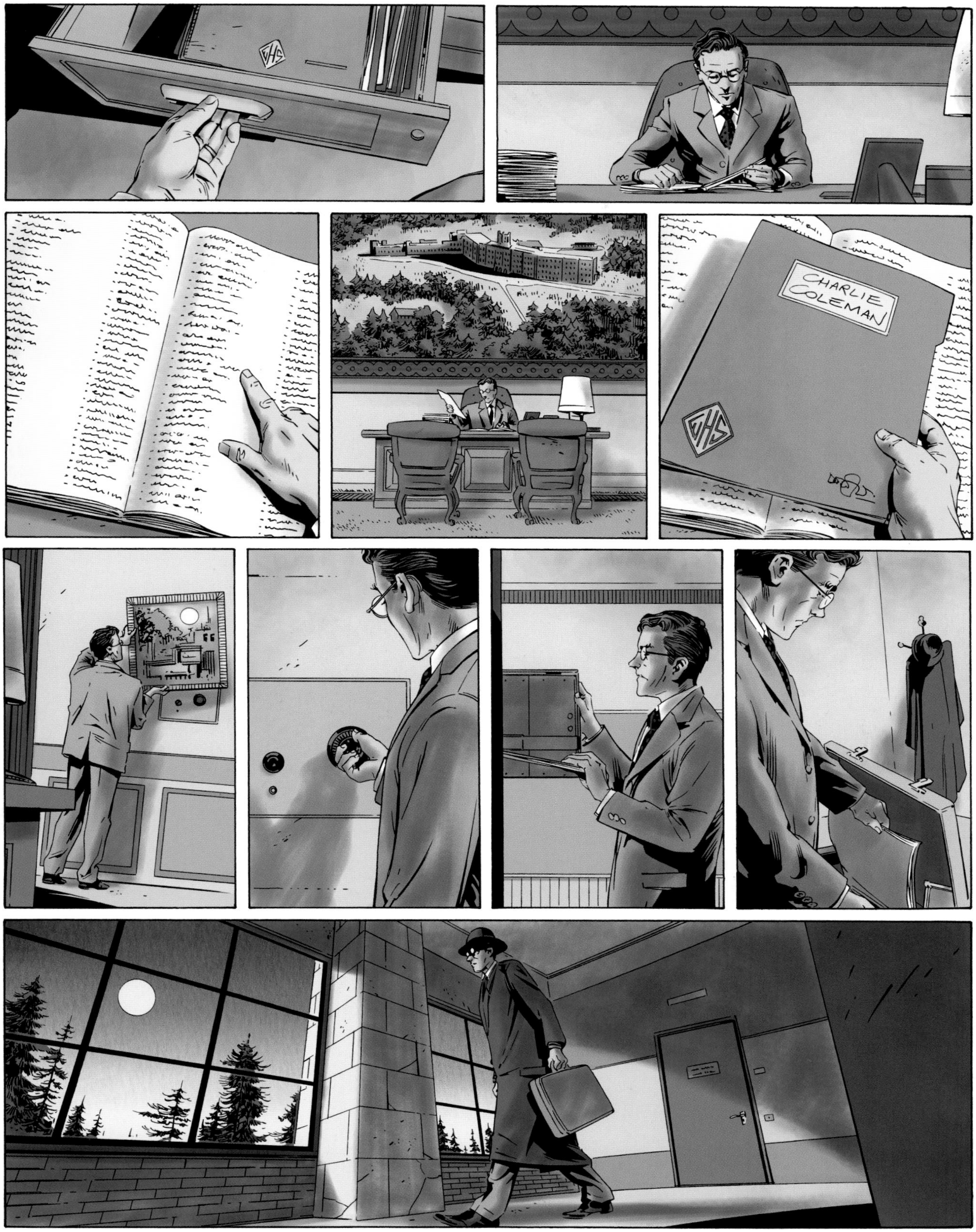
CHARLIE
COLEMAN

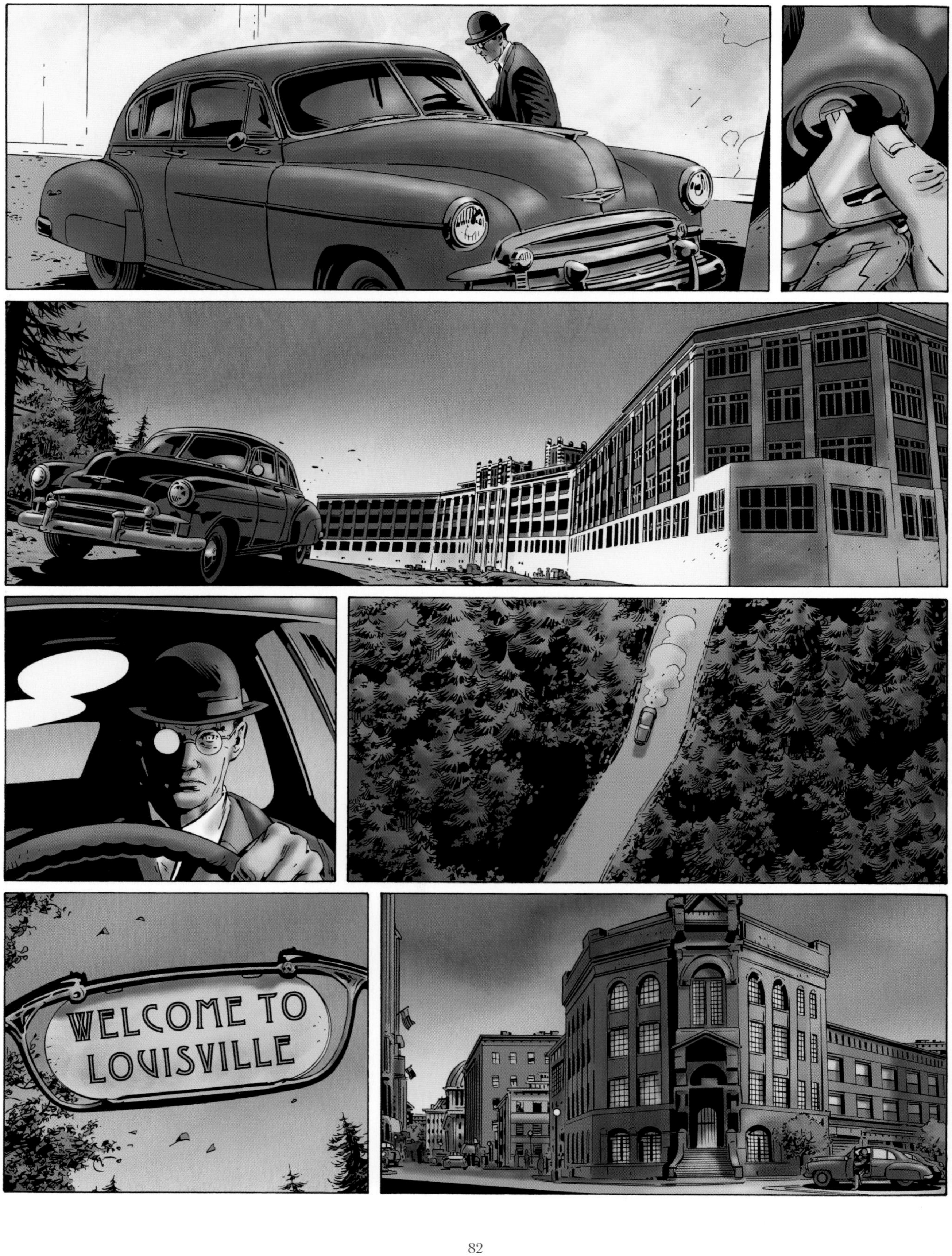
WELCOME TO
LOUISVILLE

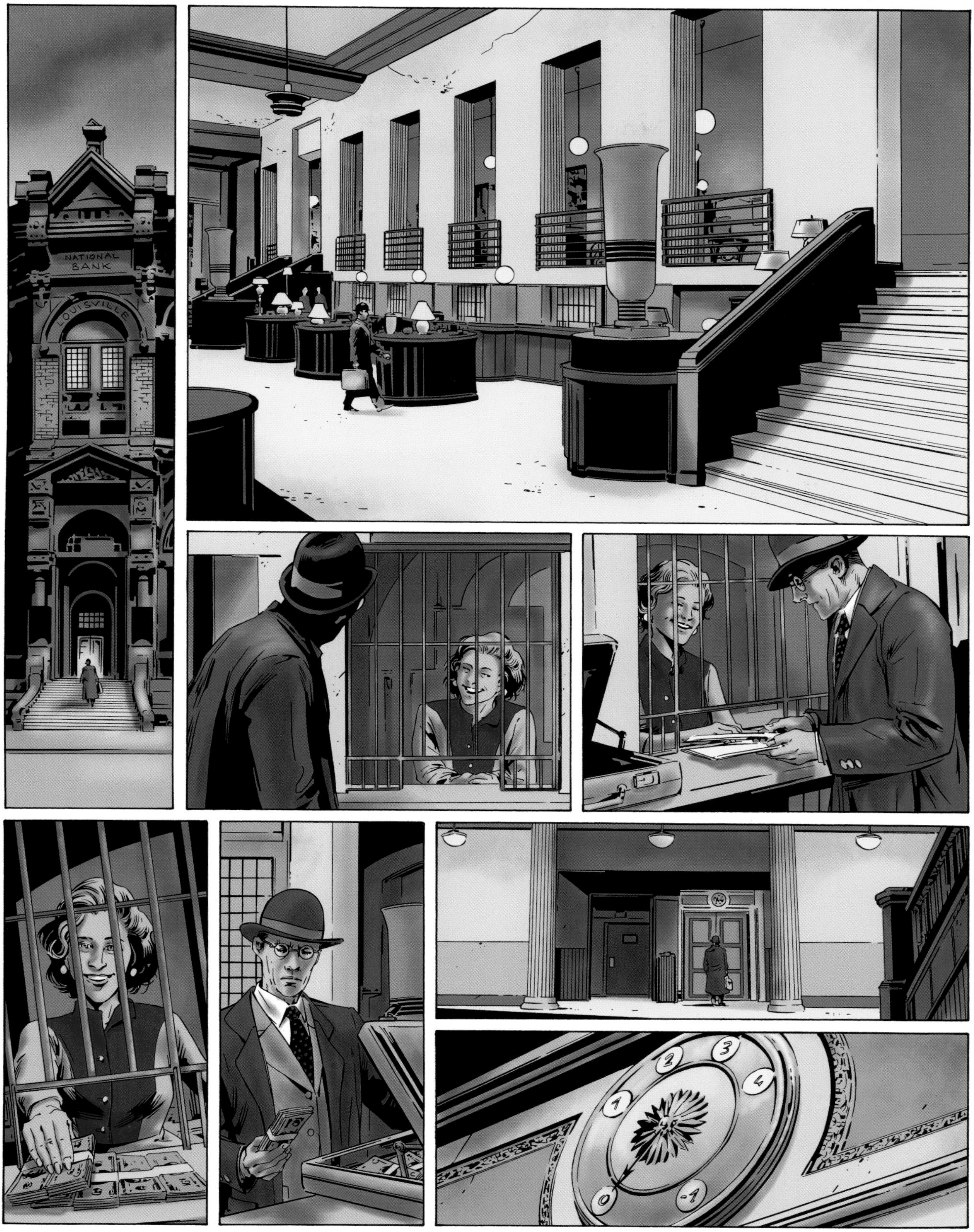
NATIONAL BANK
LOUISVILLE

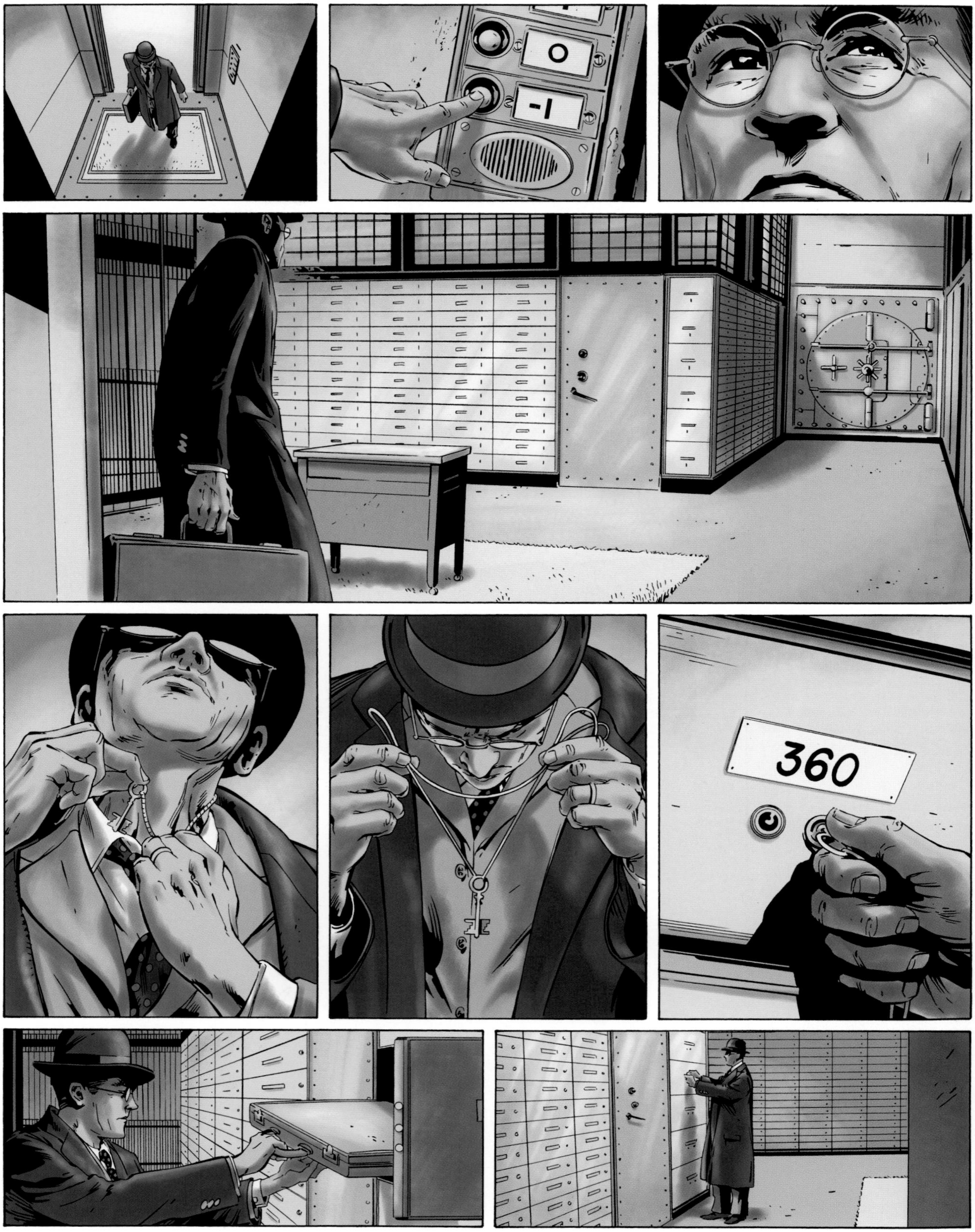
0
-1
360

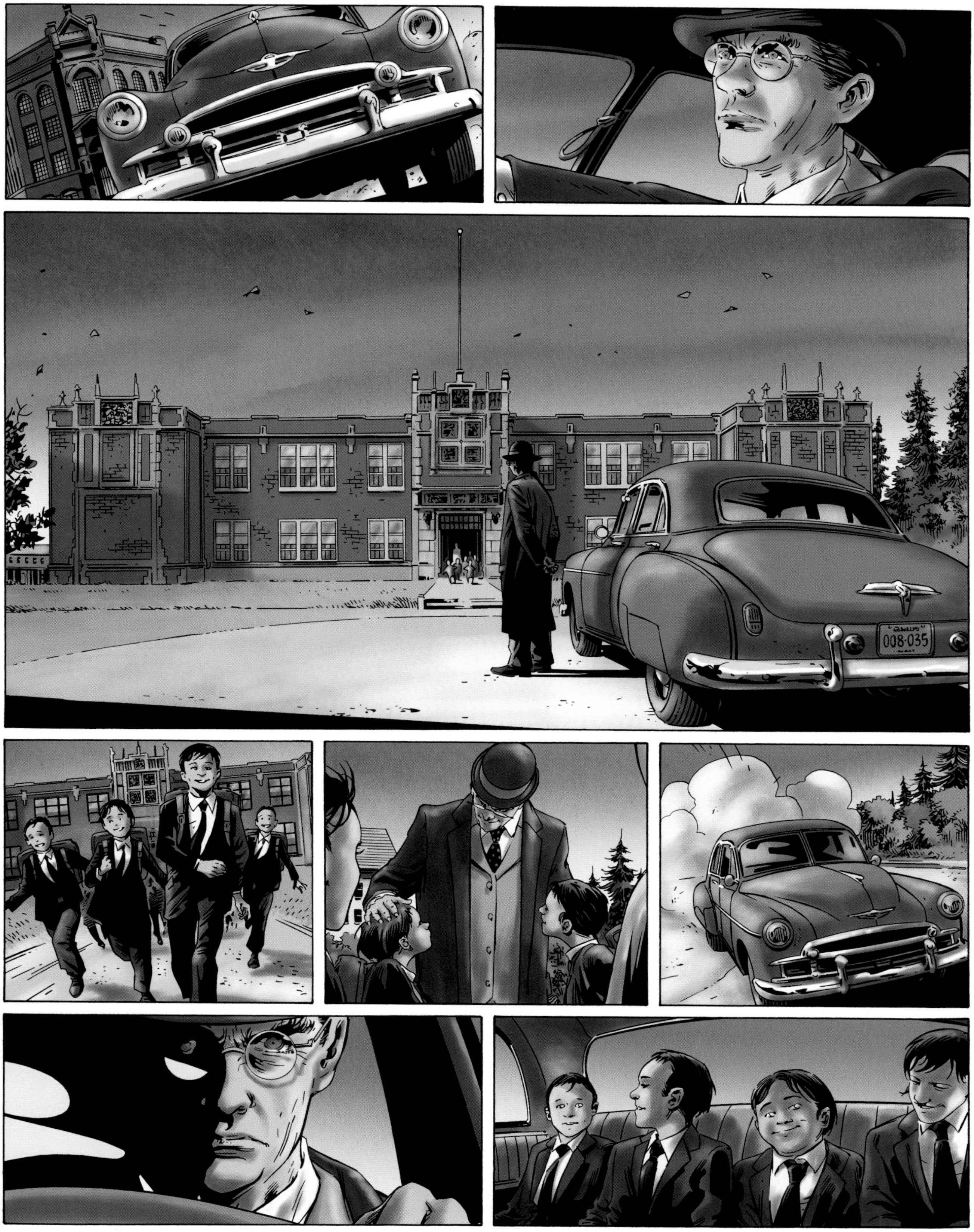
008·035

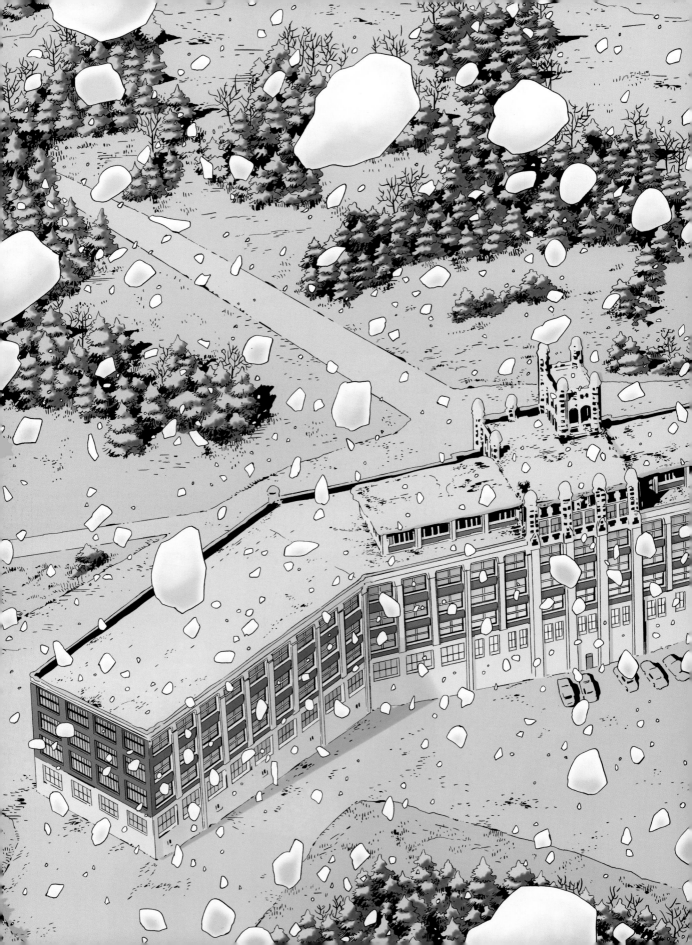

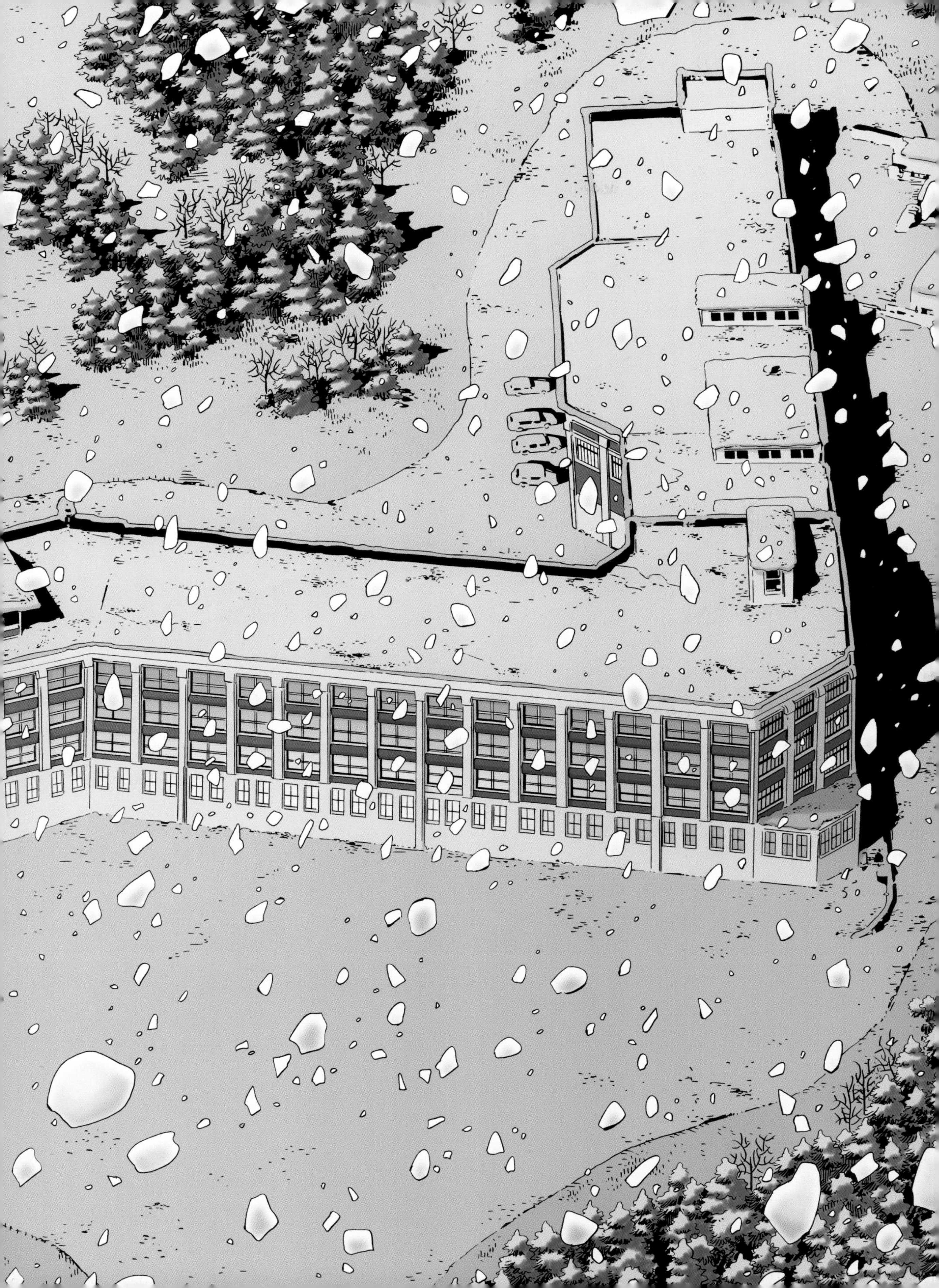

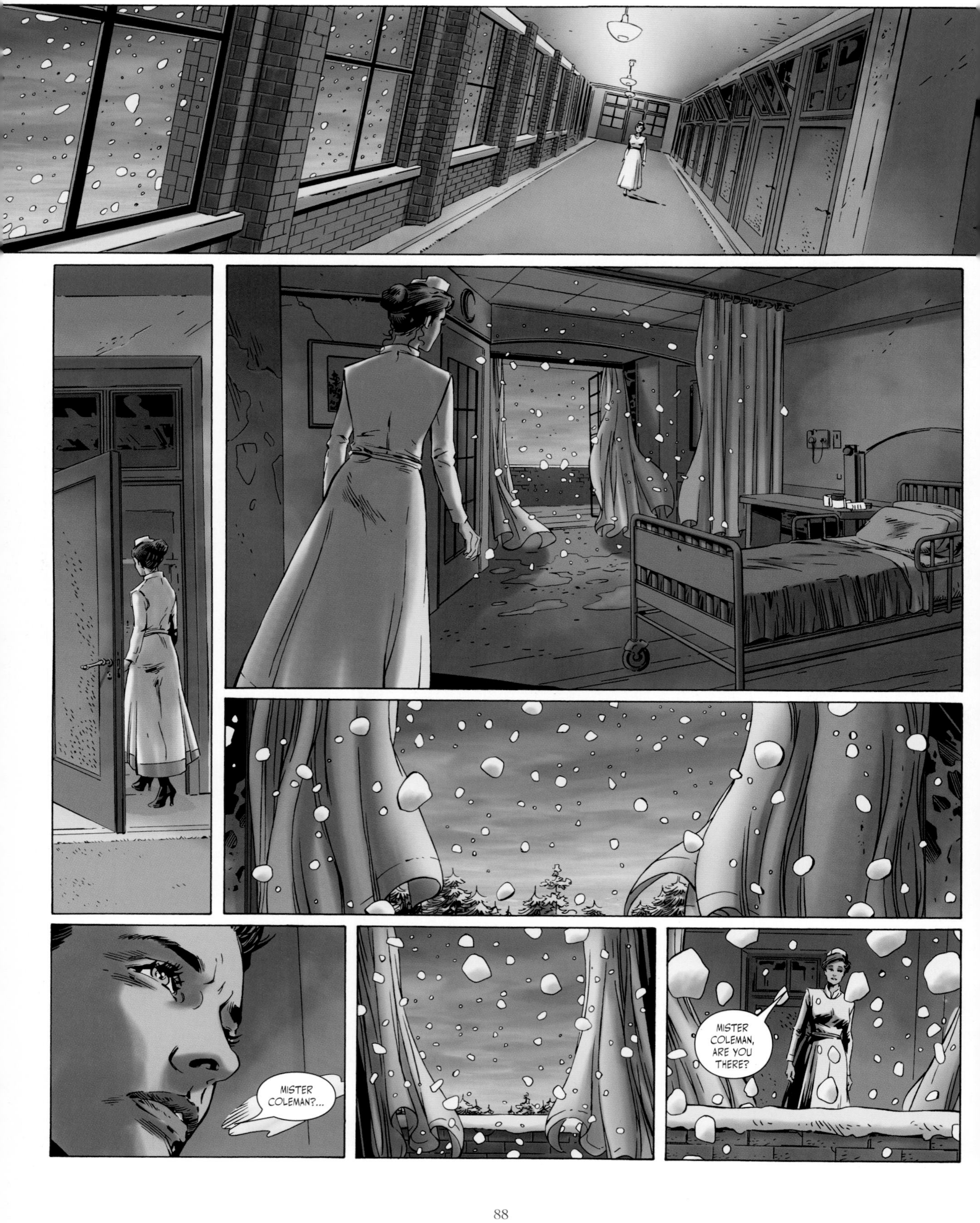
MISTER COLEMAN?...
MISTER COLEMAN, ARE YOU THERE?

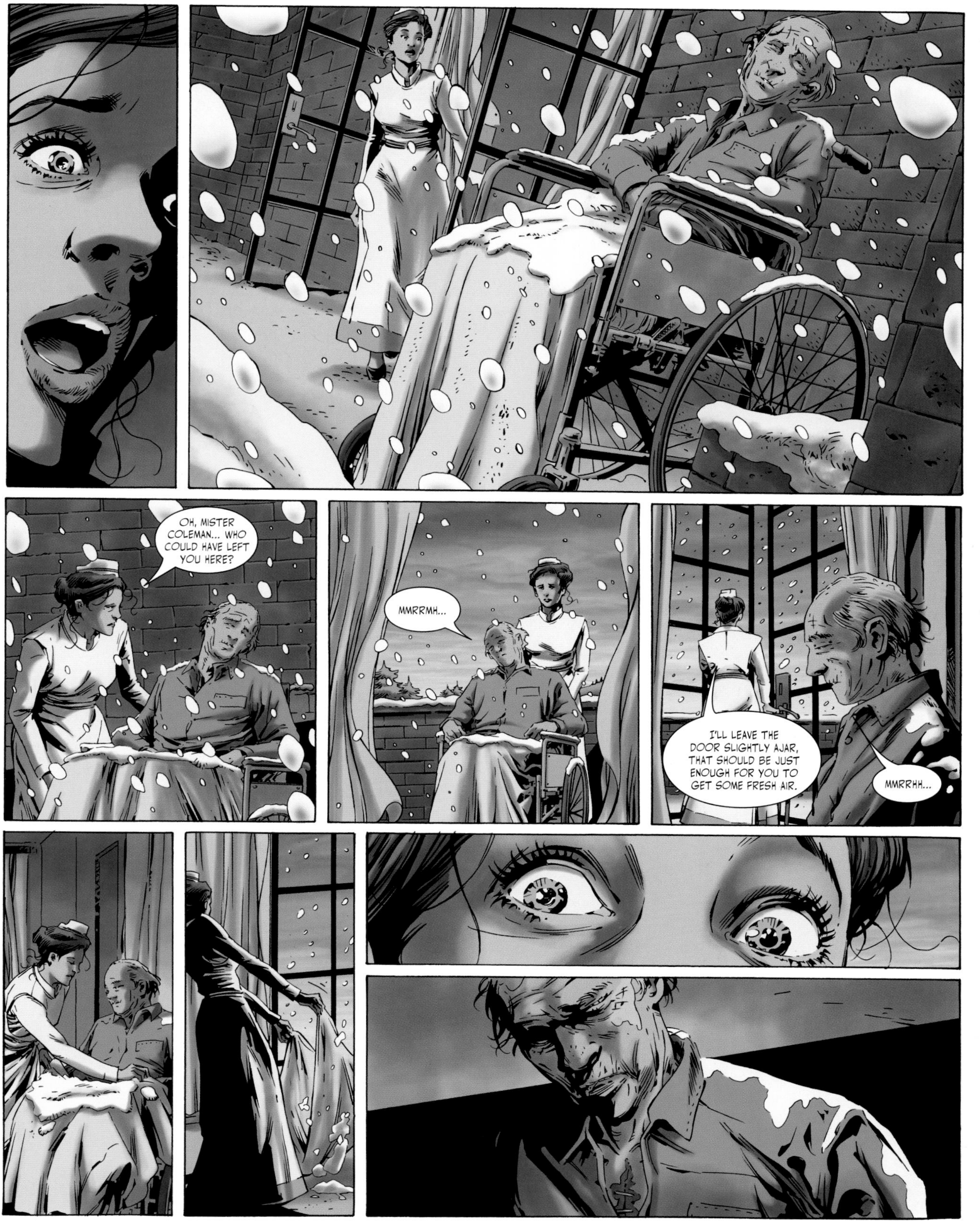
OH, MISTER COLEMAN... WHO COULD HAVE LEFT YOU HERE?
MMRRMH...
I'LL LEAVE THE DOOR SLIGHTLY AJAR, THAT SHOULD BE JUST ENOUGH FOR YOU TO GET SOME FRESH AIR.
MMRRHH...

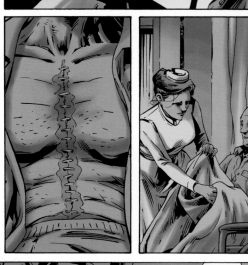

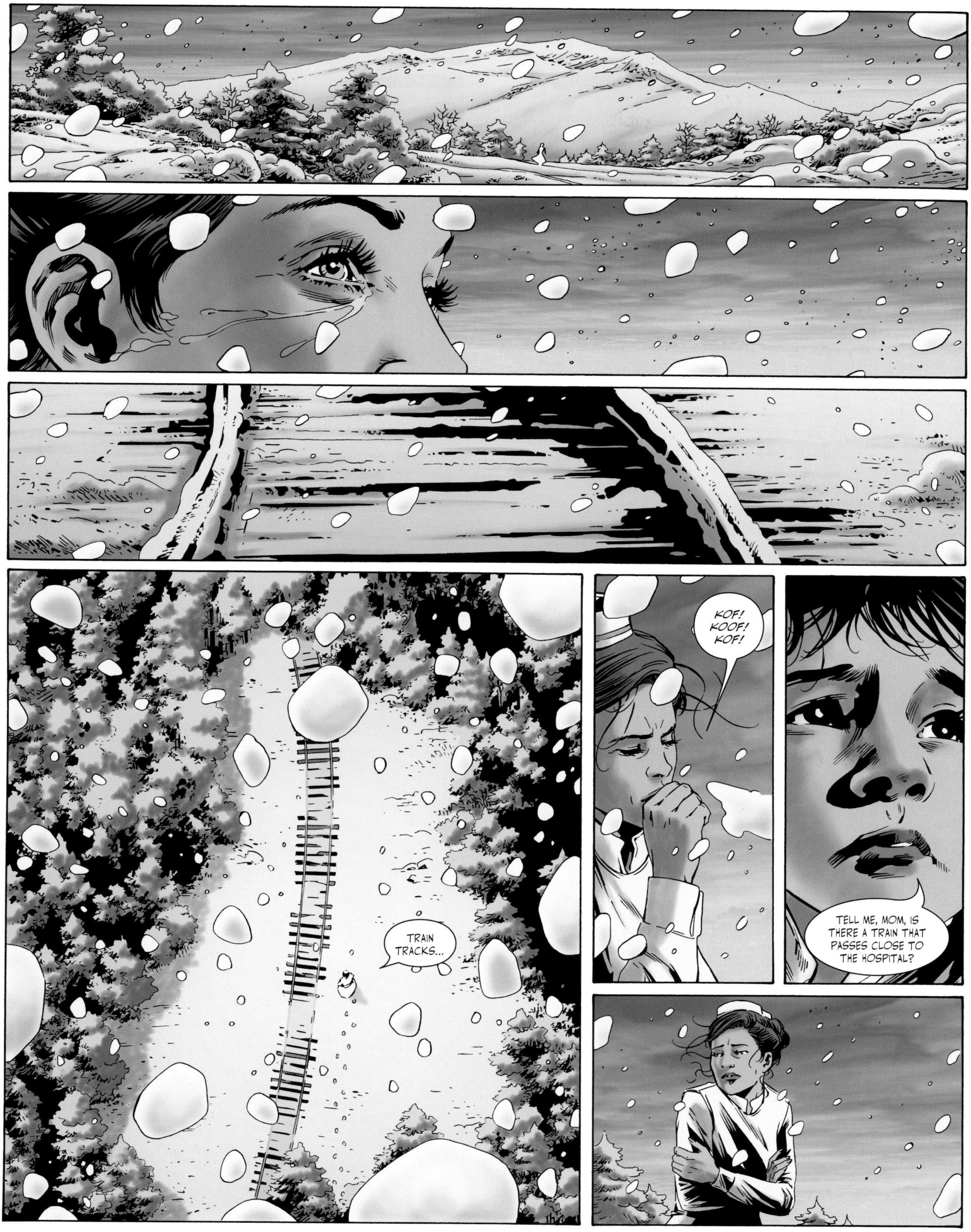
TRAIN TRACKS...
KOF! KOOF! KOF!
TELL ME, MOM, IS THERE A TRAIN THAT PASSES CLOSE TO THE HOSPITAL?

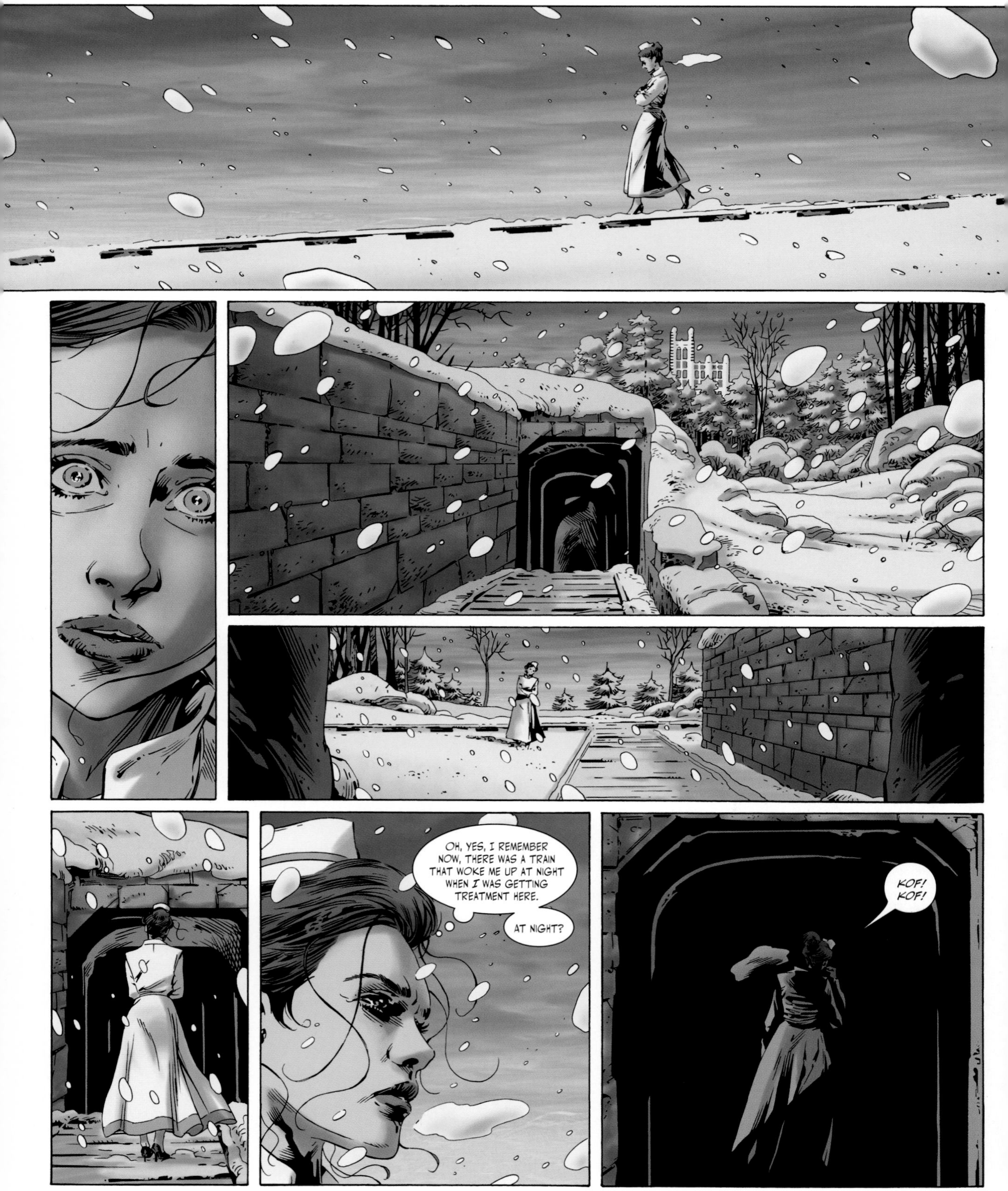

OH, YES, I REMEMBER NOW, THERE WAS A TRAIN THAT WOKE ME UP AT NIGHT WHEN I WAS GETTING TREATMENT HERE.
AT NIGHT?
KOF! KOF!

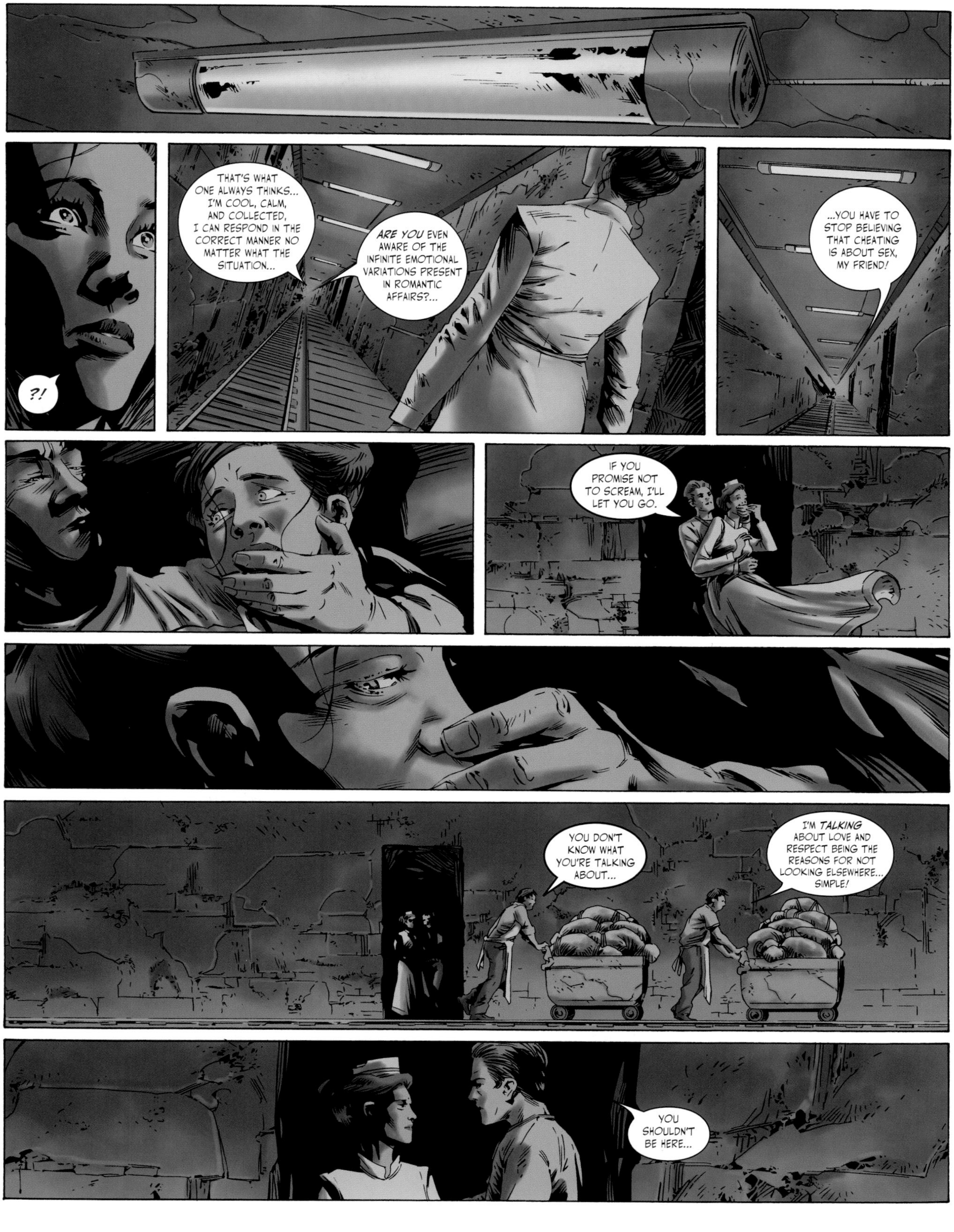
?!
THAT'S WHAT ONE ALWAYS THINKS... I'M COOL, CALM, AND COLLECTED, I CAN RESPOND IN THE CORRECT MANNER NO MATTER WHAT THE SITUATION...
ARE YOU EVEN AWARE OF THE INFINITE EMOTIONAL VARIATIONS PRESENT IN ROMANTIC AFFAIRS?...
...YOU HAVE TO STOP BELIEVING THAT CHEATING IS ABOUT SEX, MY FRIEND!
IF YOU PROMISE NOT TO SCREAM, I'LL LET YOU GO.
YOU DON'T KNOW WHAT YOU'RE TALKING ABOUT...
I'M TALKING ABOUT LOVE AND RESPECT BEING THE REASONS FOR NOT LOOKING ELSEWHERE... SIMPLE!
YOU SHOULDN'T BE HERE...

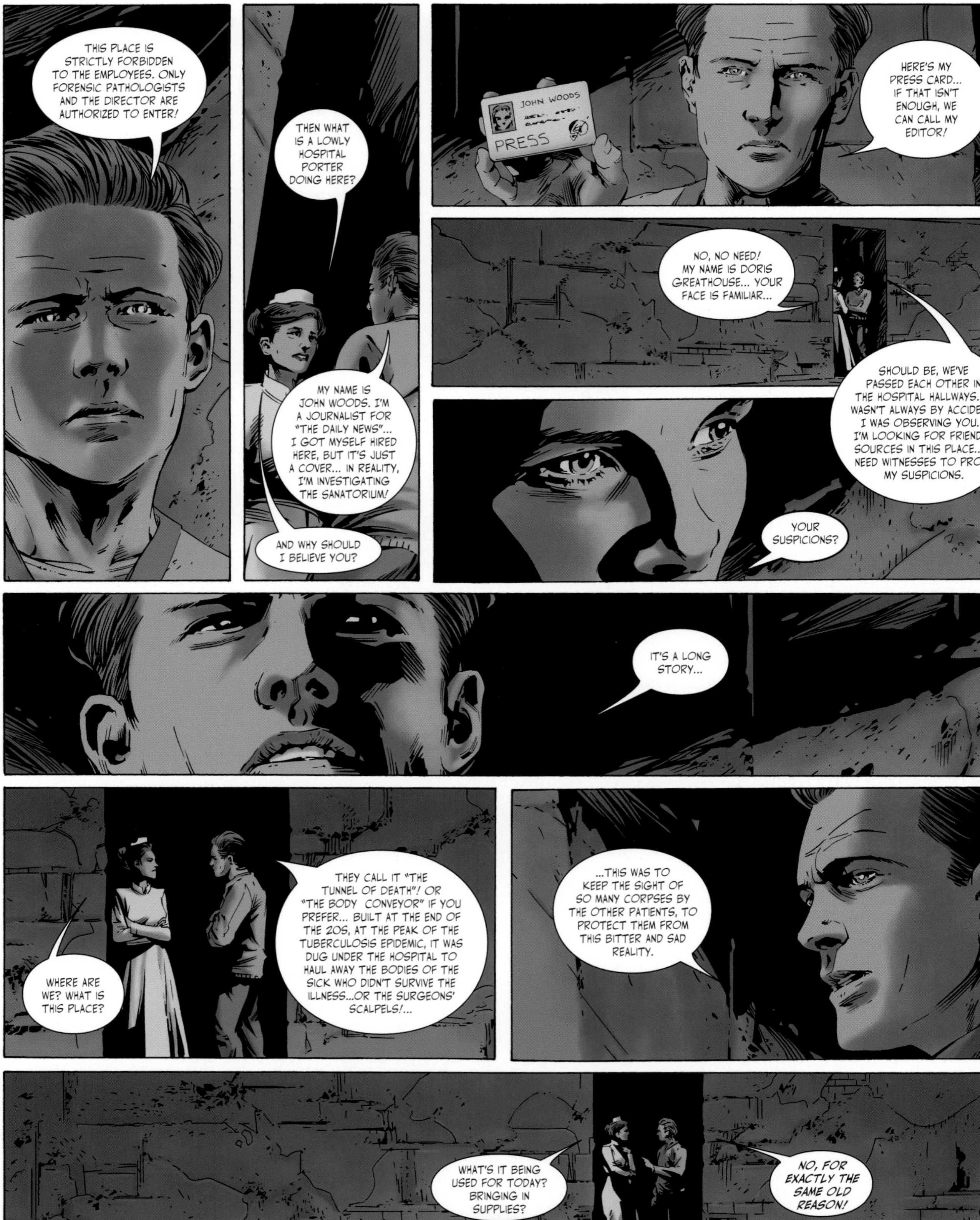
THIS PLACE IS STRICTLY FORBIDDEN TO THE EMPLOYEES. ONLY FORENSIC PATHOLOGISTS AND THE DIRECTOR ARE AUTHORIZED TO ENTER!
THEN WHAT IS A LOWLY HOSPITAL PORTER DOING HERE?
MY NAME IS JOHN WOODS. I'M A JOURNALIST FOR "THE DAILY NEWS"... I GOT MYSELF HIRED HERE, BUT IT'S JUST A COVER... IN REALITY, I'M INVESTIGATING THE SANATORIUM!
AND WHY SHOULD I BELIEVE YOU?
JOHN WOODS
PRESS
HERE'S MY PRESS CARD... IF THAT ISN'T ENOUGH, WE CAN CALL MY EDITOR!
NO, NO NEED! MY NAME IS DORIS GREATHOUSE... YOUR FACE IS FAMILIAR...
SHOULD BE, WE'VE PASSED EACH OTHER IN THE HOSPITAL HALLWAYS. IT WASN'T ALWAYS BY ACCIDENT. I WAS OBSERVING YOU... I'M LOOKING FOR FRIENDLY SOURCES IN THIS PLACE... I NEED WITNESSES TO PROVE MY SUSPICIONS.
YOUR SUSPICIONS?
IT'S A LONG STORY...
WHERE ARE WE? WHAT IS THIS PLACE?
THEY CALL IT "THE TUNNEL OF DEATH"! OR "THE BODY CONVEYOR" IF YOU PREFER... BUILT AT THE END OF THE 20S, AT THE PEAK OF THE TUBERCULOSIS EPIDEMIC, IT WAS DUG UNDER THE HOSPITAL TO HAUL AWAY THE BODIES OF THE SICK WHO DIDN'T SURVIVE THE ILLNESS...OR THE SURGEONS' SCALPELS!...
...THIS WAS TO KEEP THE SIGHT OF SO MANY CORPSES BY THE OTHER PATIENTS, TO PROTECT THEM FROM THIS BITTER AND SAD REALITY.
WHAT'S IT BEING USED FOR TODAY? BRINGING IN SUPPLIES?
NO, FOR EXACTLY THE SAME OLD REASON!

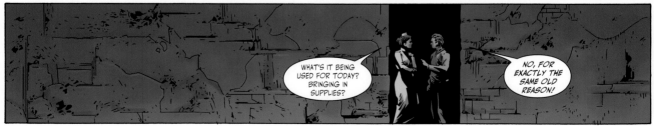

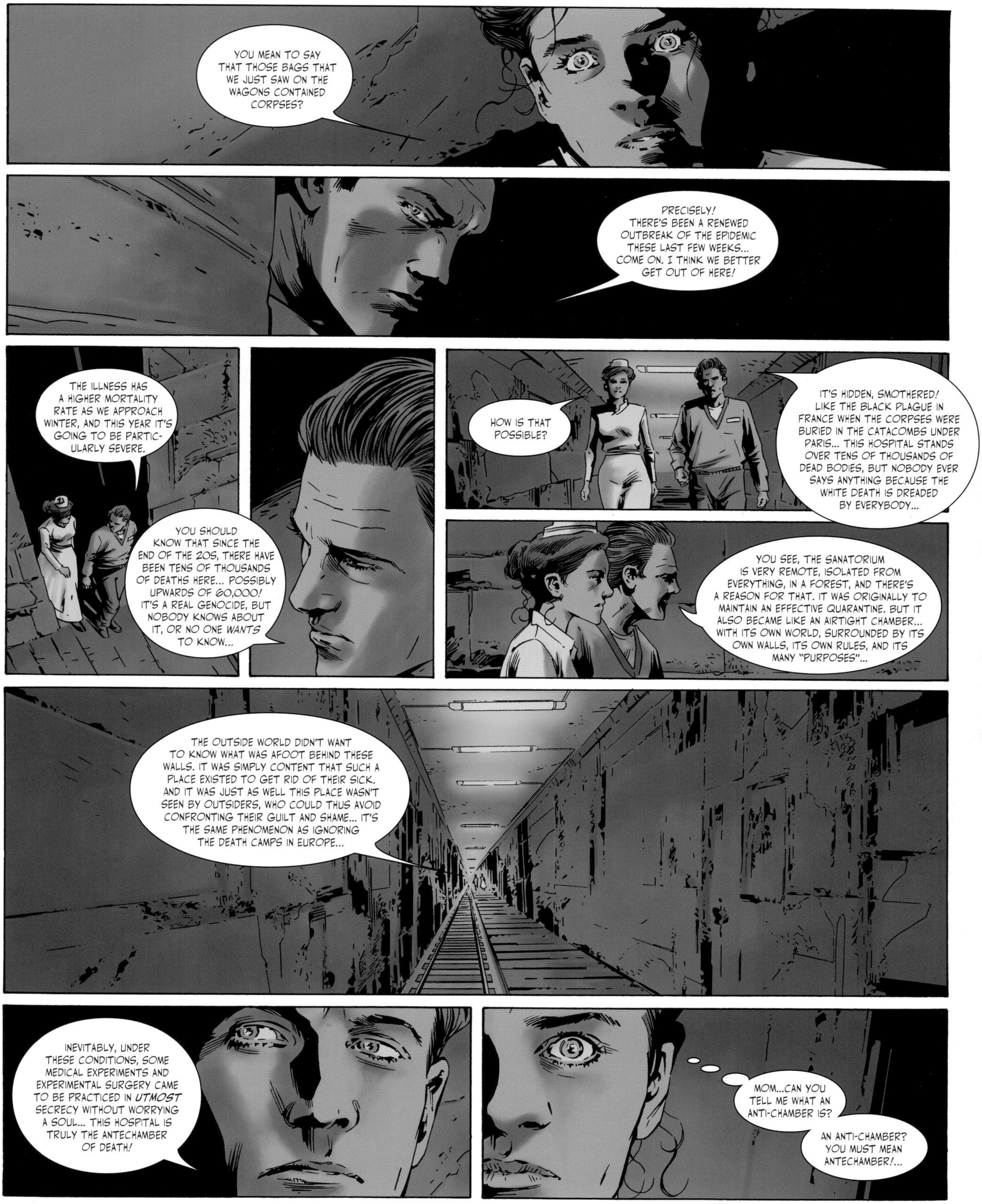
YOU MEAN TO SAY THAT THOSE BAGS THAT WE JUST SAW ON THE WAGONS CONTAINED CORPSES?
PRECISELY! THERE'S BEEN A RENEWED OUTBREAK OF THE EPIDEMIC THESE LAST FEW WEEKS... COME ON. I THINK WE BETTER GET OUT OF HERE!
THE ILLNESS HAS A HIGHER MORTALITY RATE AS WE APPROACH WINTER, AND THIS YEAR IT'S GOING TO BE PARTIC-ULARLY SEVERE.
YOU SHOULD KNOW THAT SINCE THE END OF THE 20S, THERE HAVE BEEN TENS OF THOUSANDS OF DEATHS HERE... POSSIBLY UPWARDS OF 60,000! IT'S A REAL GENOCIDE, BUT NOBODY KNOWS ABOUT IT, OR NO ONE *WANTS* TO KNOW...
HOW IS THAT POSSIBLE?
IT'S HIDDEN, SMOTHERED! LIKE THE BLACK PLAGUE IN FRANCE WHEN THE CORPSES WERE BURIED IN THE CATACOMBS UNDER PARIS... THIS HOSPITAL STANDS OVER TENS OF THOUSANDS OF DEAD BODIES, BUT NOBODY EVER SAYS ANYTHING BECAUSE THE WHITE DEATH IS DREADED BY EVERYBODY...
YOU SEE, THE SANATORIUM IS VERY REMOTE, ISOLATED FROM EVERYTHING, IN A FOREST, AND THERE'S A REASON FOR THAT. IT WAS ORIGINALLY TO MAINTAIN AN EFFECTIVE QUARANTINE. BUT IT ALSO BECAME LIKE AN AIRTIGHT CHAMBER... WITH ITS OWN WORLD, SURROUNDED BY ITS OWN WALLS, ITS OWN RULES, AND ITS MANY "PURPOSES"...
THE OUTSIDE WORLD DIDN'T WANT TO KNOW WHAT WAS AFOOT BEHIND THESE WALLS. IT WAS SIMPLY CONTENT THAT SUCH A PLACE EXISTED TO GET RID OF THEIR SICK. AND IT WAS JUST AS WELL THIS PLACE WASN'T SEEN BY OUTSIDERS, WHO COULD THUS AVOID CONFRONTING THEIR GUILT AND SHAME... IT'S THE SAME PHENOMENON AS IGNORING THE DEATH CAMPS IN EUROPE...
INEVITABLY, UNDER THESE CONDITIONS, SOME MEDICAL EXPERIMENTS AND EXPERIMENTAL SURGERY CAME TO BE PRACTICED IN **UTMOST** SECRECY WITHOUT WORRYING A SOUL... THIS HOSPITAL IS TRULY THE ANTECHAMBER OF DEATH!
MOM...CAN YOU TELL ME WHAT AN ANTI-CHAMBER IS?
AN ANTI-CHAMBER? YOU MUST MEAN ANTECHAMBER!...

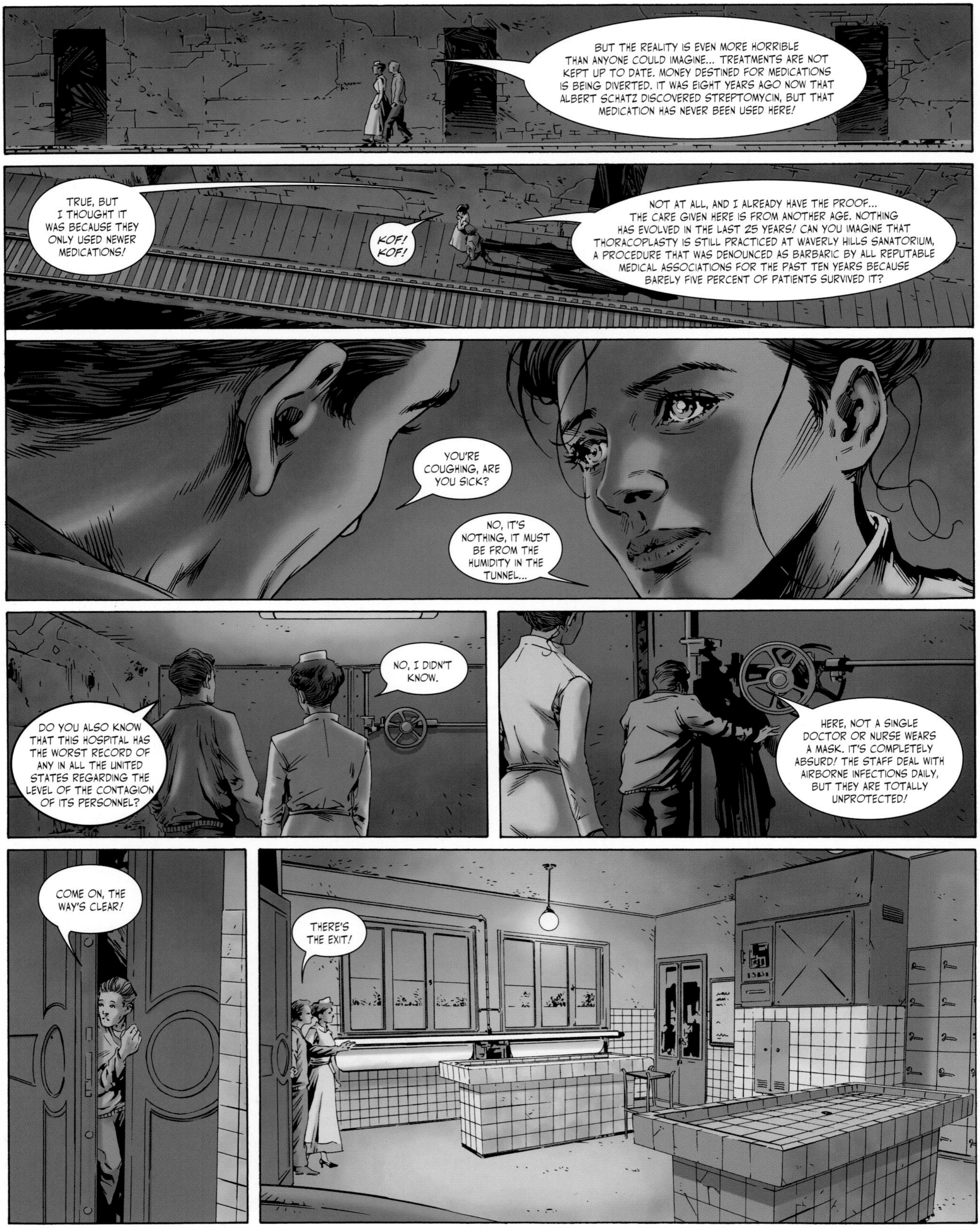
BUT THE REALITY IS EVEN MORE HORRIBLE THAN ANYONE COULD IMAGINE... TREATMENTS ARE NOT KEPT UP TO DATE. MONEY DESTINED FOR MEDICATIONS IS BEING DIVERTED. IT WAS EIGHT YEARS AGO NOW THAT ALBERT SCHATZ DISCOVERED STREPTOMYCIN, BUT THAT MEDICATION HAS NEVER BEEN USED HERE!
TRUE, BUT I THOUGHT IT WAS BECAUSE THEY ONLY USED NEWER MEDICATIONS!
KOF! KOF!
NOT AT ALL, AND I ALREADY HAVE THE PROOF... THE CARE GIVEN HERE IS FROM ANOTHER AGE. NOTHING HAS EVOLVED IN THE LAST 25 YEARS! CAN YOU IMAGINE THAT THORACOPLASTY IS STILL PRACTICED AT WAVERLY HILLS SANATORIUM, A PROCEDURE THAT WAS DENOUNCED AS BARBARIC BY ALL REPUTABLE MEDICAL ASSOCIATIONS FOR THE PAST TEN YEARS BECAUSE BARELY FIVE PERCENT OF PATIENTS SURVIVED IT?
YOU'RE COUGHING, ARE YOU SICK?
NO, IT'S NOTHING, IT MUST BE FROM THE HUMIDITY IN THE TUNNEL...
DO YOU ALSO KNOW THAT THIS HOSPITAL HAS THE WORST RECORD OF ANY IN ALL THE UNITED STATES REGARDING THE LEVEL OF THE CONTAGION OF ITS PERSONNEL?
NO, I DIDN'T KNOW.
HERE, NOT A SINGLE DOCTOR OR NURSE WEARS A MASK. IT'S COMPLETELY ABSURD! THE STAFF DEAL WITH AIRBORNE INFECTIONS DAILY, BUT THEY ARE TOTALLY UNPROTECTED!
COME ON, THE WAY'S CLEAR!
THERE'S THE EXIT!

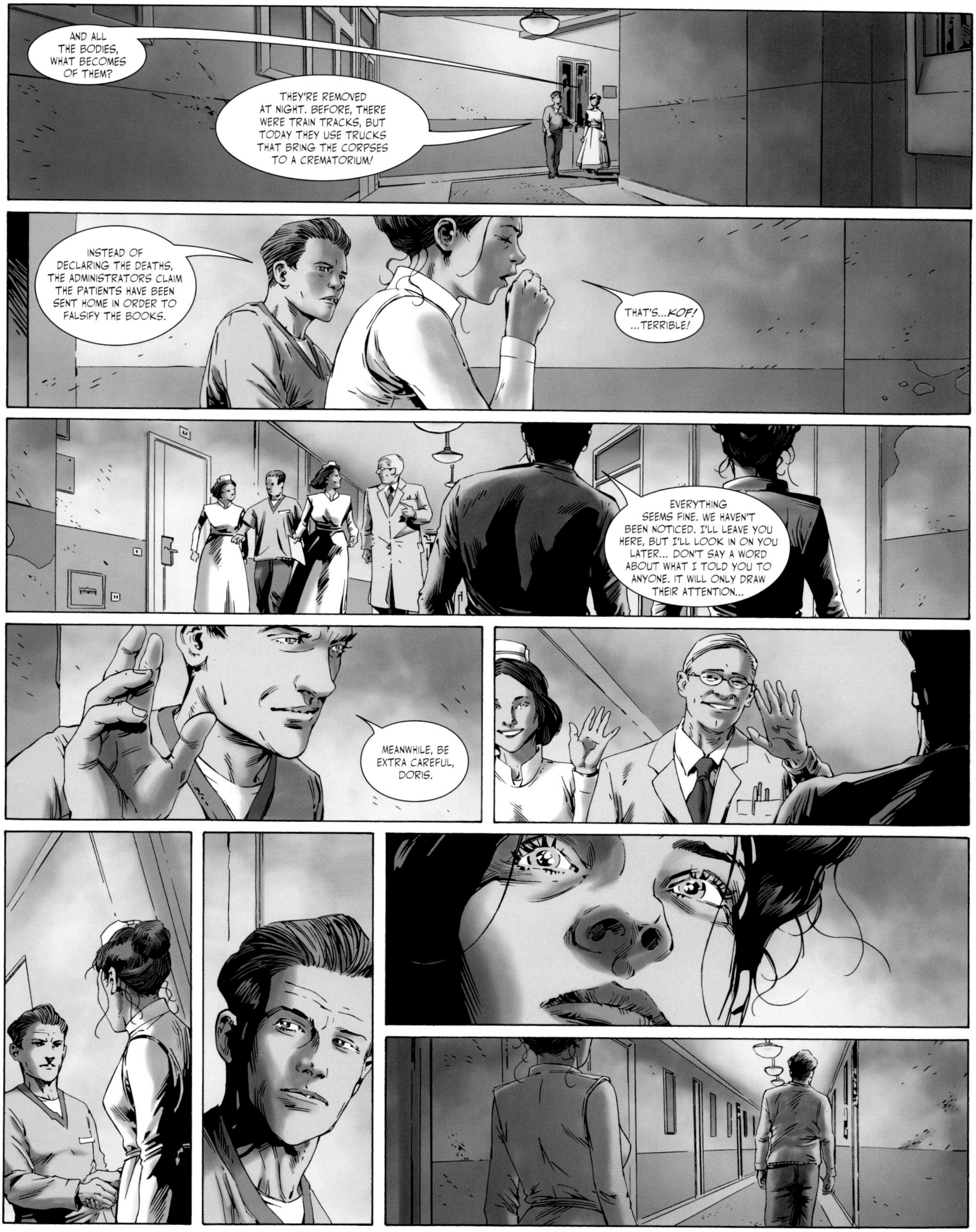

AND ALL THE BODIES, WHAT BECOMES OF THEM?
THEY'RE REMOVED AT NIGHT. BEFORE, THERE WERE TRAIN TRACKS, BUT TODAY THEY USE TRUCKS THAT BRING THE CORPSES TO A CREMATORIUM!
INSTEAD OF DECLARING THE DEATHS, THE ADMINISTRATORS CLAIM THE PATIENTS HAVE BEEN SENT HOME IN ORDER TO FALSIFY THE BOOKS.
THAT'S...*KOF!* ...TERRIBLE!
EVERYTHING SEEMS FINE. WE HAVEN'T BEEN NOTICED. I'LL LEAVE YOU HERE, BUT I'LL LOOK IN ON YOU LATER... DON'T SAY A WORD ABOUT WHAT I TOLD YOU TO ANYONE. IT WILL ONLY DRAW THEIR ATTENTION...
MEANWHILE, BE EXTRA CAREFUL, DORIS.

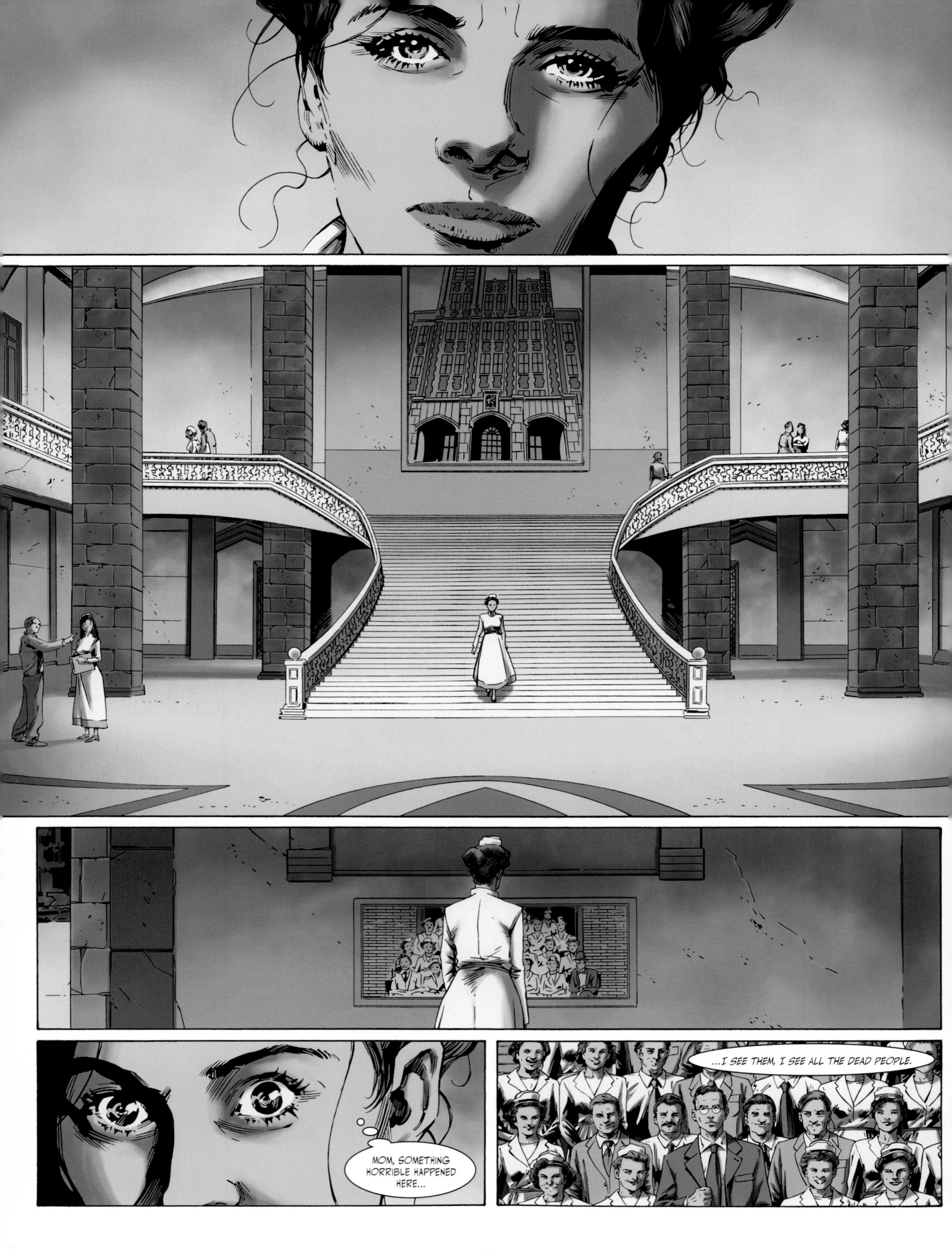
MOM, SOMETHING HORRIBLE HAPPENED HERE...
...I SEE THEM, I SEE ALL THE DEAD PEOPLE.

MMMM... CAN YOU SMELL THE DELICIOUS AROMA OF COFFEE AND TOAST?...

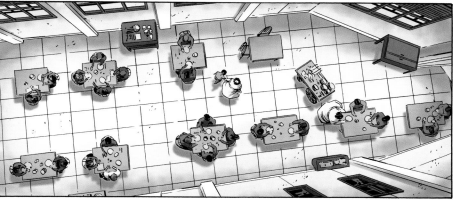

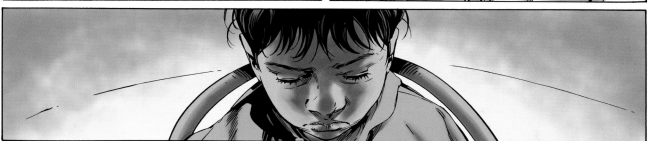

WHAT'S BOTHERING YOU, BABY?... IS IT THIS FIRST SESSION OF THE ULTRA VIOLETS THAT'S UPSETTING YOU?... FRED SAID IT'S PAINLESS, SO DON'T WORRY, SWEET PEA.

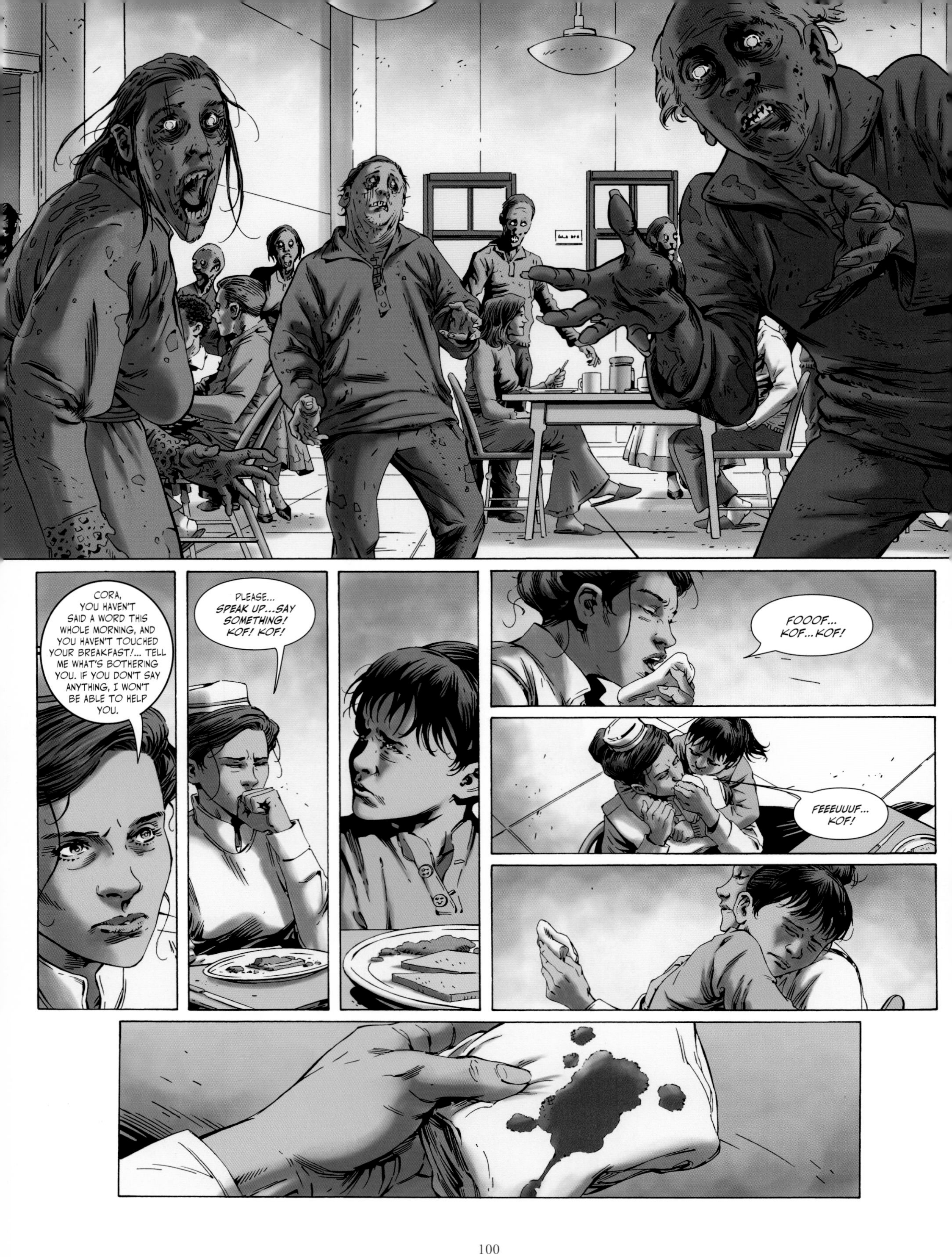

CORA, YOU HAVEN'T SAID A WORD THIS WHOLE MORNING, AND YOU HAVEN'T TOUCHED YOUR BREAKFAST!... TELL ME WHAT'S BOTHERING YOU. IF YOU DON'T SAY ANYTHING, I WON'T BE ABLE TO HELP YOU.
PLEASE... SPEAK UP...SAY SOMETHING! KOF! KOF!
FOOOF... KOF...KOF!
FEEEUUUF... KOF!

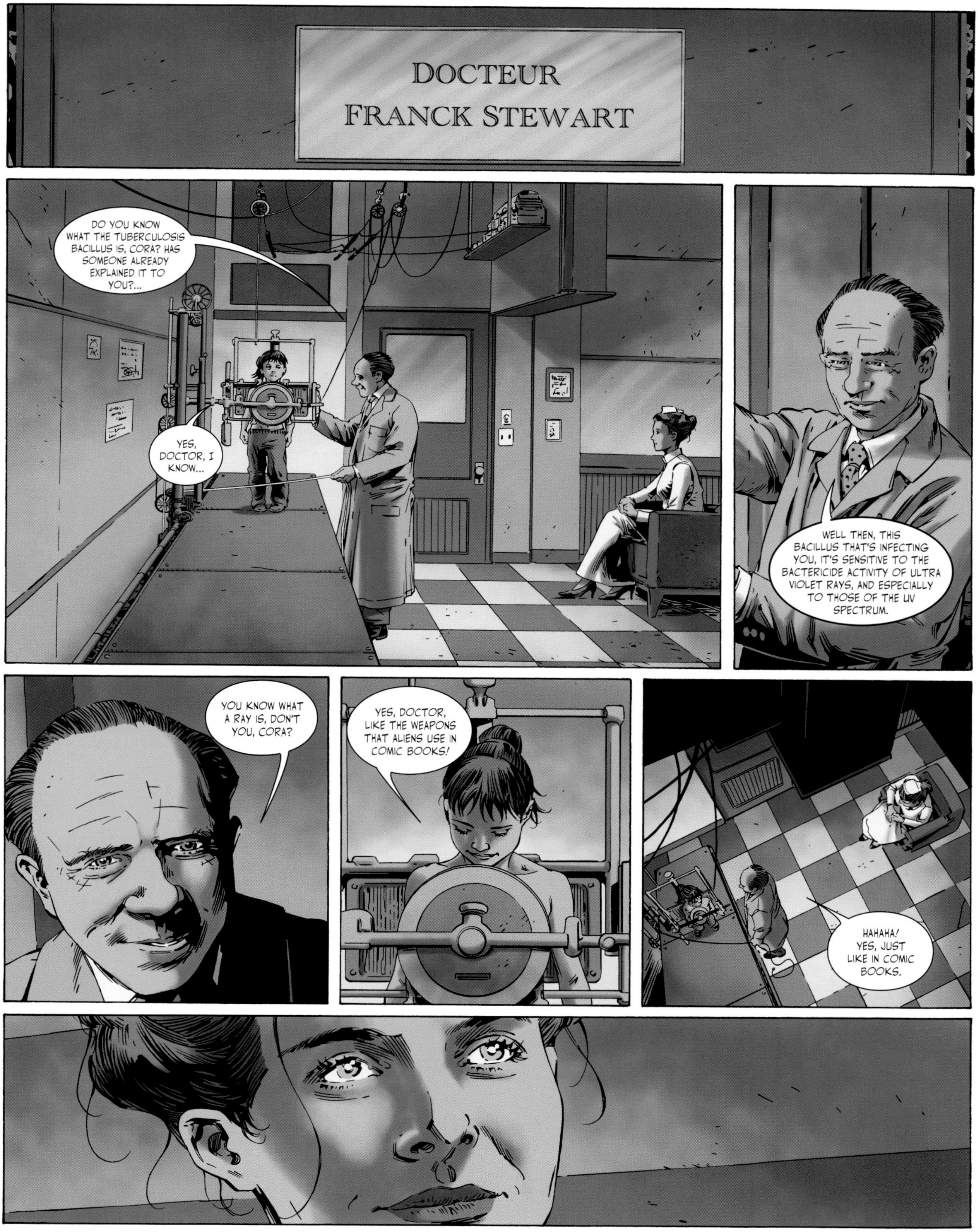
DOCTEUR
FRANCK STEWART
DO YOU KNOW WHAT THE TUBERCULOSIS BACILLUS IS, CORA? HAS SOMEONE ALREADY EXPLAINED IT TO YOU?...
YES, DOCTOR, I KNOW...
WELL THEN, THIS BACILLUS THAT'S INFECTING YOU, IT'S SENSITIVE TO THE BACTERICIDE ACTIVITY OF ULTRA VIOLET RAYS, AND ESPECIALLY TO THOSE OF THE UV SPECTRUM.
YOU KNOW WHAT A RAY IS, DON'T YOU, CORA?
YES, DOCTOR, LIKE THE WEAPONS THAT ALIENS USE IN COMIC BOOKS!
HAHAHA! YES, JUST LIKE IN COMIC BOOKS.

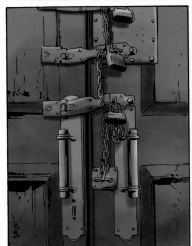

EVEN IF IT IS TERRIBLE TO HAVE TO GET TO THIS POINT, WHAT ELSE CAN WE DO?...

I HAVE NO OTHER CHOICE.

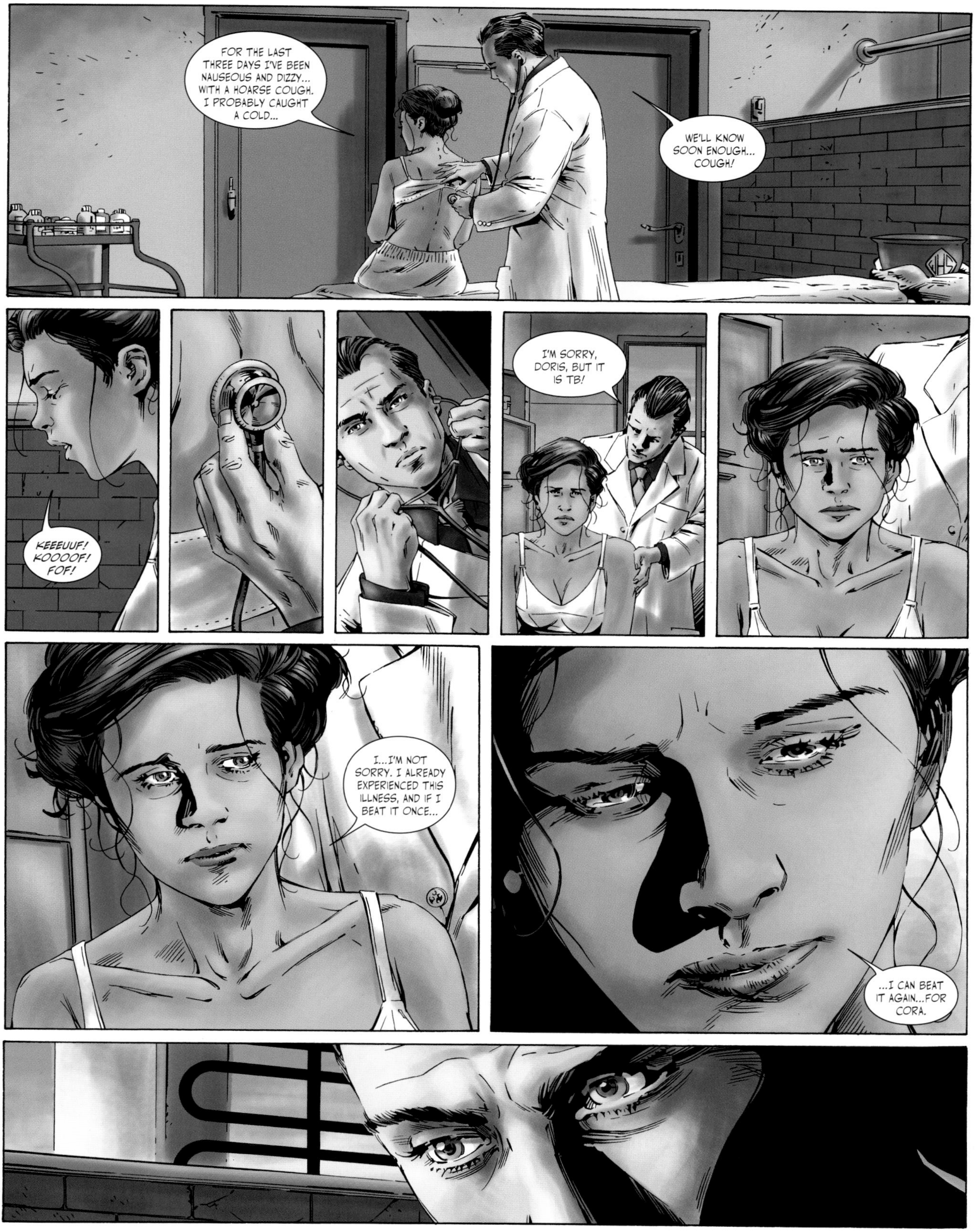
FOR THE LAST THREE DAYS I'VE BEEN NAUSEOUS AND DIZZY... WITH A HOARSE COUGH. I PROBABLY CAUGHT A COLD...
WE'LL KNOW SOON ENOUGH... COUGH!
KEEEUUF! KOOOOF! FOF!
I'M SORRY, DORIS, BUT IT IS TB!
I...I'M NOT SORRY. I ALREADY EXPERIENCED THIS ILLNESS, AND IF I BEAT IT ONCE...
...I CAN BEAT IT AGAIN...FOR CORA.

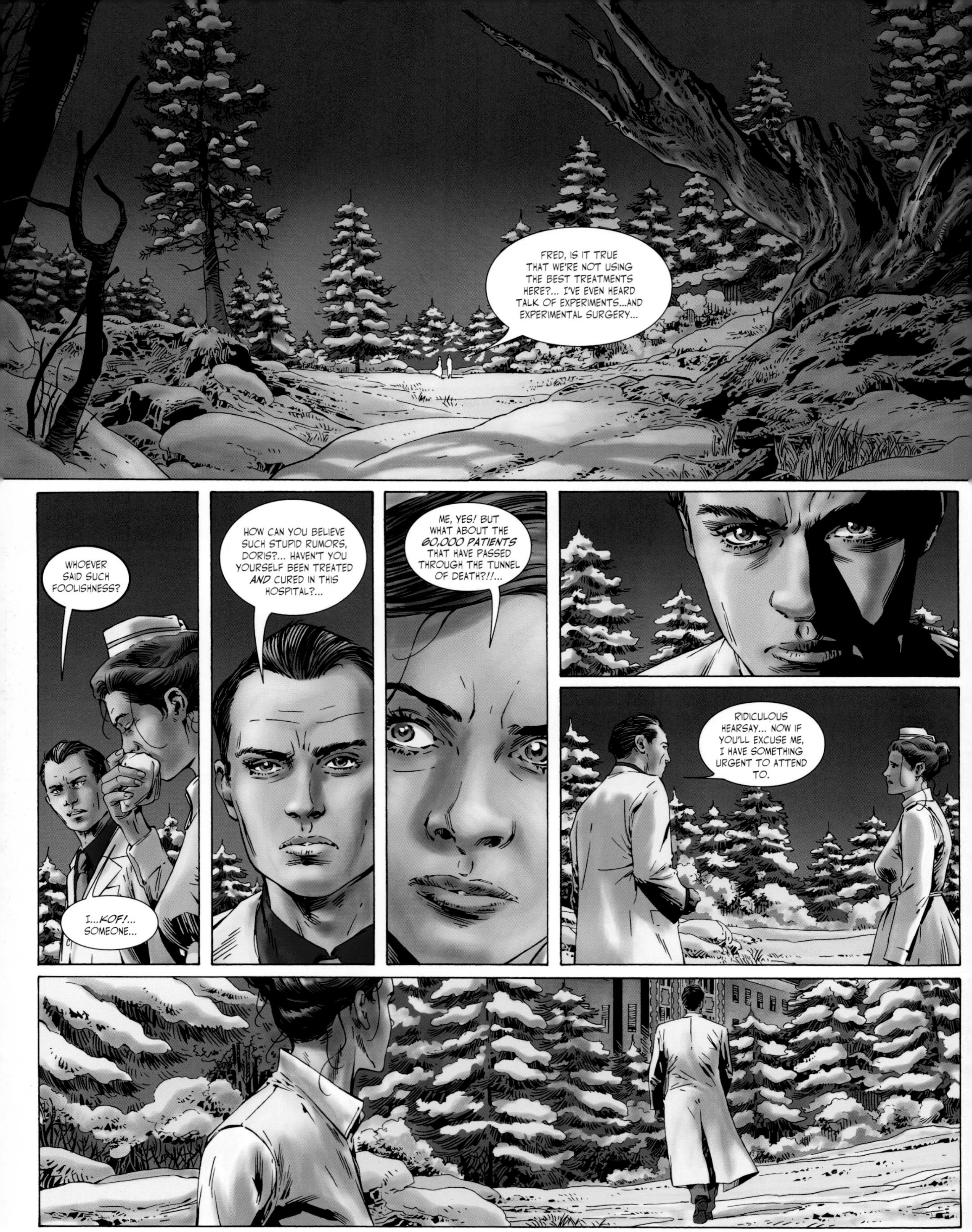
FRED, IS IT TRUE THAT WE'RE NOT USING THE BEST TREATMENTS HERE?... I'VE EVEN HEARD TALK OF EXPERIMENTS...AND EXPERIMENTAL SURGERY...
WHOEVER SAID SUCH FOOLISHNESS?
I...KOF!... SOMEONE...
HOW CAN YOU BELIEVE SUCH STUPID RUMORS, DORIS?... HAVEN'T YOU YOURSELF BEEN TREATED AND CURED IN THIS HOSPITAL?...
ME, YES! BUT WHAT ABOUT THE 60,000 PATIENTS THAT HAVE PASSED THROUGH THE TUNNEL OF DEATH?!!...
RIDICULOUS HEARSAY... NOW IF YOU'LL EXCUSE ME, I HAVE SOMETHING URGENT TO ATTEND TO.

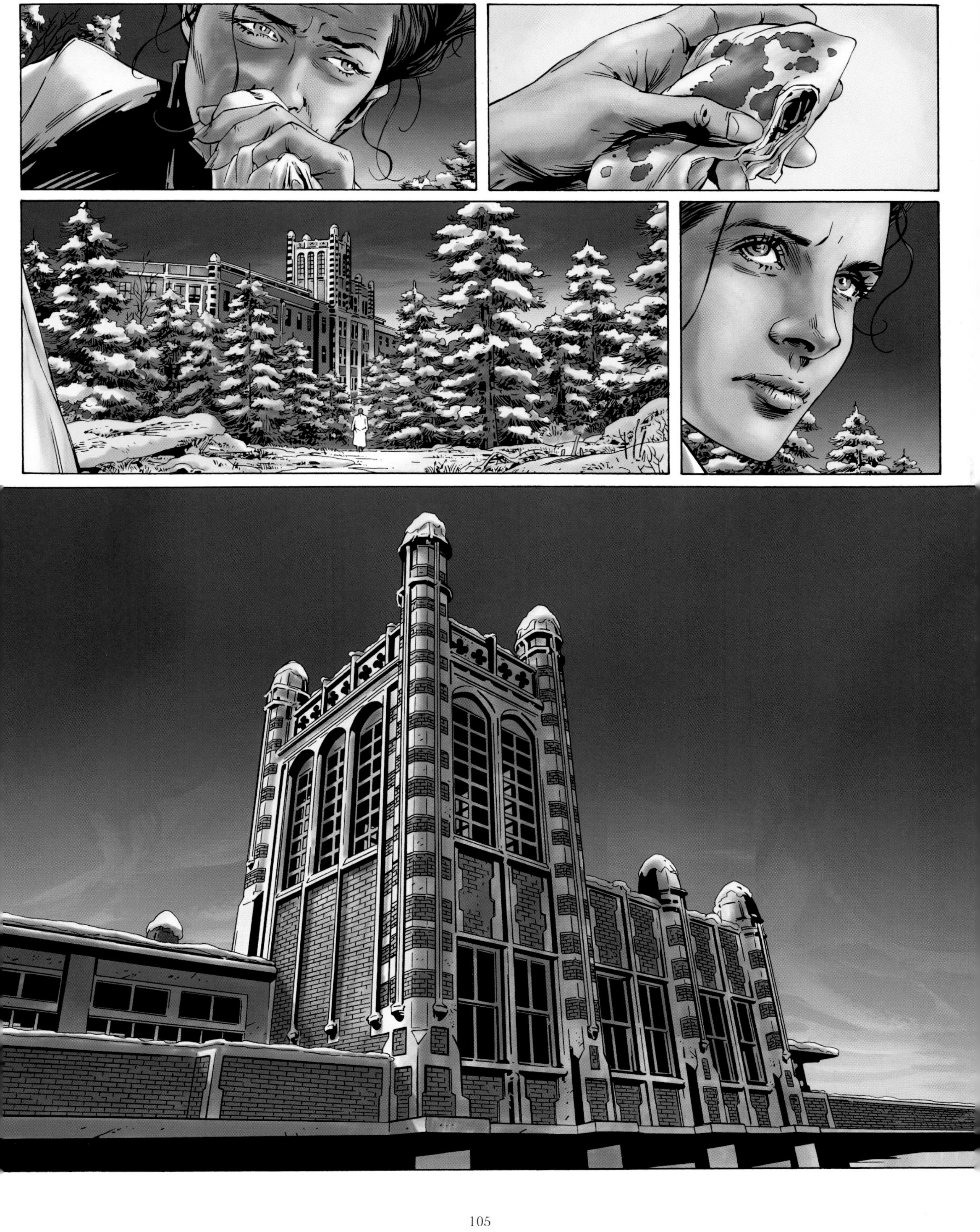

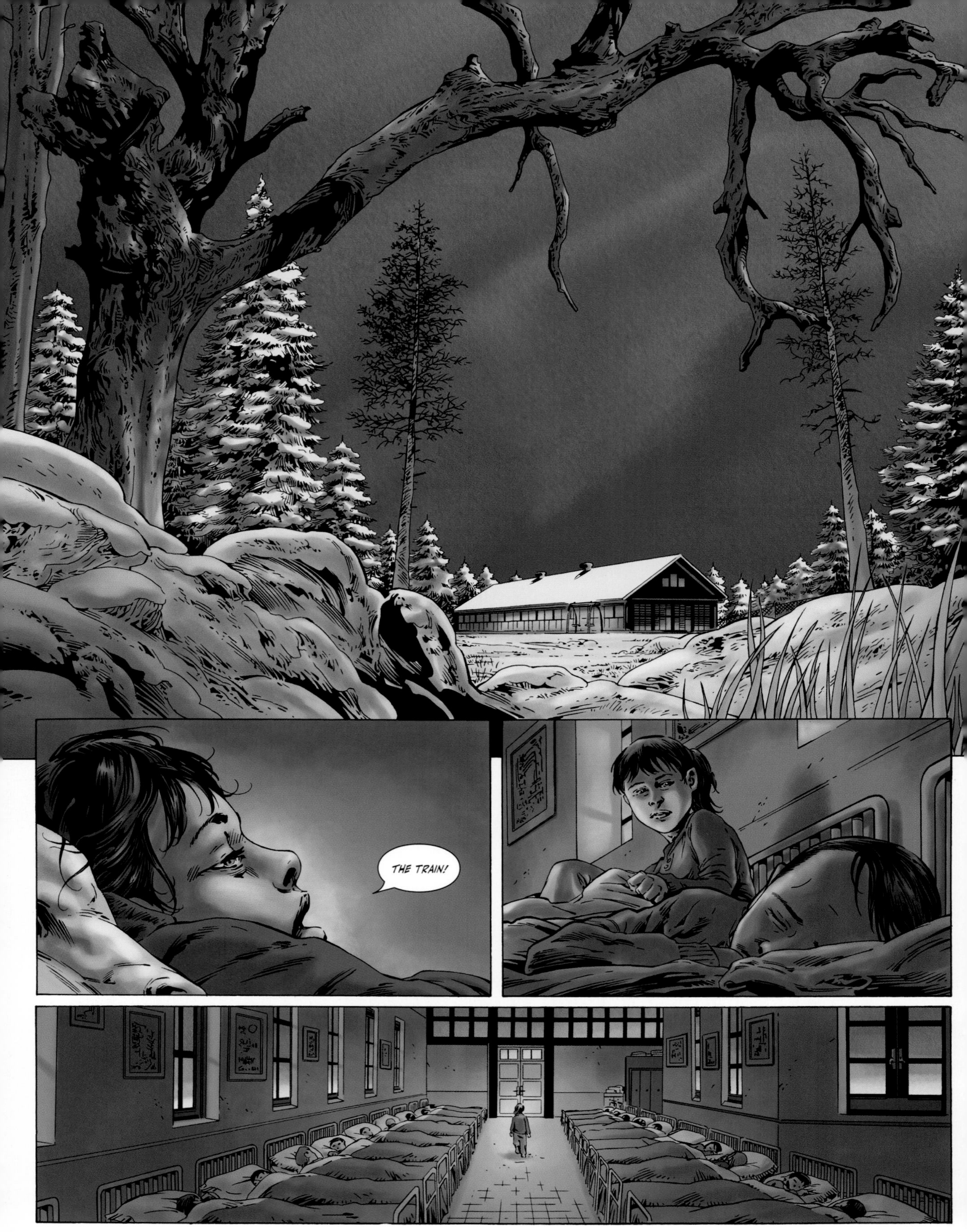
THE TRAIN!

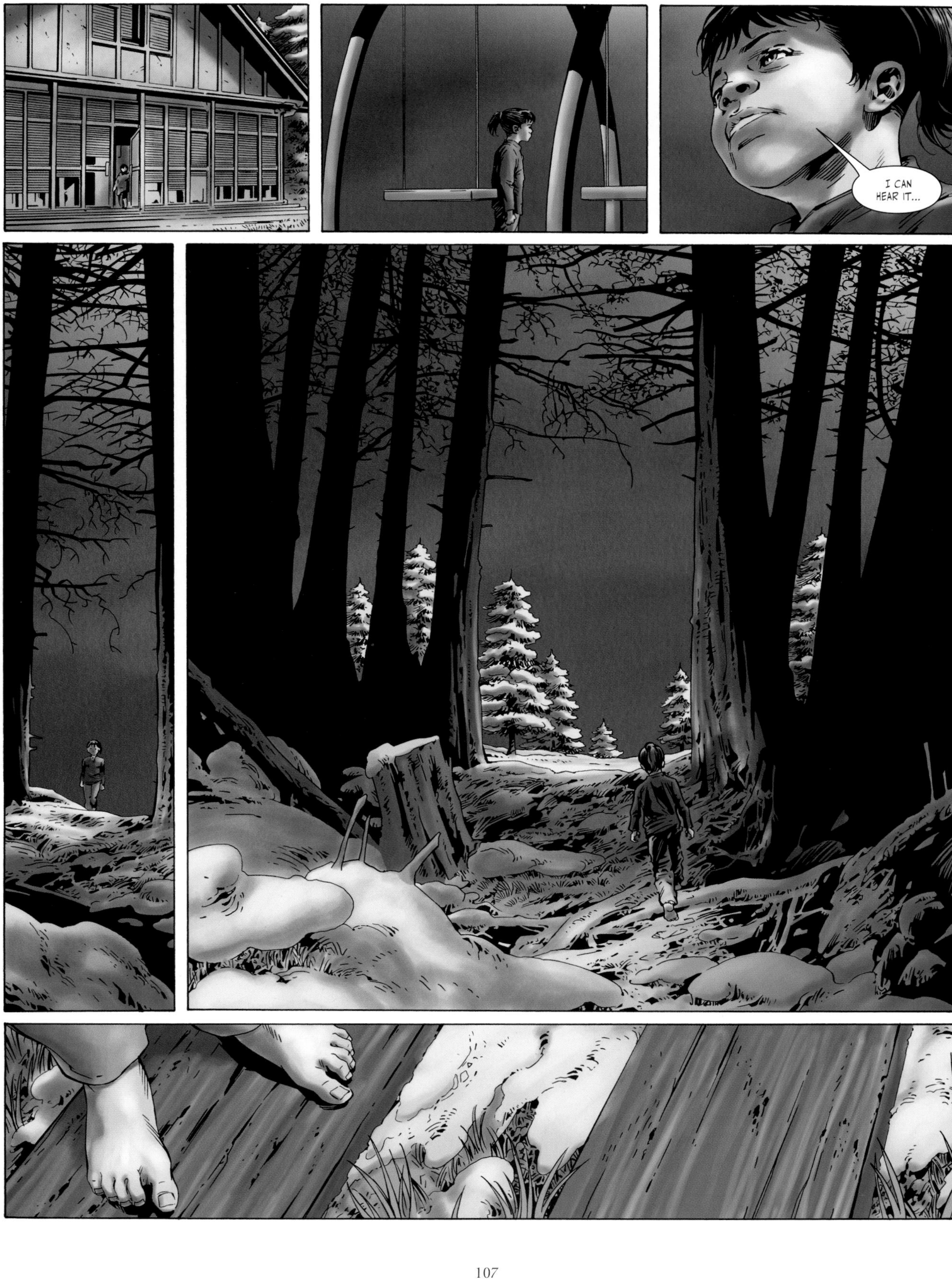
I CAN
HEAR IT...

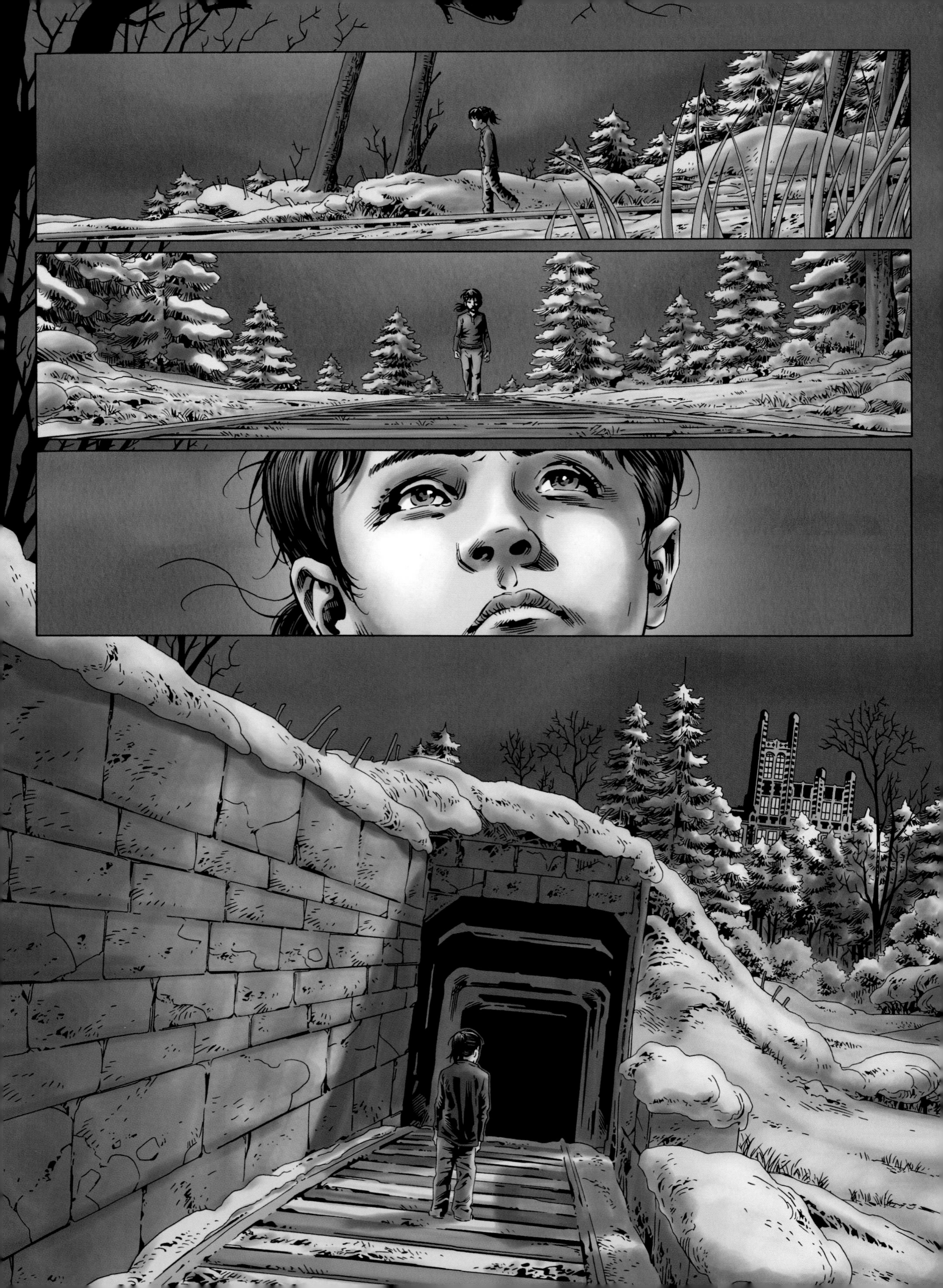

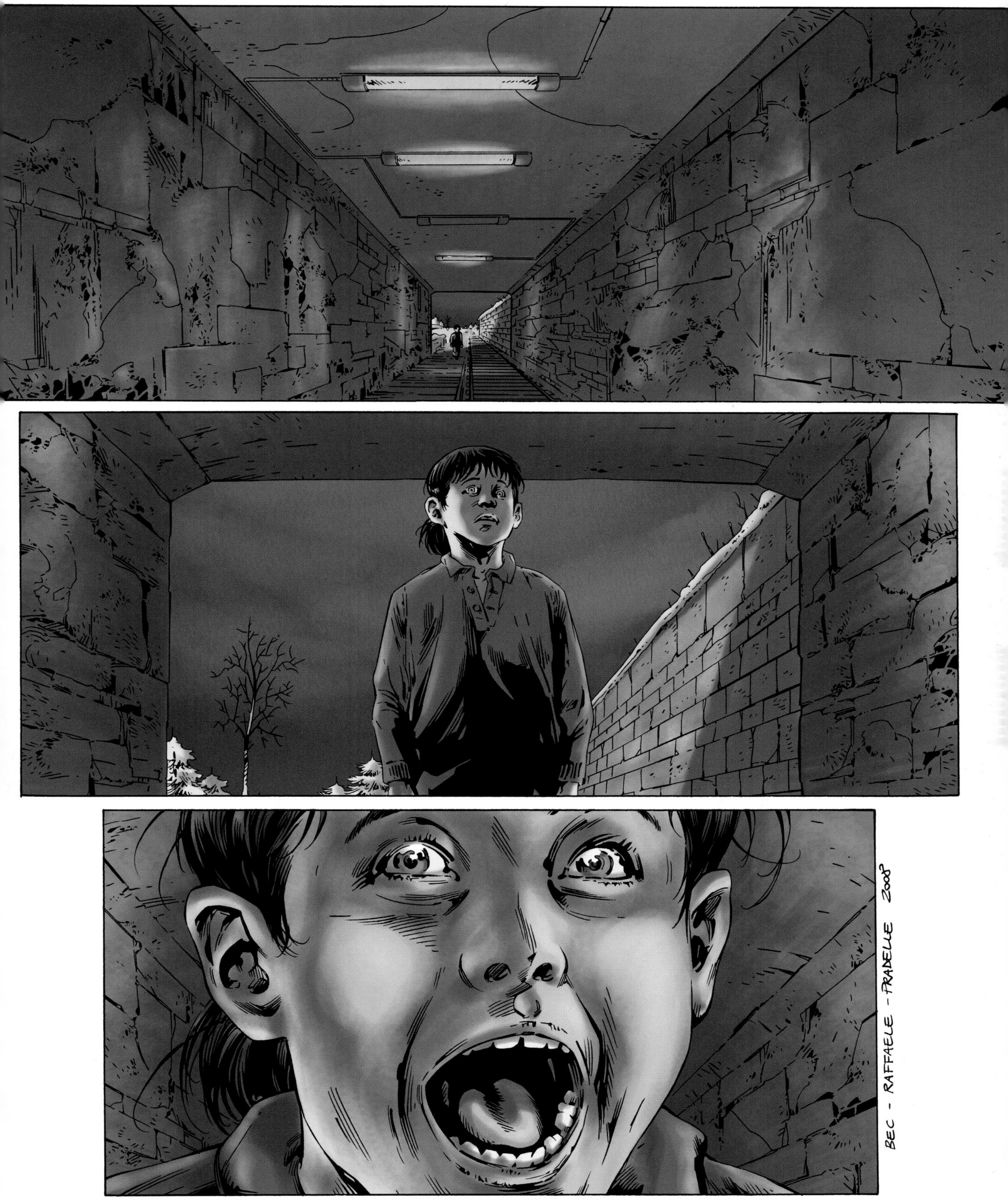
BEC - RAFFAELE - PRADELLE 2008

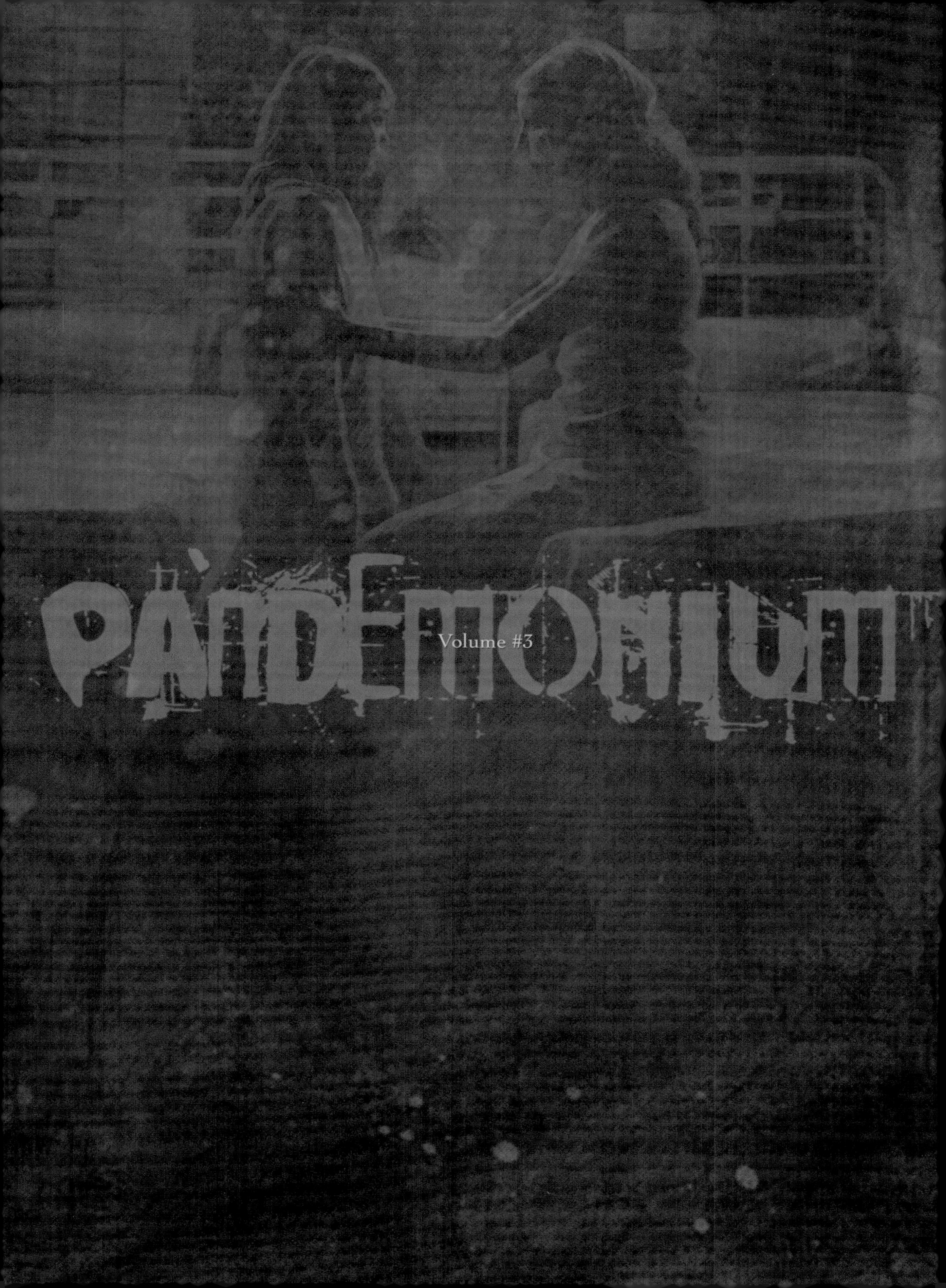
PANDEMONIUM
Volume #3

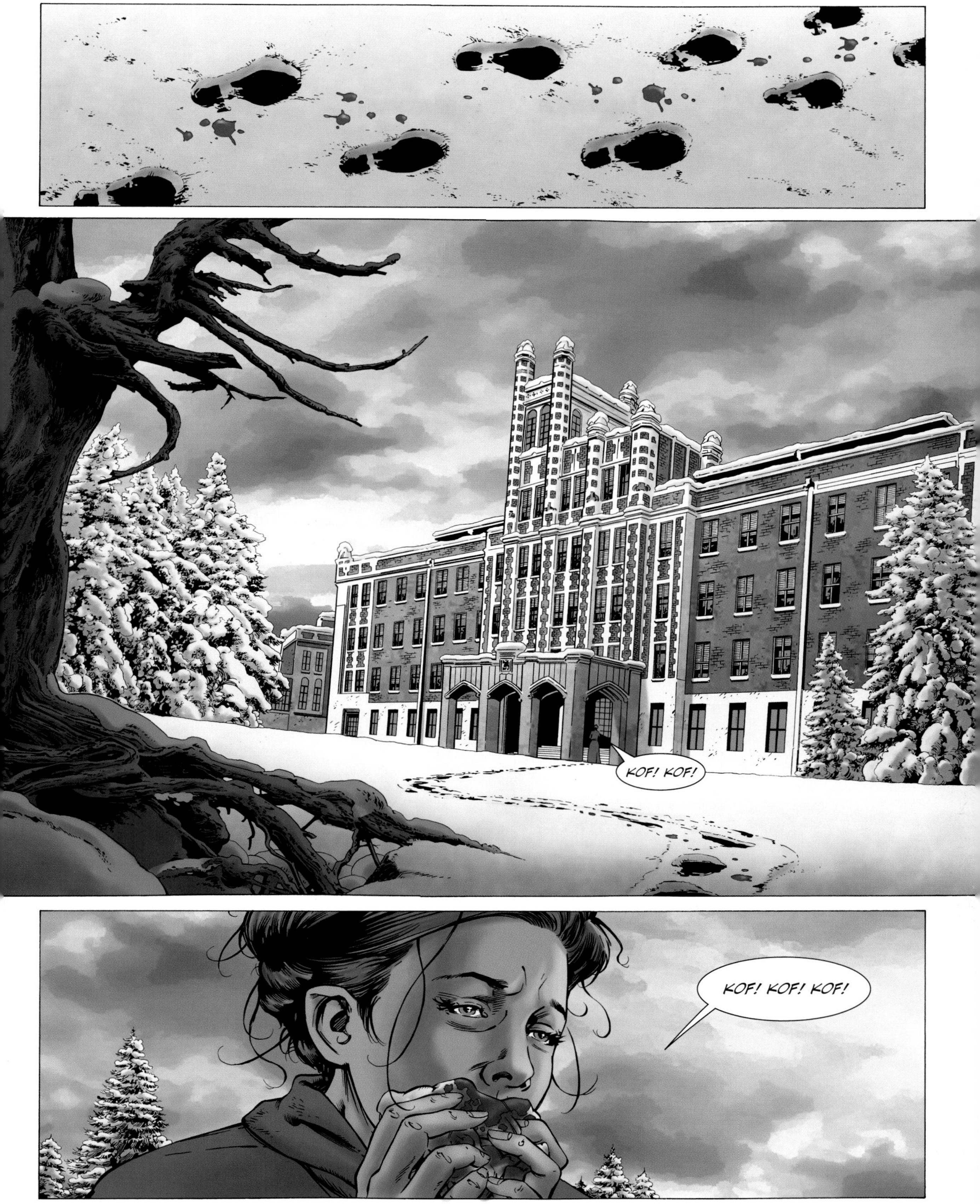
KOF! KOF!
KOF! KOF! KOF!

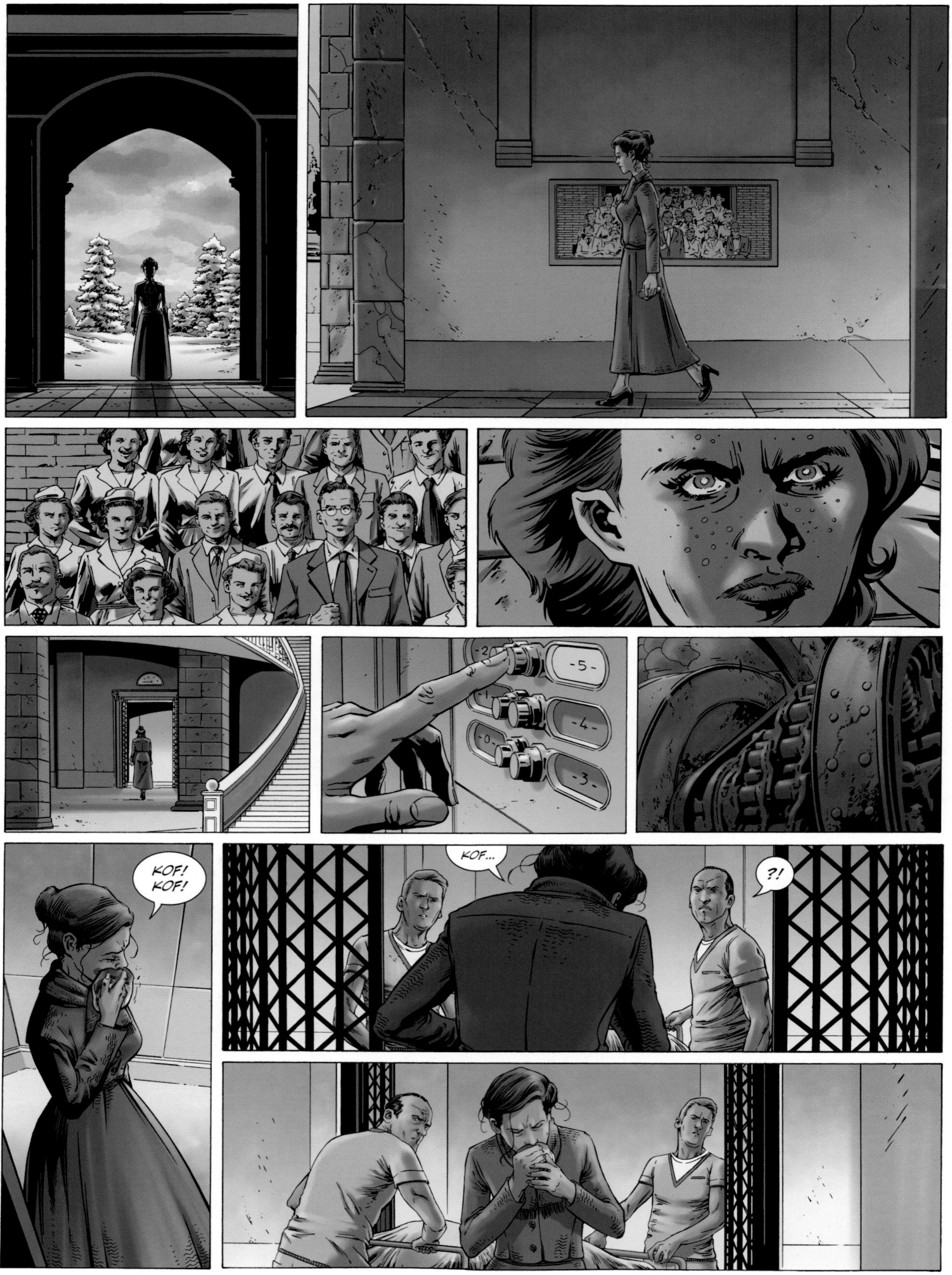
KOF!
KOF!
KOF...
?!

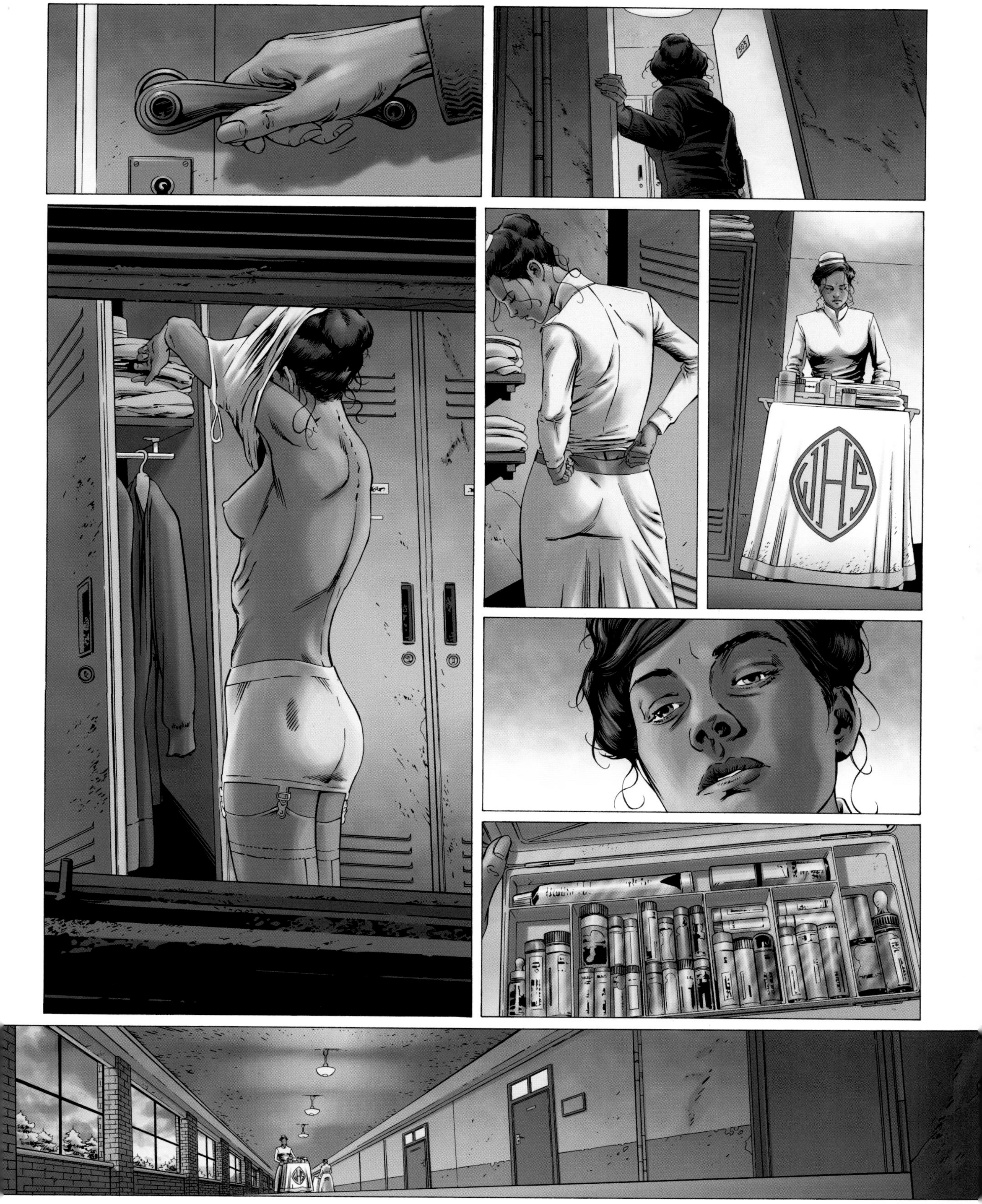

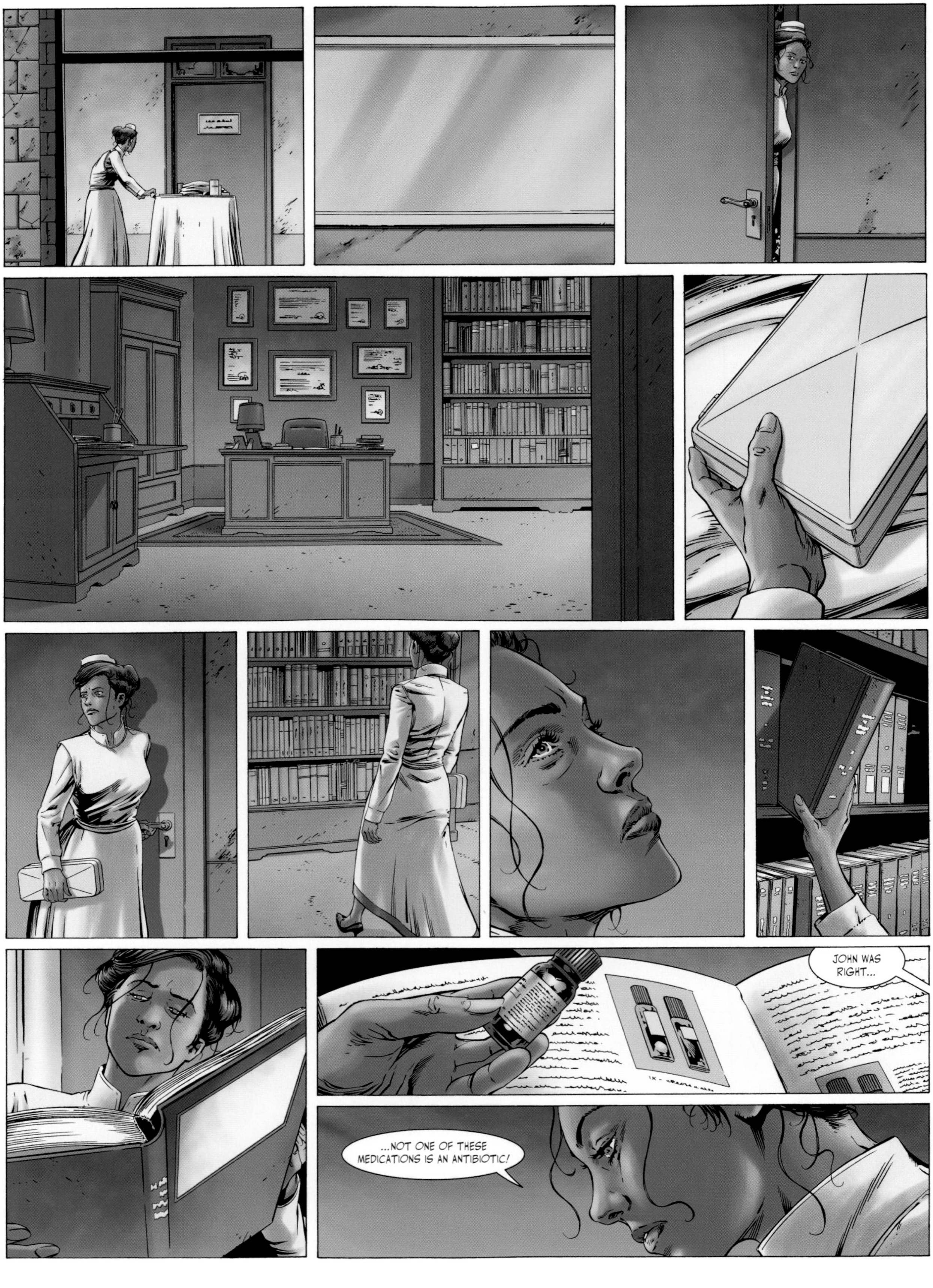
JOHN WAS RIGHT...
...NOT ONE OF THESE MEDICATIONS IS AN ANTIBIOTIC!

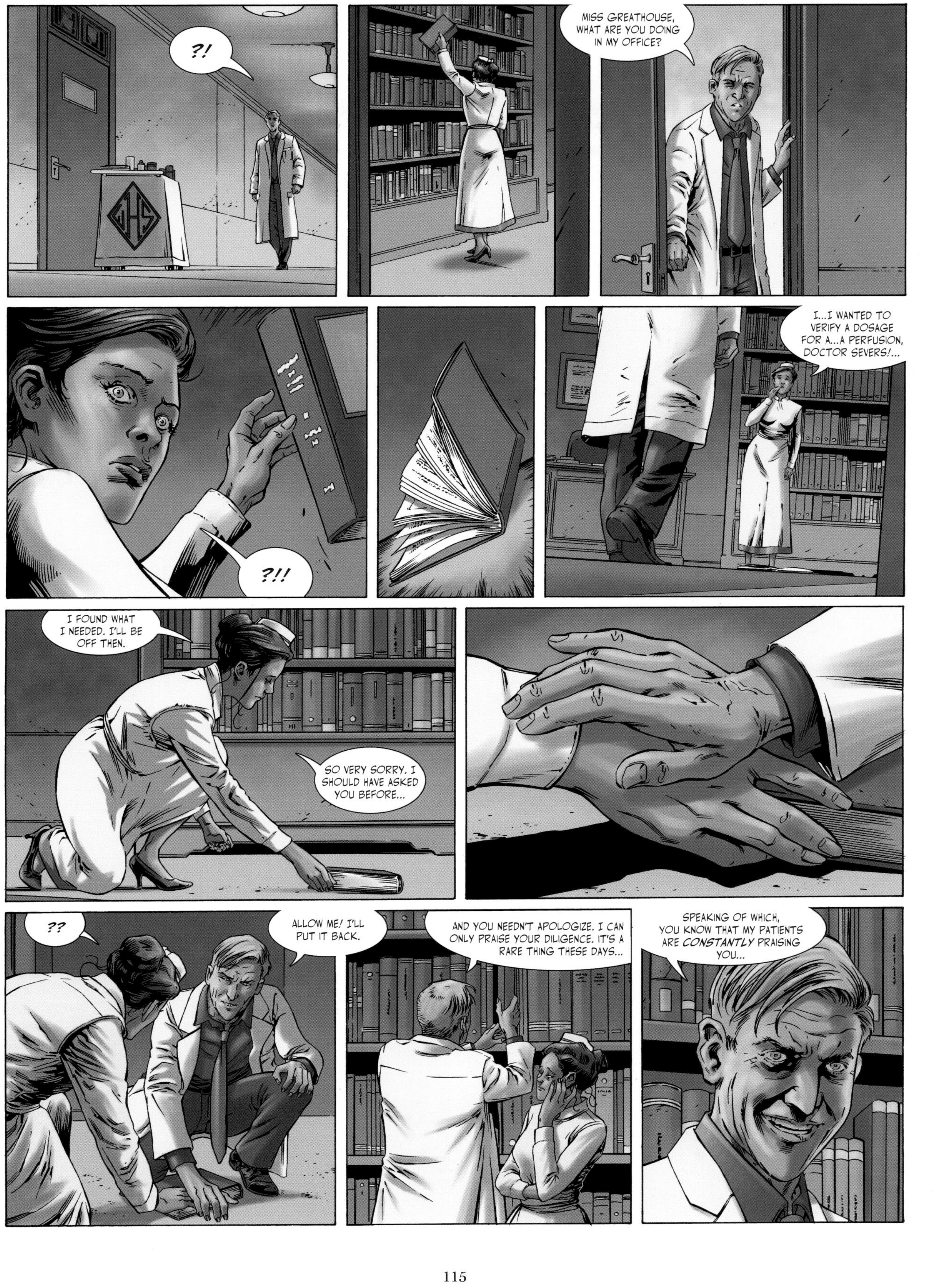
?!
MISS GREATHOUSE, WHAT ARE YOU DOING IN MY OFFICE?
?!!
I...I WANTED TO VERIFY A DOSAGE FOR A...A PERFUSION, DOCTOR SEVERS!...
I FOUND WHAT I NEEDED. I'LL BE OFF THEN.
SO VERY SORRY. I SHOULD HAVE ASKED YOU BEFORE...
??
ALLOW ME! I'LL PUT IT BACK.
AND YOU NEEDN'T APOLOGIZE. I CAN ONLY PRAISE YOUR DILIGENCE. IT'S A RARE THING THESE DAYS...
SPEAKING OF WHICH, YOU KNOW THAT MY PATIENTS ARE *CONSTANTLY* PRAISING YOU...

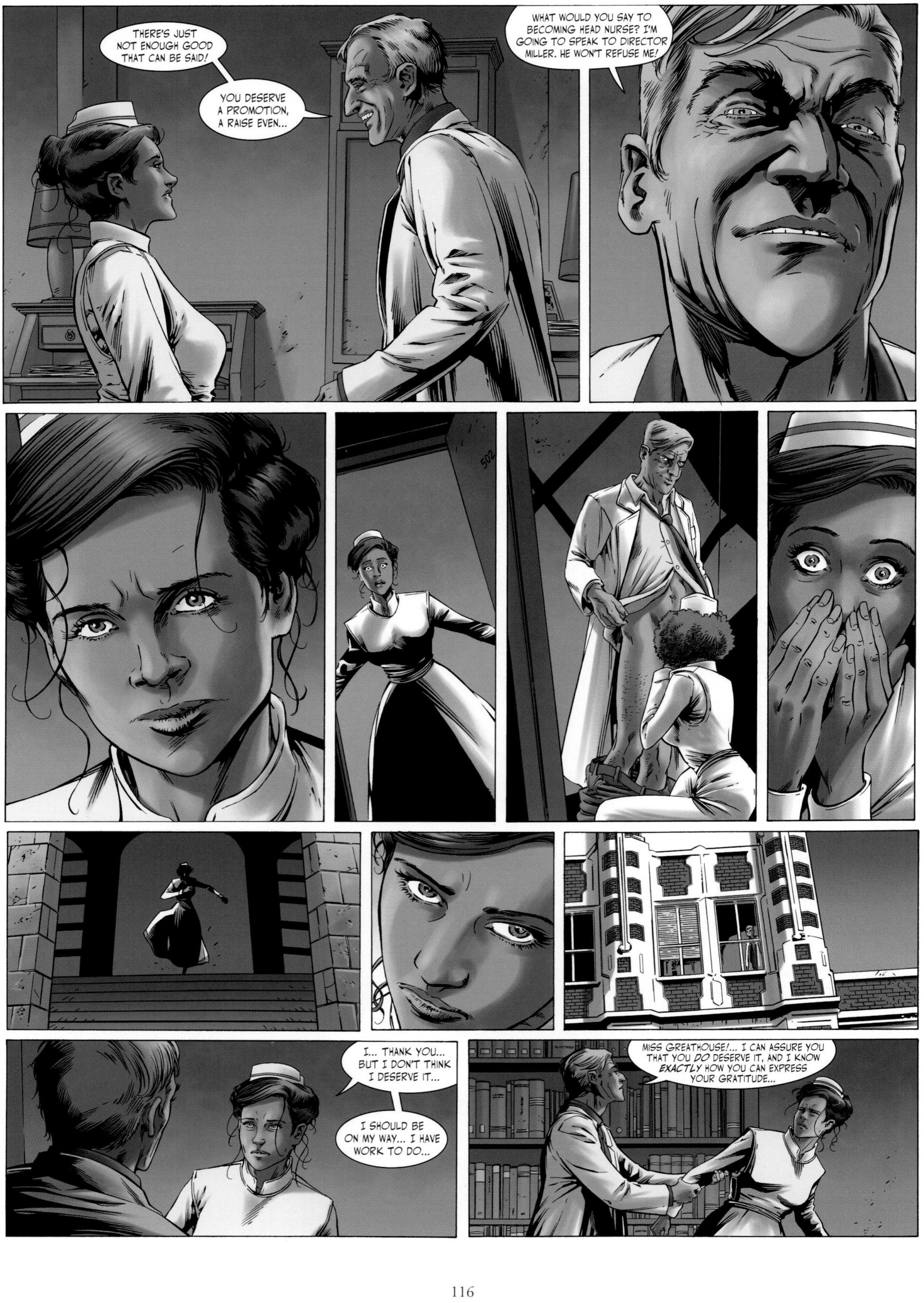
THERE'S JUST NOT ENOUGH GOOD THAT CAN BE SAID!
YOU DESERVE A PROMOTION, A RAISE EVEN...
WHAT WOULD YOU SAY TO BECOMING HEAD NURSE? I'M GOING TO SPEAK TO DIRECTOR MILLER. HE WON'T REFUSE ME!
502
I... THANK YOU... BUT I DON'T THINK I DESERVE IT...
I SHOULD BE ON MY WAY... I HAVE WORK TO DO...
MISS GREATHOUSE!... I CAN ASSURE YOU THAT YOU *DO* DESERVE IT, AND I KNOW *EXACTLY* HOW YOU CAN EXPRESS YOUR GRATITUDE...

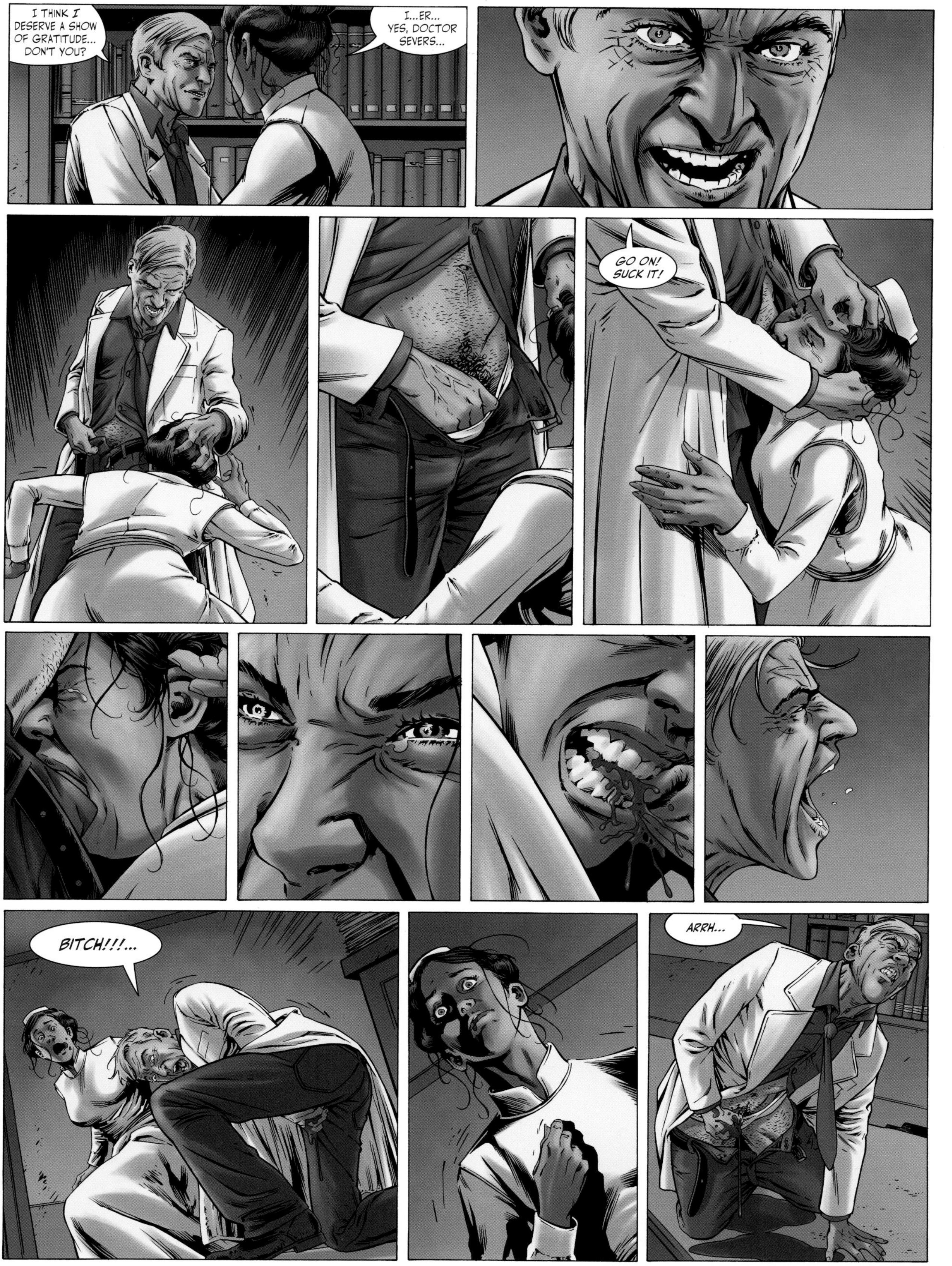
I THINK *I* DESERVE A SHOW OF GRATITUDE... DON'T YOU?
I...ER... YES, DOCTOR SEVERS...
GO ON! SUCK IT!
BITCH!!!...
ARRH...

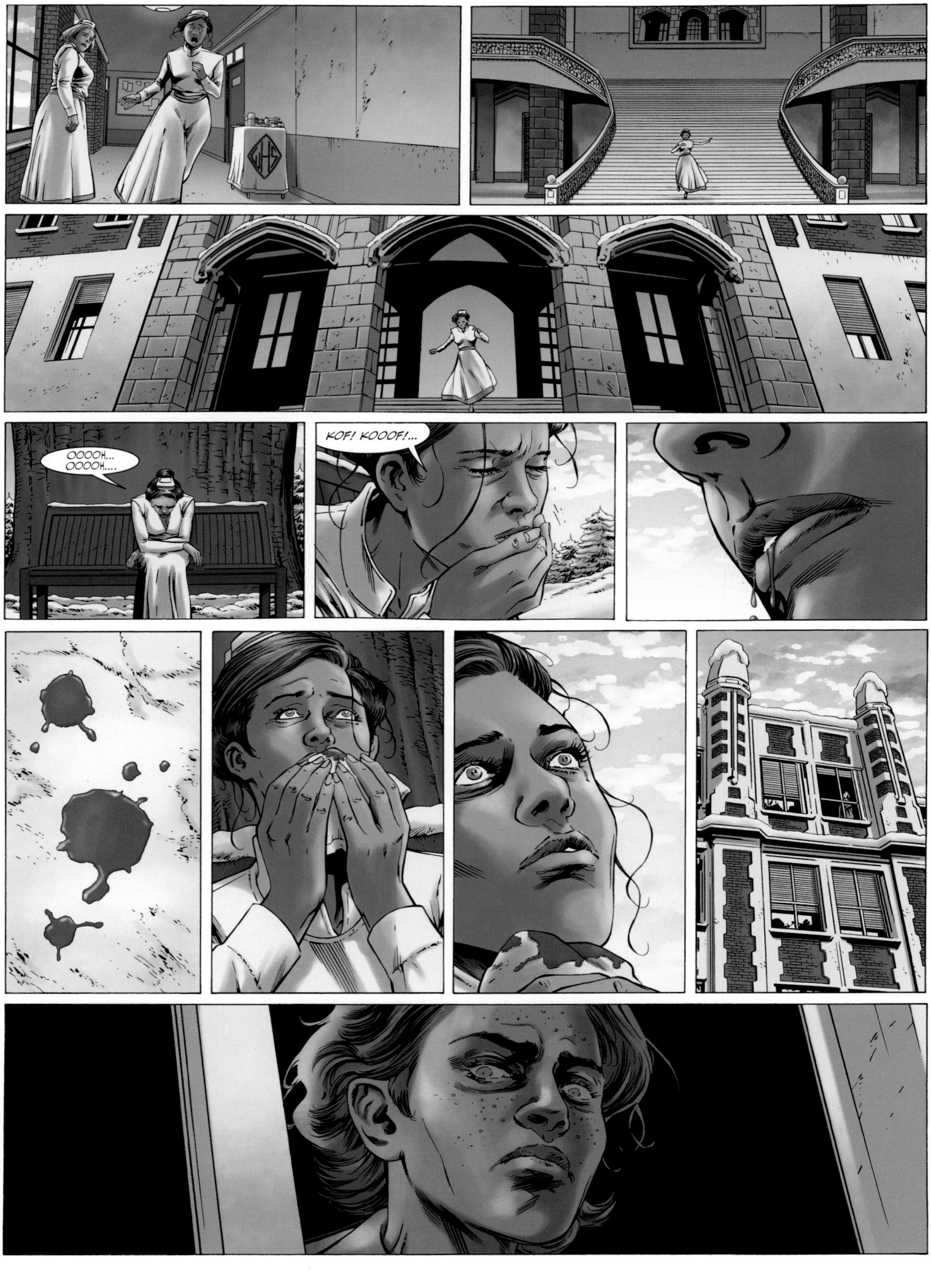
OOOOH...
OOOOH....
KOF! KOOOF!...

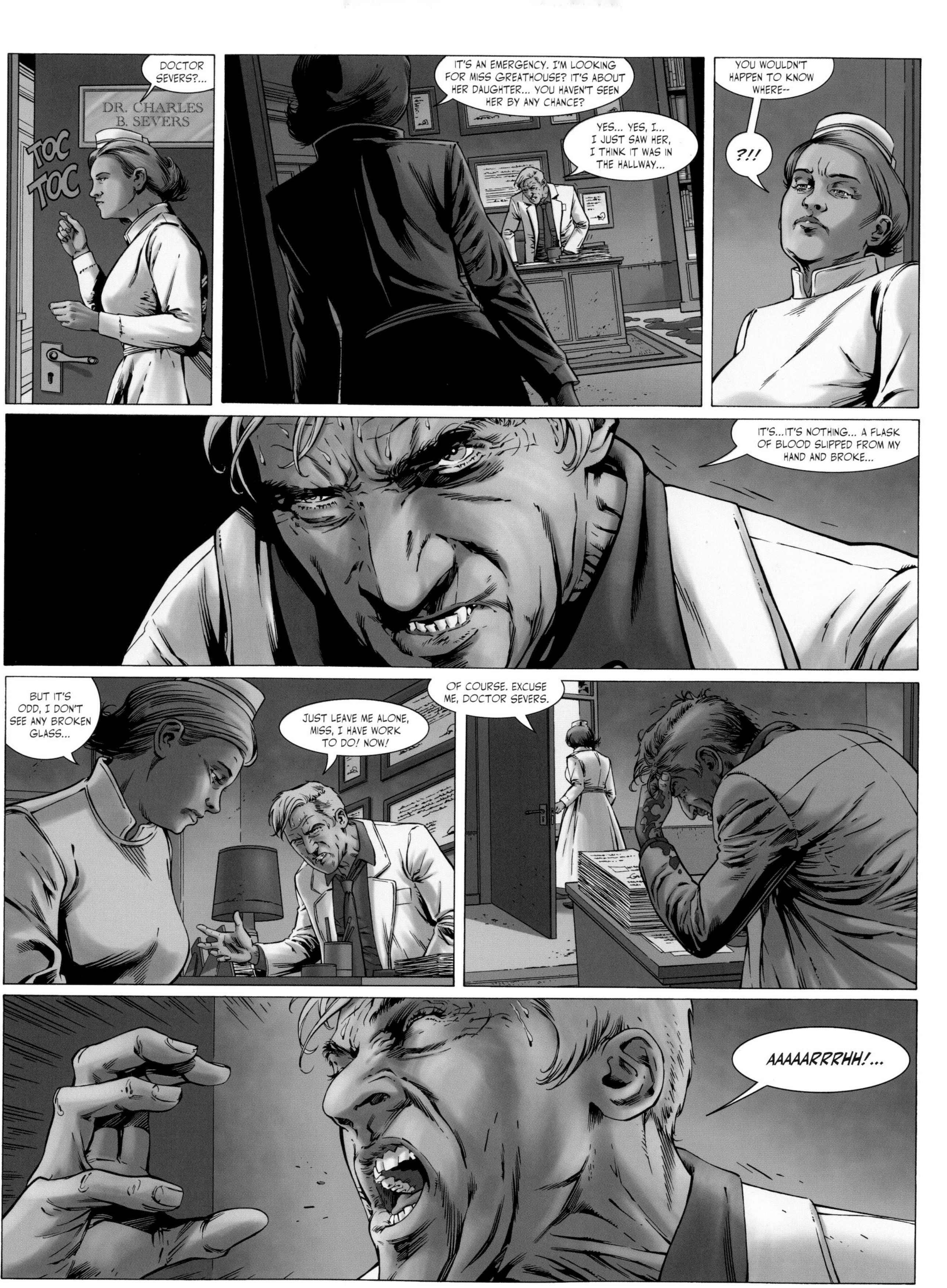
DOCTOR SEVERS?...
DR. CHARLES B. SEVERS
TOC TOC
IT'S AN EMERGENCY. I'M LOOKING FOR MISS GREATHOUSE? IT'S ABOUT HER DAUGHTER... YOU HAVEN'T SEEN HER BY ANY CHANCE?
YES... YES, I... I JUST SAW HER, I THINK IT WAS IN THE HALLWAY...
YOU WOULDN'T HAPPEN TO KNOW WHERE--
?!!
IT'S...IT'S NOTHING... A FLASK OF BLOOD SLIPPED FROM MY HAND AND BROKE...
BUT IT'S ODD, I DON'T SEE ANY BROKEN GLASS...
JUST LEAVE ME ALONE, MISS, I HAVE WORK TO DO! NOW!
OF COURSE. EXCUSE ME, DOCTOR SEVERS.
AAAAARRRHH!...

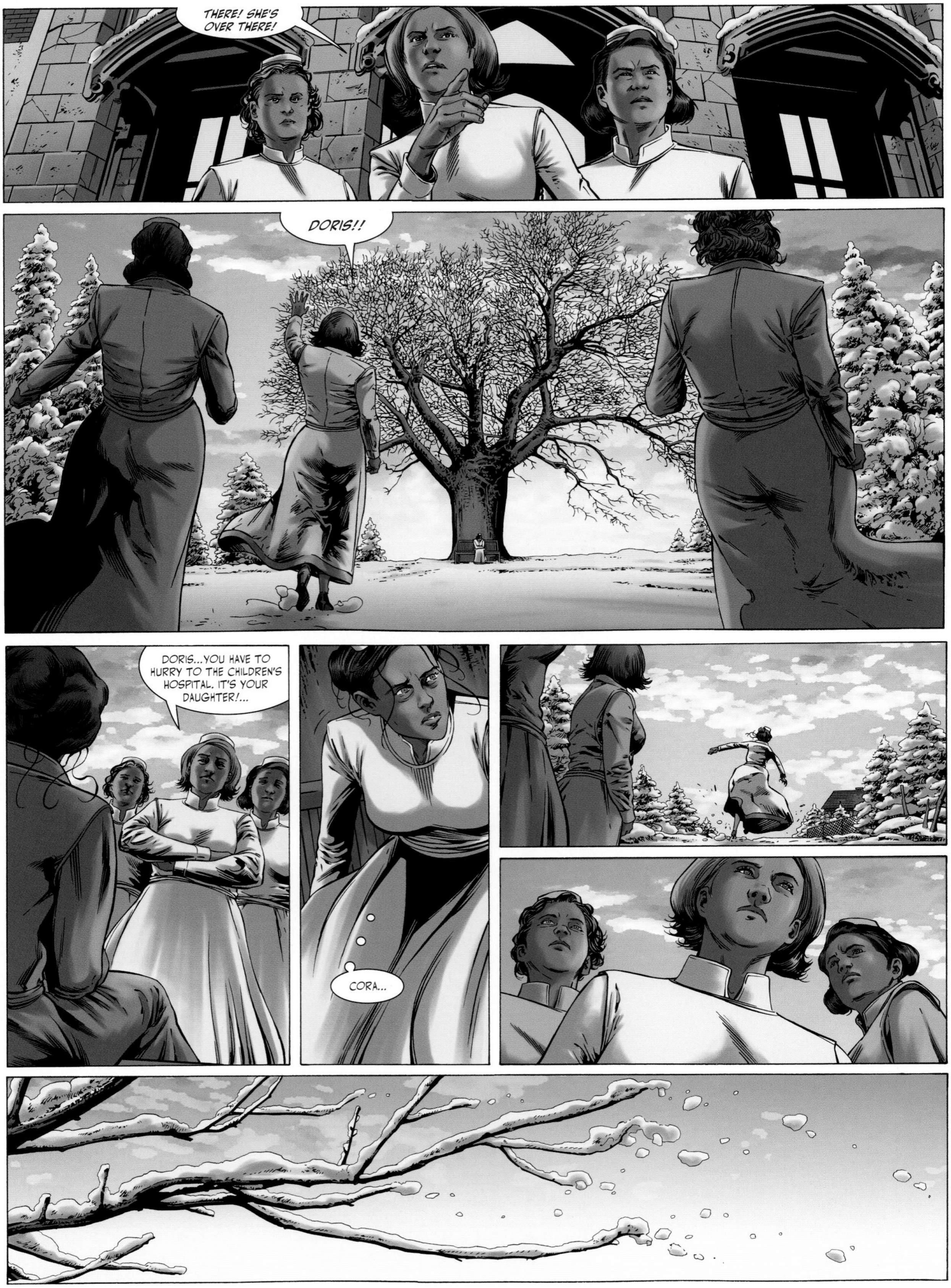
THERE! SHE'S OVER THERE!
DORIS!!
DORIS...YOU HAVE TO HURRY TO THE CHILDREN'S HOSPITAL. IT'S YOUR DAUGHTER!...
CORA...

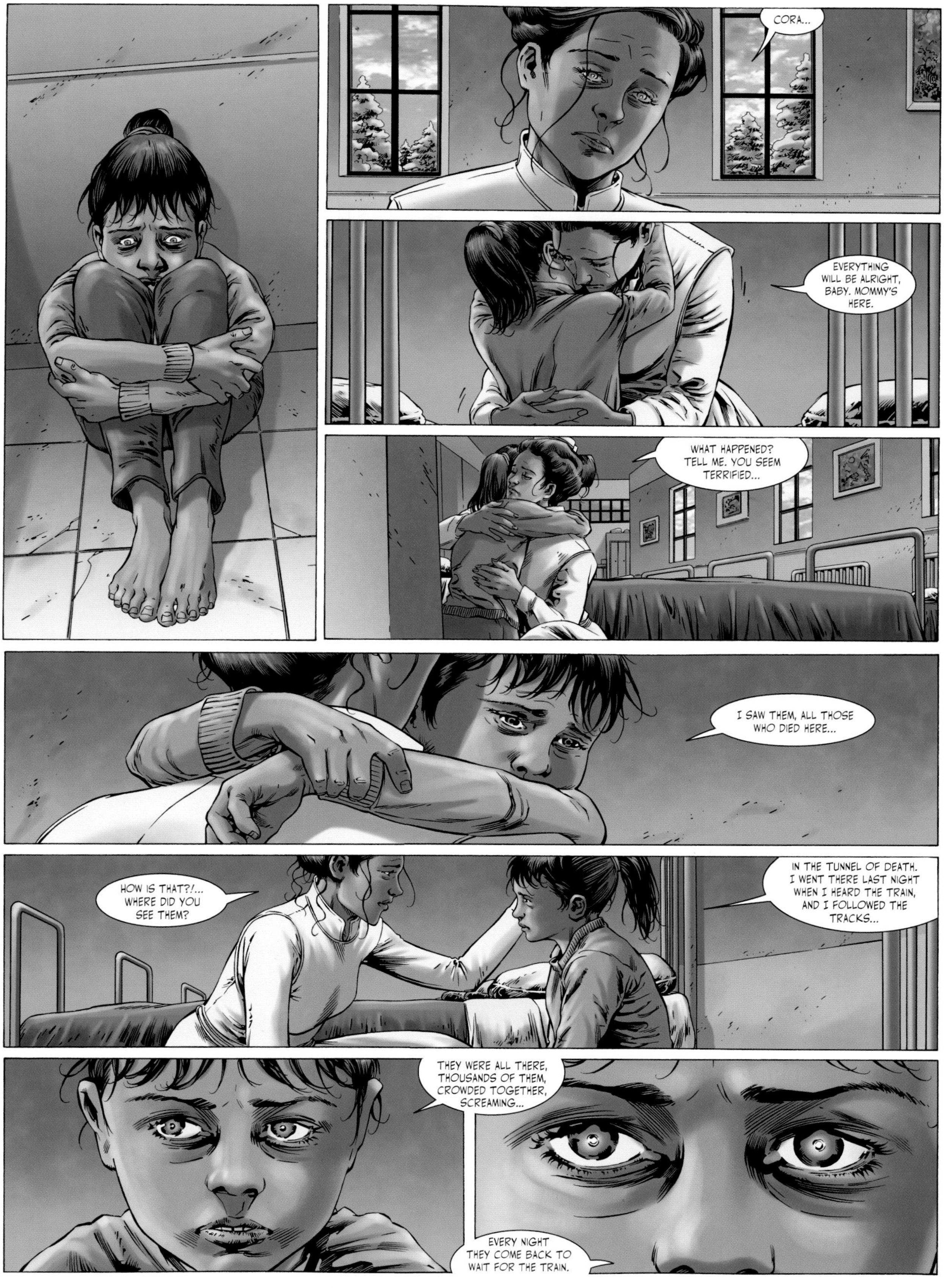
CORA...
EVERYTHING WILL BE ALRIGHT, BABY. MOMMY'S HERE.
WHAT HAPPENED? TELL ME. YOU SEEM TERRIFIED...
I SAW THEM, ALL THOSE WHO DIED HERE...
HOW IS THAT?!... WHERE DID YOU SEE THEM?
IN THE TUNNEL OF DEATH. I WENT THERE LAST NIGHT WHEN I HEARD THE TRAIN, AND I FOLLOWED THE TRACKS...
THEY WERE ALL THERE, THOUSANDS OF THEM, CROWDED TOGETHER, SCREAMING...
EVERY NIGHT THEY COME BACK TO WAIT FOR THE TRAIN.

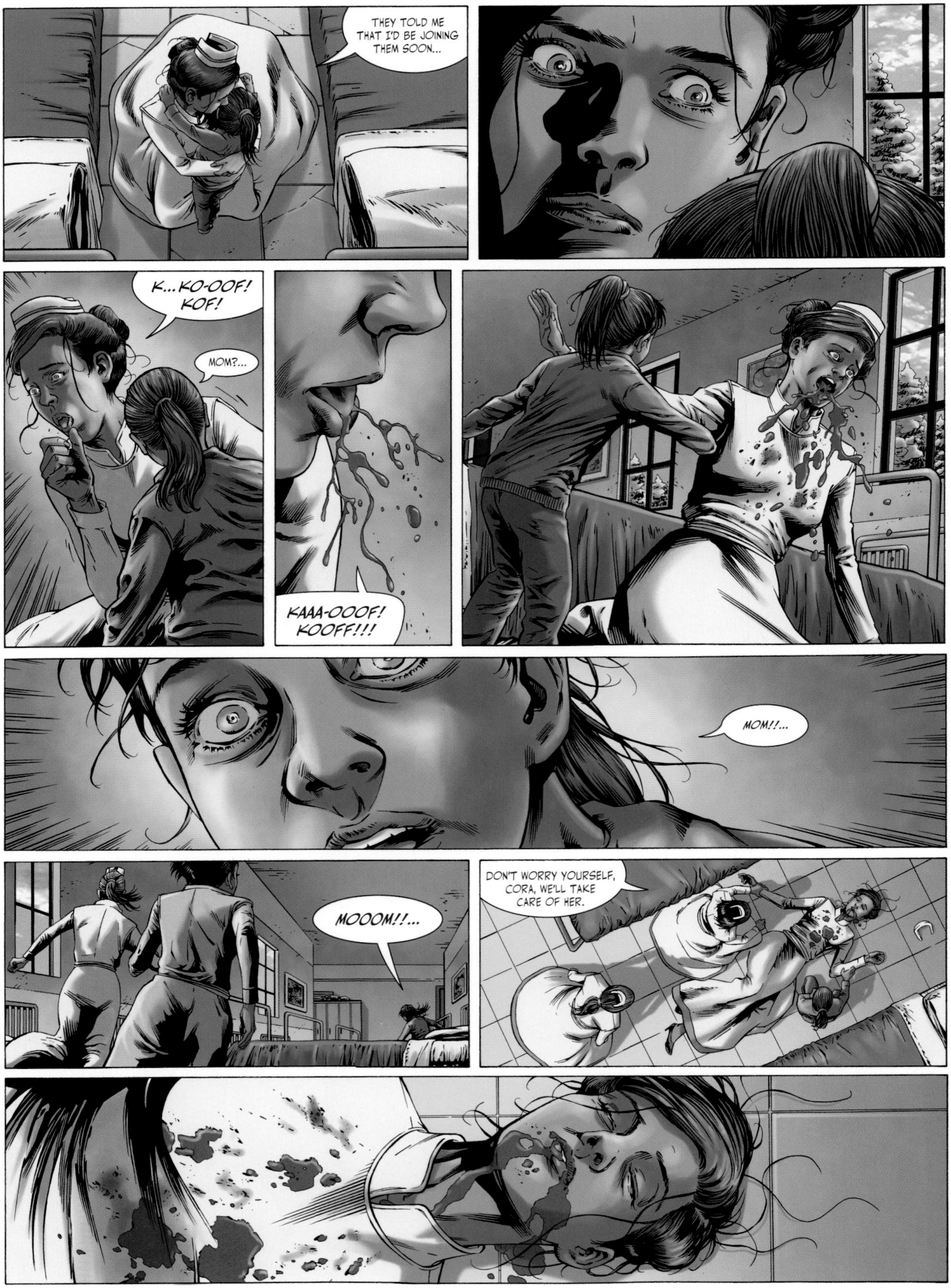
THEY TOLD ME THAT I'D BE JOINING THEM SOON...
K...KO-OOF! KOF!
MOM?...
KAAA-OOOF! KOOFF!!!
MOM!!...
MOOOM!!...
DON'T WORRY YOURSELF, CORA, WE'LL TAKE CARE OF HER.

?!!

WHEN I DISCOVERED THAT YOU HAD FAINTED, MISS GREATHOUSE, I BROUGHT TO BEAR ALL MY INFLUENCE WITH DIRECTOR MILLER SO THAT I COULD *PERSONALLY* ATTEND TO YOU...

NOOO...

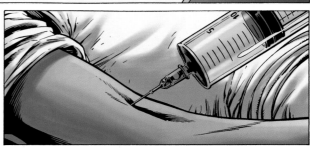

DO YOU REALIZE THAT I MIGHT'VE LOST MY MASCULINITY BECAUSE OF YOU!... AND BE IMPOTENT FOR THE REST OF MY LIFE...

BUT LUCKILY, IT WAS LESS SERIOUS THAN I ORIGINALLY HAD FEARED. I WON'T BE ABLE TO MANAGE AN ERECTION FOR THE NEXT THREE MONTHS, BUT SO BE IT...

AND WHILE I'LL BE UNABLE TO PENETRATE YOU, *DORIS*...

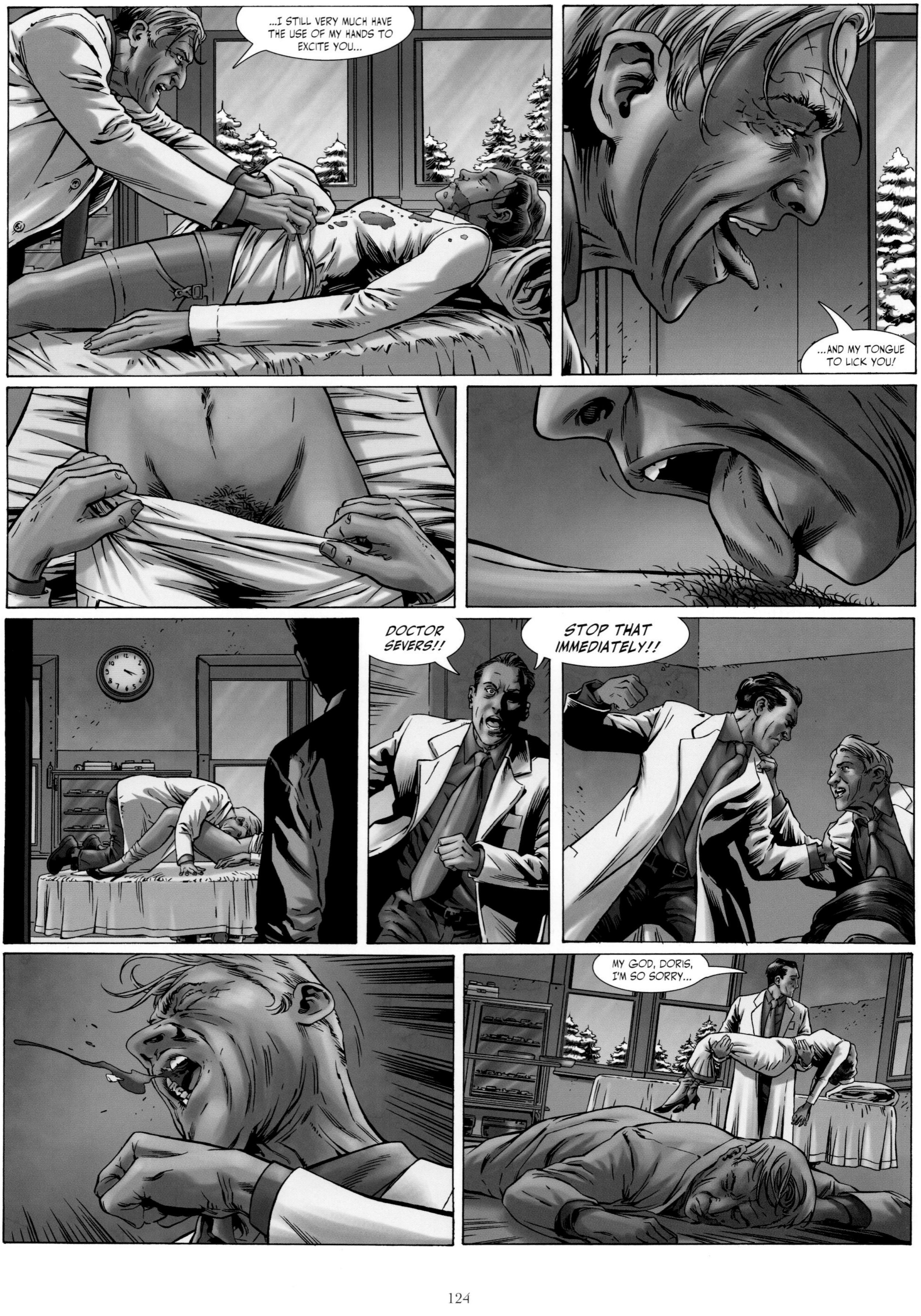
...I STILL VERY MUCH HAVE THE USE OF MY HANDS TO EXCITE YOU...
...AND MY TONGUE TO LICK YOU!
DOCTOR SEVERS!!
STOP THAT IMMEDIATELY!!
MY GOD, DORIS, I'M SO SORRY...

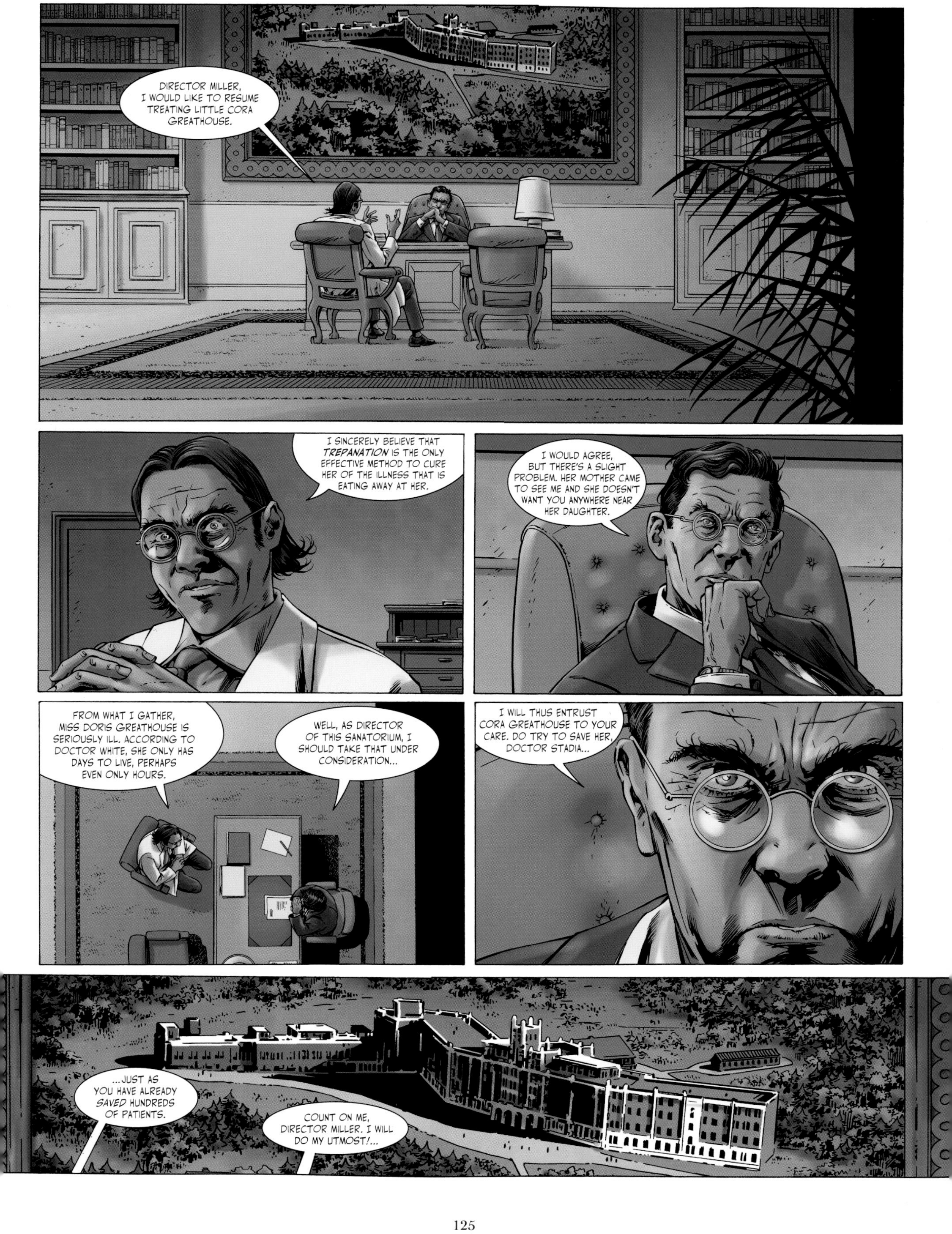
DIRECTOR MILLER, I WOULD LIKE TO RESUME TREATING LITTLE CORA GREATHOUSE.
I SINCERELY BELIEVE THAT *TREPANATION* IS THE ONLY EFFECTIVE METHOD TO CURE HER OF THE ILLNESS THAT IS EATING AWAY AT HER.
I WOULD AGREE, BUT THERE'S A SLIGHT PROBLEM. HER MOTHER CAME TO SEE ME AND SHE DOESN'T WANT YOU ANYWHERE NEAR HER DAUGHTER.
FROM WHAT I GATHER, MISS DORIS GREATHOUSE IS SERIOUSLY ILL. ACCORDING TO DOCTOR WHITE, SHE ONLY HAS DAYS TO LIVE, PERHAPS EVEN ONLY HOURS.
WELL, AS DIRECTOR OF THIS SANATORIUM, I SHOULD TAKE THAT UNDER CONSIDERATION...
I WILL THUS ENTRUST CORA GREATHOUSE TO YOUR CARE. DO TRY TO SAVE HER, DOCTOR STADIA...
...JUST AS YOU HAVE ALREADY *SAVED* HUNDREDS OF PATIENTS.
COUNT ON ME, DIRECTOR MILLER. I WILL DO MY UTMOST!...

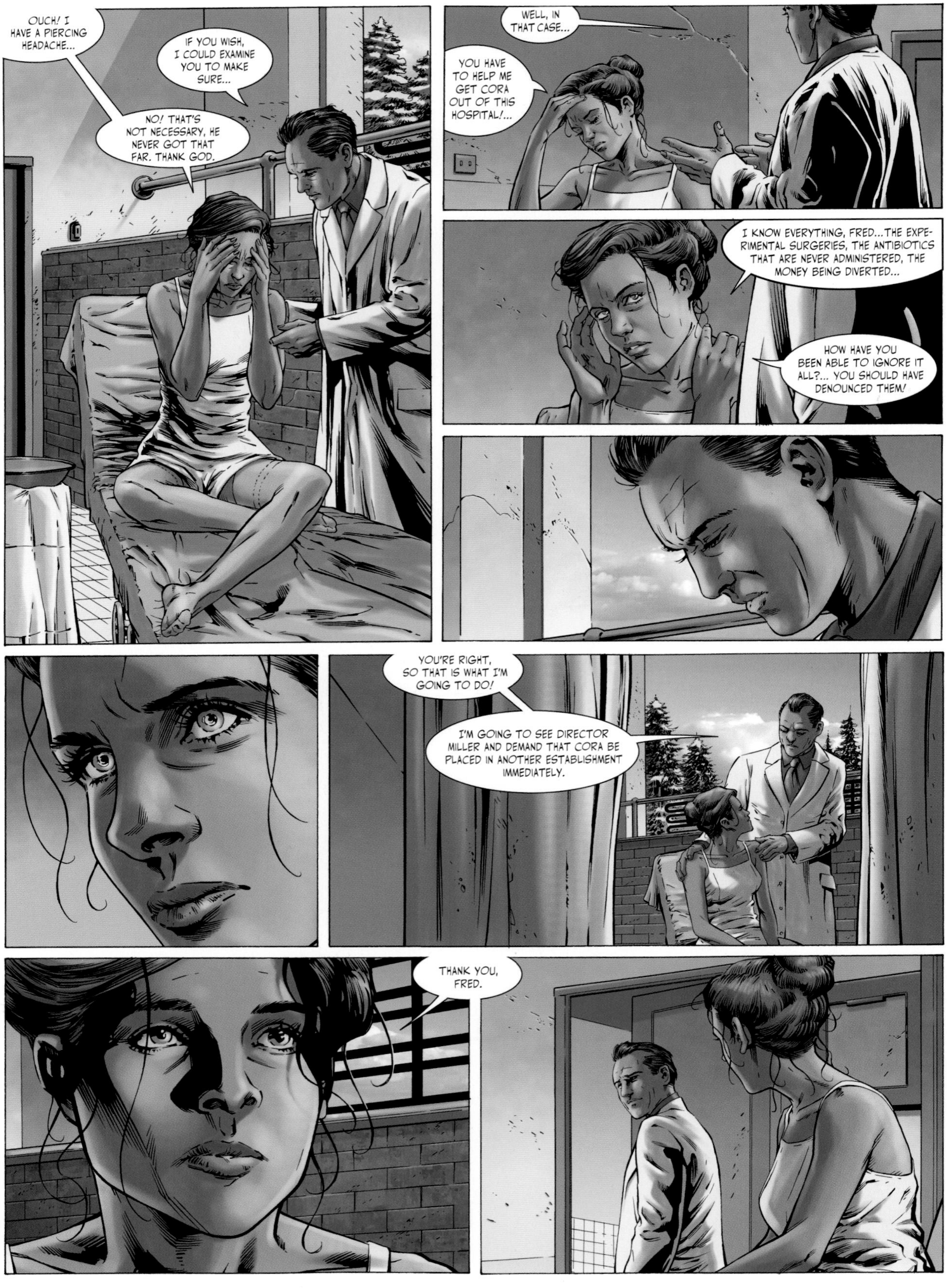
OUCH! I HAVE A PIERCING HEADACHE...
IF YOU WISH, I COULD EXAMINE YOU TO MAKE SURE...
NO! THAT'S NOT NECESSARY, HE NEVER GOT THAT FAR. THANK GOD.
WELL, IN THAT CASE...
YOU HAVE TO HELP ME GET CORA OUT OF THIS HOSPITAL!...
I KNOW EVERYTHING, FRED...THE EXPERIMENTAL SURGERIES, THE ANTIBIOTICS THAT ARE NEVER ADMINISTERED, THE MONEY BEING DIVERTED...
HOW HAVE YOU BEEN ABLE TO IGNORE IT ALL?... YOU SHOULD HAVE DENOUNCED THEM!
YOU'RE RIGHT, SO THAT IS WHAT I'M GOING TO DO!
I'M GOING TO SEE DIRECTOR MILLER AND DEMAND THAT CORA BE PLACED IN ANOTHER ESTABLISHMENT IMMEDIATELY.
THANK YOU, FRED.

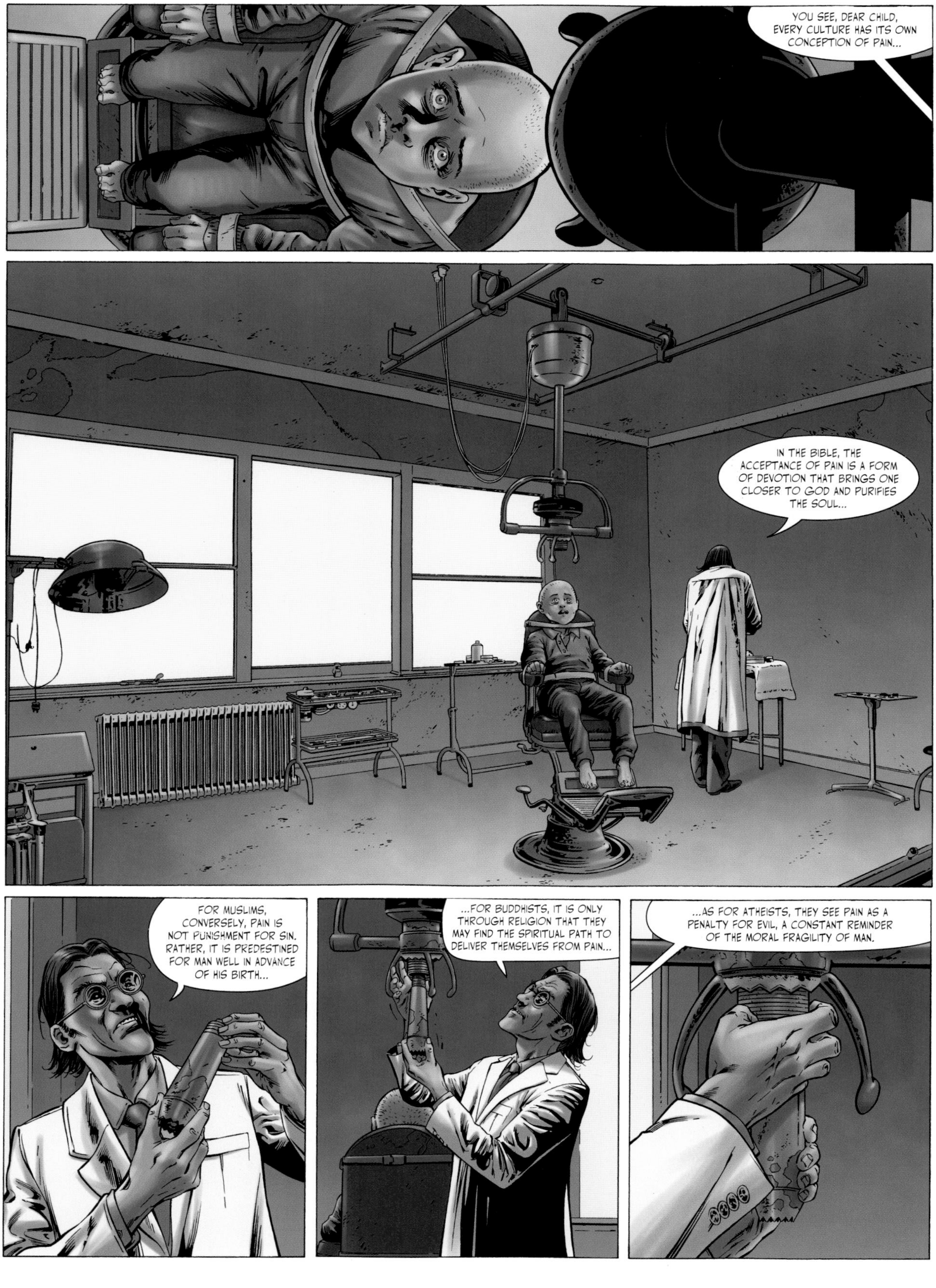
YOU SEE, DEAR CHILD, EVERY CULTURE HAS ITS OWN CONCEPTION OF PAIN...
IN THE BIBLE, THE ACCEPTANCE OF PAIN IS A FORM OF DEVOTION THAT BRINGS ONE CLOSER TO GOD AND PURIFIES THE SOUL...
FOR MUSLIMS, CONVERSELY, PAIN IS NOT PUNISHMENT FOR SIN. RATHER, IT IS PREDESTINED FOR MAN WELL IN ADVANCE OF HIS BIRTH...
...FOR BUDDHISTS, IT IS ONLY THROUGH RELIGION THAT THEY MAY FIND THE SPIRITUAL PATH TO DELIVER THEMSELVES FROM PAIN...
...AS FOR ATHEISTS, THEY SEE PAIN AS A PENALTY FOR EVIL, A CONSTANT REMINDER OF THE MORAL FRAGILITY OF MAN.

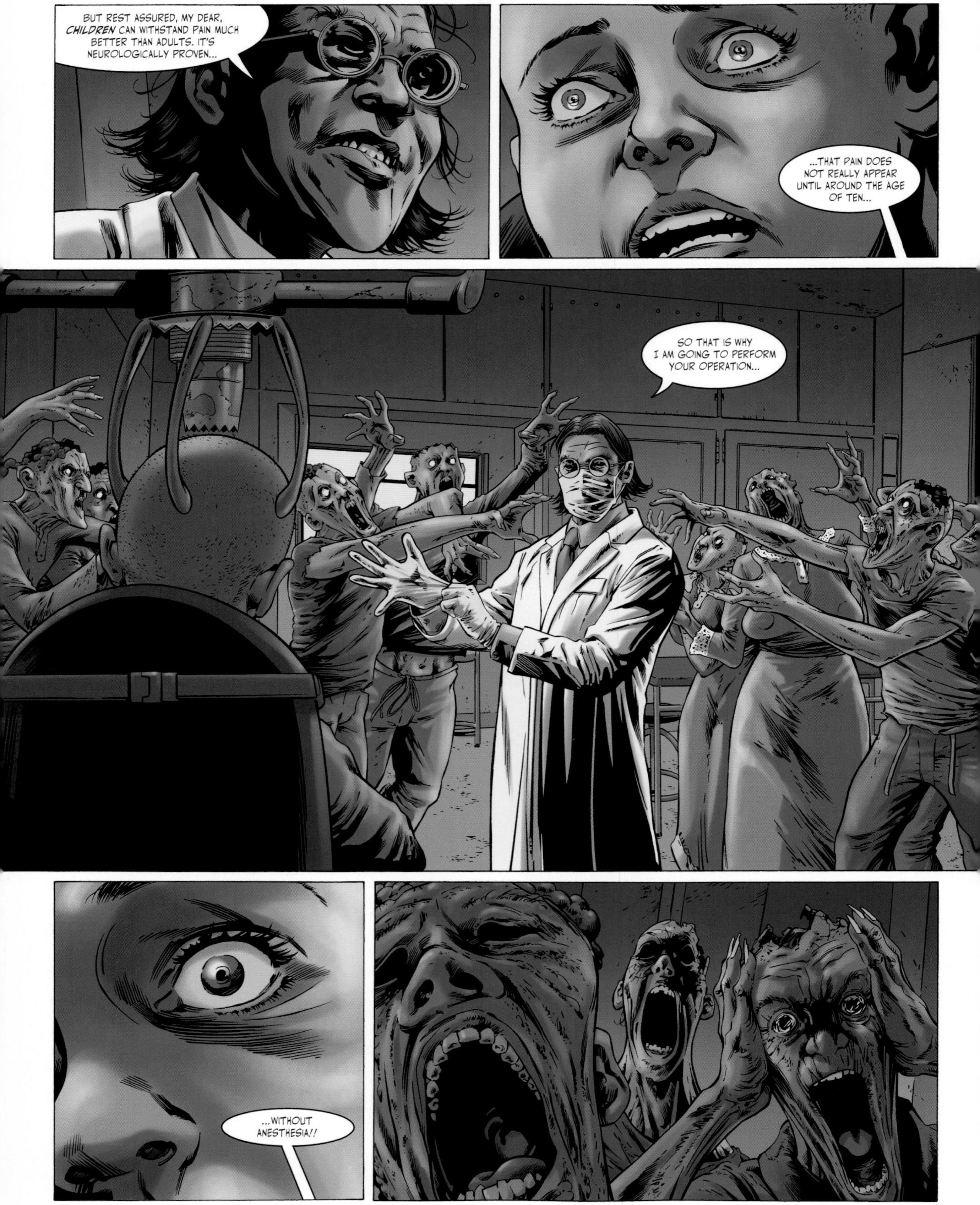
BUT REST ASSURED, MY DEAR, *CHILDREN* CAN WITHSTAND PAIN MUCH BETTER THAN ADULTS. IT'S NEUROLOGICALLY PROVEN...
...THAT PAIN DOES NOT REALLY APPEAR UNTIL AROUND THE AGE OF TEN...
SO THAT IS WHY I AM GOING TO PERFORM YOUR OPERATION...
...WITHOUT ANESTHESIA!!

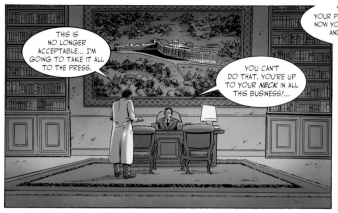
THIS IS NO LONGER ACCEPTABLE... I'M GOING TO TAKE IT ALL TO THE PRESS.

YOU CAN'T DO THAT. YOU'RE UP TO YOUR *NECK* IN ALL THIS BUSINESS!...

YOU'VE BEEN FATTENING YOUR POCKETS OVER THE YEARS, AND NOW YOU WANT TO BETRAY EVERYONE AND JUST WASH YOUR HANDS OF IT ALL ?!...

THAT'S *NOT* HOW IT WORKS, OLD FRIEND! NOT LIKE THAT AT ALL!...

I DON'T GIVE A *DAMN* ABOUT THE CONSEQUENCES!

OH, I GET IT, YOU WANT SOMETHING. WHAT IS IT?

TO TAKE CORA GREATHOUSE OUT OF THIS HOSPITAL!

IS THAT ALL?

YES! IF YOU DO THAT, I WON'T REVEAL ANYTHING.

DONE! BUT YOU DO UNDERSTAND THAT UNDER THESE CONDITIONS, I HAVE NO OTHER CHOICE THAN LETTING YOU GO.

I'LL GIVE YOU YOUR SEVERANCE IMMEDIATELY...

YOU BELIEVED ME, YOU DAMN FOOL?

BLAM

...THAT *I* WAS GOING TO TRUST A *TRAITOR* LIKE *YOU* WITH ANYTHING?!

NOBODY MUST EVER KNOW...

NOBODY!

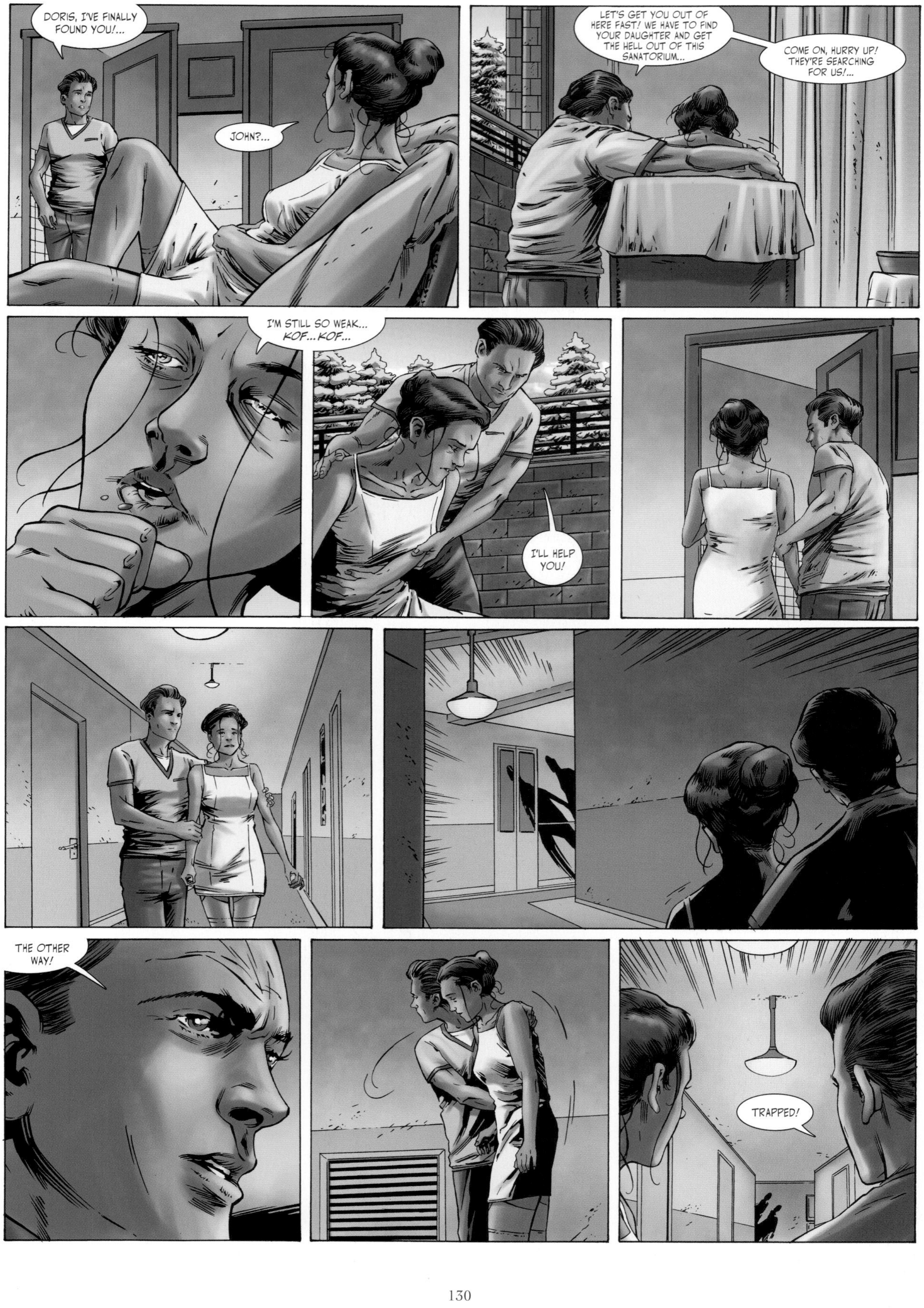
DORIS, I'VE FINALLY FOUND YOU!...
JOHN?...
LET'S GET YOU OUT OF HERE FAST! WE HAVE TO FIND YOUR DAUGHTER AND GET THE HELL OUT OF THIS SANATORIUM...
COME ON, HURRY UP! THEY'RE SEARCHING FOR US!...
I'M STILL SO WEAK... KOF...KOF...
I'LL HELP YOU!
THE OTHER WAY!
TRAPPED!

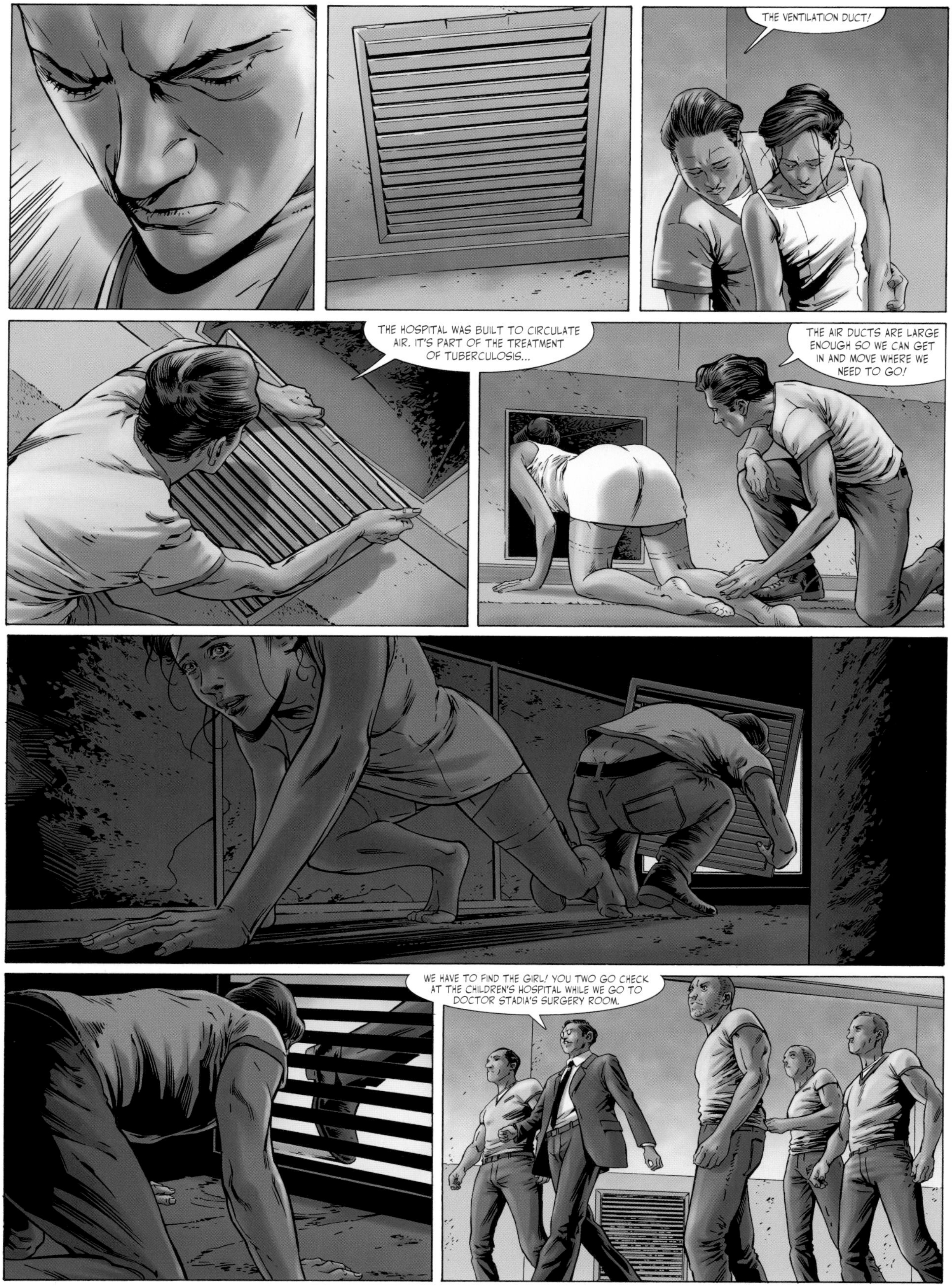
THE VENTILATION DUCT!
THE HOSPITAL WAS BUILT TO CIRCULATE AIR. IT'S PART OF THE TREATMENT OF TUBERCULOSIS...
THE AIR DUCTS ARE LARGE ENOUGH SO WE CAN GET IN AND MOVE WHERE WE NEED TO GO!
WE HAVE TO FIND THE GIRL! YOU TWO GO CHECK AT THE CHILDREN'S HOSPITAL WHILE WE GO TO DOCTOR STADIA'S SURGERY ROOM.

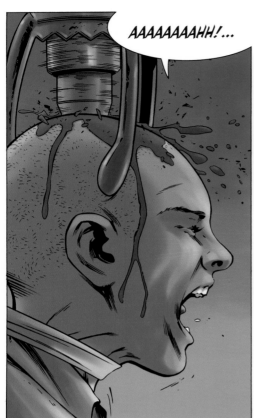

AAAAAAAHH!...

DID YOU KNOW, DEAR CHILD, THAT TREPANATION IS THE OLDEST FORM OF SURGERY?

THE EXAMINATION OF SKULL FOSSILS SHOWS THAT OPERATIONS OF THIS KIND WERE PRACTICED BACK IN BOTH THE NEOLITHIC AND MESOLITHIC PERIODS...

HIPPOCRATES HIMSELF WROTE EXTENSIVELY ON THE METHODOLOGY OF TREPANATION!

FOR THE TIBETANS, TREPANATION WAS THE ROAD TO DISCOVERING THE THIRD EYE...

IN THE MIDDLE AGES, IT WAS A MEANS OF DRIVING OUT EVIL SPIRITS FROM THEIR HOST...

SO, IN A WAY, THIS IS WHAT WE ARE DOING, MY DEAR...

WE ARE GOING TO EXPEL THE EVIL SPIRIT FROM WITHIN YOUR SKULL!

132

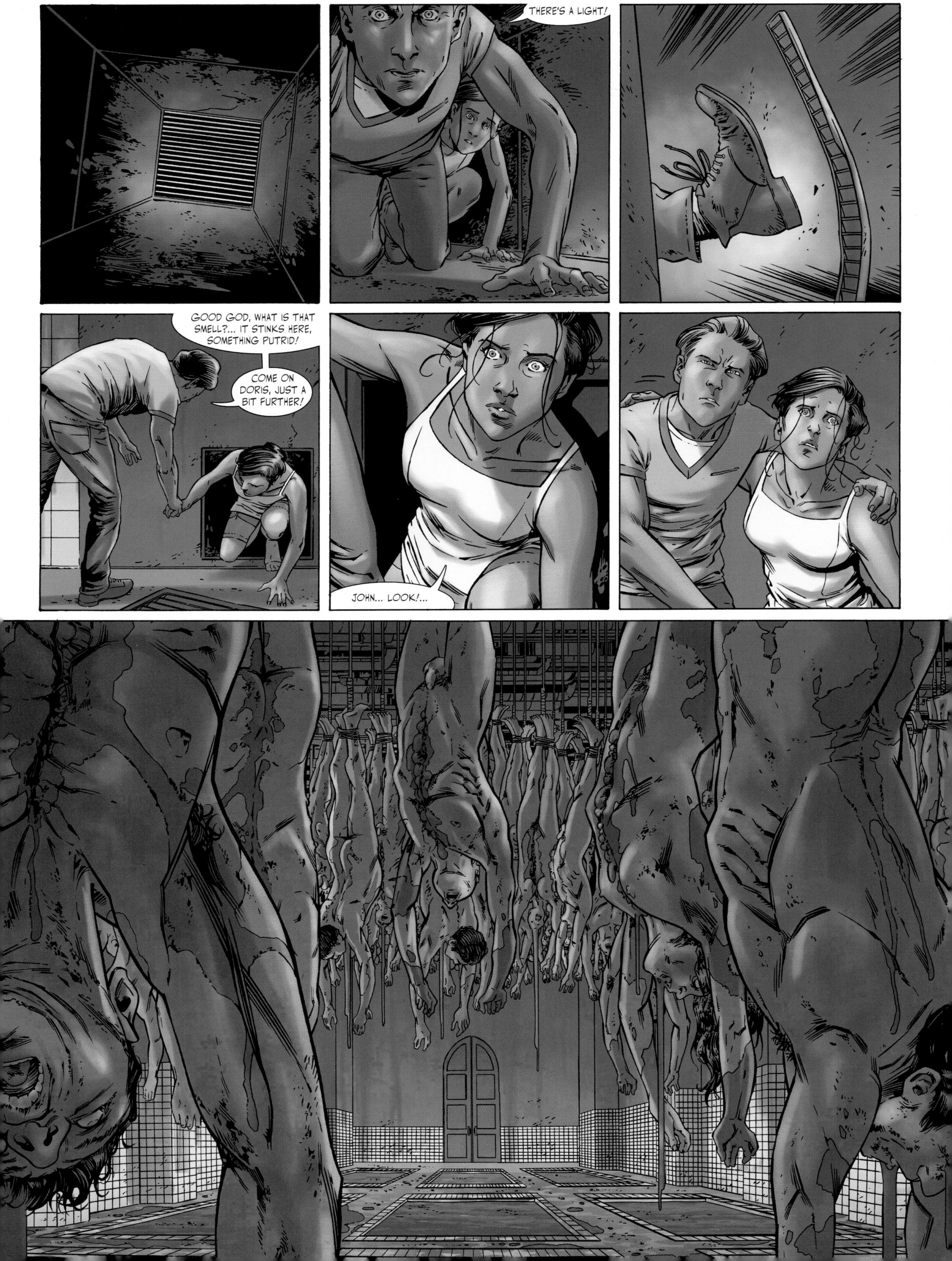
THERE'S A LIGHT!
GOOD GOD, WHAT IS THAT SMELL?... IT STINKS HERE, SOMETHING PUTRID!
COME ON DORIS, JUST A BIT FURTHER!
JOHN... LOOK!...

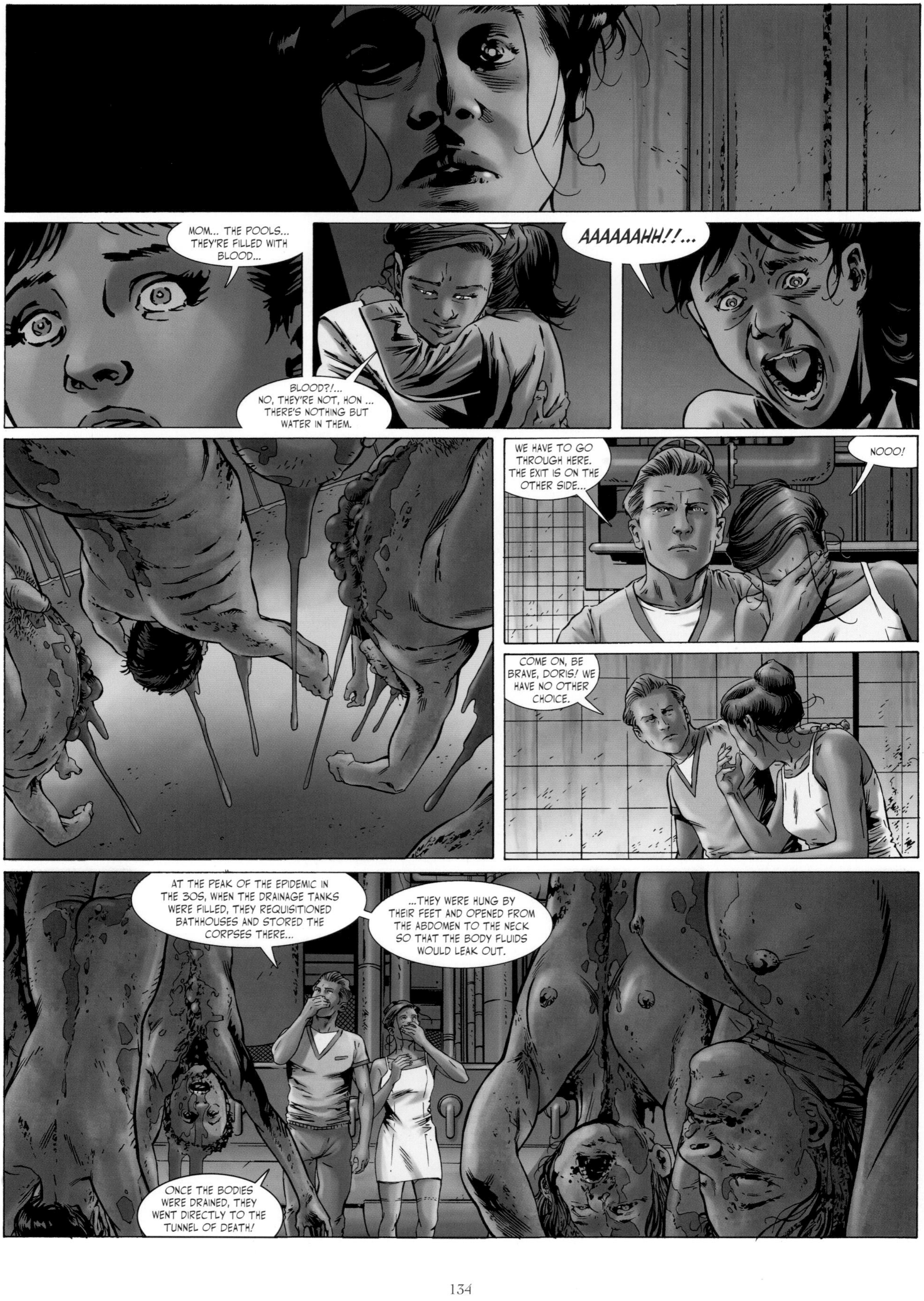
MOM... THE POOLS... THEY'RE FILLED WITH BLOOD...
BLOOD?!... NO, THEY'RE NOT, HON ... THERE'S NOTHING BUT WATER IN THEM.
AAAAAAHH!!...
WE HAVE TO GO THROUGH HERE. THE EXIT IS ON THE OTHER SIDE...
NOOO!
COME ON, BE BRAVE, DORIS! WE HAVE NO OTHER CHOICE.
AT THE PEAK OF THE EPIDEMIC IN THE 30S, WHEN THE DRAINAGE TANKS WERE FILLED, THEY REQUISITIONED BATHHOUSES AND STORED THE CORPSES THERE...
...THEY WERE HUNG BY THEIR FEET AND OPENED FROM THE ABDOMEN TO THE NECK SO THAT THE BODY FLUIDS WOULD LEAK OUT.
ONCE THE BODIES WERE DRAINED, THEY WENT DIRECTLY TO THE TUNNEL OF DEATH!

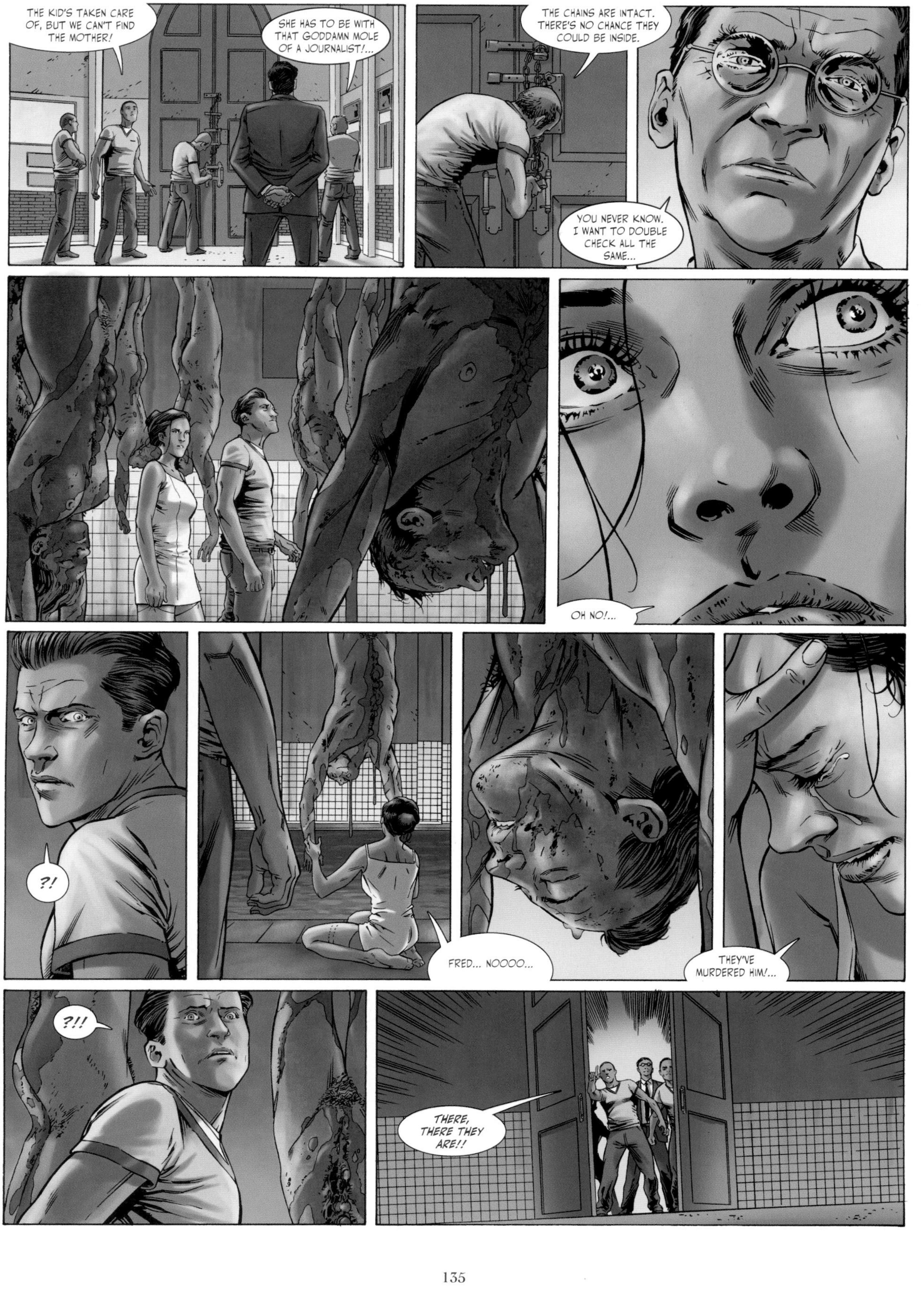
THE KID'S TAKEN CARE OF, BUT WE CAN'T FIND THE MOTHER!
SHE HAS TO BE WITH THAT GODDAMN MOLE OF A JOURNALIST!...
THE CHAINS ARE INTACT. THERE'S NO CHANCE THEY COULD BE INSIDE.
YOU NEVER KNOW. I WANT TO DOUBLE CHECK ALL THE SAME...
OH NO!...
?!
FRED... NOOOO...
THEY'VE MURDERED HIM!...
?!!
THERE, THERE THEY ARE!!

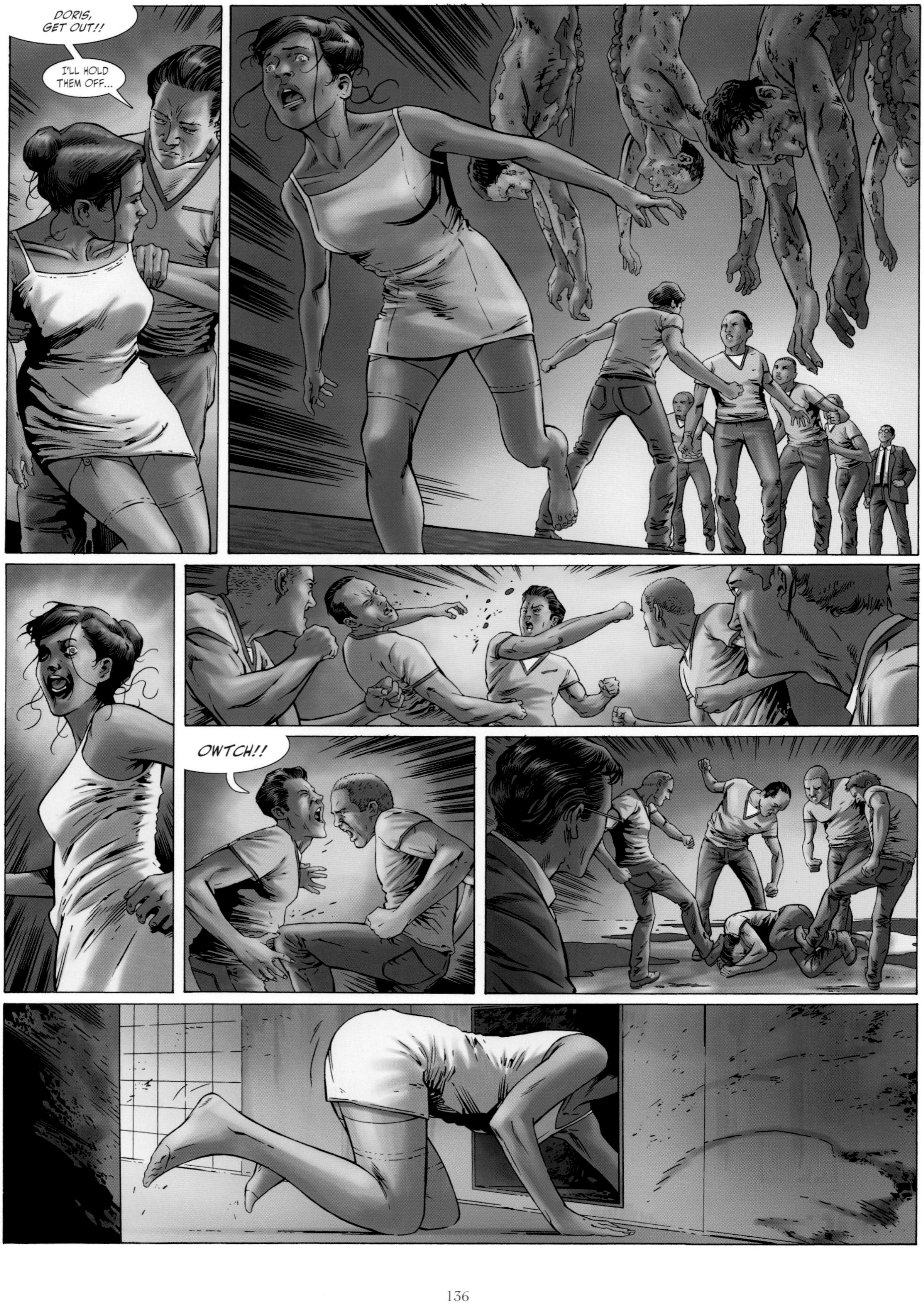
DORIS, GET OUT!!
I'LL HOLD THEM OFF...
OWTCH!!

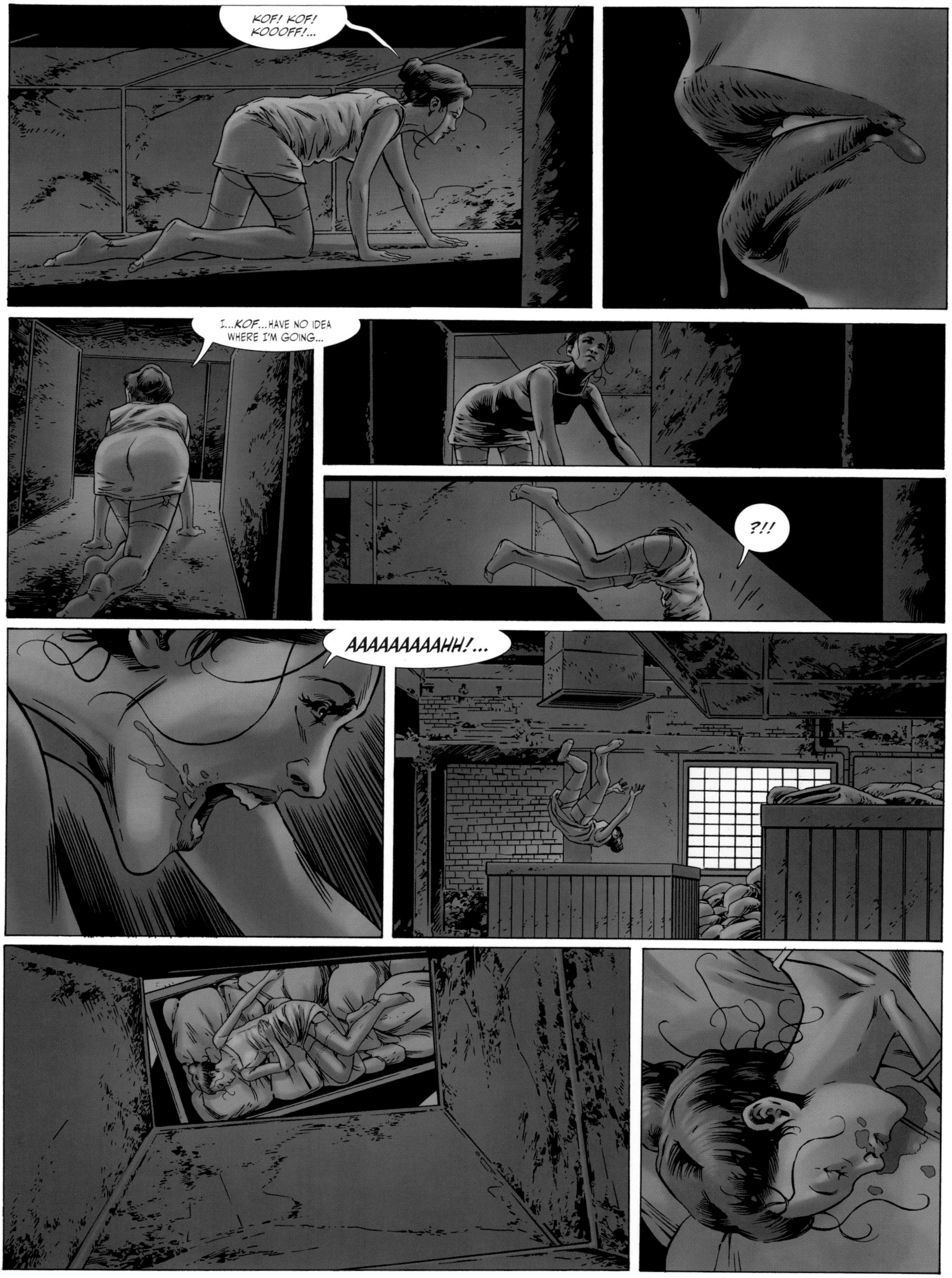
KOF! KOF! KOOOFF!...
I...KOF...HAVE NO IDEA WHERE I'M GOING...
?!!
AAAAAAAAAAHH!...

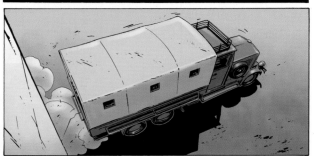

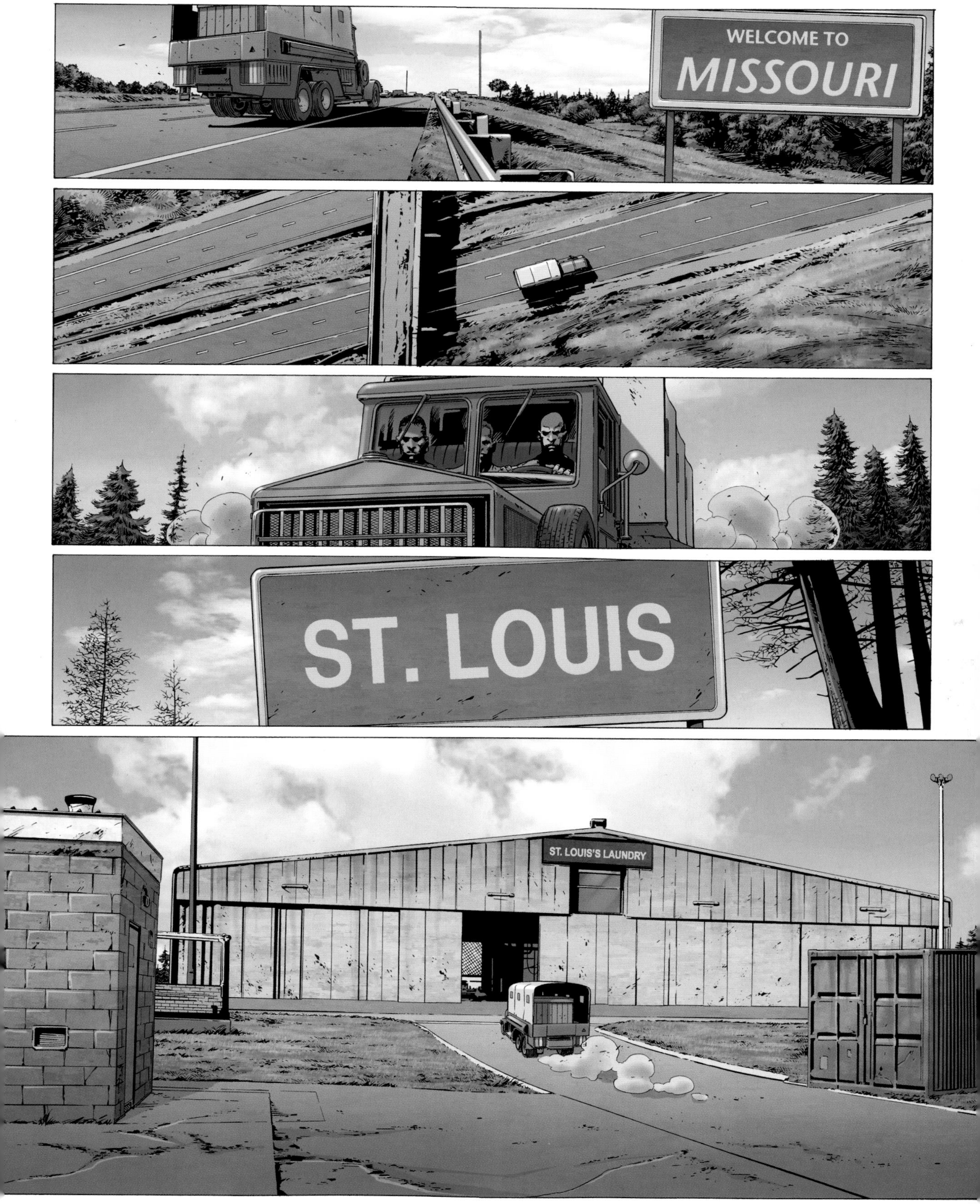
WELCOME TO
MISSOURI
ST. LOUIS
ST. LOUIS'S LAUNDRY

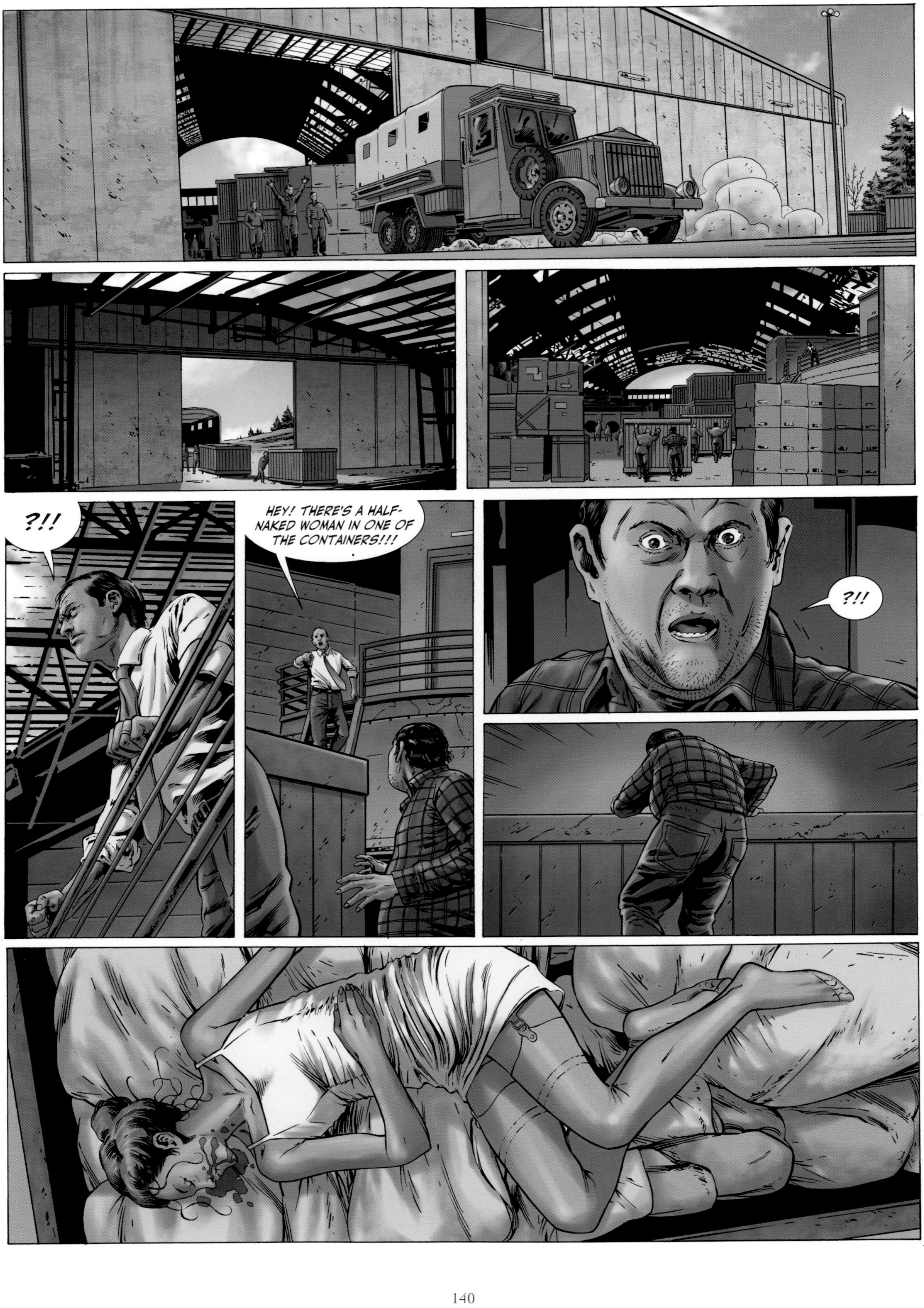
?!!
HEY! THERE'S A HALF-NAKED WOMAN IN ONE OF THE CONTAINERS!!!
?!!

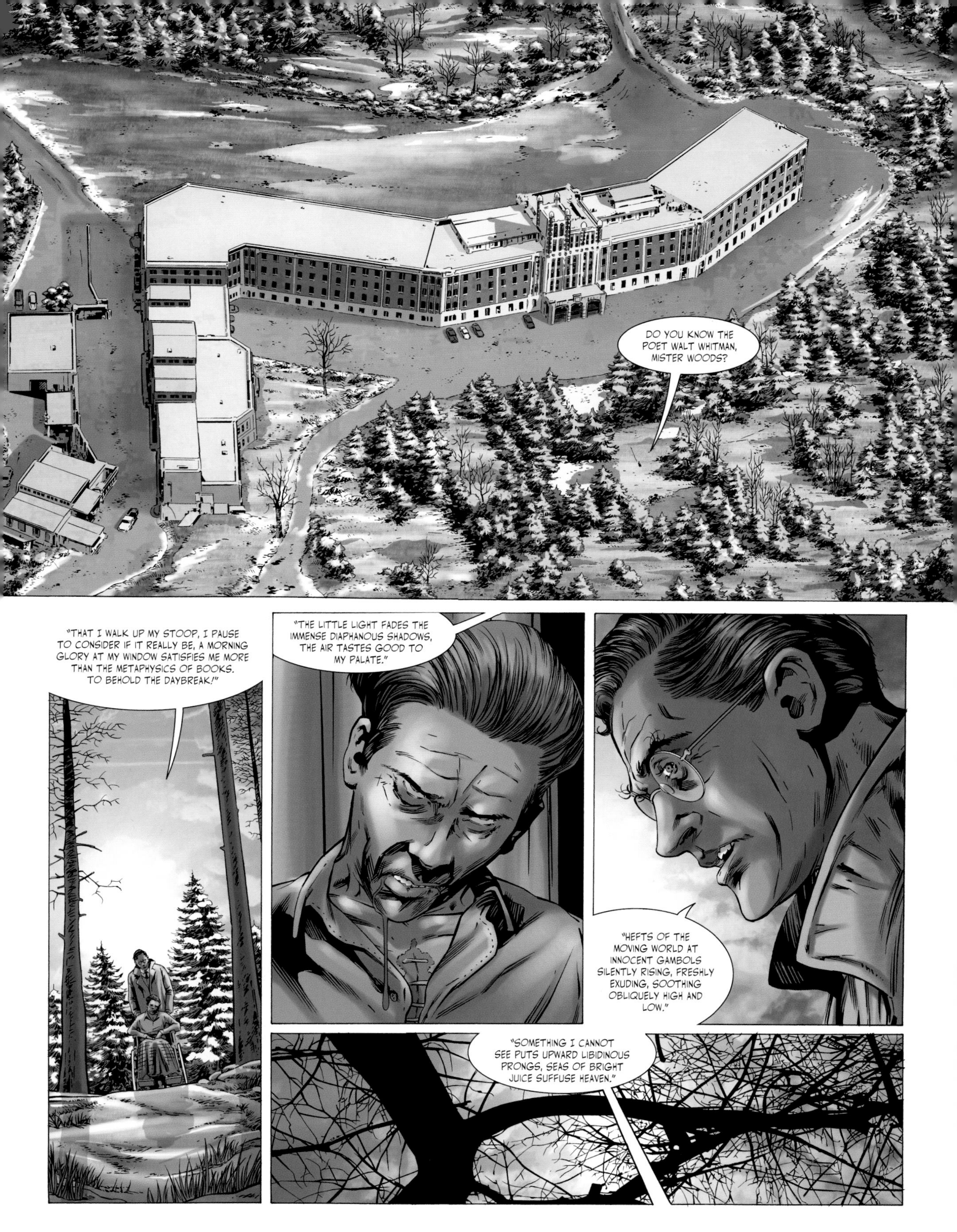
DO YOU KNOW THE POET WALT WHITMAN, MISTER WOODS?
"THAT I WALK UP MY STOOP, I PAUSE TO CONSIDER IF IT REALLY BE, A MORNING GLORY AT MY WINDOW SATISFIES ME MORE THAN THE METAPHYSICS OF BOOKS. TO BEHOLD THE DAYBREAK!"
"THE LITTLE LIGHT FADES THE IMMENSE DIAPHANOUS SHADOWS, THE AIR TASTES GOOD TO MY PALATE."
"HEFTS OF THE MOVING WORLD AT INNOCENT GAMBOLS SILENTLY RISING, FRESHLY EXUDING, SOOTHING OBLIQUELY HIGH AND LOW."
"SOMETHING I CANNOT SEE PUTS UPWARD LIBIDINOUS PRONGS, SEAS OF BRIGHT JUICE SUFFUSE HEAVEN."

"THE EARTH BY THE SKY STAYED WITH, THE DAILY CLOSE OF THEIR JUNCTION. THE HEAVED CHALLENGE FROM THE EAST THAT MOMENT OVER MY HEAD,"...

"THE MOCKING TAUNT, SEE THEN WHETHER YOU SHALL BE MASTER!"

BEAUTIFUL, ISN'T IT?

YOU SEE, MISTER WOODS, YOU SHOULD NEVER HAVE STUCK YOUR NOSE IN OTHER PEOPLE'S BUSINESS!

SO IN THE END, THIS THOROCOPLASTY SURGERY, EVEN IF YOU WEREN'T SICK...

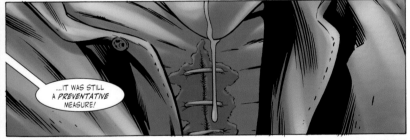

...IT WAS STILL A *PREVENTATIVE* MEASURE!

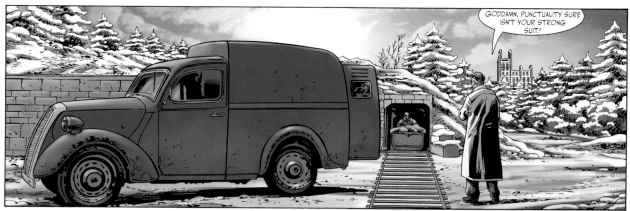

GODDAMN, PUNCTUALITY SURE ISN'T YOUR STRONG SUIT!

THIS JOB'S ONLY GETTING WORSE. I STILL HAVE ANOTHER FIFTEEN BODIES! GOD KNOWS WHERE TO PUT THEM. THE FRIDGES ARE FILLED TO OVERFLOWING CAPACITY, AND THE DIRECTOR HIMSELF REQUISITIONED THE SWIMMING POOLS FOR THE SURPLUS!

THEN TO MAKE MATTERS WORSE, WILL YOU LOOK AT THAT...THIS HAS TO BE THE BODY OF A KID, ONLY SEVEN OR EIGHT, CAN'T BE ANY OLDER...

THAT'S NOT A GOOD SIGN WHEN YOU START FEELING SORRY FOR THEM... YOU MIGHT THINK ABOUT PUTTING IN FOR RETIREMENT.

YEAH, BUT FOR YOU ON THE OTHER HAND, BUSINESS IS THRIVING, AIN'T IT, PAL!

I CAN'T COMPLAIN.

UNTIL TOMORROW, SAME TIME, SAME PLACE!

RIGHT, 'TIL TOMORROW.

TWO DAYS LATER.

DOCTOR! THE LADY IN 508, SHE'S AWAKE!

GOOD NEWS! THERE'S ONE THAT'S COME BACK FROM THE DEAD.

I'LL BE RIGHT THERE!...

LET ME GO! I HAVE TO FIND MY DAUGHTER!

MADAM, CALM YOURSELF!... YOU'RE IN A HOSPITAL IN ST. LOUIS, MISSOURI. YOU WERE BROUGHT HERE IN VERY SERIOUS CONDITION.

YOU'RE QUITE SICK, BUT WE'VE TREATED WITH YOU THE APPROPRIATE ANTIBIOTICS.

WHAT IS YOUR NAME, AND WHERE DID YOU COME FROM?

DORIS...DORIS GREATHOUSE! I'M A NURSE AT WAVERLY HILLS SANATORIUM IN LOUISVILLE...

PLEASE, LISTEN, I HAVE TO RETURN THERE. MY DAUGHTER IS IN DANGER!

MRS. GREATHOUSE, BE REASONABLE!... PLEASE!

NOOO!

I CANNOT ALLOW YOU TO LEAVE THIS ROOM. YOU ARE IN NO STATE TO LEAVE. TO DO SO MIGHT PROVE FATAL!!

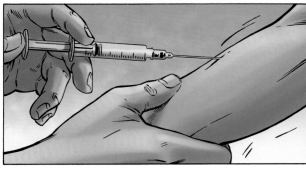

NOOOO!!

144

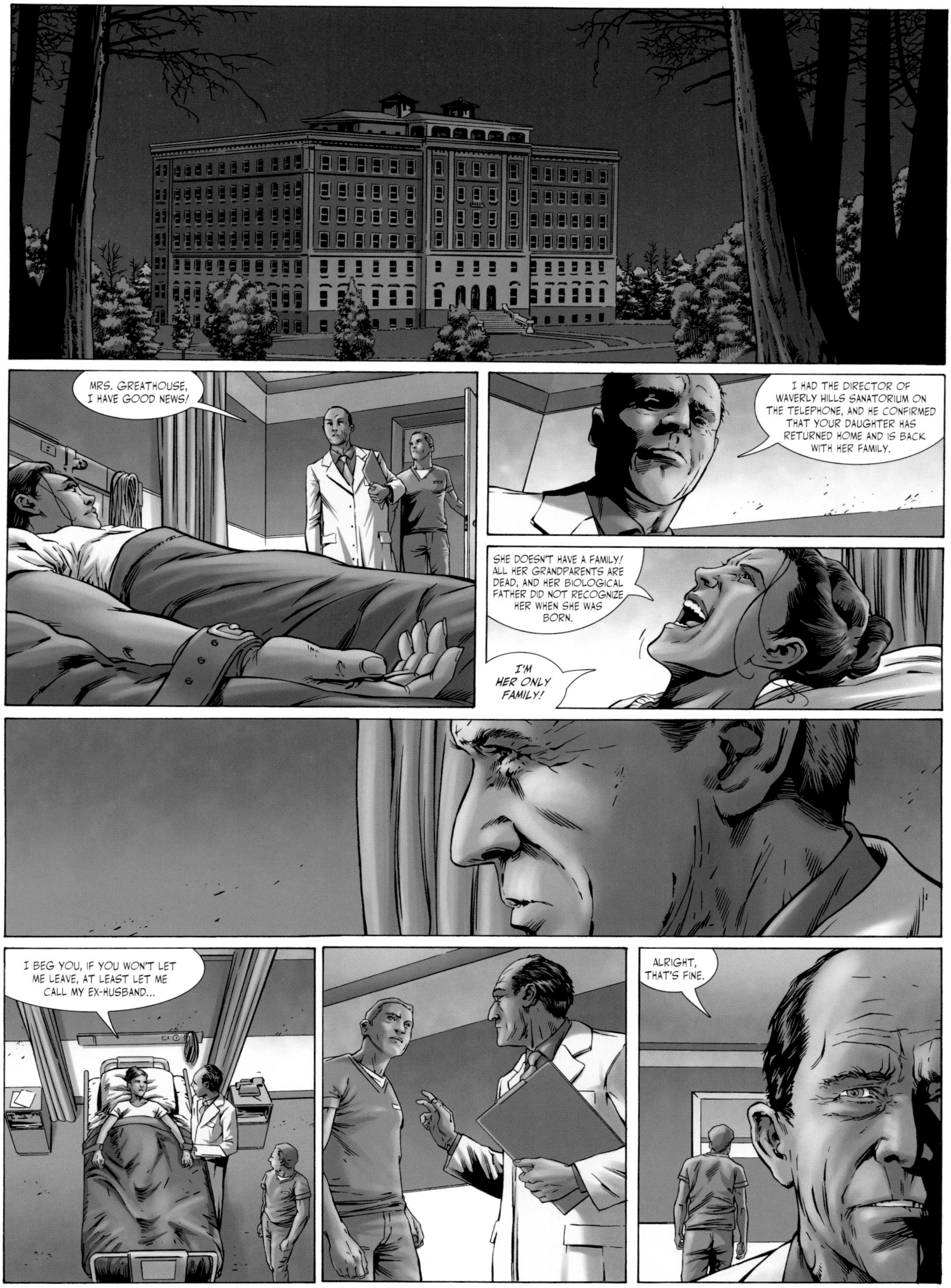
MRS. GREATHOUSE, I HAVE GOOD NEWS!
I HAD THE DIRECTOR OF WAVERLY HILLS SANATORIUM ON THE TELEPHONE, AND HE CONFIRMED THAT YOUR DAUGHTER HAS RETURNED HOME AND IS BACK WITH HER FAMILY.
SHE DOESN'T HAVE A FAMILY! ALL HER GRANDPARENTS ARE DEAD, AND HER BIOLOGICAL FATHER DID NOT RECOGNIZE HER WHEN SHE WAS BORN.
I'M HER ONLY FAMILY!
I BEG YOU, IF YOU WON'T LET ME LEAVE, AT LEAST LET ME CALL MY EX-HUSBAND...
ALRIGHT, THAT'S FINE.

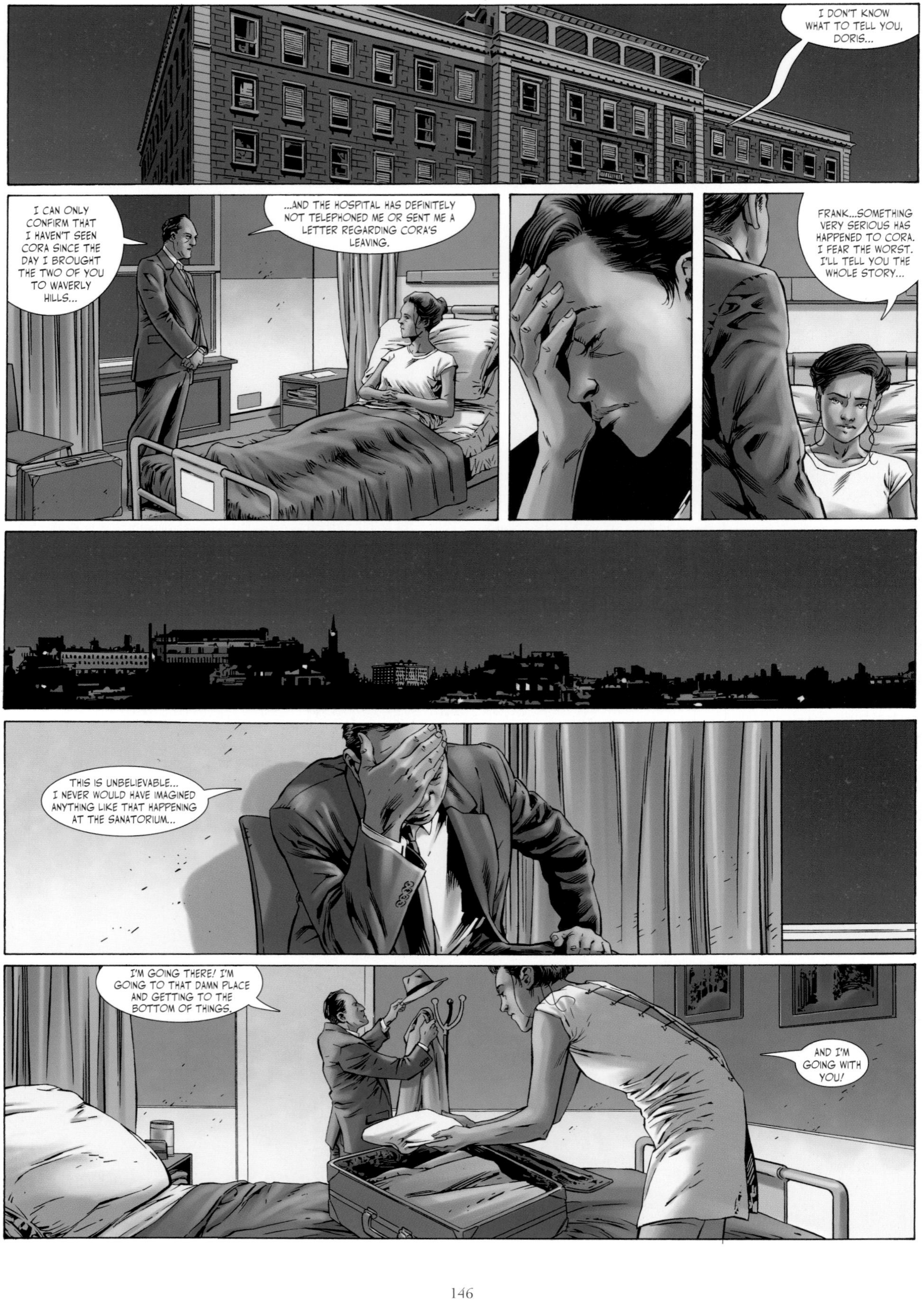
I DON'T KNOW WHAT TO TELL YOU, DORIS...
I CAN ONLY CONFIRM THAT I HAVEN'T SEEN CORA SINCE THE DAY I BROUGHT THE TWO OF YOU TO WAVERLY HILLS...
...AND THE HOSPITAL HAS DEFINITELY NOT TELEPHONED ME OR SENT ME A LETTER REGARDING CORA'S LEAVING.
FRANK...SOMETHING VERY SERIOUS HAS HAPPENED TO CORA. I FEAR THE WORST. I'LL TELL YOU THE WHOLE STORY...
THIS IS UNBELIEVABLE... I NEVER WOULD HAVE IMAGINED ANYTHING LIKE THAT HAPPENING AT THE SANATORIUM...
I'M GOING THERE! I'M GOING TO THAT DAMN PLACE AND GETTING TO THE BOTTOM OF THINGS.
AND I'M GOING WITH YOU!

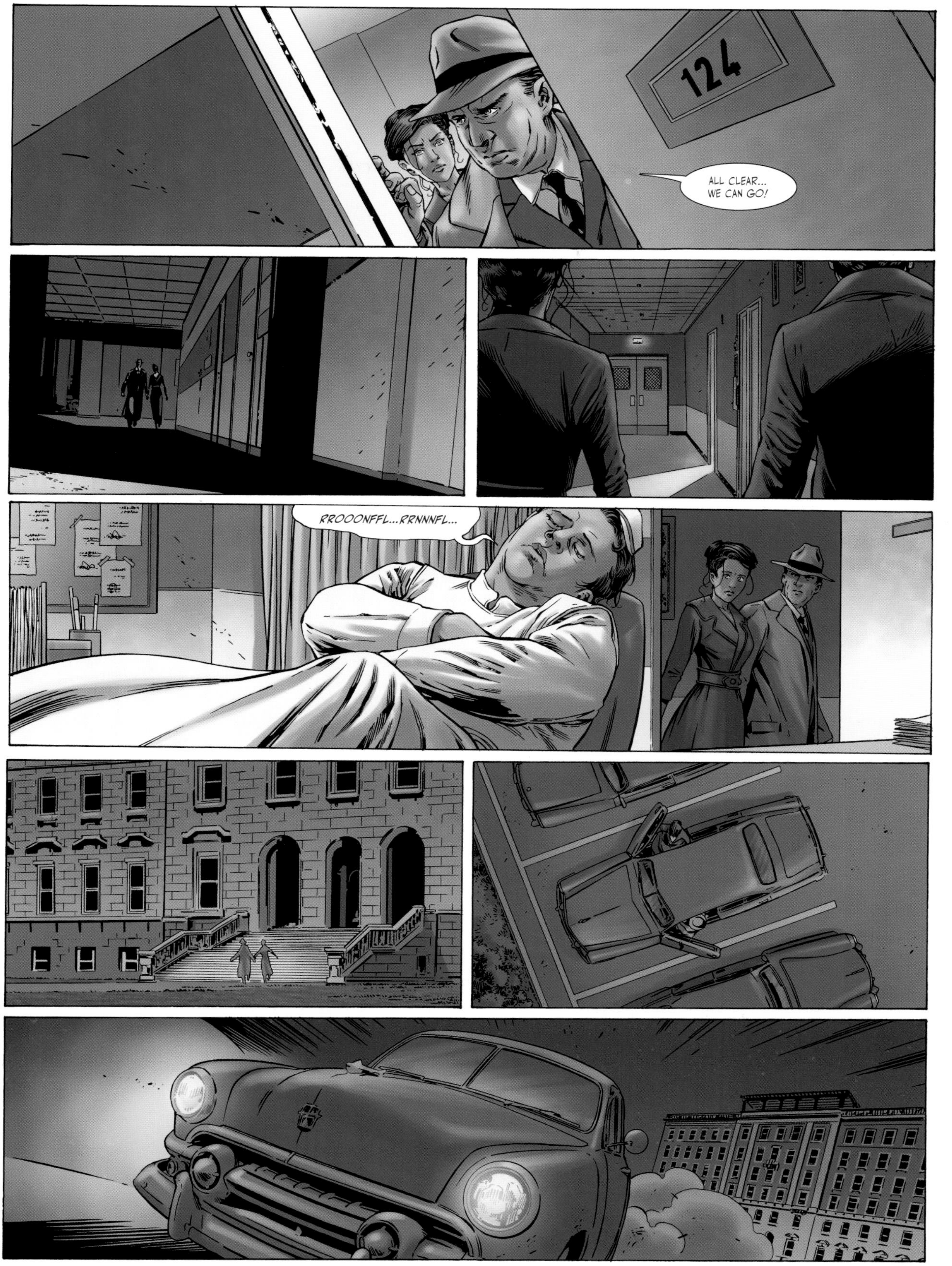
ALL CLEAR... WE CAN GO!
RROOONFFL...RRNNNFL...

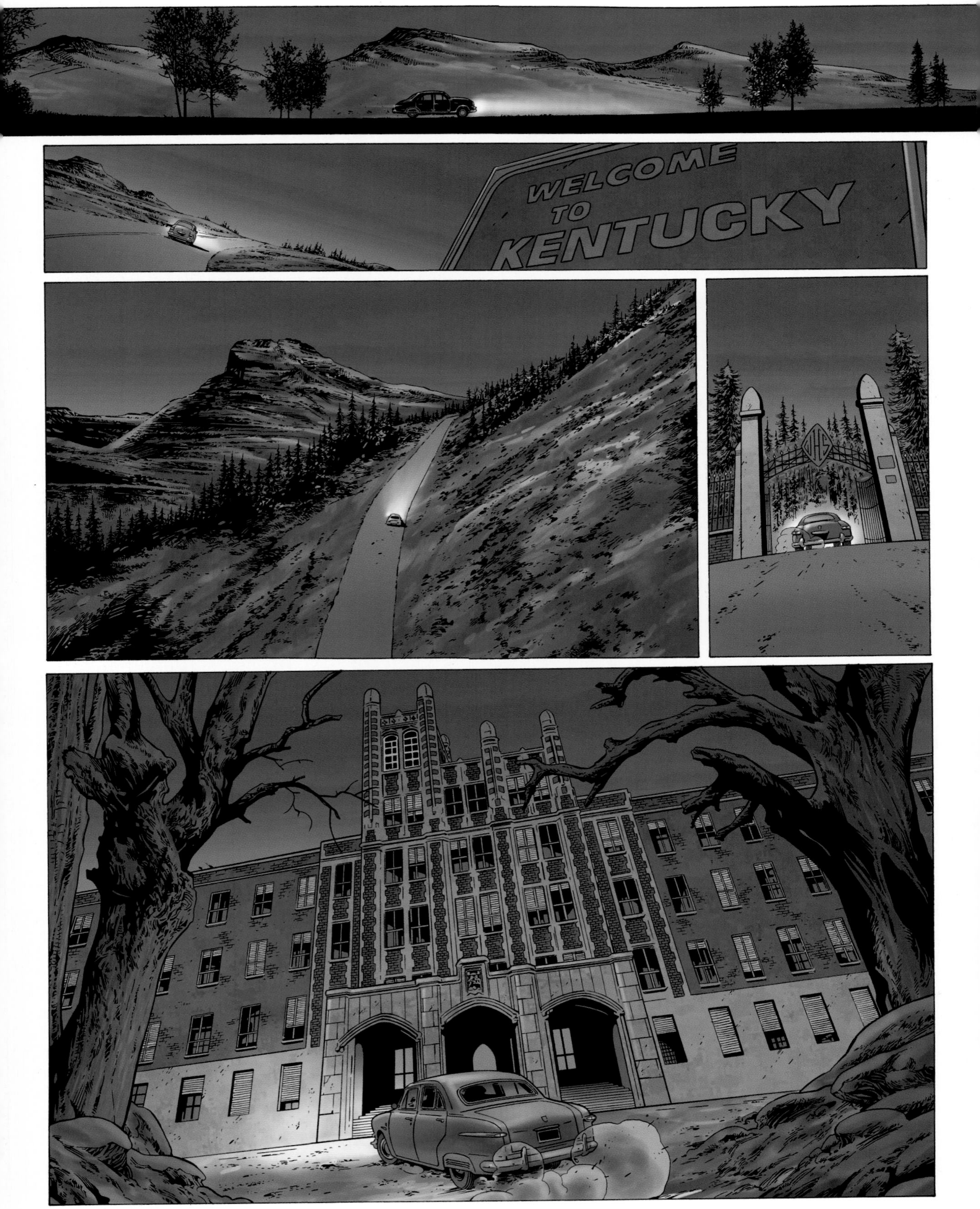
WELCOME TO KENTUCKY

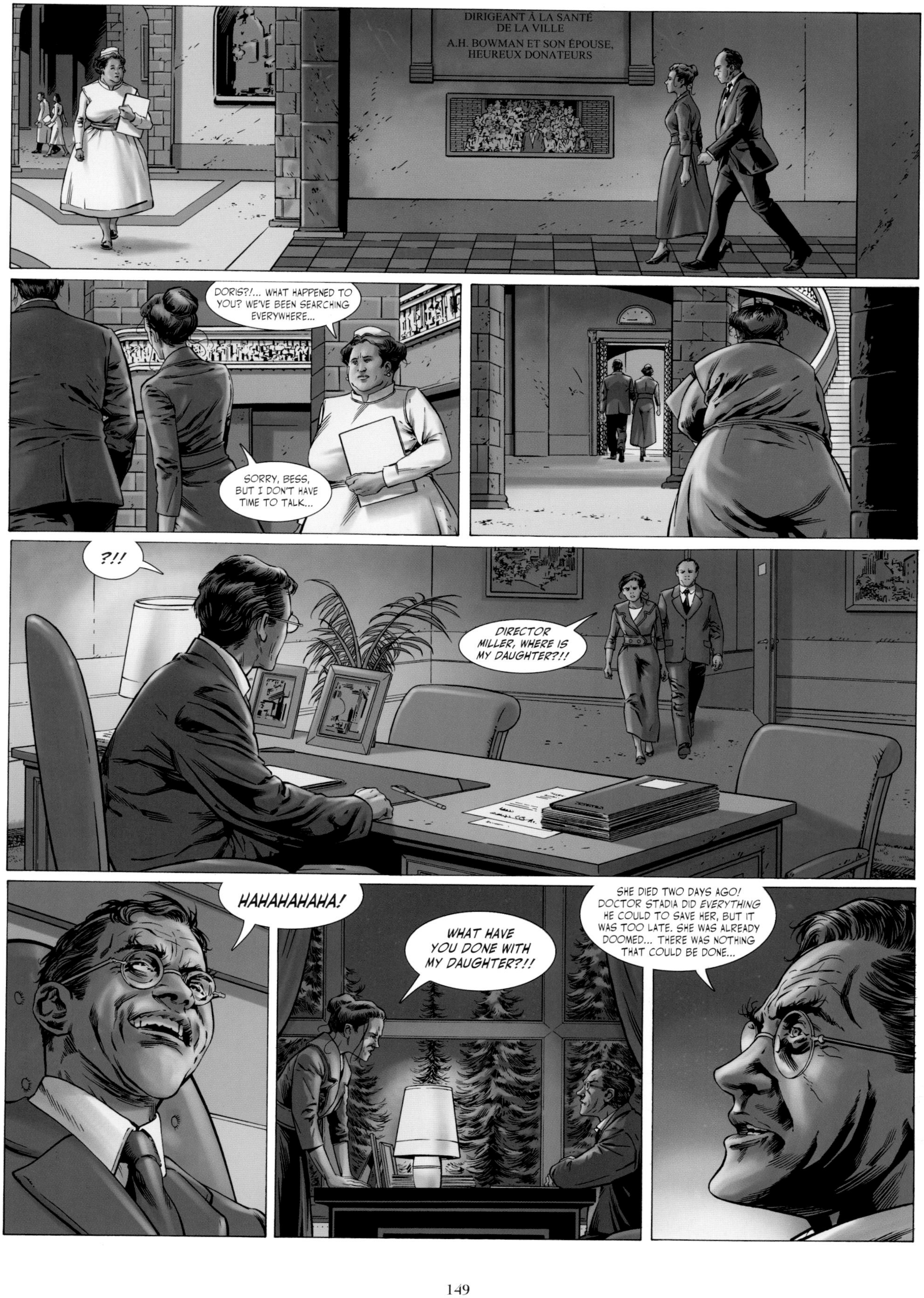

DIRIGEANT À LA SANTÉ DE LA VILLE
A.H. BOWMAN ET SON ÉPOUSE, HEUREUX DONATEURS
DORIS?!... WHAT HAPPENED TO YOU? WE'VE BEEN SEARCHING EVERYWHERE...
SORRY, BESS, BUT I DON'T HAVE TIME TO TALK...
?!!
DIRECTOR MILLER, WHERE IS MY DAUGHTER?!!
HAHAHAHAHA!
WHAT HAVE YOU DONE WITH MY DAUGHTER?!!
SHE DIED TWO DAYS AGO! DOCTOR STADIA DID EVERYTHING HE COULD TO SAVE HER, BUT IT WAS TOO LATE. SHE WAS ALREADY DOOMED... THERE WAS NOTHING THAT COULD BE DONE...

WHAT?! YOU ALLOWED HIM TO TOUCH HER?!... I HAD FORBIDDEN YOU!...

YOU ARE THE ONE IN CHARGE... YOU ARE RESPONSIBLE FOR HER DEATH!!...

HER BODY... WHERE IS HER BODY?!...

IT WENT DOWN WITH THE OTHER PACKAGES ON THE BODY SLIDE.

WHERE DO THOSE PACKAGES GO?!

TO THE CREMATORIUM IN CINCINNATI.

	21649			
	21650	FREEMAN,	ADAM	
	21651	CAMPBELL,	ANDREW	
	21652	GREATHOUSE,	CORA	
	21653	LLOYD,	WILLIAM	
	21654	WRIGHTSON,	BEN	

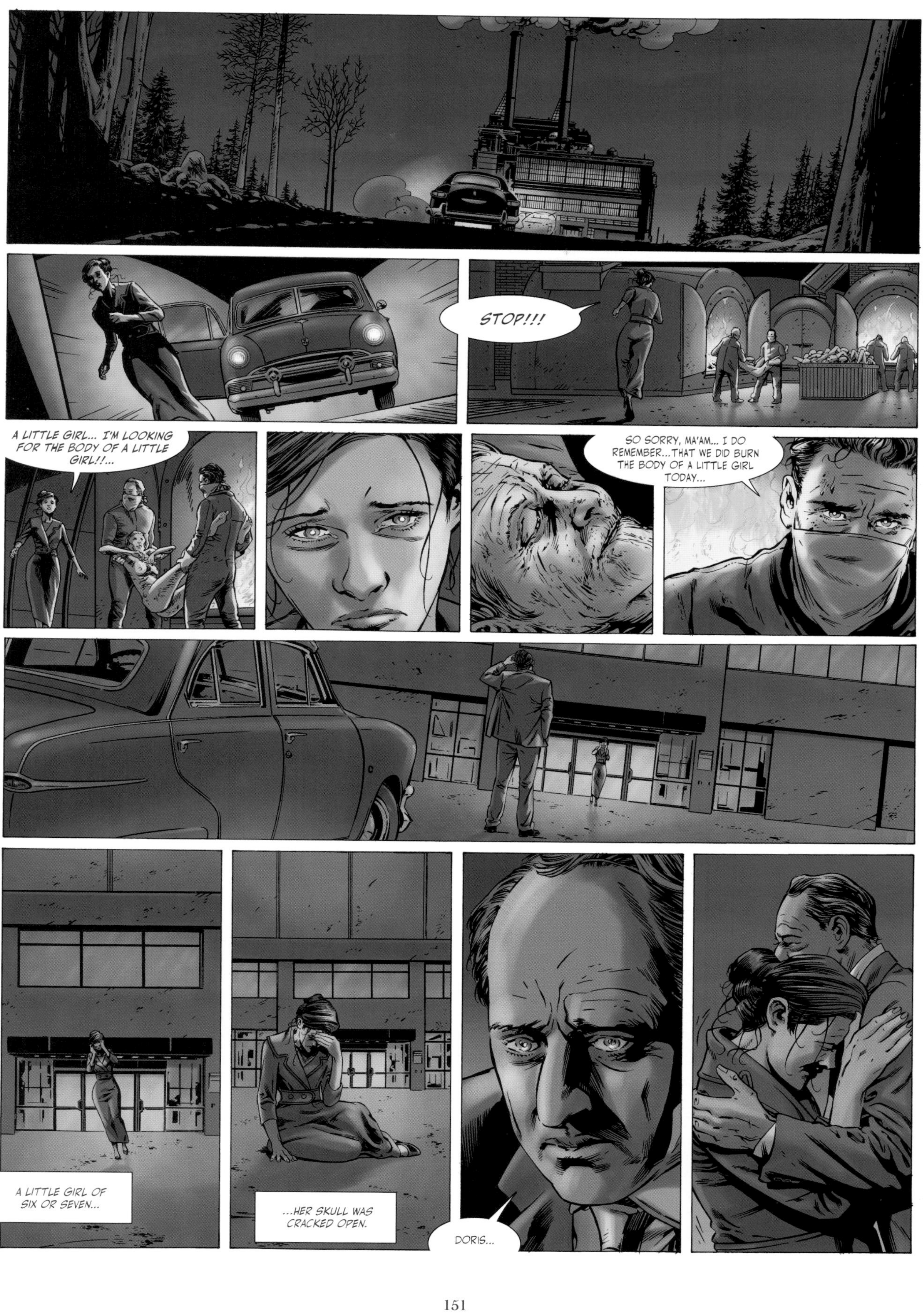

STOP!!!
A LITTLE GIRL... I'M LOOKING FOR THE BODY OF A LITTLE GIRL!!...
SO SORRY, MA'AM... I DO REMEMBER...THAT WE DID BURN THE BODY OF A LITTLE GIRL TODAY...
A LITTLE GIRL OF SIX OR SEVEN...
...HER SKULL WAS CRACKED OPEN.
DORIS...

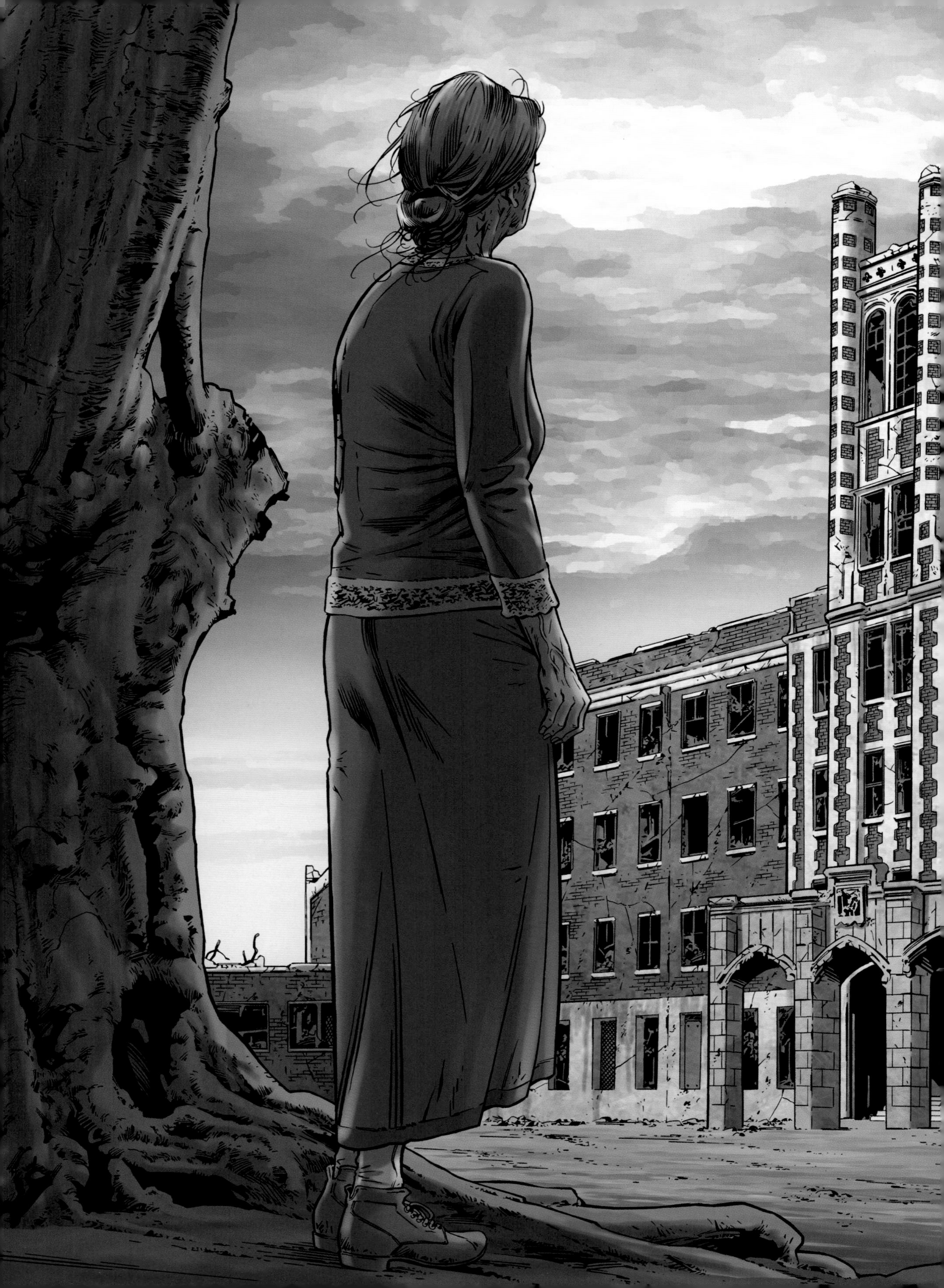

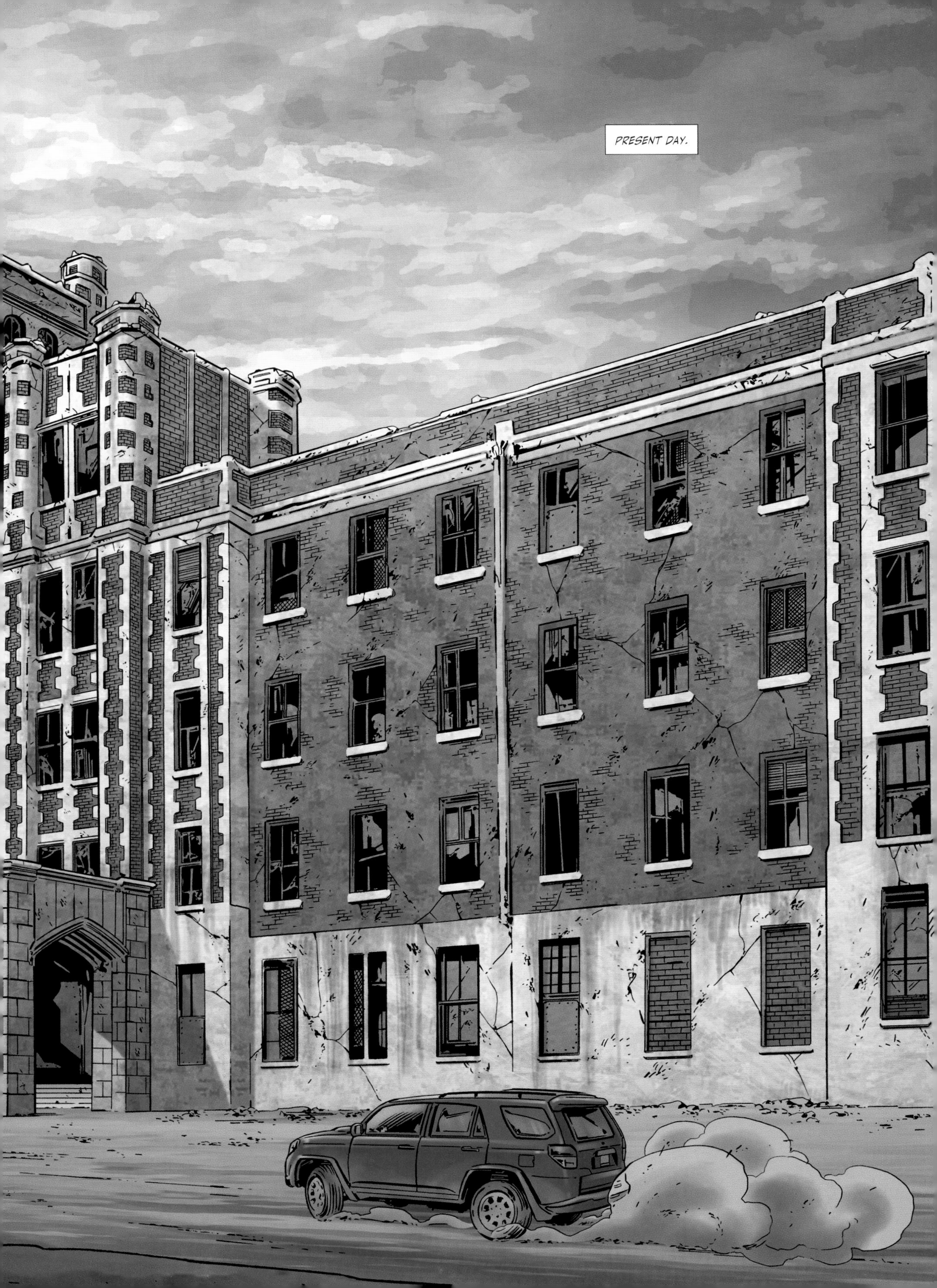
PRESENT DAY.

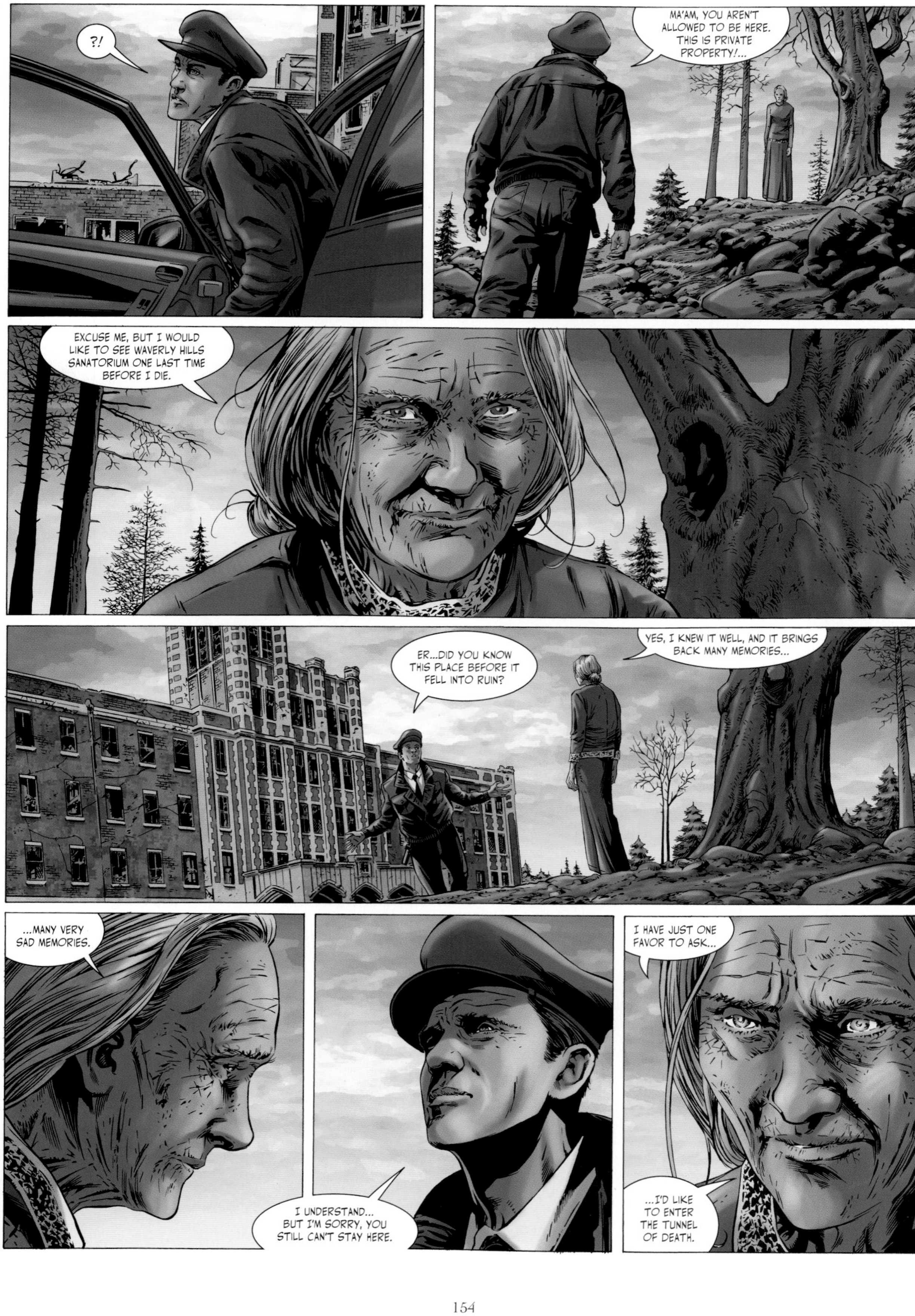
?!
MA'AM, YOU AREN'T ALLOWED TO BE HERE. THIS IS PRIVATE PROPERTY!...
EXCUSE ME, BUT I WOULD LIKE TO SEE WAVERLY HILLS SANATORIUM ONE LAST TIME BEFORE I DIE.
ER...DID YOU KNOW THIS PLACE BEFORE IT FELL INTO RUIN?
YES, I KNEW IT WELL, AND IT BRINGS BACK MANY MEMORIES...
...MANY VERY SAD MEMORIES.
I UNDERSTAND... BUT I'M SORRY, YOU STILL CAN'T STAY HERE.
I HAVE JUST ONE FAVOR TO ASK...
...I'D LIKE TO ENTER THE TUNNEL OF DEATH.

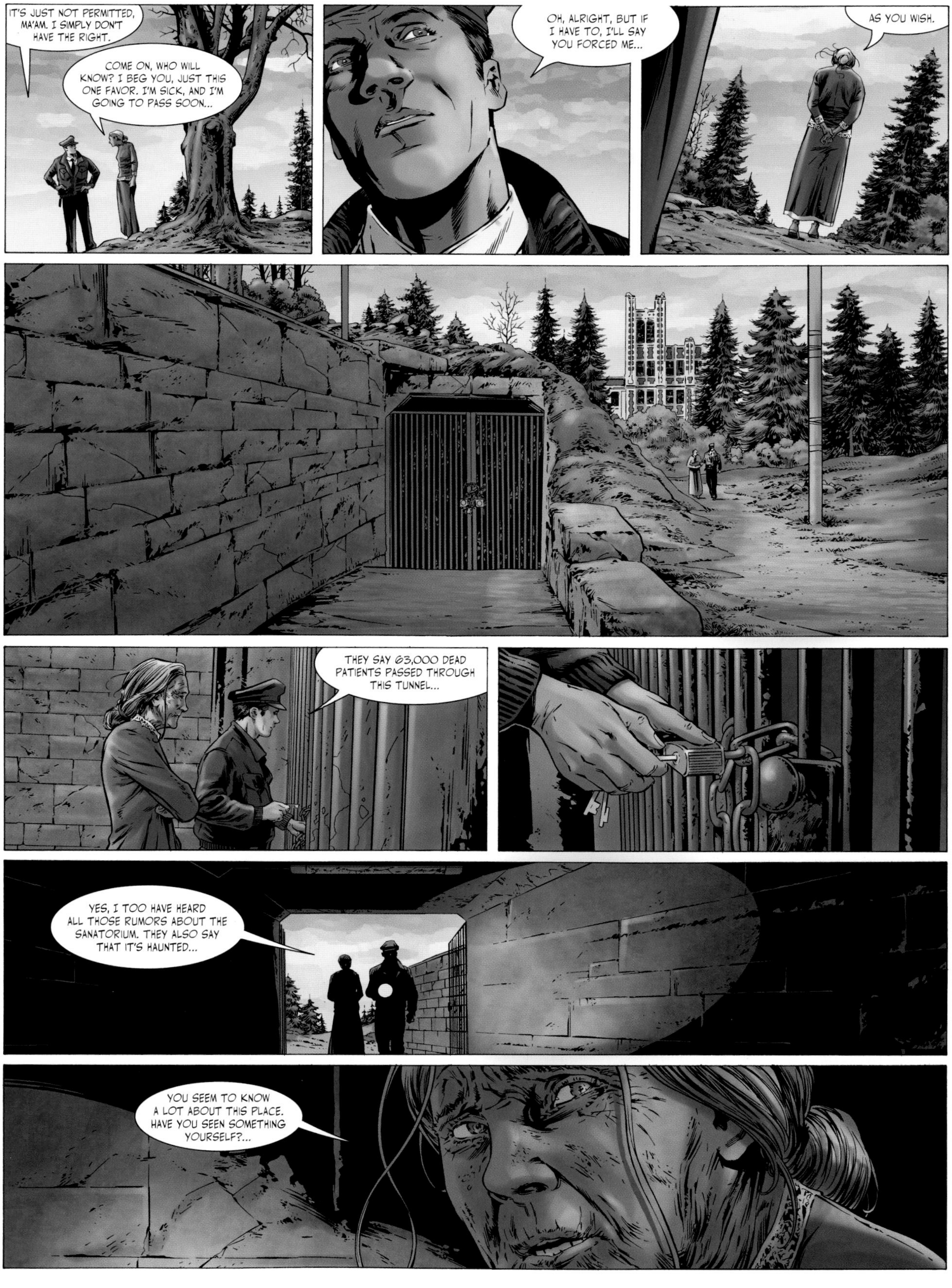
IT'S JUST NOT PERMITTED, MA'AM. I SIMPLY DON'T HAVE THE RIGHT.
COME ON, WHO WILL KNOW? I BEG YOU, JUST THIS ONE FAVOR. I'M SICK, AND I'M GOING TO PASS SOON...
OH, ALRIGHT, BUT IF I HAVE TO, I'LL SAY YOU FORCED ME...
AS YOU WISH.
THEY SAY 63,000 DEAD PATIENTS PASSED THROUGH THIS TUNNEL...
YES, I TOO HAVE HEARD ALL THOSE RUMORS ABOUT THE SANATORIUM. THEY ALSO SAY THAT IT'S HAUNTED...
YOU SEEM TO KNOW A LOT ABOUT THIS PLACE. HAVE YOU SEEN SOMETHING YOURSELF?...

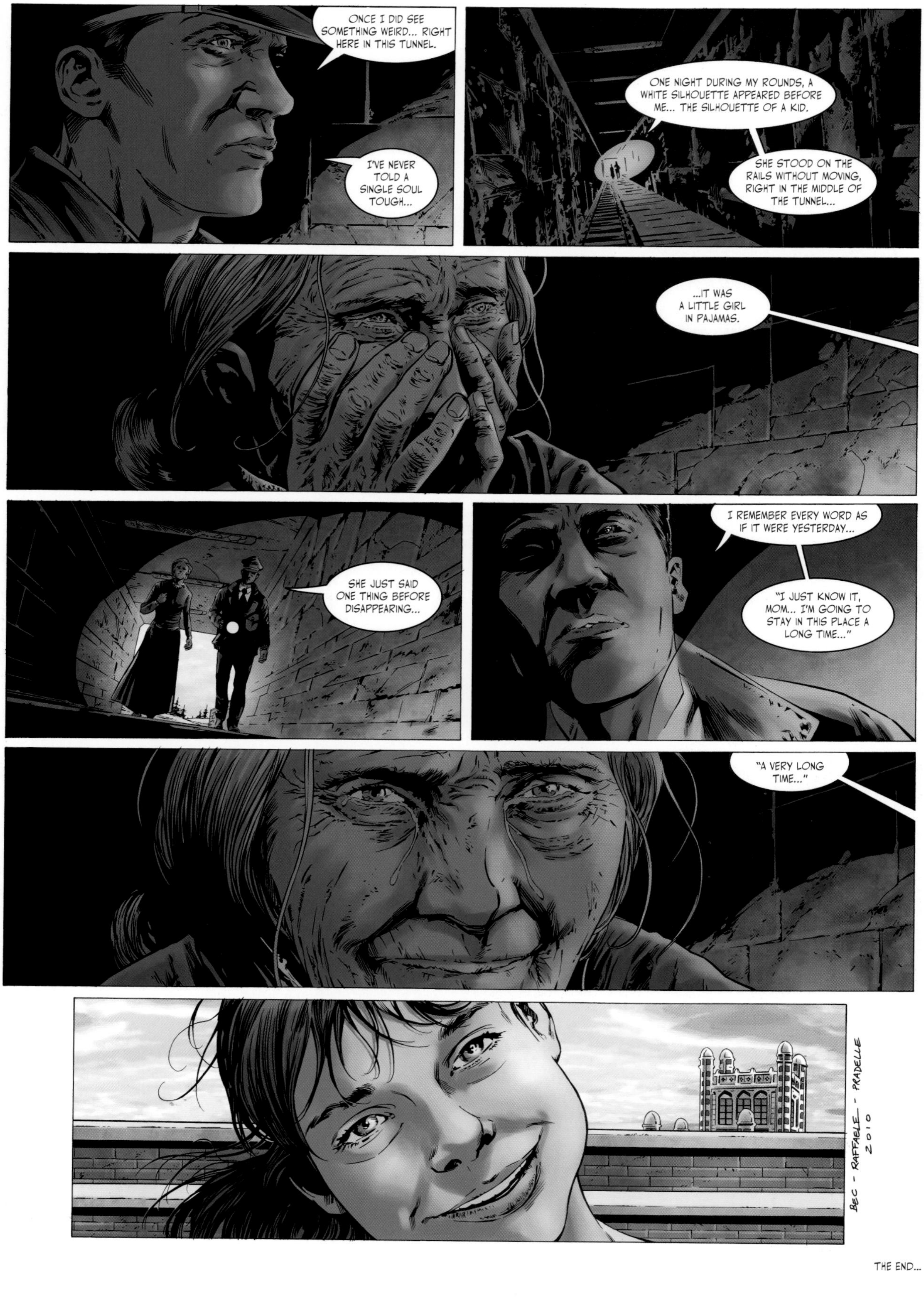
ONCE I DID SEE SOMETHING WEIRD... RIGHT HERE IN THIS TUNNEL.
I'VE NEVER TOLD A SINGLE SOUL TOUGH...
ONE NIGHT DURING MY ROUNDS, A WHITE SILHOUETTE APPEARED BEFORE ME... THE SILHOUETTE OF A KID.
SHE STOOD ON THE RAILS WITHOUT MOVING, RIGHT IN THE MIDDLE OF THE TUNNEL...
...IT WAS A LITTLE GIRL IN PAJAMAS.
SHE JUST SAID ONE THING BEFORE DISAPPEARING...
I REMEMBER EVERY WORD AS IF IT WERE YESTERDAY...
"I JUST KNOW IT, MOM... I'M GOING TO STAY IN THIS PLACE A LONG TIME..."
"A VERY LONG TIME..."
BEC - RAFFAELE - PRADELLE 2010

THE END...

PANDEMONIUM
Postscript

Assuming that this graphic novel can stand alone, I have chosen not to rehash my version of the story of Waverly Hills Sanatorium in this bonus section, but rather to write about the actual history of the site.

Many readers in France, after reading the three individual books, wanted to know what happened next, what transpired after our story. At the time, I didn't agree to comment on this because "Pandemonium" was and still is for me the story of Doris and her daughter Cora, and that is definitely over.

But this subject of "what happened next" is now ideal for this postscript.

I'm going to pick up the real story of Waverly Hills Sanatorium where it stopped in the graphic novel, that's to say at the end of the winter of 1952…

The establishment, whose plans had been drawn by the architects James J. Gaffney and Xavier Murphy,and that had initially been dedicated to the treatment of Tuberculosis closed its doors in June 1961. Thanks to the pharmacological progress made in the field of medicine during that period, Streptomycin had become the most effective medication in the battle against the terrible sickness. Thus, sanatoriums were less in demand, and WHS itself was no longer profitable (in 1955, each patient costs the Sanatorium $5.19 per day).

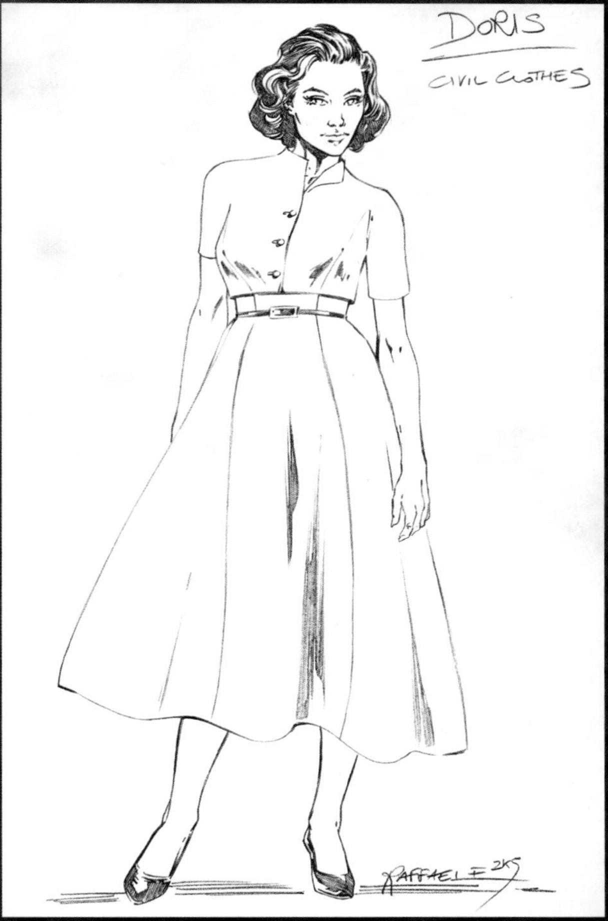
DORIS
CIVIL CLOTHES
RAFFAELE 2K5

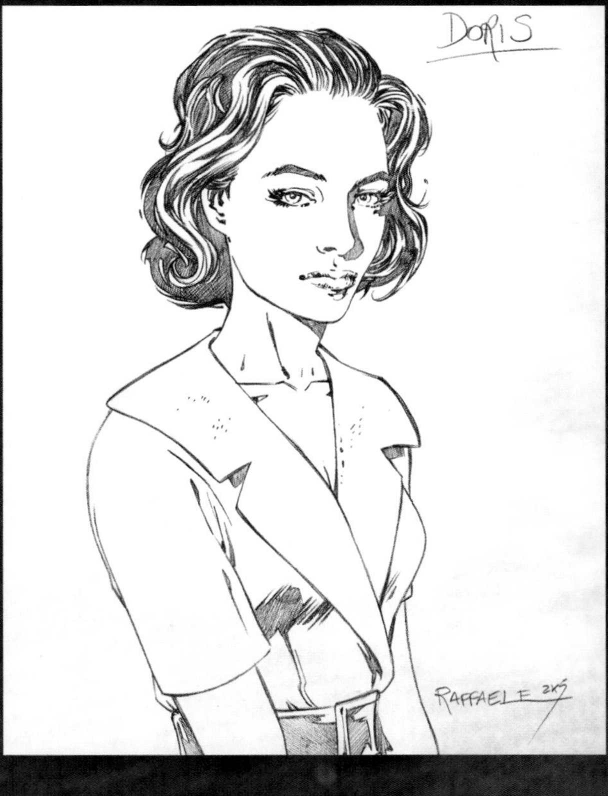
DORIS
RAFFAELE 2K5

The buildings would be reopened in 1962 under the name of Woodhaven Geriatrics Hospital as a geriatric center. Following many complaints regarding the improper treatment of patients, this hospital would finally close its own doors in 1981. Other sources allege that the cause was one particular and very serious medical error… In any case, it was from that point on that the urban legend claiming that it had became a lunatic asylum was born. That never actually occurred.

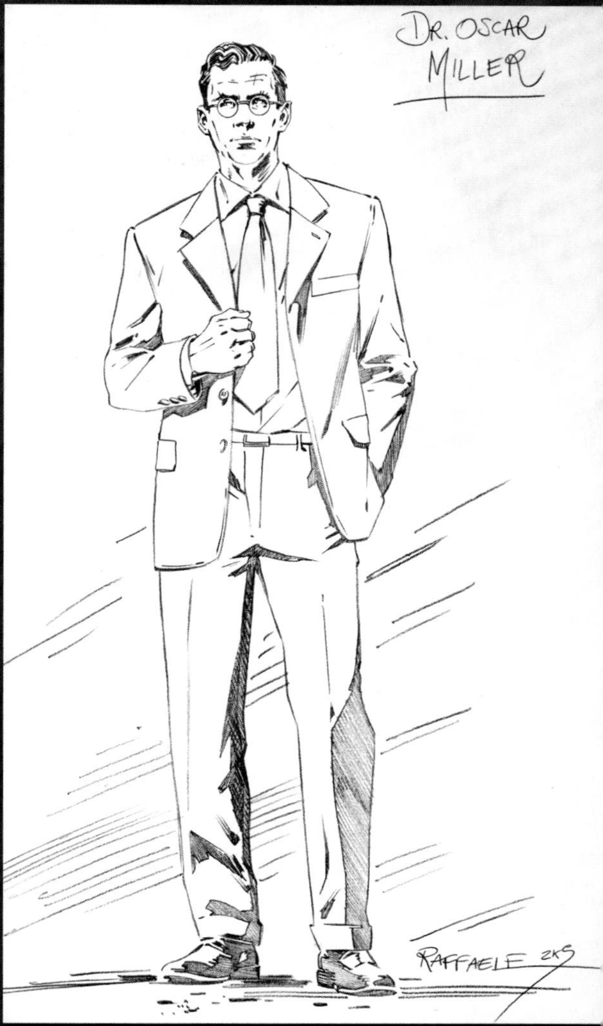
DR. OSCAR MILLER
RAFFAELE 2K5

In 1983, two years following the closing of Woodhaven, the property was purchased by Clifford Todd, who had plans to convert it into a state prison. This plan failed. Seeking to make the best of his purchase, Clifford next tried to convert the site into an apartment complex. This last plan also floundered due to a lack of financing.

In 1996, Robert Alberhasky acquired Waverly Hills and its surrounding property. He had a two stage plan. The first phase involved erecting a 500-foot high statue representing Jesus Christ, based on the famous Christ Redeemer Statue that stands over Rio de Janeiro in Brazil (mention of this was made in the first pages of the book you now hold). The second phase was designed to turn profits and included a chapel, a souvenir store, and shops. Once again, like all the other previous projects, this came to naught. Alberhasky then let the property fall into ruin over the years, leaving it to the mercy of vandals who ransacked the interior of the buildings.

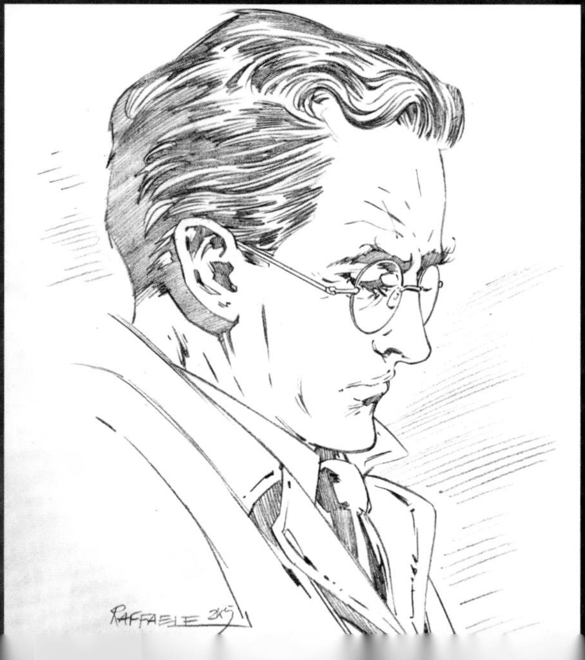
RAFFAELE 2K5

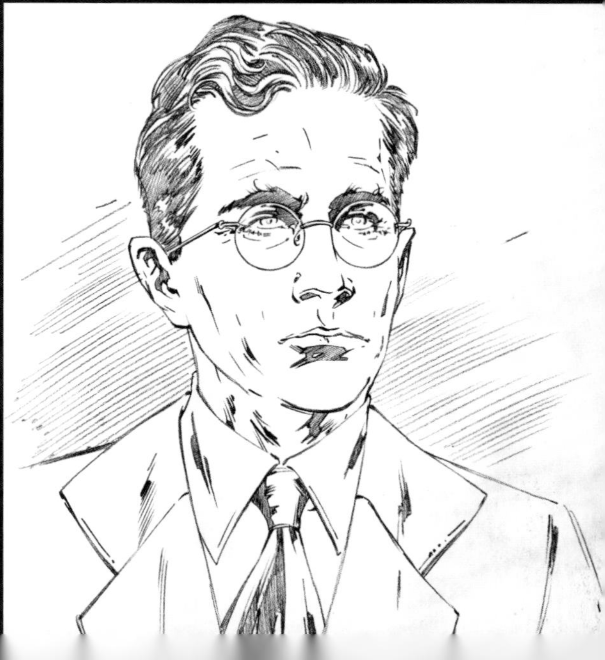

After a year of failed attempts to recuperate his investment, Alberhasky tried to destroy the buildings by mining the basement of the main structure with the goal of completely razing it in hopes of selling the land for a good price. He was stopped short by a restraining court order sought by the National Register of Historic Places.

In 2001, new owners, Mr. and Mrs. Mattingly, purchased the site with the goal of transforming it into a luxury four-star hotel.

The restoration work, however, was colossal, especially in the north wing which was in particularly poor condition. During four years, the work site was continuously plagued by health risks tied to asbestos.

Today, Waverly Hills Sanatorium is still being restored by its present owners. They offer a variety of tours and holiday stays at the Sanatorium. The location, quite popular within the United States, is called "the most haunted in America." It has been used dramatically in many television programs, notably those tied to ghost hunting. Some quite disturbing images were and continue to be filmed there…

– Christophe Bec
Albi, France, October 2011

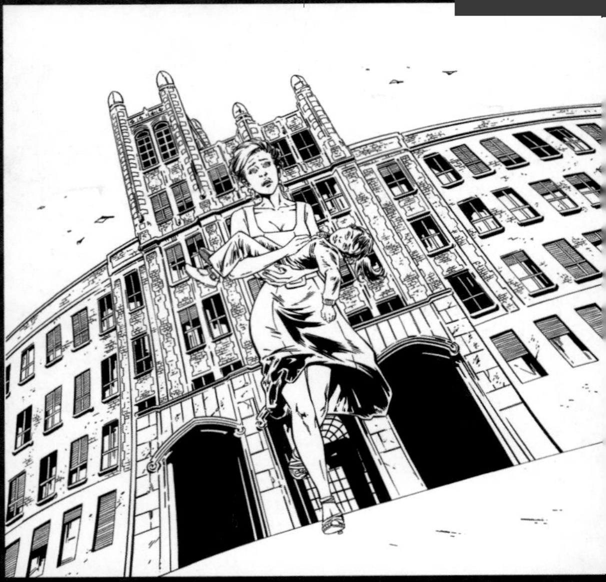

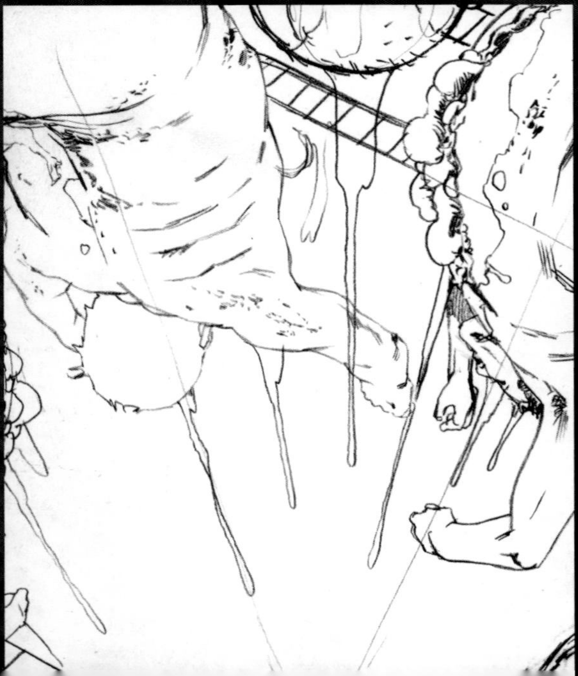

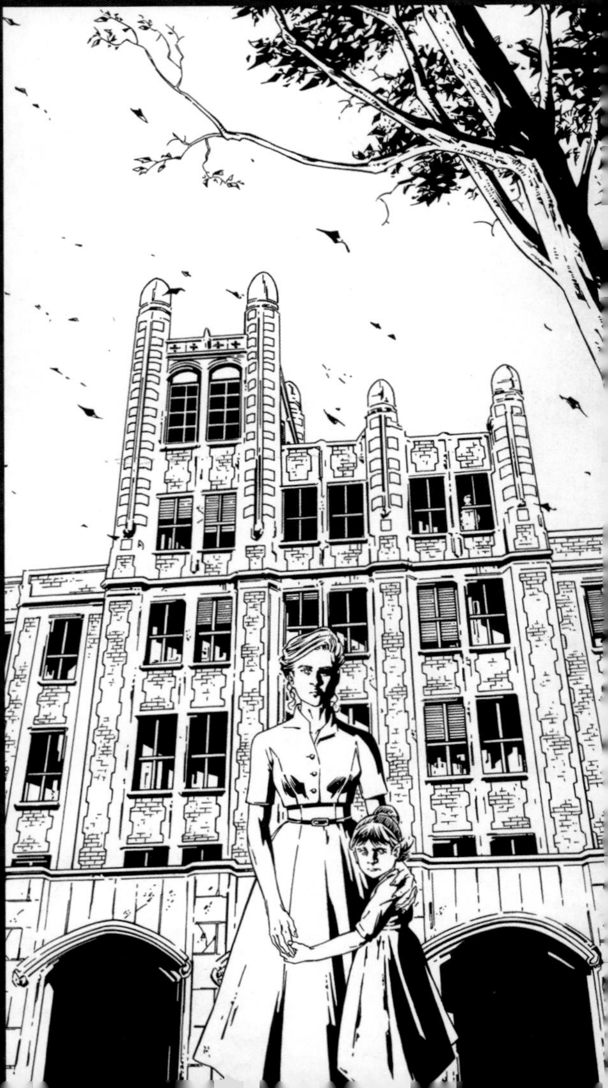